GREENSEA

ISLA[illegible]ERY OF TH[illegible]ST

VICTOR BRIDGES

ZINC READ

Published by
This edition copyright © 2024 by Zinc Read
Design and setting By Zinc Read
Email- zincread@gmail.com
ISBN-978-93-6137-519-4

CONTENTS

CHAPTER ONE

I was leaning over the starboard railing, waiting for a boat, when Ross, the ship's doctor, came sauntering along the deck, puffing contentedly at a large Manilla cigar.

"Hullo, Dryden!" he observed, in that pleasant drawling voice of his. "Busy as usual?"

Having just completed five hours' strenuous toil, supervising the unlading of cargo, I could afford to treat his effort at sarcasm with the contempt that it deserved.

"Are you coming ashore?" I asked.

He shook his head. "I'm not the second officer of the *Neptune*; I've got work to do. We are expecting another bundle of Dagoes on board at three o'clock, and I must be around to examine their beastly eyes." He knocked off the end of his cigar, which fluttered down into the blue water of Leixoes Harbour. "Besides," he added, "what on earth's the good of going ashore? There's nothing fresh to see in Oporto."

"There's probably something fresh to smell," I replied hopefully. "Anyhow, I'm going. I'm sick to death of the ship, and I want to stretch my legs."

His glance travelled ironically downwards.

"I should have thought they were quite long enough already," he said. "If you grow any bigger you will have to give up the sea, or else join the White Star. There will be no room for you on the Planet Line."

"Well, I shan't break my heart about it," I returned, laughing. "I've had quite enough of the gay and bounding ocean to last me the rest of my time."

He nodded sympathetically. "It's a dog's life," he admitted. "I have often thought of chucking it myself and setting up as a Harley Street specialist. The only objection is my incurable honesty and truthfulness."

"In about a week," I remarked, "you would be packing up and bundling off to Timbuctoo or Yokohama or somewhere. You've not got a simple, restful nature like mine; you are one of those people who have to keep on wandering about because their consciences won't let them rest."

"It's not my conscience," he replied cheerfully. "I knocked the nonsense out of that years ago. It's nothing but a silly habit I've drifted into. If one paddles about the world long enough one gets a sort of taste for it into one's blood, and when once that happens a man's lost. It's worse than drink or opium." He leaned back against the rail and surveyed me with mock seriousness. "Let my fate be a warning to you, Dryden. If you feel any yearnings for a nice little wife, and some chickens in the back garden, and a corner seat in the parish church, you get out of this while you're still young and innocent. Otherwise, in a few years' time, you will be just such another case as I am."

"It's the horrible possibility of that," I explained, "that makes me want to go ashore."

He laughed good-humouredly. "Well, go ashore then; and while you're about it you might see if you can pick me up a new pipe. My old one's getting positively insanitary." He glanced down it at the boat which was coming alongside.

"By the way," he added, "you may come across the beautiful Miss de Roda if you're lucky. She went off about half an hour ago."

"What, alone?" I asked.

"Quite alone," he returned encouragingly. "Uncle's still too seedy to go bucketing about as a chaperon."

"Well, I wonder he allowed her on shore by herself," I remarked. "It's the last thing I should have expected considering the way he has bottled her up all the blessed voyage."

Ross smiled indulgently. "He probably thinks she's safe against ordinary temptations. I expect it's only romantic-looking second officers that he's frightened of." He walked with me to the head of the ladder. "I suppose you'll want a boat to fetch you," he added. "Don't forget we sail at six sharp."

"Oh, that will be all right," I replied, preparing to descend. "I'm not sure what time I shall be back, so I'll get one of those ruffians on the beach to bring me off."

I climbed down and took my place along with a couple of passengers who had also been seized with a belated desire to set foot on the soil of Portugal. A minute later we were moving rapidly across the harbour towards the long stone jetty.

All the way in, despite the chatting of my companions, my thoughts kept flitting persistently round the two people Ross and I had been discussing. One meets many and various types of humanity on a South American liner, but from the very first Señor de Roda and his niece had aroused my especial interest.

They had joined the ship at Manaos, and I had happened to be standing on the deck at the very moment when they had come on board. Two things had struck me about them instantly; one was the fact that de

Roda himself looked wretchedly ill, and the other that his niece, on whose arm he leaned heavily as he came up the gangway, was quite the prettiest girl I had ever seen in my life. I am not much of a hand at describing anyone's appearance, but if you can imagine yourself coming face to face with one of Greuze's most lovely pictures, suddenly brought to life and a little sunburned, you will get some faint idea of my sensations at that particular moment. I am glad that no one was with me, for I know that I stood there gaping at her with a sort of stupefied admiration of which I should never have heard the last during the remainder of the voyage.

To de Roda, on the other hand, I had only devoted the briefest of glances. That, however, had left me with the impression of a tall, powerfully built man of middle age, prematurely bent by illness, and with a sallow face, from which two dark eyes looked out with a curious and rather forbidding intensity.

The next moment they had passed me, and with an effort I had jerked myself back into something like my usual self-possession.

Later on the same day, when I had happened to run across the purser, I had made some enquiries concerning the new arrivals. Except for supplying me with their names, however, he had been unable to give me any information, beyond the fact that they had booked through for the full voyage to London, and that they had taken the two best cabins still available.

It was from Ross that I subsequently gleaned the few further particulars I knew about them. His medical services had been called in the first evening, and he had been in fairly regular attendance throughout the whole voyage from Manaos to Oporto.

From one or two remarks he let drop I gathered that de Roda was suffering from some form of heart trouble, and that although this might, and probably would, get better for a time, any permanent recovery was out of the question. The girl, it appeared, was his patient's niece, and, unlike her uncle, who was an obvious South American through and through, she herself was half English, and spoke the language as fluently and readily as she did Spanish or Portuguese.

Ross declared that she was as charming to talk to as she was beautiful to look at, but this was a statement that so far I had no opportunity of putting to a practical test. Throughout the entire voyage both uncle and niece had kept as strictly to themselves as any two people could possibly do on an ocean-going steamer. For the first day or so de Roda's state of health had rendered it advisable that all his meals should be served in his cabin, and it was not until we were half way across that either of them had appeared in the saloon. Even then they had made arrangements with the steward that they should have a private table, and so far as I knew they were only on the barest speaking terms with any of the other passengers.

Very occasionally they would stroll round the deck in each other's company, de Roda invariably holding his niece's arm and staring out in front of him with a sombre look that was distinctly discouraging to any casual advances. Now and then in the afternoons Miss de Roda would establish herself in a quiet corner with a book and a deck chair, but the few more intrusive spirits who had attempted to take advantage of this fact did not seem to have met with any startling success.

Personally, I had made no effort to follow in their steps. I will confess straight away that this was not due to any indifference on my part, for she occupied my thoughts in a curiously persistent and disturbing fashion. My duties, however, left me little time for talking to the passengers, and, apart from that, I had no wish to try and force my acquaintance upon a girl who so obviously desired to be left alone. At times I could not help wondering whether her attitude in the matter was not dictated rather by loyalty to her uncle's wishes than by any natural inclination for solitude; but still, that made no difference to the facts of the case, which were sufficiently obvious for any but the most thick-skinned individual.

So far as I was concerned, this slight touch of mystery only added to her attractiveness. In spite of our never having spoken to each other, I found that with each day of the voyage my interest in her increased rather than lessened, a circumstance which I had been at some particular pains to keep entirely to myself. As a rule I have not the least objection to being chaffed, but for once in a way I rather shrank from the raillery which Ross would certainly have indulged in if he had had the remotest inkling of my real feelings.

In the middle of these meditations of mine we came alongside the jetty, from which two or three nondescript longshoremen had been eyeing our arrival with apathetic interest. For its size, Leixoes seems to contain a remarkable number of leisured citizens, whose only source of income appears to be the scanty earnings of their hard-working wives.

My two companions were anxious to have a look round the village before proceeding farther, so, leaving them to their own devices, I walked up the beach and boarded an electric tram which was just about to start for Oporto. Half an hour's run along the sandy road brought me to that straggling city, which, with its mediæval charm and shoddy, unfinished modern "improvements," gives one an illuminating picture of Portuguese history.

I descended in the old quarter on the quay, where the tall, tumble-down houses, with their quaint open fronts, still stare out picturesquely over the broad waters of the Douro. A glass of excellent iced beer in a neighbouring café washed away most of the dust which had collected in my throat, and then, feeling remarkably at peace with the world, I strolled off up the hill in the blazing glare of an almost tropical sunshine.

For perhaps an hour I wandered leisurely about the town, buying one or two things which I wanted—including Ross's pipe—and thoroughly enjoying the sensation of being once more on solid ground. Then, having nothing better to do, I turned my steps to the English Club, where, through the kindness of the members—a very genial and hospitable crowd—any officer of the Planet Line was always a welcome guest.

Here I found one or two old acquaintances, including the British Consul. All of them hailed me in the friendliest fashion. What with cigars and talk and more iced drinks, the time slipped away so rapidly that I suddenly woke up to the fact that I was cutting things rather fine with regard to the return journey. I had intended to walk back to Leixoes, but this was out of the question now, so, bidding my kind hosts a hasty good-bye, I made my way to the celebrated Rolling Square, where I found another obliging tram waiting my convenience.

As I stepped inside, the very first person who met my eyes was Miss de Roda. For the time I had quite forgotten that she was on shore, and the spectacle of her sitting there quietly in the corner gave me such a start that with a sudden unintentional movement I trod heavily upon the conductor's toe. The explosion that followed, punctuated by my apologies, naturally attracted her attention. She glanced up with a half-suppressed smile quivering round the corners of her lips, and behind it I thought I could detect a faint trace of friendly recognition. Anyhow, I hesitated no longer. Taking my courage in both hands, I walked up the tram to where she was sitting and raised my cap.

"I hope you won't mind my introducing myself," I said. "I am the second officer of the *Neptune*, and I think that you are one of our passengers."

A slight but charmingly graceful movement of her head encouraged me to take the vacant seat beside her.

"My name," I added, "is Dryden—John Dryden—the same as the poet."

She looked at me with a faint gleam of amusement still lurking in the depths of her beautiful brown eyes.

"I know you by sight, Mr. Dryden," she said. "I have seen you on the ship." Then she paused. "You must be proud of your name," she added. "It is a very distinguished one."

"It was very nearly extinguished just now," I replied. "At least, judging by what I could understand of the conductor's remarks."

She laughed softly—a low musical laugh that gave me a curious little stab of pleasure.

"One can't blame him," she remarked. "You must be a dreadfully heavy weight to come down suddenly upon anyone's toe."

I could hardly explain to her the real reason for my clumsiness, so I took refuge in a piece of shameless dishonesty.

"I was in a hurry," I explained. "I had been talking to some friends in the English Club, and I suddenly realised I should only just have time to get back. Hence the catastrophe!"

She glanced at her watch. "We have left it rather late," she admitted. "I have been doing some commissions for my uncle, and they kept me a good deal longer than I expected." She looked up at me with a slight trace of anxiety. "I suppose there is really no danger of our missing the ship?" she asked.

I shook my head. "None at all. If there were I should have taken a taxi. We shall be at Leixoes by half-past five, and it's only a ten minutes' row to where the *Neptune's* lying."

"Provided that we can get a boat," she added.

"Oh, there'll be no difficulty about that," I said. "There are generally plenty on the beach, and if it came to the worst we could always signal to the ship."

My reassurances seemed to have the desired effect, for she leaned back in her seat with a relieved expression, and obviously dismissed the matter from her thoughts.

It is not an easy thing to carry on a natural and unbroken conversation in a Portuguese tram, handicapped as one is by the pace at which the vehicle travels and the perpetual gong-ringing in which all drivers so joyously indulge. Still, considering the difficulties under which we laboured, we certainly got along together remarkably well. Long before we reached Leixoes I was in full agreement with Ross's statement that my companion was just as charming to talk to as she was beautiful to look at, and all the way I was secretly blessing the lucky accident which had given me the chance of making her acquaintance.

One thing I noticed, however, and that was that although she talked freely about the voyage and about her impressions of Oporto, she made no further reference either to her uncle or to her own affairs. I need hardly add that I was particularly careful to avoid saying anything which might sound like an attempt to introduce either topic, but the fact only strengthened my previous opinion that her self-imposed solitude on board was due to some private reason rather than to any natural aversion to society.

This belief was increased by the faint but curious suggestion of reserve which seemed to linger in the background, even when she was speaking about the most unimportant matters. It gave me the impression that she regarded our conversation as a sort of unexpected holiday—a holiday which for some mysterious reason she had no real right to indulge in. Its only effect, however, was to render her still more attractive, and I felt quite resentful against the unnecessary efficiency of the Portuguese tram service, when we gonged our way noisily into Leixoes five minutes after the appointed time for our arrival.

Disentangling ourselves from the rest of the company, we made our way down to the beach. Out in the harbour we could see the *Neptune* busily engaged in getting up steam, while a few trading boats still clustered round her side, making a final effort to coax money out of her now wary passengers.

As we reached the shore a swarthy and rather truculent-looking gentleman, decorated with silver ear-rings, came forward to meet us.

"You want to go to sheep?" he enquired, waving a dirty hand in the direction of the *Neptune*.

I eyed him with some disfavour, but there appeared to be only one boat on the beach, so it was no good being too fastidious.

"Bring her along to the edge of the jetty," I said, "and we'll get in there."

With a shrill whistle through his fingers he summoned another and equally unattractive individual to his aid, and the pair of them commenced to haul their boat down into the water.

Miss de Roda and I walked along the causeway.

"I'm sorry I can't find you a handsomer crew," I said, "but it's a question of Hobson's choice."

"Oh, they will do very well," she answered, smiling. "They are probably the most respectable people really." Then she paused. "It's a bad habit to judge by appearances," she added, with what seemed to me the least touch of bitterness in her voice.

I looked at her steadily. "Perhaps you're right," I admitted. "All the same, it's one of those bad habits that I'm rather a believer in."

To this remark she returned no answer, and the next minute the boat, with its two unprepossessing occupants, came drifting alongside. We took our places in the stern, facing the gentleman with the silver ear-rings, who was pulling stroke. At closer quarters I thought I had never seen a more sinister-looking rascal in my life, an impression which was in no way mitigated by a large, businesslike-looking knife, which he wore stuck in a sheath suspended from his belt.

At a very leisurely pace we moved away from the jetty and headed in the direction of the ship. Neither of the men appeared to be putting the least energy into his work, and at any other time I should have called their attention to the fact in pretty straight language. As it was, the prospect of spending a few more minutes in my companion's society reconciled me to their slackness, though the furtive way in which they kept glancing at us annoyed me almost beyond endurance.

We had covered about half the distance, and were still some two hundred yards from the *Neptune*, when, without any warning, both men suddenly ceased rowing and rested their oars on the water.

I looked up at them sharply. "What are you doing?" I said. "Get on at once."

The fellow with the silver ear-rings eyed me with provoking insolence.

"No—no," he said. "You pay us now. You pay us two pound and then we take you to sheep."

Now the proper fee for a harbour boat at Leixoes is two shillings, so for a moment the audacity of this demand almost took away my breath. I suppose my face showed what I felt, for before I could speak Miss de Roda leaned across and touched me on the arm.

"Please don't let my being with you make any difference, Mr. Dryden," she said. "Do exactly what you think best."

I had quite recovered myself by this time, and the cool way in which she accepted the situation filled me with secret pleasure.

I addressed myself to the leader of the mutiny.

"I shall pay you your exact fare," I said, "and if you take my advice you will go on at once."

He met my gaze with an expression of truculent defiance.

"Two pound," he repeated, "or we take you over there and leave you." He waved his hand in the direction of the desolate sandbanks which stretched along the farther side of Leixoes harbour. "You not get boat then," he added, grinning maliciously; "you stop there and lose sheep."

It has always been an axiom of mine that when you have got to have a row the quicker and more vigorously you start work the better. The man's face was only a few feet away from me, and, without a second's hesitation, I made a swift lunge forward, and struck out with all the force that I was capable of. He saw what was coming and grabbed for his weapon, but just as he drew it from its sheath the blow crashed home on the point of his chin, and sent him reeling over backwards into the arms of his companion. Slipping from his hand, the knife tinkled down on to the floorboard of the boat, and the next instant I had snatched it up and was standing over the confused heap of arms and legs which represented the vanquished enemy.

"Now," I said, "are you going on, or am I going to chuck you both into the harbour?"

For a moment there was no answer; then, with an effort, the gentleman in the bow slithered out from under his companion and sat up, blinking and gasping. He was evidently a poor-spirited ruffian compared with the other, for his face had gone the colour of putty, and he eyed me with absolute terror.

"You had better make up your mind quickly," I added.

He nodded his head vigorously. "Yes, yes," he exclaimed; "we take you to sheep"; and, without waiting for any further developments, he seized hold of his discarded oar and plunged it furiously into the water.

"Well, you won't do it by rowing round in a circle," I observed. "We must try what first aid for the injured will do."

I picked up a rusty tin from under one of the seats, and, filling it with water, poured the contents over the head of the sleeping beauty, who still lay in a huddled mass between the two seats. For such a simple remedy it worked with surprising efficiency. There was a grunt, followed by a convulsive start, and then, shaking himself like a drenched Newfoundland dog, the patient slowly arose from his recumbent attitude.

I scowled at him ferociously. "Oh, you've waked up, have you?" I said. "Catch hold of your oar, and don't let me hear another word from you before we reach the ship."

If looks could kill I should have dropped dead in the boat, but, nature having fortunately arranged otherwise, no such unpleasant tragedy occurred. Without a word he proceeded to carry out my instructions, and the next moment we were moving on towards the *Neptune* at a considerably brisker pace than we had hitherto achieved.

Going back to my place in the stern, I reseated myself beside Miss de Roda.

"You have made me change my opinion," she said, in a delightfully tranquil voice. "In future I shall attach more importance to first impressions."

"I hope you didn't mind," I answered apologetically. "I couldn't think of anything else to do for the moment."

She shook her head, with the same gleam of amusement in her eyes that I had seen before.

"On the contrary," she said, "I am extremely obliged to you. I have the greatest possible objection to being cheated." She paused, and, bending sideways, looked out ahead of us. "I wonder if anybody on the ship saw what happened," she added. "There seem to be several people leaning over the side."

I fancied I could detect a faint trace of anxiety in her voice, as though she rather dreaded the possibility she referred to.

"I don't suppose so," I said comfortingly. "The sun's in their eyes, and we were some distance off."

"It's only my uncle I am thinking of," she exclaimed. "As long as no one says anything to him it doesn't matter in the least. He is not very well, you know, and I shouldn't like him to be upset or—or annoyed."

She brought out the last word with some hesitation, and then stopped, as though rather regretting that she had made use of it.

"I'm sure it will be all right," I repeated. "There's something very deceptive about the Portuguese atmosphere. If anybody imagines they saw anything, I shall let them know that they were making a mistake."

By this time we had drawn close enough to the *Neptune* to be able to distinguish the small group of people who were watching our approach. It was with a certain feeling of discomfort that I recognised amongst them the burly figure of Ross, for I knew that, whatever the others might have missed, nothing would have escaped his singularly observant eye. Still, I comforted myself with the thought that he was the last person who would be likely to gossip unnecessarily, and that it was only I myself who would be the victim of his amiable banter.

As our two boatmen brought us alongside the ship in sullen silence, a sailor who had been waiting at the top of the ladder ran down and caught hold of the gunwale. I guessed from his expression that he also had been an intelligent witness of our little disturbance, a suspicion which was fully confirmed by his opening remark.

"Been 'avin' trouble with 'em, sir?" he enquired.

I assisted Miss de Roda out of the boat, and collected the one or two small parcels which I had brought with me.

"It was a case of sudden illness," I explained. "One of our friends here was taken faint, and I had to pour some water over his head. He is feeling better now."

The sailor said nothing, but I saw him glance with an appreciative grin at the scowling face of the supposed invalid, which was beginning to show distinct traces of its recent contact with my fist. This scowl became even darker when I handed over a two shilling piece, and stepped up unconcernedly on to the bottom rung of the ladder, leaving the knife lying behind me on the seat. I fancy that its owner would have given all his earthly possessions to jump up after me and plunge it into my back, but if so his longing had to share the fate of many another splendid aspiration in this disappointing world.

As I reached the deck, under a fire of rather curious glances from the small knot of passengers who had gathered there, I noticed Miss de Roda, a little distance apart from the others, apparently waiting to speak to me. Ross, who was still leaning over the rail, made no effort to attract my attention, so, passing through the group, I walked up to where she was standing.

"Here is my shilling, Mr. Dryden," she said, holding out her hand; "and thank you very much for saving me the other nineteen."

I took the coin she offered me and put it into my pocket.

"I think I shall bore a hole in it," I said, "and wear it as a medal. A naval victory like ours deserves some recognition."

She laughed softly. "There will always be one person who remembers it," she said, "if that's any satisfaction."

Something prompted me to take a bold step.

"May I come and talk to you sometimes when I see you on deck?" I asked. "Please tell me straight out if you would rather I didn't."

A troubled look came into her eyes, and for a moment she hesitated.

"It isn't a question of what I should like," she said slowly. "You see, I have to think of my uncle. He is not at all well, and he has a very strong objection to our making any fresh acquaintances on board."

I daresay my face showed what I thought of Señor de Roda, for she continued a little hastily: "You mustn't imagine that he is unkind or disagreeable. Indeed, in a way I—I agree with him. Please don't think me ungrateful, but it will be much the best if we just say good-bye now."

There was something almost wistful in the way she spoke, which at once softened my resentment without in any way altering my disappointment.

"Couldn't we split the difference?" I suggested. "Let me have one more talk with you, and then, if it's got to be good-bye, I'll try and say it as cheerfully as possible."

There was a moment's pause. "Very well," she said. "I sometimes go up on deck for a few minutes before breakfast. If you care to come and talk to me to-morrow morning, please do."

I took off my cap, and with a very slight bow she turned towards her cabin, leaving me standing there in a tangle of interesting, and, so far as I was concerned, quite novel emotions.

I woke up to perceive Ross sauntering towards me, with his hands in his pockets and a mischievous twinkle in his grey eyes.

"Hullo!" he observed. "Got my pipe?"

I nodded. "I have bought you a beauty," I said. "You will be a credit to the ship."

"There's a telegram for you in your cabin," he went on; "a cable from England, I think. It came on board just after you had gone ashore."

"A cable from England!" I repeated. "I wonder who the Dickens it's from."

He chuckled softly. "Can't say," he replied, "unless it's a message from King Arthur offering you a seat at the Round Table. I believe they're getting devilish short of knights errant."

I stepped up to him and took him gently but firmly by the arm.

"I think you want a drink, Ross," I said. "You had better come along down with me, and I'll give you a whisky and soda."

CHAPTER TWO

I led him across the deck until we reached the companion, when I released my grip on his elbow.

"Tell me, you old scoundrel," I said, "did anyone except you and that confounded sailor see what was going on?"

He chuckled again. "What can you expect," he enquired, "if you will choose the public ocean on which to perform these feats of chivalry?"

"There wasn't any chivalry about it," I said. "The blighters tried to blackmail us into giving them a couple of quid. In fact, they had the infernal cheek to threaten to put us ashore on the sands if we didn't pay up."

Ross smiled provokingly. "I should have thought that would have just suited you," he observed. "You would make a very nice Paul and Virginia."

"It wouldn't have suited Miss de Roda," I returned. "As it is, she's worried to death with the idea that someone will go and tell her uncle about that scrap in the boat. She thinks it will give him another heart attack, and, seeing the sort of doctor we've got on board, I must say I rather sympathize with her."

He took my shaft quite imperturbably.

"I thought you would get the poor girl into trouble sooner or later," he remarked. "Still, thanks to me, it's not as bad as it might have been. I was the only one on board with a pair of glasses, and, when the others asked me what was happening, I told them the gentleman you sloshed on the jaw had managed to catch a crab. It was some crab, by the way, wasn't it? I hate lying, but I knew that your natural modesty would shrink from anything like a public ovation."

I stopped outside my cabin. "Ross," I said feelingly, "you may be a bad doctor, but you're a damned good pal. You shall have a double whisky for this."

I led the way in and closed the door behind us.

"Besides," he continued, settling himself down on my bunk, "there's no risk of Uncle Philip dropping dead. He has bucked up a lot the last day or two, thanks to my extraordinary skill."

I mixed a generous peg, and brought it across to where he was sitting.

"I can't quite make out the Señor de Roda," I said. "He looks as if he had something on his mind—something he was always brooding over."

Ross took a long and appreciative drink. "He has had a rotten time somehow," he replied; "that's quite certain. I should put him down as a naturally healthy man who had been broken up by bad feeding and rough living." He paused. "But I expect you're pretty well up in the family history now?" he added drily.

"That's the weak point of your profession," I retorted. "When you don't know you generally guess wrong. As a matter of fact I only met Miss de Roda in the tram coming down from Oporto. There wasn't much time for private enquiry work, even if I had felt like it."

"You didn't do so badly," returned Ross, wagging his head. "There is nothing women like so much as a little display of primitive brutality. It's just your luck to have had the chance. That sort of thing never comes my way." He finished his drink and put down the tumbler. "Aren't you going to open your wire?" he asked. "There it is on the table."

"By Jove!" I exclaimed. "I'd forgotten all about it."

I crossed the cabin, and, slitting the flap of the little blue envelope, pulled out the flimsy sheet of paper inside. It was headed "London, May 26th," and underneath was the following message:

> "Regret inform you your uncle, Richard Jannaway, died 17th inst. As next of kin you inherit. Please call 117 Bedford Row as soon as you reach England.—Wilmot and Drayton, solicitors."

For several seconds I stood there contemplating this document, in such complete surprise that at last Ross got up a little anxiously from where he was sitting.

"Nothing wrong, I hope?" he asked.

Without a word I handed him the slip, and he in turn read through its contents.

"My sainted aunt!" he exclaimed. "Have you come into a fortune or what?"

"I haven't the faintest notion," I said.

There was a short pause. Then once more he glanced through the message which he was still holding in his hand. "Who was Mr. Richard Jannaway?" he demanded. "And what's all the mystery about?"

I picked up the whisky and helped myself to a drink.

"He was my mother's brother," I said. "I know hardly anything about him besides that. I was under the impression that he was dead years ago."

"Haven't you ever seen him?"

I shook my head. "He left England when I was a baby. I believe he was a pretty bad egg one way and another—the sort of black sheep that every respectable family rolls out occasionally. I have got some vague idea that he went to South America, but so far as I know there has never been any news of him from that day to this."

Ross reseated himself on the bunk and stared at me with vast enjoyment.

"You've struck the main reef, my son," he observed. "It's the sort of thing one reads about in a shilling shocker. He's probably made a huge fortune cornering castor oil or something, and when you get back you'll find yourself a prancing millionaire."

"It's much more likely he's left me a bundle of debts," I said sceptically.

"Don't you believe it," persisted Ross. "I've got a wonderful instinct for lucky people, and the very first time I saw you I smelt money. I don't suppose you'll ever do another honest day's work in your life—at least, not after you reach London."

As he spoke the jangling sound of the shore bell echoed loudly through the ship.

"Anyhow, I must go up and make a final effort at it now," I said. "I am due on the bridge in five minutes, and I shouldn't like to leave the service with a tarnished record."

Ross hoisted himself to his feet and handed me back the wire.

"I shall retire to my cabin and read Marcus Aurelius," he announced. "He is very consoling with regard to the favouritism and injustice of life."

As people go I don't think I am very easily upset, either by good luck or the reverse. Still, I must admit that, in spite of what I said to Ross, the totally unexpected news which Messrs. Wilmot and Drayton had been kind enough to forward me had certainly set my heart beating a little more briskly than usual. There is something peculiarly stimulating in the thought that one may have come into a fortune—especially to a second officer in the Merchant Service, whose capital consists of about seventy pounds in cash and a miscellaneous collection of shore-going clothes.

All through my watch, while we were creeping out of Leixoes harbour, and thrashing our way up the desolate coast of Spain, the pleasant possibilities of the situation kept turning themselves over in my mind. As I had told Ross earlier in the afternoon, I was sick of my present life—sick to death of it. Ever since the war I had been helping to trundle the *Neptune* backwards and forwards between London and Brazil, and any faint attraction the job might once have possessed had long since vanished into thin air. I had already practically made up my mind to chuck it at the first favourable opportunity, and now it looked as if Fate were suddenly offering me a chance such as I had never hoped for even in my wildest dreams. If this mysterious uncle of mine had really left me anything worth having I could start out on my fresh career with all the advantages of a leisurely and deliberate choice. What that choice would be I had not exactly determined. When one is twenty-six, and as fit as a fiddle, the world contains so many delightful openings, it is difficult to decide in a hurry which is the most congenial.

Even when I was back in my cabin and stretched out comfortably in my bunk, I still found my mind sufficiently busy to keep me wide awake. Another and highly interesting thought had suddenly dawned upon me, and that was that if Ross's predictions were in any way right, I should now be in a much more justifiable position to pursue my acquaintance with Miss de Roda.

Lying there in the dark, I seemed to see her face as plainly as if she were standing just in front of me. Those wonderful eyes and the soft curve of her lips stood out before me with a strange, bewitching vividness. Slowly and with a curious pleasure I went through again all our conversation during the drive down from Oporto. It had been simple enough on the surface—the mere exchange of ordinary cheerful commonplaces suitable to the situation—but once more I seemed to catch that faint, tantalising atmosphere of reserve and mystery which was none the less real for being so utterly intangible.

The more I thought it over the more certain I felt that in her own opinion there was some impenetrable barrier which cut her off from the possibility of making friends with anyone on board. Her uncle's wishes may have had something to do with it, but there seemed to me little doubt that she herself shared his views in the matter, and was fully determined to carry them out.

It was not exactly an encouraging conclusion, but I refused to let it depress me. Barriers, after all, are only made to be attacked, and on the whole I rather like a certain amount of opposition. It adds so enormously to the value of the prize after one has succeeded in getting one's own way.

I meditated upon this satisfactory truth a little longer, and at last with a feeling of drowsy contentment over the prospect of seeing and talking with her the next morning, I turned over comfortably on my side and dropped off to sleep.

It is not always that nature is so obliging as to harmonize with one's feelings, but from what I could see through the porthole when I woke up the next morning it appeared to me that the weather was thoroughly in keeping with my own good spirits. When I reached the deck I found no reason for changing my opinion. Under a sky of cloudless blue and through a sparkling, sunlit sea the *Neptune* was steadily churning her way northwards, leaving a broad white wake of foam stretching away half a mile behind her. Even the usually expressionless face of the first officer was wreathed in a satisfied smile as he paced slowly up and down the bridge.

By half-past seven one or two passengers had already made their appearance, but it was not until a few minutes after eight that I at last caught sight of Miss de Roda. She was standing by herself looking out over the stern railing, and the sudden thrill that ran through me when I recognised her showed me that my feelings must have been travelling at a very creditable pace during the last twenty-four hours.

There was not much time before breakfast, so, without any unnecessary delay, I at once made my way aft. She looked up as I approached, and the swift fear I felt that she might have repented making the appointment vanished immediately before the friendly smile with which she returned my greeting.

"Good morning, Mr. Dryden," she said, "and if you've any consideration for my feelings, please don't tell me it's a beautiful day. I have heard that from three different people already."

I looked at her with deep contentment. She was wearing a plain linen frock that showed off the graceful lines of her figure, and altogether she was as fresh and delightful a picture as ever gladdened the eye of sinful man.

"I am sorry," I said regretfully. "I had made up one or two very bright remarks on the subject, but under the circumstances I'll keep them for somebody else." I paused. "How is Señor de Roda this morning?" I asked. "I hope he hasn't heard anything about our adventures in the harbour?"

She shook her head. "Not a word apparently. I am beginning to think that nobody saw us after all, except the sailor who spoke to you."

In a few words I acquainted her with what Ross had told me the previous evening—a piece of information which she received with obvious thankfulness.

"I have always liked Dr. Ross," she said. "He is so kind and cheery. Is he a special friend of yours?"

"We have been together for a dozen voyages," I explained, "and so far we have managed to get along without squabbling."

"A dozen voyages!" she repeated, opening her eyes. "You must be getting a little tired of the *Neptune*, aren't you?"

"She has lost some of her first charm," I admitted frankly. "I have been thinking of applying for a separation for some time."

She looked up at me with a friendly interest that I found very refreshing.

"What are you going to do?" she asked.

"I don't know exactly," I replied. "It depends to a certain extent upon Messrs. Wilmot and Drayton."

There was a short pause.

"They sound like two very important people," she said, wrinkling her forehead, "but I am afraid I have never heard of either of them."

"Neither had I until I got back yesterday," I returned. "Then I found a cable from them in my cabin telling me that my uncle was dead."

She gave a little exclamation of sympathy. "Oh, I am so sorry," she began. "I'm afraid——"

"It's quite all right," I interrupted cheerfully. "I never saw him in my life, and I believe he was several kinds of a blackguard. The only reason they wired to me was because I happen to be the next of kin, and as he died without making a will I suppose I come into his goods and chattels—if there are any to come into."

"But don't you know? Didn't they give you any details?"

I shook my head. "Nothing at all. I may be a millionaire, or he may have left me a parrot and an old suit of clothes. I should think the latter was much the more likely of the two, but Ross won't have it at any price. He says that he has got a kind of second sight about money matters, and that he's always felt I was born to be one of the idle rich."

She laughed easily. "I do hope he's right. Aren't you tremendously excited about it?"

"I am trying not to be," I said. "You see, the more one expects the greater the disappointment."

"Who was your uncle?" she asked, after a moment's silence. "Another namesake of the poet?"

"He wasn't a Dryden at all," I explained. "He was my mother's brother, and his name was Richard Jannaway."

I had given my answer quite casually, but its effect was so startling that for a moment I stood there petrified with astonishment. Every vestige of colour had fled from my companion's face, and she was staring at me with an expression of incredulous horror.

"Good heavens!" I exclaimed involuntarily. "What is it? What's the matter?"

By a tremendous effort of will she managed to pull herself together.

"It's nothing," she answered, with amazing coolness. "I—I once knew somebody of that name, but it couldn't possibly have been the same person."

"I don't know," I said slowly; "there can't be very many Richard Jannaways in the world." Then I paused. "My uncle spent most of his life in South America," I added deliberately.

I saw her hand tighten on the railing that she was holding until the knuckles stood out white and distinct under the skin.

"South America?" she repeated in a low whisper.

The same panic-stricken look had come back into her face, as though the two words confirmed all the strange dread which the first mention of my uncle's name had suddenly aroused.

I came a step nearer to her. "For God's sake tell me what's the matter," I said again. "If there's anything in the world——"

I was interrupted by the noise of the breakfast gong, which came booming up from below in a loud, insistent clamour.

With another obvious effort my companion regained her self-control, and, letting go of the railing stood up in front of me, white and breathless.

"Mr. Dryden," she said, "please don't ask me any questions. There is something I can't explain to you now—something I can never explain. I can only assure you that what you have told me makes no real difference between us. It was always quite impossible that we could ever be friends."

"Nothing is impossible unless one admits it," I returned doggedly.

She made a little despairing gesture with her hands.

"You don't understand," she said; "and, please God, you never will."

For one moment we remained facing each other in a strained, unnatural silence; then, without another word, she turned away towards the companion, and disappeared down the steps into the saloon.

To say that I was utterly flabbergasted would be nothing but the literal truth. It had all happened so unexpectedly, and with such astounding abruptness, that for a second or so I felt like a man who had inadvertently dropped a lighted match into a large can of petrol. Indeed, no actual explosion could have reduced me to such a complete state of amazed bewilderment as that in which I stood staring at the spot where she had vanished.

Then, quite suddenly, my senses seemed to come back to me. I caught sight of several passengers advancing towards the companion, and, taking out my case, I lighted myself a cigarette, and strolled very slowly in the direction of the stern. At this hour the stretch of deck behind the donkey engine house was absolutely deserted. A better place for a little quiet meditation could scarcely have been found, and, leaning over the railing, I set about the process with as much steadiness as my disturbed faculties would permit.

One thing seemed absolutely certain. Whatever Miss de Roda's original views may have been as to the wisdom of continuing her friendship with me, it was her sudden discovery about my uncle which had been wholly responsible for the extraordinary change in her manner. If I had told her that I was the nephew of Judas Iscariot the result could hardly have been more striking. The mere mention of Richard Jannaway's name had been sufficient to fill her with such amazement and horror that she had been quite incapable of making any attempt at hiding her feelings.

This fact of itself would have been sufficiently remarkable, but to me its significance was doubly increased by the way she had behaved the previous day during our little discussion with the boatmen. Any girl who could have shown such perfect coolness under the circumstances must be gifted with a spirit and nerve that were not easily shaken. I was, therefore, convinced that it must have taken some very real and urgent sense of danger to upset so completely her usual self-control.

Having arrived at this point, I found myself utterly at sea. Beyond the fact that the mystery was in some way or other connected with my uncle I had practically nothing to go upon. If the family recollections of that distinguished gentleman could be trusted, he had probably thrown himself heartily into all kinds of mischief during the course of his South American career, and since the de Rodas came from that part of the world it was quite possible that the name of Richard Jannaway might be connected with some black, unwholesome memory which overshadowed both their lives.

Señor de Roda was just the sort of man who suggested a mysterious past. His obvious avoidance of any sort of society, and the brooding depression which always haunted his sallow face, were exactly in keeping with the idea. The more I thought it over the more probable it seemed that at some period in his life he had been mixed up with my disreputable relation, and I began to feel an acute desire for a little genuine information about the tatter's history.

The most likely people to be able to gratify this curiosity appeared to be Messrs. Wilmot and Drayton. However secretive their late client may have been, they would at least know more about him than I did, and such facts as they possessed might well be the starting-point for further discoveries.

There was no other chance of enlightenment that I could see except by renewing my interrupted conversation with Miss de Roda. This plan, difficult as it might be to put into practice, appealed to me on two grounds. In the first place, I was ready to jump at any suggestion which would bring me into further contact with her, and secondly, I felt perfectly certain that if she chose she could give me a good deal more interesting information than I was likely to get in Bedford Row.

The abrupt way she had left me was not exactly an encouraging omen, but it was possible that after she had recovered from her first agitation she might take a different view of the matter. Anyhow, I made up my mind that if an opportunity came along I would be ready enough to grasp it, and with this resolve I at last tossed away the burned-out stump of my cigarette, and went off to hunt up a belated and much-needed breakfast.

It is one thing to come to a sound decision, however, and quite another to get the chance of carrying it out. All the rest of that day, though I kept a particularly watchful eye upon every likely part of the deck, I never so much as caught a glimpse of the one figure that I was looking for. The remainder of the passengers promenaded up and down in the sunshine with maddening persistence, but Miss de Roda herself remained as obstinately invisible as though she had vanished from the ship.

At one time I almost made up my mind to send along a note to her cabin asking her to meet me. Second thoughts, however, soon led me to abandon the idea. She could be in no possible doubt about my feelings on the matter, and if she didn't choose to gratify them, any attempt to persuade her would be worse than futile. There was nothing to do but to put up with the situation as philosophically as I could, a course of action in which I was assisted by a natural and happy tendency not to worry unnecessarily about anything that cannot be helped.

Late in the day, after we had rounded Ushant and were making our way up Channel, the fine weather which had so far kept us company suddenly petered out. We ran into a grey, drizzling mist, which, although not thick enough to retard our speed to any great extent, was a most unpleasant change after the perfect conditions of the last twenty-four hours. Things got worse rather than improved as we drew nearer to the mouth of the Thames, and when we stopped to pick up our pilot off the Nore the rain was coming down with a pitiless energy that would have damped the ardour of the most enthusiastic patriot.

Under these depressing conditions we crept up the river and came to our berth off the docks. We were not due to make our entrance until eight o'clock the next morning, and it was with a feeling of thorough thankfulness for the fact that I went down to my cabin, and, throwing off my wet clothes, took the chance of a few hours' well-earned sleep.

It was still raining dismally when I turned out, but the short rest had restored me to my usual good spirits. While dressing, I determined that before going on deck I would write a brief line to Miss de Roda wishing her good-bye. I knew that, even if she were willing to see me, which was very unlikely, I should probably be much too busy for the next hour or so to attend to anything but my immediate duties. A second officer is never likely to run short of work while his ship is entering a harbour dock.

I therefore routed out a sheet of notepaper and an envelope, and, sitting down on my bunk, scribbled the few following words by the grey light which filtered in through the porthole:

> "DEAR MISS DE RODA,—As you will probably be leaving the ship before I get a chance of seeing you, I am sending you a line to say good-bye—for the present. I am not going to ask you any questions, as you don't want me to, but I should like you to know that there is nothing in the world which I should allow for a moment to stand in the way of my friendship with you. Whatever the difficulties are, I mean to find them out and put an end to them. Till then I shall have to content myself with thinking about you, as I can't see you; but please

remember that always and any time, if I can be of the slightest service to you, you have only got to let me know. For the next few days I shall be staying on the ship; after that a letter addressed to the head office of the Planet Line in Cockspur Street will always reach me.

"Yours sincerely,

"JOHN DRYDEN."

In reading this through I felt that it was not altogether what I had wanted to say; but I am not much of a hand at letter-writing, and, anyhow, it was too late to start altering it. I put it in the envelope, and on my way along the corridor I gave it to one of the stewardesses, and asked her to hand it on privately to Miss de Roda. Then, having done all I could, I went up on deck and set about the task of earning my inadequate salary.

In a shroud of mist we crept in through the grey dock entrance, amidst the usual bustle and excitement which always accompanies the process of coming alongside. Passengers were already trooping up with their hand-bags and lining the rail nearest the shore, but I was much too occupied with my various duties to have any time to try and distinguish one from the other. Bit by bit we sidled slowly into our appointed berth, while a small crowd of people who had gathered on the dock under dripping umbrellas began to exchange cheerful greetings with their expectant friends on board.

At last the warps were made fast, and up the lowered gangways came the customary knot of port officials. Knowing that I should be wanted, I left my station in the bows, where everything was now secured, and started to come back aft. On my way I ran into Ross, who, hidden in a long mackintosh and smoking his new pipe, was watching the scene with his usual good-tempered indifference.

"Anything I can do for you ashore, Dryden?" he asked.

I stopped. "Are you landing at once?" I asked.

He nodded. "I've got to go up to the office with my papers. I shall be back in about half an hour."

I unbuttoned my coat and took out the cable from Messrs. Wilmot and Drayton.

"Well, if you can manage it," I said, "you might ring up these people and make an appointment for me. Any time after twelve will do."

He took the wire and stuffed it away in his pocket.

"Leave it to me, my lad," he said. "I'll see they have a red carpet down for you all right."

I passed on through the jostling crowd of passengers, and, going down below, proceeded to lend a hand in the various formalities which attend the arrival of an incoming vessel. This process must have occupied the best part of an hour, and by the time I was free Ross had got through his business and returned to the ship. I came across him at the entrance to the smoking-room, where he was squatting peacefully on an upturned cabin trunk.

"It's all right about your appointment," he observed. "Half past twelve's the time, and you can take it from me that you're on a red hot winner. They nearly fell down when I mentioned your name.

"You're a fine liar, Ross," I said sceptically, "but I'm much obliged to you all the same."

By eleven o'clock we had got everything cleared up, and, as my services were no longer required, I went down to my cabin to change into shore-going kit. On my way I met the stewardess to whom I had entrusted my note for Miss de Roda. In reply to my enquiry she informed me that it had been safely delivered, but that the "young lady" had left the ship without giving her any message or answer. This, however, was only what I had expected, so I was able to accept the news with becoming fortitude.

The rain was still falling heavily when I set foot on the dock, but a pleasant tingle of excitement over my approaching interview lifted me above the consideration of such trifles. I made my way to the nearest underground station, and established myself in the corner of a first-class smoker in company with an excellent cigar on which I had omitted to pay duty. I felt that on such a critical occasion a little extravagance was distinctly permissible.

On reaching the Temple I changed into a taxi, and instructed the driver to take me to the address which Messrs. Wilmot and Drayton had given me. It was a slow journey, for the Strand and Chancery Lane were both under repair, as usual, a state of affairs which necessitated frequent and abrupt stoppages. At last, however, we managed to worm a passage across Holborn, and a few minutes later we swung round the corner into the sedate and peaceful atmosphere of Bedford Row.

No. 117 was the last house in the street—a large, old-fashioned Georgian building, that seemed to breathe out a reassuring air of comfortable respectability. I threw away the stump of my cigar, and, getting out on to the pavement, handed the driver his fare. As I did so, or rather, as I turned towards the house, I suddenly caught sight of a man who was leaning up against the railings a few yards farther on. Under ordinary circumstances I don't suppose I should have given him a second glance, but there was something in his manner—some curious suggestion of a furtive interest in my movements—which at once attracted my attention. Not being handicapped by any natural shyness, I stopped where I was and had a good square look at him. He was not what you would call an attractive individual, and any faint claims to beauty he might once have possessed had been seriously marred by a broken nose, which even at that distance was distinctly visible.

As soon as he caught my eye he turned away with an air of badly assumed indifference, and sauntered off up the street. I watched him for a second or two, wondering whether I could have been mistaken, or whether he was really as interested in me as he seemed. I even had some momentary idea of going after him, and asking him what the devil he wanted, but since he made no attempt to stop or look back, I came to the conclusion that he was not worth bothering about. It seemed wildly improbable that a complete stranger could be hanging around there with a deliberate purpose of spying on me; and, anyhow, if I ever ran across him again I should certainly recognise him at once by his broken nose.

With this reflection I dismissed the incident from my mind, and, pushing open the door of No. 117, stepped forward into the hall.

CHAPTER THREE

I found myself in a broad passage, panelled on each side, and ending in a solid-looking stone staircase which led up to the floor above. There was a partly open door on my right, and through the aperture I could see the head of an elderly gentleman peering forward over a desk. He looked up at the sound of my footsteps.

"Good morning," I said. "My name's John Dryden, and I want to see either Mr. Wilmot or Mr. Drayton."

He got up in a leisurely fashion and came round from his seat.

"If you will take a chair," he observed, "I will see whether Mr. Drayton is disengaged. Mr. Wilmot has been defunct for the past seven years."

I was about to offer my condolences, but, without waiting to hear what I had to say, he shuffled past me, and in a crab-like fashion began to ascend the staircase. I filled in the interval by strolling across to the fireplace and looking at the books which decorated the mantelpiece. They were a jolly lot, beginning with Webster's Dictionary, and working up through a rising grade of frivolity to Whitaker's Almanack, which last was carefully encased in a brown paper cover, as though to disguise its rather unseemly tendencies. I was just wondering which of them was the old gentleman's favourite reading when the sound of his returning steps became audible outside. A moment later he reappeared on the threshold.

"If you will accompany me," he observed, "Mr. Drayton will see you."

Placing my umbrella in the stand, I followed him up to the next landing, where he pushed open a door in front of us, and then stood back to allow me to enter.

It was a large, lofty room, lighted by three long windows facing into Bedford Row. Apart from several rather dilapidated easy chairs and a number of black tin boxes, its only furniture appeared to be an enormous table, plentifully strewn with papers and one or two musty packets of deeds.

Mr. Drayton, who was sitting at this table, rose on my entrance and stepped forward to meet me. He was a well-dressed man of about forty-five, with a strong, humorous face and a pair of very honest blue eyes. I took a fancy to him at once.

"How d'you do, Mr. Dryden?" he said, offering me his hand. "You received my cable all right then?"

"I did," I replied, exchanging grips with him, "and I've come along as soon as I could manage it. We only got in at eight o'clock this morning."

He pulled forward an easy chair. "Sit down," he said; "sit down and make yourself comfortable. By the way, have a cigar?" He came back to the table, and, picking up a box of excellent-looking Larenagas, held them out for my inspection.

"Well, I've only just this moment finished one," I said, "but still, that's no reason why I shouldn't have another."

"Certainly not," he remarked cheerfully. "Anybody who can smoke two cigars running ought to take full advantage of the gift."

He lighted one for himself, and then, pulling up a second chair, sat down opposite me.

"I am sorry we were not able to communicate with you sooner," he began, in a rather more serious tone, "but as a matter of fact we had some difficulty in finding out your address. Your uncle seems to have known nothing about you beyond the bare fact of your existence."

"I am not surprised," I said. "I was in much the same blissful position with regard to him."

The lawyer nodded. "Yes," he observed drily, "I gathered that. To be quite candid with you, Mr. Dryden, your uncle had no particular wish that you should benefit by his death. He omitted to make a will because he was utterly indifferent about the disposal of his property. He told me, to use his exact words, that he didn't 'care a curse what happened to it after he was dead.'"

"He seems to have been a genial sort of chap," I said. "How did you run across him?"

Mr. Drayton tilted his chair in the direction of the table, and picked up a bundle of miscellaneous papers fastened together by a clip.

"He came to us originally in rather a peculiar fashion. About two years ago we had been acting in a police court case on behalf of a man called Bascomb—a professional boxer. Bascomb had had a fight in the street with another fellow, whom he accused of cheating him, and, according to the doctor's evidence, he'd come within an inch or two of murder. Luckily for him there had been nothing against him before, and, as the other fellow was known to be a bad lot, we managed to get him off with a month's hard labour.

"The next day Mr. Jannaway called here at the office. He had seen an account of the case in one of the papers, and he wanted us to give him Bascomb's address. He told me quite frankly that as soon as the month was up he was ready to engage the man as a servant."

"He must have had a sporting taste in domestics," I observed with interest.

"Well, perhaps it wasn't quite so extraordinary as it sounds," continued Mr. Drayton, with a laugh. "Bascomb had been in the Marines before taking up with the ring, and he'd had some experience in that class of job. Indeed, one naval officer he had worked for came and gave evidence for him at the court."

"How did it turn out?" I asked curiously.

"As far as I know it was a complete success. Bascomb seemed very grateful for the unexpected chance, and as he has been in your uncle's employment ever since, I suppose he must have proved quite satisfactory. Anyhow, Mr. Jannaway appeared to be perfectly contented with him." He paused and turned over two or three of the papers which he was holding in his hand. "All this is a little beside the point, however. Our real dealings with Mr. Jannaway, so far as you are concerned, began last November. On the third of that month he came to see me again, and asked me if I would act for him in a matter of business. There was an island being advertised for sale off the Essex coast. It was a place called Greensea—a small property of about six and a half acres in the mouth of the Danewell River."

"Greensea!" I echoed. "Why, I know it quite well! I was in the Harwich Patrol the last part of the war, and we were always running in and out of the estuary."

"That's very interesting," said Mr. Drayton, "and, what's more, it saves me a good deal of trouble. If you are already acquainted with your new estate, there's no need for me to try and describe it for you."

I sat up pretty sharply in my chair. "Do you mean to say that Greensea Island belongs to me?" I exclaimed.

"It certainly does," he answered smilingly, "unless someone else turns up with a better claim to it. Your uncle bought the place through us on November the tenth, and, like all the rest of his effects, it goes to his next of kin."

For a moment I sat there, hardly able to believe my ears. If I had been asked to name any legacy more entirely to my taste I think I should have had some difficulty in doing so. All my life, ever since I was quite a small boy, I have had a curious longing to be the owner of an island. I think it was reading one of Anthony Hope's books which originally implanted this desire in my soul, but anyhow, it has always been a secretly cherished dream of mine which I hoped some day to be able to put into practice. To find a life-long wish like this suddenly and unexpectedly gratified was such a startling experience that it was only natural I should be momentarily "knocked out."

"What special attraction your uncle saw in the place," continued Mr. Drayton, "I haven't the remotest notion. There is nothing on the island except the house, and even at low water it's cut off completely from the shore. Personally, I can't imagine a more unpleasant spot to settle down in! Still, there it was; he had evidently made up his mind to buy it, and, as he raised no objection about the cost, we hadn't much difficulty in fixing things up for him. We gave two thousand three hundred and sixty pounds for it, and a very good price too—from the previous owner's point of view."

I reached out for the matches and re-lit my cigar, which in the absorption of the moment I had allowed to go out.

"And what did he do with it when he'd got it?" I demanded. "Go and live there?"

Mr. Drayton nodded. "He went straight down the day after the agreement was signed. There were a few improvements and alterations which he wanted done, but they were all carried out after he was in the house. As far as I know he never left the place again."

I felt my interest in this remarkable uncle of mine increasing with each fresh discovery about him.

"Was he all alone?" I asked. "Hadn't he got anyone living with him?"

"Only Bascomb and a dog," replied Mr. Drayton, "a great savage brute as big as a small donkey. It used to run about loose most of the time, and from what I saw of it I should imagine that nobody would have dared to set foot on the island even if he had been invited. Not that it made much difference, because, as a matter of fact, your uncle never invited anyone. He shut himself up entirely, and, except for Bascomb and the local doctor who attended him in his last illness, I don't believe he ever saw or spoke to another living soul."

"What was the matter with him?" I enquired. "Was he off his chump?"

The lawyer shrugged his shoulders. "More or less, I should think. At least, it's difficult to account for his conduct any other way. Up till then he had been living the life of an ordinary middle-aged man about town. One doesn't throw up all that sort of thing suddenly and go and bury oneself in a God-forsaken place like Greensea unless one's got a screw loose somewhere." He paused. "Besides," he added, "there's no doubt that his mind gave way during his last illness. He was quite incapable of recognising me when I went down to see him, and, according to Dr. Manning, he remained in exactly the same state until he died."

"When was that?" I enquired. "You didn't tell me in your cable."

Once again Mr. Drayton referred to his papers.

"He was taken ill suddenly on March the twenty-third. I think he got a chill, or something of the sort; anyhow, Bascomb wired to me the next day that he was very seedy, and I ran down there in the afternoon. I found him delirious, and altogether about as bad as anyone could possibly be. Bascomb had got hold of a doctor—a fellow called Manning, who spends most of his time on a barge in the river, which he has fitted up as a kind of shooting-box. He doesn't practise as a rule, but when he saw how urgent the matter was he had very kindly come over and taken up his quarters in the house. He seemed to be doing everything that was possible, and as he declared that he was quite ready to stay there as long as he was wanted I decided to leave the case in his hands.

"I heard nothing more for two days; then, on the afternoon of the twenty-eighth, I got a telegram to say that your uncle had died rather unexpectedly in the morning. I sent back a wire to say I would come down at once. In a strictly legal sense I had no real authority to act, but, since there appeared to be nobody else, I thought I had better take the responsibility.

"Dr. Manning was still in the house when I arrived, which of course simplified matters to a very great extent. He had been in charge of the case since the beginning, so there was no need for an inquest or anything of that sort. He was able to certify that the cause of death was heart failure on the top of double pneumonia, and between us we fixed up all the necessary arrangements for the funeral.

"The next thing I did was to go through your uncle's papers. I knew very little about him, and I hoped that I might come across something which would put me in touch with his family. He had never given me the faintest hint about his private affairs—except for once mentioning that he had a nephew called John Dryden, whom he believed to be his next of kin.

"Well, to cut a long story short, I was very little wiser at the end of my search than I was at the beginning. I found practically nothing, except a few receipted bills and one or two business letters which dealt entirely with money matters. If he had any private papers he had evidently put them away somewhere or other in safe custody before leaving London.

"Under the circumstances I acted as best I could. I stayed there until the funeral was over, and then I locked up everything and left Bascomb in charge, with instructions that he wasn't to allow anyone in the house without a written permission from me. He's a queer, sullen sort of fellow, but he seemed to have plenty of sense in his way, and, as far as I could make out, to be thoroughly loyal and trustworthy.

"When I got back to London my first step was to go and see your uncle's bankers. I explained the position to them, and I found them quite ready to give me all the assistance in their power. This didn't amount to much, however. They had no private documents or anything of that sort; in fact, all they could really do was to let me have a complete statement of the actual cash and securities in their possession.

"I saw then that the only practical course was to get into communication with you as soon as possible. It was a bit of a proposition, considering that I knew nothing whatever about you except your name, but luckily I was able to secure the services of a retired Scotland Yard Inspector called Martin Campbell, who is quite the smartest man in London at that sort of thing. (He is coming here this morning, by the way, so you will probably meet him.) Well, he set to work, and in something less than three weeks he had managed to run you to earth—or perhaps I should say to sea! Anyhow, he found out that you were second officer on the *Neptune,* and as the Planet people told us that your ship was expected in Oporto on the third of May, I decided to wait and cable you there.

"Meanwhile I went ahead with the business of establishing your claim to the estate. It was plain enough sailing now I had once got on to your track, and by the time you reached Oporto all the preliminary steps were more or less completed. Of course, there are still a number of legal formalities to be gone through. You won't be able to touch the money in the bank for some little while, but that is a difficulty we can probably come to some arrangement over. If you are short of cash I have no objection to making you a personal advance. As far as the actual title to the property is concerned, you can take it from me that your position is a perfectly sound one."

He tossed the bundle of papers he had been holding on to the table, and leaned back in his chair with an air of reassuring friendliness.

"It seems to me," I said gratefully, "that I'm pretty deeply in your debt already. I don't know why you should have taken all this trouble on my account, but I'm sure I'm devilish obliged to you."

"There's nothing to thank me for," he returned whimsically. "You can put it down to professional enterprise. Mr. Jannaway was a client of mine, and it seemed to me I might as well make sure of you before anyone else butted in! We're an unscrupulous lot in Bedford Row as far as business is concerned."

"It's lucky for me you are," I retorted, "otherwise I might have gone on chasing about the world without any idea that I had suddenly become a bloated capitalist." I paused. "By the way," I added curiously, "how much money is there in the bank?"

Once again his eyes twinkled. "I was waiting for that question," he said. "It's a great tribute to your self-control that you haven't asked it before."

"To be quite honest," I confessed, "it's only just come into my head. I was so interested in what you were telling me about my uncle that I haven't been able to think of anything else."

He got up from his chair, and, retrieving his discarded papers, took a seat on the corner of the table.

"Well, as a matter of fact," he began, "the position is rather odd. If the estate only consists of what the bank holds, it amounts, roughly speaking, to about ten thousand pounds. That, of course, is not counting in the value of Greensea Island."

There was a pause.

"What do you mean 'if'?" I asked. "Is there a chance of some more turning up?"

"There doesn't seem to be," he admitted; "all the same, it's very difficult to fit in the present sum with the way in which your uncle was living. Ever since he opened the account he has kept about the same balance, while on the lowest estimate he must have been spending at least two thousand a year."

"But surely the bank must have some idea where he got it from!" I objected.

"That's just what they haven't. In the whole of that period—practically four years—there were only three credit entries. One is for twelve thousand, one for three thousand, and the other for four thousand eight hundred. On each occasion these sums were paid in over the counter—in cash!"

"In cash!" I repeated half incredulously. "Why he must have been blackmailing Rothschild!"

My companion threw back his head and laughed boisterously. "Well, if that's the case," he replied, "it's a pity he hasn't left you the family secret. It's worth learning evidently."

I knocked off the ash of my cigar and sat back comfortably in my chair.

"Oh, I don't know," I remarked. "I'm not greedy. Five hundred a year will do very nicely for my simple needs."

"It will come to more than that," said Mr. Drayton. "There is one rather satisfactory piece of news I have been keeping in reserve." He paused. "I have been lucky enough to get you a tenant for Greensea Island. He is willing to pay a rent of two hundred and fifty, and take it over just as it stands."

He brought out this offer with an air of satisfaction which showed me plainly enough that he expected me to jump at it. For a moment I refrained from disillusioning him.

"Who is it?" I enquired with some curiosity.

"Well, as it happens, it's the very man we have been talking about—Dr. Manning. He wants to start a new yachting club, and he thinks the island would make an ideal headquarters. He seems to be as keen as mustard on the idea, but of course I couldn't give him any definite answer until I had seen you. I told him that you would very probably be here this morning, and he is going to ring me up at half-past two and find out if you will accept his proposal. I must say I don't think you are likely to get a better one."

"I don't want a better one," I said. "If Greensea Island really belongs to me, I haven't the smallest intention of letting it. I mean to go and live there myself."

There was a brief silence.

"Are you serious?" demanded Mr. Drayton.

"Rather," I replied cheerfully. "I've always wanted to have a private island of my own, and now I've got one you don't suppose I'm going to hand it over to anyone else?"

Something in my manner evidently convinced him that I was in earnest.

"Well, *chacun à son goüt?*" he observed, with a humorous shrug of his shoulders. "I can't see the attraction myself, but I suppose a taste for that sort of thing runs in the family."

"Oh, I've no intention of becoming a hermit like my uncle," I explained. "There must be plenty of decent fellows in the neighbourhood, and I've no doubt that I shall get all the society I want. It's the shooting and sailing and fishing that will be the chief attraction to me."

"What about your engagement with the Planet people?" he asked.

"I am under a contract of sorts with them," I said, "but they'll probably let me off if I ask them nicely. There's no shortage of second officers in the world."

"In that case," he remarked, "you can please yourself. The property will be yours in a few weeks, and if you want to go down there straight away no one's likely to raise any objection." He paused. "At least, no one except Dr. Manning," he added. "I am afraid he'll be rather disappointed. He seems to have set his heart on the idea."

"I am sorry to spoil his plans," I said, "but, after all, I suppose he can start his club somewhere else. Anyhow, it's no use his thinking about Greensea; you might make that quite plain to him when he rings up."

Mr. Drayton nodded. "I will," he said, "and another thing I had better do is to drop a line to Bascomb. I presume you will be going down there to have a look at the place as soon as possible, and it would be just as well to let him know that you're the new owner. By the way, do you intend to take Bascomb over with the other fixtures?"

"I am quite ready to," I replied, "if he likes to come, and I can afford to pay his wages. I shall want someone to look after me, and he sounds the right sort of chap."

Mr. Drayton tossed the stump of his cigar into the fireplace.

"How are you actually situated with regard to money?" he enquired.

"I have got seventy or eighty pounds of my own," I said "It's not exactly a fortune, but it ought to be enough to carry on with for the present."

He relinquished his place on the edge of the table and sat down again in the chair which he had been occupying when I first entered the room.

"Well, it's just as you like," he remarked, "but if you are really serious about this idea of yours, I think you had better let me make you a small advance. You needn't have any scruples, you know, because I shall charge you interest on it. There are bound to be a certain number of things you will want to buy, and there's no particular point in running yourself short of cash." He looked round at me enquiringly. "What would you say to a couple of hundred pounds at six per cent.?"

"I should say thank you," I replied promptly. "It's rather a lukewarm sort of a phrase, but I can't think of anything better for the moment."

He pressed a small electric bell in the wall beside him.

"No need for thanks," he repeated. "I shouldn't suggest it if it wasn't a perfectly sound investment from my point of view. I hope to make a lot of money out of you before we've finished."

The door opened, and a solemn-faced young man with a large pair of spectacles on his nose insinuated himself into the room.

"Are you busy, Sandford?" enquired Mr. Drayton, looking up from the cheque that he was writing.

"Not particularly, sir," replied the solemn-faced young man.

"Well, this is Mr. John Dryden, whom I was speaking to you about. We are advancing him the sum of two hundred pounds at six per cent. interest on the Jannaway estate. You might make out a receipt for him to sign and bring it in here as soon as it's done."

"Very good, sir," responded Mr. Sandford meekly; then he paused. "Inspector Campbell is downstairs, sir," he added. "He says he will wait until you are disengaged."

The lawyer nodded. "I shan't be very long," he replied.

Mr. Sandford withdrew as noiselessly as he had entered, and, tearing off the cheque that he had written, my companion turned back to me.

"Now let me see," he observed thoughtfully; "what's the next thing we've got to do?"

"The next thing," I said firmly, "is to go out together and have some lunch. I always make a point of giving a lunch party when I come into a fortune."

"It's not a bad habit," he admitted, smiling. "Unfortunately, I have got this man Campbell waiting to see me."

"Bring him along too," I suggested. "You can talk to him while we're eating."

Mr. Drayton got up from his chair. "We'll put it to him anyway," he said. "I don't suppose he'll say no. One can generally trust a Scotchman not to miss anything that's worth having."

He folded the cheque across in the middle and handed it to me.

"How about the receipt?" I asked.

"You can come back this afternoon and sign that. There are one or two other papers I shall have ready for you by then."

"That will just suit me nicely," I said. "I can go round to Cockspur Street first and interview the Planet people, then I shall know exactly where I am."

Taking his hat from a peg behind the door, Mr. Drayton led the way downstairs. In the small room on the ground floor a large, burly man with a close-cropped moustache and a chin like the toe of a boot was standing with his back to the fireplace.

"Morning, Campbell," said Mr. Drayton. "Let me introduce you to Mr. John Dryden, whom you were clever enough to find for me."

The Inspector stepped forward.

"Pleased to meet you, sir," he observed, extending an enormous hand.

"Mr. Dryden has invited us both out to lunch," continued the lawyer. "He wants us to assist him in celebrating his sudden accession to wealth."

The Inspector moistened his lips with the tip of his tongue.

"Always glad to oblige a friend of yours, Mr. Drayton," he replied affably.

"Well, come along then," returned the other, picking up his umbrella from the stand. "I've got to be back by half-past two, and I hate to hurry over a meal when somebody else is paying for it." He turned to me. "The Holborn's the nearest place," he added, "and the head waiter is one of my clients."

"Providence is with us," I answered hopefully.

We stepped out into the misty drizzle of Bedford Row, and, making our way down a couple of side alleys, emerged into the crowded main thoroughfare almost opposite our destination. A few minutes later we were comfortably seated at a corner table in the big restaurant, while the head waiter—an impressive gentleman with side whiskers—hovered benignly in the foreground.

"I have come into a fortune," I explained to him, "and I want a lunch which will be worthy of the occasion."

With the air of a man who is fully accustomed to deal with such emergencies he picked up the menu card and began to offer suggestions, commencing with cocktails and oysters, and wandering on in a mellow way through saddle of mutton, roast duckling, and Stilton cheese. I accepted them *en bloc*, and crowned the order by demanding a bottle of his best champagne—a finishing touch which brought a wonderfully human expression into the naturally stern face of the Inspector.

"I was doing a better day's work than I bargained for when I ran across this gentleman's track," he announced contentedly.

"The Jannaway estate," observed Mr. Drayton, "has certainly passed into the right hands."

"By the way," I said, turning to the Inspector, "when you were hunting around after me did you happen to make any discoveries in connection with my uncle? He seems to have been a queer sort of customer."

The Inspector passed his hand across his scrubby moustache. "Aye, sir," he said drily, "he was all of that and a bit over. I can't say I ever remember a gentleman who managed to keep his affairs more to himself."

"But surely you picked up some information about him?" I persisted.

"Only what I passed on to Mr. Drayton," he replied. "It didn't amount to much, as he's probably told you."

"It certainly left one or two things to be explained," assented the lawyer. "Greensea Island, for instance. I was just saying that Mr. Jannaway's sudden resolve to imitate Robinson Crusoe was one of the most extraordinary puzzles I've ever come across."

The Inspector pulled his chair closer to the table.

"I may be wrong," he said quietly, "but it's my belief that he was frightened—frightened stiff, if you ask me."

I felt a sudden tingle of excitement in my heart, but I don't think I showed any outward sign of it.

"Why do you think that?" I asked as coolly as possible. "What on earth could he have to be frightened of?"

The Inspector made a slight gesture with his hands. "That I can't tell you, sir. I only know that when a man suddenly shuts himself up on an island, and won't allow a living soul to land there without his permission, he generally has some pretty good reason at the back of it."

"Perhaps, after all, it was only a family weakness for solitude," struck in Mr. Drayton. "Dryden here intends to do the same thing as soon as he can arrange it."

"Well, hardly that," I said, forcing a laugh. "I mean to go and live there certainly, but there won't be any man-traps on my territory."

As I spoke the waiter came up with the cocktails, and in the short but agreeable pause that followed I rapidly made up my mind that it would be better for the moment not to press my enquiries about my uncle any farther. It would be difficult to do so without relating the story of my meeting with Miss de Roda, and that was a step which I had no intention of taking. If she were really mixed up with some sinister mystery concerning the dead man, I would at least take care that her name should not be dragged into the matter as long as I was able to prevent it.

Accordingly, with the arrival of the oysters, I took the chance of steering the conversation into a rather less delicate channel by asking the Inspector how he had managed to track me down with such remarkable promptitude. He was ready enough to describe his methods, and from this point we drifted into a general conversation on detective work and other exciting topics, which lasted us all through the remainder of lunch.

Both my companions proved to be excellent talkers, as well as thoroughly good fellows, and I felt quite sorry when at last Mr. Drayton suddenly glanced at his watch and announced that it was time for him to be getting back to the office.

"It's on your account," he explained, buttoning his coat. "Our friend the doctor will be ringing me up in a minute to find out whether you are prepared to do a deal with him."

"Tell him I'm sorry," I said, "and say that if he can manage to forgive me I shall look forward to making his acquaintance. I don't want to start by quarrelling with my nearest neighbour, especially after the decent way he has behaved."

"I shouldn't think there was much fear of that," returned the lawyer reassuringly. "He seems to be a most amiable person, judging from what I saw of him." He held out his hand. "Thanks for an A1 lunch," he added, "and I shall expect you back at the office some time between four and five."

I paid my bill, and we parted from each other on the pavement outside, but not before I had extracted from the Inspector (who had confessed to being "partial to a day's shooting") a promise that he would come down and spend a week-end with me at Greensea as soon as I was comfortably settled in. There was something about his stolid but shrewd personality which distinctly appealed to me, and, in addition to that I felt that, in view of the curious atmosphere which appeared to brood over my new inheritance I might find him an uncommonly useful friend.

My two companions started off together across Holborn, and, turning down Chancery Lane, I set out for Cockspur Street, where the head offices of the Planet Line are situated. It was not without certain misgivings that I mounted the big flight of stone steps and sent in my card by one of the clerks with a request for an interview with the secretary. In spite of what I had said to Mr. Drayton, I was in reality none too certain in my own mind that the management would be sufficiently obliging to relieve me from the remainder of my contract. The prospect of another long, monotonous voyage to Manaos and back was anything but an attractive one, and I waited for my summons in the outer office with considerable anxiety.

Luck, however, proved to be on my side. One of the principal directors, whom I knew quite well to speak to, happened to be engaged with the secretary at the very time when I was shown into the latter's room. Like myself, both these big-wigs had evidently lunched well, and when I told them my story and put forward my request they received it in the friendliest fashion possible.

"You may set your mind quite at rest, Mr. Dryden," said the director, with a sort of pompous affability. "I will lay your application before the Board myself, and you can take it from me that there is not likely to be any opposition. We shall be sorry to lose you, of course, but I am sure that none of my fellow directors would wish to stand in your way. Your record since you have been with us is one which entitles you to every consideration."

Stifling a modest blush, I expressed my thanks as well as I could manage; and after a little more conversation I shook hands with them both and took my leave.

I went down the steps and into the street, feeling rather like a man who has been unexpectedly released from gaol. As if by the wave of a fairy's wand, everything I wanted seemed suddenly to have come tumbling into my lap. I had an absurd desire to throw up my hat into the air and indulge in a triumphant dance round the Nelson Column, but the cold eye of a neighbouring policeman just saved me from this social indiscretion.

A glance at my watch showed me that it was close on half-past three, so, making my way across the square, I started back for Bedford Row. This time I was not kept waiting on the ground floor. Directly I arrived the old clerk conducted me upstairs to Mr. Drayton, whom I found fully prepared for me, with the papers that he wished me to sign laid out on his desk.

"Well," he said, "you're a bit early, but I'm ready for you. How did you get on with your resignation?"

I told him of the gratifying fashion in which I had been received, and he nodded his head, with the half-whimsical expression to which I was becoming accustomed.

"Nobody could help being civil to you, Dryden," he said. "You're so refreshingly straightforward."

I thought of the reserve I had practised on him with regard to my relations with Miss de Roda, and for a moment I felt very much of a humbug.

"What happened about the doctor?" I asked, by way of covering my embarrassment. "Was he very upset when he found that I wouldn't accept his offer?"

"He seemed a bit disgruntled; at least, it sounded like it over the telephone. I rather think he means to have another shot at you himself."

"I suppose you made it quite plain to him that I was in earnest?" I asked.

"Quite," returned the lawyer, "but he's evidently one of those obstinate cusses who won't take no for an answer. Anyhow, he insisted on pressing me for your address. I told him that as far as I knew you were staying on the *Neptune* for the present, so perhaps he'll turn up and plead his cause in person."

"He'll have a journey for nothing if he does," I said. "Still, that's his pigeon, not mine."

I took a seat at the table, and, after reading through the various documents, which Mr. Drayton explained to me in turn, I signed the lot one after the other.

"Now we can go straight ahead," he observed, "and get the whole business cleared up. I have sent a line to Bascomb telling him that you are his new employer, so you will be able to go and inspect your property without any fear of his setting the dog on you."

"That's comforting," I said with a laugh. "It would be a rotten beginning to be torn in pieces on one's own landing-stage." I rose from my chair and began to collect my hat and umbrella. "I shall run down there to-morrow or the next day," I added. "It just depends how soon I can leave the ship."

"Well, let's hear how you get on," he said, giving me his hand, "and if I can be of the slightest use to you in any way don't hesitate to let me know. That's the only excuse for a lawyer's existence."

I thanked him once more with a gratitude that was entirely genuine, and, feeling how extraordinarily lucky I was to have dropped across such a good friend just when I needed him, I turned up my collar and set out again on my return journey to Charing Cross.

A clammy, drizzling mist still pervaded everything, but, disdaining a cab in my present high spirits, I strode briskly along over the wet pavements. My inward cheerfulness must to some extent have been reflected in my face, for on two occasions I noticed a draggled-looking passer-by glance rather curiously at me, as though he wondered what on earth I could find to be so happy about on such a damnable afternoon.

When I reached the station I found that my luck was still in. The train I wanted was standing at the platform, and a minute later I was being whirled eastwards in the comfortably padded seat of a half-empty smoker. It had certainly been a well-arranged and satisfying day.

A short walk from Mark Lane, where I got out, brought me to the Docks entrance. The fog here was thicker than ever, and a general air of murky desolation showed that work for the day had come to a compulsory standstill. I had taken my bearings in the morning, however, and, without much fear of missing my way, I struck out into the uninviting gloom.

On the near side of where the *Neptune* was lying there was a long stretch of empty dock, with a tall, double lamp-post guarding its extreme point. I made this landmark safely, and, keeping the edge of the basin in view on my right, I advanced carefully along the wet cobblestones.

I had covered perhaps some thirty yards, and was just thinking of the hot whisky and water that I would order as soon as I got on board, when I suddenly became conscious of a quick shuffle of footsteps behind me. Before I could so much as blink an eyelash something dull and heavy came down with a sickening whack on the back of my head. The soft hat that I was wearing was driven down violently over my face, and, half-stunned by the blow, I stumbled forward on to my hands and knees.

What happened after that will always remain a trifle blurred. I have a vague impression of trying to scramble to my feet, and of receiving a violent shove which sent me sprawling sideways, with one arm and leg dangling over the edge of the parapet. I remember making a frantic clutch at the slippery stone in a vain effort to save myself; then the ground seemed to give way beneath me, and I went lurching wildly down through space into the black water below.

CHAPTER FOUR

I am a pretty good swimmer as people go, but when one is fully clothed and three parts dazed, a sudden plunge into a dirty dock is apt to prove a trifle disconcerting. I went under completely, and, although I struck out at once with the blind instinct of self-preservation, it was several moments before I managed to struggle back to the surface.

Fortunately for me my hat had come off in the fall, and, treading water with frantic energy, I was able to take a hasty survey of my position. Everything was more or less hidden by the mist, but a few yards away I could just make out the black face of the dock wall rising up dimly through the gloom.

If I hadn't been hampered by a sopping overcoat I could have covered the distance in two or three strokes. As it was, that cursed garment clung round my legs with a persistency that nearly finished off my career for good and all. Twice I was dragged under again entirely, and it was in a very exhausted state that I at last reached out a hand and grabbed hold of a slimy iron ring that was sticking out of the wall a foot or so above my head.

I was so utterly done that I could not have gone another foot. I just clung to this support, shaking the water out of my eyes, and gulping down mouthfuls of fresh air into my half-choked lungs. For all I knew the gentleman who had shoved me in might still be standing on the parapet above waiting to finish me off with a convenient brickbat, but for the moment I was too occupied in getting my breath to worry about him or anything else.

As that first feeling of suffocation passed off, however, the full extent of my danger suddenly came home to me. I realised with a sort of dull shock that nothing except the ring stood between me and death. If I once let go my hold I knew that I should sink like a stone, and, giddy and exhausted as I was, I could hardly expect my strength to last out for more than a few minutes.

Taking a firmer grip with both hands, I stared up desperately at the face of the wall. There was not much encouragement there, for the six feet of smooth and slippery concrete that met my eyes showed no trace of a crack throughout its entire surface. As far as I could see, I was trapped like a rat in a bucket, and for the first time in my life I felt a numbing chill of despair creeping through my heart.

With a last effort I twisted myself round and faced out into the grey void of the dock.

"Help!" I shouted at the top of my voice. "Help!"

With a staggering unexpectedness that nearly made me let go my grip, an answering hail came back through the mist.

"Wot's the matter? Were are you?'

"Here!" I sung out frantically. "In the water. Up against the wall."

"'Ang on, then," holloaed a gruff, encouraging voice. "'Ang on! mate! I'm a-comin'."

From a little way off I heard the sudden splash and creak of oars, and no music could have rivalled the beauty of that familiar sound. Nearer and nearer it came, while with deadened fingers I clasped the ring and battled fiercely against a growing feeling of faintness. At last, just when I felt that I could not hold on for another second, a vague blur of light broke out before me in the darkness. The ghostly outline of a boat's stern loomed up suddenly into view, and then, almost before I knew what was happening, a strong hand had gripped me by the elbow, and I was being dragged in over the gunwale. Grateful but helpless, I flopped down on to the wet floorboards, where I lay dripping and panting like a newly landed fish.

"Seems to me I come along about the right time, eh, mate?"

The gleam of a lantern flickered close above my head, and a bearded, friendly face, half hidden by a sou'-wester, peered down into mine.

"A drop o' rum's wot you want," continued my rescuer. "'Ere, 'ave a go at this; that'll put some guts into yer."

He produced a small flat bottle from his pocket, and, kneeling down beside me, tilted some of its contents into my mouth. The stuff was raw spirit of the fiercest kind, and as a prescription it certainly carried out his prophecy. With a spluttering gasp I struggled up into a sitting position, while, replacing the cork, the owner of the bottle contemplated his handiwork with an approving smile.

"Nothin' like a drop o' rum," he observed. "There's many a bloke walkin' round now who'd be dead and buried if them blarsted teetotallers 'ad their way."

In a dazed fashion I began to try and express my gratitude, but he cut me short by clapping me on the shoulder.

"That's orl right, mate! You ain't the fust I've pulled out o' this 'ere dock—not by a long way."

He thrust the bottle back into his pocket, and, slipping an arm under my shoulder, hoisted me up on to one of the seats.

"Reg'lar death trap in a fog," he went on, "an' I've told 'em so a score o' times. They ought to 'ave a chain along the edge be rights, but Lor' love yer, they don't care 'ow many's drownded—not they!"

He picked up the lantern and replaced it in the bows.

"Were was you tryin' to get to, mate?" he enquired.

Once more I fought back the stupor which was stealing over my brain.

"Do you know the *Neptune*?" I asked. "She came in early this morning."

"The *Neptune*!" he repeated. "W'y, she's lyin' just above us."

"I'm the second officer," I said, "and if you'll see me aboard I'll be devilish grateful to you. I've had a crack on the head that's knocked me a bit silly."

"I'll get yer there orl right, sir," he replied at once, with a sudden tinge of respectfulness in his voice. "Just you sit quiet and leave it to me, sir. I'll 'ave yer back inside of a couple o' minutes."

He seized his sculls, and the next moment we were moving, rapidly along through the mist under the shadow of the dock wall. I sat there in a kind of half-conscious state, watching his figure swaying backwards and forwards, and wondering vaguely how long it would be before I slipped down again into the bottom of the boat.

I have a dim recollection of arriving at the foot of some dark, slimy steps, and of scrambling feebly up with the help of my companion's arm. Then we were stumbling endlessly forward over the cobblestones, till at last the mist changed into a yellow haze, and the huge bulk of the *Neptune* reared itself up on our right.

By a fierce effort of will I just summoned enough strength to drag my failing legs up the gangway. Beyond that I know nothing, for as my feet touched the deck the world suddenly swayed round beneath me, and I felt myself dropping helplessly into a black and bottomless gulf.

*

"Well, my lad, and what have you got to say for yourself?"

The voice sounded curiously familiar, and, opening my eyes, I blinked up vaguely into the genial face of Ross. For a second or two I lay staring at him in a kind of dull perplexity. Then, as if by magic, all my drowsiness seemed to clear away, and I started up with a jerk that sent a sharp stab of pain shooting through my head.

Ross put out a restraining hand. "Whoa there!" he said. "Take it easy. Take it easy."

I had already made a couple of interesting discoveries. I was in pyjamas, and I was sitting up in my bunk in my own cabin, with a broad shaft of sunlight streaming in on me through the open porthole.

"Hullo!" I said, looking round. "How long have I been here?"

Ross consulted his watch. "It's twelve o'clock now," he replied, "all but a few minutes. You have been wallowing in exactly fifteen hours of sweet and refreshing slumber." He sat down on the edge of my bunk and placed his fingers on my pulse. "How do you feel now?" he asked.

I considered the problem with some care. "I've got a rotten head," I said, "and I feel devilish hungry."

He let go my wrist and rose to his feet.

"Let's have a look at your nut," he remarked.

He bent down over me and very carefully parted the hair at the back of my head.

"You'll do," he announced, after a brief inspection. "You've had a nasty bump of some kind, but there's no real damage done. That's the best of these thick skulls!"

In view of his medical services I allowed the insult to pass.

"Tell me, Ross," I said, "what happened when I got on board? I remember crawling up the gangway, but after that everything's a complete blank."

"The most important thing that happened," he replied, "was the interruption of my tea. I was just sitting down peacefully when someone came bursting in with the news that you were throwing fits on the deck. With my usual unselfishness I at once hurled down my bread and butter and bundled up to render first aid. I found you stretched out like a piece of wet tripe, in charge of a whiskered old fossil, who told me he had found you floating about the next door dock. His own view of the case was that you'd 'basked your napper up agin a bit o' stone,' and from what I could see his diagnosis appeared to be more or less accurate. Anyhow, I gave him five bob for his trouble—I thought you were worth that—and then I got hold of the purser, who was still on board, and between us we carted you down here and conducted a little post-mortem on our own. There didn't seem to be a vast lot the matter. You certainly had a pretty healthy bruise on the back of your head, but knowing that you'd got a skull like an ox I wasn't much worried about that. I thought you would be all right if I let you sleep it off, so we shoved you into pyjamas and tucked you up nice and comfy in your little white cot."

He paused, and, lighting himself a cigarette, contemplated me with a humorous smile.

"There you have been ever since," he finished, "snoring away in the most disgusting fashion. They started shifting cargo at six o'clock, and making the devil's own row about it, but it seemed to act on you as a sort of lullaby. You've simply lain there smiling and grunting like a new-born infant, while I've had to hang around all the morning waiting for you to wake up and make your apologies."

"You won't regret it," I said consolingly. "I've got something in the way of yarns for you that you don't hear every day in the week."

"Well, you had better get some grub inside you before you start it," he interrupted. "No one can be really chatty on an empty stomach." He moved towards the door. "I believe there is still a cook lurking about the premises somewhere," he added. "You lie quiet and I'll go and forage around and see what I can find."

He left the cabin, and, sinking back in a rather gingerly fashion, I took up a comfortable position amongst the pillows. In spite of a racking headache, my mind itself seemed to be in excellent working order. The various events of the previous afternoon stood out clear and distinct in my memory, and, lying there with my eyes shut, I allowed my thoughts to travel slowly and carefully over the whole of my experiences up to the moment when I had fallen unconscious upon the *Neptune's* deck.

From this retrospective effort one fact emerged with startling clearness. However wild and incredible it might seem, someone had undoubtedly attempted to murder me. There had been a whole-hearted efficiency about the attack which rendered any other conclusion impossible. If I had merely been knocked on the head from behind I might have attributed the kind attention to some prowling dock rat who had suddenly seen the chance of picking up a little money, but the recollection of that extra shove which had sent me sprawling into the water put this explanation altogether out of court. It was murder, not loot, which had been my assailant's object, and nothing but the providential thickness of my skull had robbed him of success.

So far from clearing up the riddle, however, this only made things more unaccountable than ever. Why on earth anyone in the world should be thirsting for my blood was a problem for which I could find no conceivable solution. No doubt I have managed to make some enemies amongst the various crews I have had to handle in my time, but, after all, people don't attempt to split one's skull unless they have a rather more pressing reason than mere personal dislike.

Gradually, and with a kind of half-incredulous hesitation, my thoughts began to turn in another direction. Could it be possible that this adventure was in some way or other connected with my new inheritance? Ever since I had received that unexpected telegram at Leixoes I seemed to have been moving in a vague atmosphere of mystery and danger, which increased rather than lessened with each fresh discovery that I made. My interview with Miss de Roda had been a strange enough opening to the whole business, while the various facts that I had subsequently picked up from Mr. Drayton only served to strengthen the impression left on me by that amazing incident.

There was now little doubt in my mind that my late lamented uncle had been a pretty complete blackguard, and that in attributing his passion for solitude to a guilty conscience the detective had been more or less on the right track. Quite possibly, as I had originally guessed, de Roda himself had been mixed up with some of his shady transactions, in which case it was only natural that the former's niece should have been a trifle upset on hearing my news. This at least was a possible explanation, and, so far as I could see, the only one that fitted in with the facts of the case.

Where it failed to be particularly illuminating, however, was with regard to my attempted assassination. Why my uncle's sins—if they were sins—should be visited upon me in this prompt and drastic fashion was a bewildering question which I was quite unable to answer. After all, I had had nothing to do with his confounded past, and, unless there was another heir lurking in the background, it was difficult to see how my departure from this planet could possibly benefit anybody.

Besides, even if it did, there still remained the problem of my assailant's identity. With the exception of Ross and Mr. Drayton himself no one had known of my appointment in Bedford Row, while even I myself had been quite unaware what time I should be likely to return to the ship. If the attack had been deliberately planned, it seemed almost certain that someone must have been spying on my movements, since no other theory would account for their being on the right spot at the right moment.

Suddenly, as if it were a sort of inspiration, there came back to my memory the one incident of the previous day which so far I had overlooked. Who was the gentleman with the broken nose who had been lounging about so suspiciously in the neighbourhood of Mr. Drayton's office? Had he really been waiting there for me, and could it have been his hand that had stretched me out in that particularly neat fashion upon the dock causeway? Once again I recalled the furtive eagerness with which he had been apparently watching my movements, and the prompt way in which he had slunk off as soon as he had seen that I was looking at him. The more I thought it over the more likely it seemed that he had been in some way or other connected with my adventure, and I could have kicked myself for not having tackled him then and there, in accordance with my first impulse.

Things being as they were, however, it was no good worrying over past mistakes. I had quite enough to occupy my attention with thinking about the immediate future, which from all appearances promised to be a singularly lively one. From a purely commonsense point of view the right thing to do was obviously to lay the whole matter in front of Mr. Drayton. I felt that I had in him a shrewd and friendly ally, who would at once take every possible step to get to the bottom of the mystery. Unfortunately, I was faced with the same difficulty as on the previous afternoon—I could not very well take him into my confidence without telling him the complete story. The same objection held good in the case of Ross, the only other person I could think of to whom I could turn for help. I should have to tell him something, of course, but, no matter what happened, I was still determined not to introduce Miss de Roda's name into the affair so long as it could possibly be avoided.

At this point in my meditations the door was pushed open, and Ross himself came back into the cabin. He was carrying a well-loaded tray, from which an appetising odour of coffee mounted up into the air.

"I didn't know what you wanted," he observed, "but I've managed to rake together something in the way of a meal."

I glanced down at the rack of nicely browned toast, the tempting heap of scrambled egg, and the little white rolls of fresh butter.

"It's not so bad," I remarked, "for a scratch effort."

"Well, you get outside it," he replied, "and then we'll hear what you have got to say for yourself. You don't mind my having a gasper, I suppose?"

He seated himself on my sea-going chest, and, feeling in his waistcoat pocket, produced a battered-looking packet of cigarettes. While he was thus engaged I set to work on the tray in front of me, and in a very little while I had polished off its contents with a thoroughness that would have done credit to a flight of locusts.

"That's better," I said, with a contented sigh. "Now take away the tray and give me one of those poisonous things you're smoking. I must keep you company, if only in self-defence."

He did as I asked him, and, having secured a light, I settled back into my old position amongst the pillows.

"Take it slow," he repeated encouragingly. "We've got all the rest of the day ahead of us."

Beginning at the moment when I left the ship, I started out to tell him the story of my previous day's experiences. I only made one omission, and that was to leave out all reference to the broken-nosed stranger in Bedford Row. My idea that the latter might be in some way or other connected with the de Rodas may have been a far-fetched one, but, as I have said before, I had no intention of taking any risks. I knew that underneath Ross's careless manner there lurked an uncommonly wide awake intelligence, and that the least hint might be sufficient to put him on the right track.

I therefore cut out that particular incident completely, and went straight ahead to a description of my meeting with Mr. Drayton and of the various adventures which had followed our interview. Step by step I related the whole proceedings, until I had brought my story right down to the moment when I had spun round and pitched headlong on the unpleasantly solid planking of the *Neptune's* deck.

Squatting on the chest and scattering tobacco ash generously all over the floor, Ross listened to me with the closest attention. He made no attempt to interrupt me until I had finished, and even then he remained for a moment peacefully smoking, and contemplating me with a sort of amused interest.

"It's a shamefully unfair world," he observed at last. "Here have I been hunting for adventure all my life, and hardly ever finding it, while, without so much as lifting a finger, you go and plop bang into the middle of the finest shilling shocker I've ever heard of." He tossed away the stump of his cigarette through the open porthole. "I always said you were born to be the hero of a romance," he added; "and, by Jove, you've struck it this time with both feet."

"I'll take your word for it," I replied ruefully. "At present I feel as if I'd struck it chiefly with my head." I raised myself on my elbow and looked across to where he was sitting. "Tell me, Ross," I said, "what do you make of it all? Do you really think this cracked skull of mine can have anything to do with the rest of the business?"

"Well, it looks a bit like it," he answered drily. "I can't imagine your having any personal enemy sufficiently savage to try and blot you off the face of the earth. You are such an amiable lad—as second officers go."

"But there's no one I can think of who would benefit a farthing by my death," I objected.

"You never know," he returned hopefully. "There may be some bloody-minded next of kin who is simply thirsting to step into your shoes." He paused. "If it isn't that," he went on, "it must be one of those family vendettas, like they have in Corsica. Your uncle probably played a rotten trick on somebody, and they've sworn an oath to exterminate the entire breed."

"Thanks," I said with a laugh. "You're a comforting sort of blighter, Ross."

He hoisted himself up, and came across to where I was lying.

"It's all right," he said. "I'm really devilish interested, and if there's any way in which I can help you can count me in to the limit." He grinned mischievously. "I couldn't help pulling your leg though; the whole thing's so gorgeously fantastic."

"I suppose it is," I admitted. "At the same time there's a good solid chunk of fact about it somewhere—at least, judging by the way my head's aching." I lay back again on the pillow to try and ease the pain. "The question is," I added, "what the deuce am I to do next?"

"The first thing to do is to get well," he answered. "Then it seems to me that your best plan will be to go down to this mysterious island of yours and have a good squint round. If there's any dirty work going on you're more likely to get on the track there than anywhere else."

"That's my notion," I agreed. "In fact, I'd pretty well fixed up to take a trip down there to-morrow. You had better come along too if you really want to make yourself useful. I'll get a car, and we'll do the thing in style."

He shook his head "Can't manage to-morrow. I have promised to go and look up my sister at Croydon. Suppose we say Thursday instead. You will be none the worse for another day's rest."

"Thursday will do just as well," I said. "It doesn't matter which day as long as I send a line to this fellow Bascomb to say we're coming."

"Right you are," he replied. "It's just the sort of thing that will suit me down to the ground. I've always felt I had a bit of a turn in the Sherlock Holmes line." He stooped down and picked up the tray off the floor. "And now," he added more seriously, "that's quite enough talking for the present. What you've got to do is to lie perfectly quiet and not worry yourself about anything. I will look in later and see how you are, and in the meanwhile you try and get to sleep again if you can. You will probably be as right as ninepence in the morning, but one mustn't take too many liberties, even with a skull like yours."

He nodded in an encouraging fashion, and, backing out carefully with the tray, closed the door behind him.

I did my best to follow his advice, though it was not altogether an easy business. When one has fallen in love for the first time, suddenly come into a fortune, and just escaped being murdered, even the best disciplined mind is apt to prove a little restive. However, in spite of my headache I managed at last to sink into a welcome state of drowsiness, which lasted until well on into the afternoon.

About five o'clock a steward brought me another light meal. By this time I was feeling distinctly better, and, after I had done justice to the food and enjoyed a comfortable pipe, I dropped off into a really sound sleep without any further difficulty.

It was broad daylight when I awoke again, to find Ross, fully dressed in shore-going kit, standing beside my bunk.

"Had a good night?" he enquired kindly.

"Not so bad," I said, stretching myself with a yawn. "What time is it?"

"Nearly nine," he answered. "I looked in after tea yesterday, but you were well down to it then, so I didn't disturb you. Headache better?"

"It's more than better," I said thankfully. "It's gone."

"Well, don't presume on it. Take things nice and easy this morning. Just potter around and order the car, and write and tell this prize-fighter gentleman of yours that we're coming down to inspect the island to-morrow. You had better give him instructions to wash the dog and shave himself properly. There's nothing like putting servants in their right place to start with."

"You needn't bother," I said with some dignity. "I know what's due to my position."

He took himself off with a parting chuckle, and, rolling out of my bunk, I made my way to the bathroom, where a refreshingly cold tub put the finishing touch to my complete recovery.

I was returning along the corridor when I ran into the steward, who was coming towards me with a note in his hand.

"I was looking for you, sir," he announced. "A special messenger has just brought this letter aboard. He said there was no answer."

He handed me the envelope, which I glanced at with some curiosity. It was addressed in a hand that was quite unfamiliar to me—a small, clear writing with a good deal of character about it.

"I hope you're better, sir?" the man added politely.

"Yes, thanks," I said. "I am quite all right this morning. You can lay breakfast for me in the saloon; I shall be along in about a quarter of an hour."

I turned into the cabin, and throwing my towel and sponge on to the table, I slit open the envelope and pulled out its contents. One glance at the signature sent a queer, familiar thrill trickling through my heart.

"DEAR MR. DRYDEN,—There is something which I feel I ought to say to you, but I cannot very well tell you in a letter. If you are still on the ship and you get this note in time, will you meet me outside the Dover Street Tube Station at half-past two this afternoon? I shall not keep you more than a few minutes.

"Yours sincerely,

"CHRISTINE DE RODA."

Christine! Christine de Roda!

Somehow or other it was exactly right—just the name I should have chosen out of all others if providence had had the happy inspiration to consult me in the matter.

Repeating it aloud to myself with a curious sense of satisfaction, I sat down on the bunk with the letter in my hand. For a moment or so the whole thing seemed almost too good to be true. In spite of the fact that I had told her to write to me if there was any way in which I could be of use, this prompt summons was about the last thing that I had really expected.

Turning to the note, I read it through a second time from start to finish. It was written on half a sheet of paper, and there was no address, and nothing to show from what part of London it had been sent off. Perhaps the messenger could have given me some information, but he had doubtless left the ship by this time, and I could hardly dash after him in my pyjamas in order to question him on the point.

What, I wondered, could the mysterious "something" be which had led her to make this sudden and apparently impulsive appointment? In her own opinion it must be a matter of urgent importance, otherwise I felt pretty certain she would not have taken such a step. Could it possibly have anything to do with my adventure in the next door dock? If that were the case, her good offices were certainly a trifle belated, though it warmed my heart to think that she might be feeling anxious on my account.

Anyhow, above everything else there emerged the one radiant fact that within a few hours I should be seeing her and talking to her again. In view of that, all other matters seemed ridiculously unimportant, and it was in a very cheerful mood that I jumped up from my bunk and set about the job of putting on some clothes.

The morning dragged horribly, as mornings have a way of doing when there is a particularly interesting afternoon ahead of them. I filled out some of the time by writing to Bascomb, telling him that I was coming down with a friend the next day to inspect my new property, and that he had better arrange to have some food ready for us. I felt no little curiosity about my uncle's queer retainer. If he were really straight, as Mr. Drayton believed, he might certainly prove a most useful ally. Up to the present, however, I was inclined to reserve judgment on the point. My recent experiences did not encourage a hasty confidence in anybody.

By half-past twelve I was so tired of hanging about that I decided to go ashore. I could lunch somewhere in town, which would be more amusing than having a solitary meal in the saloon, and there would just be comfortable time afterwards to hunt up a car for the following day's trip.

I took the train to Charing Cross, and getting out there, strolled leisurely along through the busy streets until I came to Piccadilly. I knew nothing about West End restaurants, but with such a magnificent array to choose from I felt that I could not go very far wrong. After inspecting the outside of one or two, I eventually decided on Hatchett's. It was fairly close to Dover Street, and there was a big motor establishment just opposite, which would doubtless be able to supply me with what I wanted.

I lunched handsomely, spending at least three-quarters of an hour over the operation; and then, in that tranquil frame of mind which follows such pleasant extravagance, I sauntered across the road to the garage. I was received languidly by a young man with pink socks and beautifully brushed hair. Having listened to my requirements with a bored air, he led the way to the back of the premises, where he waved his hand towards a smart and powerful-looking Napier.

"Not a bad bus," he observed wearily. "She'll get you there and back all right."

This being the exact service that I needed, I entered at once upon the question of terms. These were soon settled, and after arranging for the car to call for us the next morning, I emerged again into the roar of Piccadilly.

It was now five and twenty minutes past two. With my heart beating a shade quicker than usual, I crossed back to the corner of Dover Street and took up my position outside the Tube Station. There was another man standing there—a fat, pompous person in a bowler hat, who kept on glancing at his watch. He, too, was evidently expecting somebody, and his impatience struck me as being singularly unreasonable. Whomsoever he was waiting for, he could not possibly want to see them as much as I wanted to see Christine.

Through the open window of one of the neighbouring houses a mellow-toned clock chimed out the half-hour. The sound had hardly died away when the big doors of the lift slid noisily back, and Christine herself stepped out into the sunshine. She was dressed in white, and she looked so deliciously beautiful that I had a sudden frantic impulse to seize her in my arms and kiss her before the whole street. It was a close thing, but fortunately I just managed to recover in time. The next moment I was holding her hand and making a gallant effort to appear more or less in my senses.

"You are as punctual as a cuckoo clock," I said. "You came out exactly as the half-hour struck."

She smiled up at me in the old, delightful way, but there was a troubled expression in her brown eyes that it went to my heart to notice.

"I had to be punctual," she answered quietly. "We can only spend a few minutes together, and there are several things that I must speak to you about."

I let go her hand with some reluctance. "Well, a few minutes are better than nothing," I said as cheerfully as possible.

"Where can we go to?" she asked, with a quick glance up and down the street. "Do you know any place close by where there won't be a lot of people?"

"There's a tea-shop at the corner of Bond Street," I said. "It's not likely to be crowded at this time of day."

She nodded her head. "That will do. I can't stand and talk to you here. Somebody might see us."

"Come along then," I remarked, and, turning the corner into Piccadilly, I led the way along the crowded pavement until we reached the establishment in question.

It was a pleasant, quiet place, panelled in brown oak, and except for a solitary couple near the door we appeared to be the only customers. We walked across to the far corner and seated ourselves at one of the empty tables.

"What shall I order?" I asked, as a tall, flaxen-haired lady advanced with dignity from behind the counter.

Christine laid down the menu which I had handed her. "I don't want anything except a cup of black coffee," she said. "I have just had lunch."

"So have I," I rejoined, "and a jolly good one it was too."

I announced our simple needs to the waitress, who returned in a few minutes with the desired refreshment, and set it down in front of my companion. I could not help noticing the gleam of reluctant admiration with which she took in every detail of Christine's appearance.

The latter filled up one of the two little cups and passed it across to me.

"Mr. Dryden," she began in a low voice, "I want you if you will to tell me exactly what has happened with regard to your uncle's property. I know it must sound an extraordinary question, but I am only asking it in what I believe to be your own interests."

"Of course I'll tell you," I said. "It's the one thing I've been longing to do for the last two days."

I took a sip of the coffee and sat back in my chair.

"To put it badly," I continued, "it amounts to this. My uncle died without making a will, and unless he was married—which doesn't seem to be the case—I come into everything that he left behind him. As far as I know at present, the 'everything' consists of about ten thousand pounds in cash and a place called Greensea Island, off the Essex coast."

There was a short pause.

"Greensea Island," she repeated slowly. "Was that where your uncle lived?"

"It was where he lived," I said, "and it was also where he died. He bought the place about six months ago, and shut himself up there with a dog and a retired prize-fighter. Mr. Drayton, the lawyer, has got hold of a notion that he was frightened of somebody or something. It does look rather like it, because from all accounts he never went to the mainland, and never allowed any visitors on the island."

Her brown eyes were fixed curiously on mine.

"Have you any idea what he was frightened about?"

I shrugged my shoulders. "Not the faintest; but, from the way my father used to talk of him when I was a boy, I can quite imagine that he had all sorts of unpleasant things on his conscience."

There was another and longer pause.

"What are your plans?" she asked at length "What are you going to do?"

"I propose to carry on the family traditions," I replied. "I've chucked my job with the Planet people, and I am going to settle down on Greensea Island and see how I like it."

The look of troubled distress deepened in her face.

"You mean to live there—alone?"

"It depends how I get along with the dog and the prize-fighter," I said. "If they turn out amiable I shall probably invite them to stay on."

Christine pushed away her untasted cup of coffee and drew her chair a little nearer the table.

"Mr. Dryden," she said again, "you were telling me the truth just now. You do honestly believe that I am trying to act in your own interests?"

"I trust you from the bottom of my heart," I answered simply.

"Then, whatever you do, don't go to Greensea Island by yourself. Take some friend with you—somebody that you can absolutely rely on. I can't explain, but there are reasons which would make it very unsafe for you to be there alone." She hesitated for a moment. "It's even possible you might be in danger of your life."

"Isn't it just a little late to tell me that?" I asked.

Her hand, which was resting on the cloth, suddenly tightened.

"What do you mean?"

"Why," I said, "it's only by the grace of heaven and an exceptionally thick skull that I happen to be here now. When I was on my way back to the ship after seeing Mr. Drayton, somebody banged me on the head from behind and threw me into the dock. It was about the most honest attempt at murder that ever managed to go astray."

The horror and amazement in her eyes were quite obviously genuine.

"But it's impossible," she broke out; "impossible!"

"It's true enough," I returned. "If you don't believe me, I can show you the crack in my skull."

She stared at me with the same expression of frightened bewilderment. "I—I don't understand," she faltered.

"I am sure you don't," I said. "Neither do I. Still, the fact remains that there's someone strolling around with an unsatisfied longing for my blood, and I suppose they are just as likely as not to follow me down to Greensea." I paused. "Would you advise me not to go there at all?" I asked deliberately.

For a moment she made no answer. She seemed to be torn by some inward conflict that was plainly visible in her face.

"No, no," she replied, almost in a whisper. "The place is yours, and——" She broke off with a little helpless gesture of her hands. "Oh, I don't know what to say," she finished wretchedly. "You must go if you want to. I can't tell you any more."

"You have told me quite enough," I said gratefully. "If I don't manage to take care of myself now, I shall deserve everything I get."

The clock on the wall began to strike three. With a slight start she glanced up at it; then, pushing back her chair, she rose suddenly to her feet. I made a movement as if to accompany her.

"No, please," she said hurriedly, putting out her hand. "Don't come with me. We must say good-bye here."

"But I'm not going to say good-bye," I objected. "It's a word that doesn't exist as far as you and I are concerned." I took her hand in both of mine, regardless of the flaxen-haired lady who was surveying us coldly from behind the counter. "Tell me when I shall see you again," I demanded. "I can't let you go until you do."

She shook her head. "I don't know. Perhaps we shall never meet after this." She pulled her hand away and stood looking up into my face with wide-open, unhappy eyes. "In any case," she said, "whatever happens, will you always remember that I tried to help you?"

As she spoke she turned away, leaving me standing alone in the middle of the restaurant. The next moment she had stepped out through the open door, and disappeared into the stream of people that hurried ceaselessly past.

CHAPTER FIVE

"By Jove!" exclaimed Ross enviously. "You are a lucky ruffian!"

We had halted the car at the top of a gently rising slope, and there, stretched out below us, lay the shining expanse of the Danewell Estuary. For a couple of miles in either direction a winding belt of silver gleamed and sparkled in the bright morning sunshine. On the left it narrowed gradually towards the small tidal haven of Barham Lock, from which point one could just trace the placid course of the river Shell, meandering along idly through the marshes. On the right it opened out by degrees into an ever-broadening channel, until far away in the distance, where a faint haze brooded over everything, it merged itself imperceptibly into the grey waters of the North Sea.

I pointed to a small, irregularly shaped island which lay out in mid-stream, almost exactly ahead of us.

"That," I said, "is Greensea."

Shading his eyes with his hand, Ross gazed down at my new inheritance. One could not see very much of the house, for the straggling cluster of trees that surrounded it practically hid it from the mainland. All that was plainly visible was a neglected-looking landing-stage with a roughly built wooden boat-house alongside.

"Seems nice and private," he observed. "Just the place for a retiring nature like yours." He took another glance, and then turned to me with an air of disappointed enquiry. "I don't see the dog or the prize-fighter though. Why aren't they standing on the quay waiting for us? It is very disrespectful of them."

"Never mind," I said. "Perhaps they're getting lunch ready. That's a heap more important."

We ran down the short incline into the little hamlet of Pen Mill, and pulled up outside the old-fashioned Gunner's Arms. For a moment I sat where I was, and looked round me with contented eyes. It was nearly five years since my last visit, and to my huge satisfaction nothing seemed to have changed during the interval. There was the same village green, which had always reminded me of the cover of *Jackanapes*. The same geese, or what appeared to be the same geese, waddled happily about in the sunshine, the same clumsy boats were moored up alongside the old stone jetty, and the big bow-windows of the inn still leaned out crazily towards the water. I took in a long, deep breath, and stepped down from the car.

"I don't want to interfere in any way with the programme," remarked Ross, "but what about a drink?" He glanced up at the picturesque front of the Gunner's Arms. "I suppose they sell drink in this interesting ruin?"

"Any amount of it," I replied, brushing off the dust from my coat. "It's where my skipper—Bobby Dean—and I used to come when we were paddling around in the Harwich Patrol."

I led the way up the flight of wooden steps, and entered the low-ceilinged, panelled room, where I had spent many a cheerful half-hour in past days. Here I found the first traces of Time's handiwork. Instead of the apple-cheeked old landlady whom I remembered so well, an enormous, genial-looking man in his shirt-sleeves came forward to take our orders.

"Yes, sir," he said, in answer to my enquiry, "Mrs. Green's been dead and gone a matter o' two years come next July. Went off sudden like as you might say, and the house was put up to auction. I'd had my eye on it for some time, and I bought the whole place, lock, stock, and barrel."

He crossed to the bar, returning in a few moments with the whiskies and sodas that we had asked for.

"You've not been in these parts for some time, sir?" he hazarded.

"Not since the war," I replied; "but you will probably see something of me in future." I took a drink and set down the tumbler. "I am the new owner of Greensea Island," I added.

He looked at me with sudden curiosity. "Well I never! Is that so, sir? Why, only yesterday somebody was saying that a nephew of Mr. Jannaway's had come into the whole property."

"That's right," I said. "Mr. Jannaway was my uncle."

He received the information in silence, but I thought I could detect a faint change of expression in his face.

"Did you know him?" I asked, striking a match to light my pipe.

"No, sir, I can't say that I did. No one didn't know Mr. Jannaway, not in a manner o' speaking. I don't believe he ever come ashore, not the whole time he was on the island."

"Perhaps you have met his man—Bascomb?"

He nodded, but without any apparent enthusiasm. "He's been in here a few times, sir."

Another customer appeared in the doorway, and with a murmured word of apology he moved away to attend to his wants.

Ross sat back and surveyed me with a mischievous grin. "We don't seem to be in luck," he remarked. "Ask him if he's friendly with the dog."

My eyes travelled through the open window towards the lowlying shore and the straggling clump of trees opposite. A more peaceful scene it would have been difficult to imagine, but its outward calm did nothing to allay the ever-growing sense of danger which haunted me like a persistent shadow.

I turned back to Ross, however, with a well-assumed air of indifference.

"I expected to find that Uncle Richard had queered the pitch. I shall have to begin at the bottom and endear myself to the neighborhood gradually."

"Well, you've started the right way by bringing me along," he retorted. "It will at least show 'em that you have got some respectable friends."

I beckoned to the landlord, who was again disengaged.

"Is there a boat of any sort you could let us have?" I asked. "We want to go across to the island."

Whatever may have been the drift of his private thoughts, he was evidently prepared to be civil and obliging.

"Why, certainly, sir," he said. "There's one down alongside the jetty." He walked to the window and thrust his head out. "Jim," he shouted, "just get that boat ready. There's a couple o' gents comin' along in a minute."

I settled up for the drinks, and we made our way out of the room and down the rickety flight of steps.

We found Jim, a shock-headed youth of about eleven, unhitching the painter of a small weather-beaten dinghy.

"Will you want me, sir?" he enquired.

"Not to-day, James," I said. "We are only going over to the island. I think we can manage that between us."

He glanced at us both a little doubtfully. "You'll 'ave to row up stream a bit," he announced. "The tide runs very strong 'bout here."

I thanked him for this well-meant information, and, having given him sixpence, took my place at the sculls. With another grin Ross settled himself comfortably in the stern.

"Even the children mistrust us," he observed, as I tugged the boat out into the tideway.

It was not more than a couple of hundred yards across but so rapid was the current that it took us some little while to make the passage. I pulled well up until I was almost opposite the furthest point of the island, and then, getting into comparatively slack water, rowed down under the shelter of the shore. At last we came alongside the landing-stage, where Ross leaned over and grabbed hold of a rusty chain.

"There doesn't seem to be anyone about," he said. "I wonder if the blighter got your wire."

The words had hardly left his lips when there was a sudden rustle amongst the trees, and a huge black shape bounded out into the open. It was a dog, but the biggest dog I have ever seen—an enormous brute that looked like a cross between a great Dane and an old English mastiff.

For a second it stood there, swishing its tail and staring at us out of its bloodshot eyes, then in a menacing fashion it began to advance rapidly up the path.

With undignified haste Ross let go the chain and scrambled back into his seat. Freed from this check, the head of the boat promptly swung round, and the next moment we were drifting broadside on, with several feet of water between us and the shore.

"Don't be frightened," I said soothingly. "It's only his fun. He doesn't bite."

Before Ross could answer there was the sound of a step on the gravel, and the figure of a man came hurriedly round the bend leading from the house.

"Come 'ere," he shouted. "Come 'ere at once."

The dog pulled up as if he had been shot, and, casting a disappointed glance at us, stalked away solemnly from the bank. With a couple of strokes I managed to regain our former position.

"Good morning," I said. "Are you Bascomb?"

The newcomer, a dark, heavily built, clean-shaven man of about thirty-five, advanced quickly across the open space.

"That's me, sir," he replied. "You're Mr. Dryden, I suppose?"

I shipped my sculls and stepped up on to the landing-stage, followed by Ross.

"Yes," I said, "I'm Mr. Dryden. Did you get my wire?"

"It come along yesterday afternoon, sir. I got some lunch ready for you." He tied up the painter to an iron ring, and then glanced round at the dog, who was sitting on his haunches a few yards away, surveying us with sombre interest. "I'm sorry 'e run at you like that. 'Taint 'is fault exac'ly. He's bin trained not to allow no strangers on the island."

"He seems to have picked up the trick very nicely," I replied. "What's his name?"

"Satan, sir."

I turned to Ross. "No wonder he wanted to get hold of you," I said, laughing.

Ross stooped down and snapped his fingers. "Come on, Lucifer," he called out coaxingly. "We're all pals here."

The huge animal rose slowly to his feet, and in a very deliberate fashion strolled across to where we were standing.

"'E won't 'urt you now," observed Bascomb. "'E only wants to take stock of yer like."

As if to confirm his statement, Satan came up to each of us in turn, and sniffed enquiringly at the legs of our trousers. His inspection was evidently a success, for with a prodigious yawn he sat down between us, and stared out indifferently at the landscape.

"We've passed all right," said Ross, "but I don't think we've taken honours."

"Well, we shan't be chawed up, anyhow," I returned. "That's something to be grateful for."

"You won't 'ave no more trouble with 'im," put in Bascomb. "'E'll be as friendly as a kitten now 'e understands you belong 'ere." Then, as if anxious to change the conversation, he added quickly: "Will ye come inside straight away, sir, or would you like to take a walk round the island first?"

"Oh, we may as well see the house," I said. "There will be plenty of time for exploring after lunch."

Without any further remark my new retainer led the way up the path—a narrow walk hedged in on each side by an unkempt shrubbery of laurels. We passed through an iron gate, which brought us out into the open, and suddenly, with a little thrill of curiosity, I found myself face to face with my future home.

It was a low, rambling house of two storeys, built of red brick, and covered with a thick growth of creeper. On one side of the porch were two long windows, opening out on to a verandah. A strip of lawn with flower-beds in it ran the whole length of the front, and, except for the general air of neglect which seemed to pervade everything, it looked as charming and comfortable a place as the most exacting owner could desire.

Ross gave vent to a long whistle of approval.

"It's great!" he exclaimed admiringly. "A real dyed-in-the-wool happy little English country home! I can just picture you paddling around with the mowing machine, and sneaking out at night to murder the slugs."

Bascomb glanced at him queerly out of the corner of his eye, as if wondering whether he were quite sane; then, marching ahead of us across the grass, he pushed back the front door, which was already partly open.

We found ourselves in a large, rambling hall, fitted up as a sitting-room. One glance round showed me that it was a sort of place where I should feel absolutely at home. Like the parlour at the Gunner's Arms, it was panelled from floor to ceiling in black oak. There was a huge fireplace, with steel dogs on the hearth; a couple of big leather armchairs were ranged invitingly on each side of it; while tucked away in one corner stood a broad low couch, plentifully heaped with cushions. An old Jacobean desk, apparently locked, and a fine corner cupboard of the same period, practically completed the furniture.

Ross stood there gazing about him with the same approving smile.

"By Gad!" he remarked. "The old boy knew how to make himself comfortable."

I turned to Bascomb. "Did my uncle furnish this room himself?" I asked.

The latter shook his head. "No, sir. 'E bought these things along with the 'ouse. 'E 'ad that fireplace put in, otherwise it's just the same as when 'e come 'ere."

"I'm glad he had the good taste to leave it alone," I said. "It's more than I should have given him credit for."

Except for a rather sour glance, Bascomb made no reply. He crossed the hall to a door at the back, and, turning the handle, pushed it open.

"This is the dining-room," he announced curtly.

Ross and I walked over and followed him in. It was a pleasant apartment, with a diamond-paned bow-window looking out on to another strip of grass, where several chickens were strutting about in the sunshine. In the centre was a table laid for lunch.

"I've got a bit o' cold lamb ready when you'd like it," continued Bascomb, in the same surly tone. "But p'raps you'd rather see the rest of the 'ouse while yer about it?"

I nodded my assent, and, turning back into the hall, he conducted us up the staircase to the landing above. He stopped at one of the rooms, the door of which was already ajar.

"Mr. Jannaway used to sleep in 'ere," he said, "but there's two others if you don't fancy it."

I glanced round at the big four-poster bed and the solid, old-fashioned furniture, all of which I found distinctly pleasing. Then I moved over to the window and looked out. The room faced directly towards Pen Mill, and through a gap in the trees I could just see the rough stone jetty, and the picturesque front of the Gunner's Arms.

"This will suit me," I said. "It would take a very bad conscience to keep one awake here."

I made the remark quite carelessly, but from the expression on Bascomb's face he evidently took it to be another reflection upon his late lamented master. In dead silence, and with a scarcely concealed air of resentment, he led us through the remainder of the house; then, having brought us back to the dining-room, departed to fetch the lunch.

"Well, what do you think of it all?" I asked Ross as soon as were left alone.

He sat down on the broad cushioned seat in the window.

"It reminds me more of the hymn than anything else," he said, "'Where every prospect pleases, and only man is vile.' The place is top-hole, but of all surly brutes I've ever met, that prize-fighter of yours about takes the biscuit."

I pulled one of the chairs to the table. "He's not exactly a sunbeam," I admitted. "All the same, I think it was chiefly my fault. I ought to have been more careful what I said about Uncle Richard. From what Drayton told me this chap was devoted to him in his way, and I suppose I've managed to upset his feelings."

Ross grunted unsympathetically. "He'd go tracking jolly quick if it was my place," he observed. "I should get the blue hump if I were shut up alone in the house with a fellow like that."

Any further discussion was cut short by the sound of steps in the hall, and a moment later Bascomb himself came back into the room carrying a well-loaded tray. Without saying a word, he proceeded to set out its contents on the table, moving around with a quick noiseless tread rather surprising in a man of his size and weight. When he had finished he stood for a moment with the empty tray in his hand.

"There's a bell alongside the fireplace," he announced, "and there's some coffee comin' after. I'll be in the kitchen if you want me before then."

With this information he again took himself off, shutting the door behind him as he went out.

Ross drew up his chair opposite to mine. "It looks all right," he said, with a satisfied glance round the table. "I suppose he hasn't put poison in the salad!"

"I shall risk it, anyhow," I returned. "I'm too hungry to worry about trifles."

In spite of his suggestion, Ross seemed to share my feelings, for he certainly did full justice to the excellent meal in front of us. Besides the lamb there was cold gooseberry tart and cream, with a large slab of Cheddar cheese to fill up any remaining corners. For drink we had a bottle of good hock, a wine to which I have always had a peculiar and affectionate attachment.

By the time we had finished and rung for the coffee all Ross's usual amiability had returned.

"I like your island, my lad," he said, lighting himself a cigar. "I could even put up with the prize-fighter if he always turns out meals like this. When we come back in August you shall ask me to stay."

"Why not stay now?" I suggested.

He shook his head. "Can't be done," he said regretfully. "I have promised to take my sister to Bath. I take her there every year in May when I'm home, and I wouldn't have the heart to disappoint her. For some extraordinary reason she appears to enjoy it."

I was more than a little disappointed, for to tell the truth I had been counting a good deal on Ross's society during the next two weeks. Half the fun of settling into a new place is to have some pal to talk things over with, and he was just the sort of cheerful, easy-going chap who would have exactly filled the role.

Apart from that, Christine's warning about not being alone on the island still echoed clearly in my memory. I was not afraid, but after what had happened to me in the docks I could hardly doubt the soundness of her advice, and for a moment I could think of nobody else whom I could invite to share my solitude. It is true that Mr. Drayton's friend, Inspector Campbell, had expressed his willingness to come down for a week-end whenever I asked him, but until I had got a little firmer grip on the situation I was not particularly anxious for the presence of a detective.

As I have said before, however, I am not given to worrying over what cannot be helped, and I was on the point of making some suitable rejoinder when the door opened and Bascomb arrived with the coffee. As he set it down in front of me I took the opportunity to congratulate him upon the excellence of our lunch.

"We'll have a stroll round the island as soon as we've finished," I added. "You might come with us and show us anything there is to be seen."

"Very good, sir," he returned, in a slightly mollified voice. "I'll be outside—along by the front door."

True to his word, we found him standing on the path when we came out, with Satan in due attendance.

"If yer don't like the dog," he said, "I can tie 'im up in the yard."

"But I do like him very much," I replied. "We are going to be the best of friends, aren't we, Satan?"

I bent over and patted the huge black head, an attention which its owner accepted with a complacent grunt that was distinctly encouraging.

It seemed to me that a momentary flicker of relief passed across Bascomb's naturally wooden features, but without any further observation he led the way round to the back, where another rusty iron gate opened out on to the marshes.

From this point the whole expanse of Greensea Island was visible to our eyes. It consisted of a long stretch of saltings and swamps, only broken by occasional creeks and pools, which sparkled here and there in the bright May sunshine. To some people, I suppose, the outlook would have appeared dismal in the extreme, but for me this kind of scenery has always possessed an extraordinary charm. I love it even in the winter time, when it lies bare and desolate under a cold sky. Now, with the thrift mantling the marshes everywhere with a garment of shot satin, its strange and lonely beauty seemed to stir the very chords of my heart.

These delicate emotions were rudely interrupted by Ross, who had been watching my face with his usual amused smile.

"You look like the stage hero coming back to his long-lost village. If there was only a golden-haired damsel in white muslin picking roses, it would make a lovely fifth act for a melodrama."

"I can get along very nicely without her," I returned. "I've had quite enough melodrama to last me for the present."

I had spoken again without thinking, but once more my words appeared to have a curious effect upon Bascomb. Anyhow, I caught him staring at me suddenly, with a peculiar expression of doubt and suspicion. He turned away, however, directly he met my eyes, and, pushing open the gate, stepped back to allow us to pass.

We set out over the uneven ground, and, striking right across to the water's edge, started to make a complete circuit of the island. It was not easy walking, for the whole place was infested with puddles and patches of bog, and we were constantly making small detours or else jumping from tuft to tuft in order to avoid one or another of these obstacles.

Innumerable red-shanks and sea birds kept on popping up in front of us with shrill cries of alarm, while more than once a large heron rose slowly to his wings and flopped away with a kind of majestic indignation. I could see that in winter it must be a splendid shooting-ground, and I reflected with some satisfaction on the new gun which was one of the first things I had promised myself to buy.

We had covered about half the distance, and were skirting along the inner shore in the direction of the landing-stage, when Ross suddenly came to a standstill and pointed away up the estuary.

"Look there!" he said. "Somebody's coming to pay you a visit already."

About a couple of hundred yards distant a small petrol dinghy containing a single passenger was rapidly churning its way towards the island.

I turned to Bascomb. "Who is it?" I asked. "Anyone you know?"

Shading his eyes, he stared out at the approaching boat.

"Yes," he said. "It's Dr. Manning."

If he had said it was the devil his tone could scarcely have been more appropriate, and both Ross and I looked up in amazement at the renewed churlishness of his manner.

"Dr. Manning!" I repeated. "I thought he was in London."

Bascomb whistled to the dog, who trotted up obediently to his side.

"'E may 'ave bin there for all I know. 'E come back last night anyway. I seen 'im goin' across to the barge."

There was a short pause.

"Well, I suppose we'd better get along and meet him," I said dryly. "I know he wants to have a talk with me, and I can't very well say I'm not at home."

To this Bascomb returned no answer. He fell in behind Ross and me, with Satan at his heels, and in this order we advanced across the strip of salting which still separated us from the landing-stage.

We reached our destination at almost the same moment as the boat. Its owner brought it up alongside with a skill which showed him to be a practised hand, and, switching off his engine, leaned over and caught hold of the ring.

I don't know exactly what I had expected, but my first impression of him was a distinctly surprising one. He was a man who would have attracted attention anywhere, if only for his unusual good looks. Except on one of the early Greek coins, I don't think I have ever seen features so extraordinarily well cut. His face was burned to the colour of old mahogany, and against this dark background a pair of china blue eyes looked out with a curious and almost disconcerting brilliance. He was wearing flannels and the usual white yachting cap, and as far as age went he might have been anything between forty and forty-five.

"How do you do?" he said pleasantly. "I suppose I'm right in taking you for Mr. Dryden? I'm Dr. Manning."

"You're quite right," I answered, "and I'm very glad to see you. Won't you come ashore?"

He stepped up lightly out of the boat, and shook my hand with a grip that certainly lacked nothing in heartiness.

"I spotted you from my barge," he went on, "so I thought I would come over and introduce myself. I have been looking forward to meeting you for some little while."

"I was half-expecting to hear from you in London," I said. "Mr. Drayton told me that he had given you my address." I paused. "Let me introduce you to a brother professional," I added. "Dr. Ross, of the *Neptune*."

I saw his glance travel swiftly and keenly over my companion.

"Delighted to meet you," he said. "I was a ship's surgeon myself at one time." He turned back to me. "I should have run down to look you up at the docks, only I couldn't quite fit things in. Besides, I thought we were certain to come across each other here before long."

"Suppose we go up to the house and have a drink," I suggested.

"That's not a bad idea," he returned cheerfully. "I must just fasten up the boat first, though."

He bent down, and with a couple of quick turns hitched the painter to the ring. I was on the verge of speaking rather sharply to Bascomb, who, still standing sullenly in the background, had made no effort to come forward and assist him. For the moment, however, I thought it best to let the matter pass, and side by side we all three started up the path towards the front door.

"There's no need for ceremony," I said, as I led the way into the hall. "You probably know the house better than I do."

"Well, I was here for several days," he answered, "but most of the time I was up in your uncle's bedroom."

I mixed him a whisky and soda and passed it across.

"I know," I said, "and I haven't thanked you yet. It was uncommonly good of you to come over and look after him as you did."

"Oh, you mustn't say that," he protested. "I was very pleased to be of any use. I have given up practice for some years, but I am always ready to do anything I can in an emergency." He paused. "I only wish I had been more successful," he added. "It was one of those cases, though, in which medical skill is practically helpless. Heart failure, you know, on the top of double pneumonia."

I nodded "I never met my uncle," I said, "but I imagine that he had led a pretty hard life. I suppose that's bound to tell when it comes to the point."

His blue eyes rested curiously on mine. "You never actually met him?" he repeated. "I suppose you knew a good deal about him though?"

"Precious little," I said frankly. "He went off to South America when I was about five years old, and the next thing I heard of him was Mr. Drayton's cable telling me that he was dead."

"Why, it's quite a romance," he exclaimed in his easy, almost drawling manner. "You were evidently born under a lucky star. There are not many people who drop into a fortune from relations that they've never spoken to." His glance wandered round the room, as though noting its various features. "Not that it's everyone's property," he went on with a smile. "Jolly enough in the summer, of course, but it's a bleak and desolate place in the winter, I give you my word. I have often wondered what induced your uncle to shut himself up here."

"I suppose it appealed to him," I said. "There's no accounting for tastes."

Dr. Manning took a sip of his whisky and soda and set down the glass.

"I believe Mr. Drayton spoke to you about my proposal," he said. "I mean the idea some of us had of starting a yachting club here."

"He did mention it," I replied, "and I'm very sorry to disappoint you. The fact is that I haven't any wish to let the place. I mean to live here myself."

He took my refusal with the most perfect good humour.

"I'm delighted to hear it," he answered. "Of course, if you are particularly set on the island itself there's no more to be said. I thought, however, that you might prefer to be on the mainland. It's much more convenient and cheerful in some ways. There are one or two very jolly little places in the market that could be picked up for a mere song, and we should be prepared to give you a good rent for Greensea. You see, it's just exactly suited for what we want."

"It isn't a question of money," I said. "As far as that goes, the terms you offered through Mr. Drayton were exceedingly handsome. The point is that I am quite contented where I am. I have always wanted to have an island of my own, and now I have got one I mean to stick to it."

"Well, if that's the situation," he returned with a laugh, "we mustn't bother you about it any further." He finished his whisky and soda, and, putting his hand in his pocket, pulled out a small cigarette case.

"Won't you have a cigar?" I suggested.

He shook his head. "No, thanks. I never smoke anything but Egyptian cigarettes. A friend of mine sends them to me over from Cairo. Will you try one?"

He held out the case, and both Ross and I helped ourselves.

"I suppose you will be importing servants if you are going to settle down here?" he said. "Your uncle, you know, wouldn't have anyone else on the island except that one man of his."

"What do you think of Bascomb?" I asked.

He blew out a long wreath of smoke. "Well, it's hardly my place to criticise him," he answered, smiling, "but to be quite candid, I should get rid of him as soon as possible if I were in your shoes. I don't want to do the fellow an injustice, but from what I saw of him while I was here I mistrust him profoundly."

Ross glanced at me with rather a triumphant expression.

"I daresay you're right," I said. "He certainly doesn't err on the side of cheerfulness."

As a matter of fact, his warning, though doubtless a well-intended one, only increased my determination not to act hastily in the matter. There is a regrettable streak of obstinacy in my character which always gets up against other people's advice, and, in addition to that, I had an unaccountable feeling inside me that Bascomb was not really as black as he was painted. In spite of his surliness, he gave me the impression of being an honest fellow, and when it comes to judging character I am prepared to back my instincts against a good deal of circumstantial evidence.

Something, however, urged me to keep my ideas to myself, so, changing the conversation, I asked Manning if he could tell me anything about the prospects of wild fowling during the coming winter. I had evidently hit on the right source of information, for he at once began to discuss the subject in a fashion which showed me that he knew every creek and marsh throughout the length and breadth of the estuary.

"There's plenty of sport," he added, "any amount of it; only, if you don't mind my giving you a tip, you want to be a little careful how you go about it. The fact is that some of these fellows round here—the professional gunners, I mean—are as jealous as hell. They are a rough lot, and I wouldn't put much beyond them when they get really nasty."

I looked at him with some surprise. I had run across a certain number of these gentry when I had been messing around in the motor launch with Bobby Dean, and although they were a queer crowd in their way, I should never have suspected them of being dangerous.

"You don't mean to say they'd take a pot shot at one," I said, "or anything bloodthirsty of that sort?"

"It sounds rather a large order," he admitted. "All the same, when I first came here I had a couple of devilish narrow escapes. They may have been accidents, of course, but if so—" He shrugged his shoulders in a fashion that was sufficiently expressive.

"It doesn't seem to have interfered much with your shooting," put in Ross.

"Oh, I'm all right now," he replied easily. "I'm well in their good books because I have doctored up two or three of them when they were seedy, and I suppose they feel grateful to me in their way." He turned to me. "I thought I ought to mention it though, just to put you on your guard."

"Thanks very much," I said. "I'm not a nervous person, but I'll keep my eyes open in case anyone should mistake me for a duck."

As though suddenly thinking of the time, Dr. Manning glanced at the slim gold watch which he wore upon his wrist.

"I must be off," he announced. "I'm expecting some friends on the barge at half-past three." He rose to his feet and shook hands with both of us. "I shall see you again before very long, I suppose?" he added, addressing himself to me.

"I shall be down here for good in three or four days' time," I said.

"Well, don't forget to make use of me," he returned. "If you would like to be put up for the club at Shalston or anything of that sort you have only got to let me know."

I thanked him again, and we all walked down together to the landing-stage, where he got into his boat and started off on his return journey.

Ross and I stood for a minute watching the long wake of foam that he left behind him as he sped rapidly away into the distance.

"I am beginning well," I said. "It's something to have made friends with one's next-door neighbour."

Ross, who was still staring at the retreating dinghy, indulged in a rather doubtful grunt.

"I suppose he's all right," he said half reluctantly. "I can't say I cottoned to him much myself. He's too damned good-looking for my taste."

"There doesn't seem to be much love lost between him and Bascomb," I remarked. "I wonder what the trouble is."

"God knows," returned Ross, "but on that point at least my sympathies are with the doctor." He turned away from the water, and we strolled back side by side towards the house. "Do you think there's anything in this yarn of his about the natives? If so, it looks to me as if you were up against a pretty breezy proposition."

"I'm not worrying myself," I replied placidly. "Somebody wants to assassinate me already—that's quite plain—and a few extra hands on the job won't make much difference. After all, one can only die once."

"That's the spirit, my lad," observed Ross, slapping me on the shoulder. "All the same, I don't like to think of you stuck down here on your little lonesome. I've half a mind to chuck my sister and come and keep you company."

"No you won't," I said firmly. "You trot off to Bath like a good boy. If things get too hot I'll rout out somebody else to share the racket."

We reached the front door just as I spoke, and almost simultaneously Bascomb came into view round a corner of the shrubbery, with Satan still at his heels. I hesitated for a moment, wondering what was the best thing to do. Should I take him to task there and then, or would it be better to wait until I returned to the island and was properly settled into the house? I decided on the latter course, and, leaving Ross, walked forward to where he was standing.

"We shall be off in a few minutes, Bascomb," I said "I must leave the rest of the island until I come back."

He met my gaze quite steadily, though the same sullen expression still lingered in his eyes.

"Very well, sir," he said. "When shall I expect you?"

"I don't know for certain," I replied. "About Wednesday or Thursday, I expect, but I'll send a line and let you know." I paused. "Is there anything you want for the house—anything I can have sent down from London?"

He shook his head. "There's no trouble about gettin' food," he answered. "All the Shalston tradesmen deliver at Pen Mill, and, as far as liquor goes the cellar's just full up with it."

My opinion of Uncle Richard underwent a slight improvement.

"That's good news," I said. "How are you off for money?"

"I've got enough to go on with. Mr. Drayton gave me twenty pound last time 'e was down 'ere." He hesitated for a moment, and then added gruffly: "Beggin' your pardon, sir, but might I ask what arrangements you're thinkin' o' makin'?"

"How do you mean?" I asked.

"Well, I was wonderin' if you wanted me. Mebbe you'll be bringin' your own folk along with you."

"You looked after my uncle while he was alive, didn't you?" I asked.

"Yes," he said bluntly, "I reckon 'e was satisfied, but it don't foller you won't 'ave different ideas."

"That depends on you," I said. "If you make me comfortable I shall be quite contented with the arrangement—at all events for the present."

He was evidently rather surprised, but the satisfaction in his face was unmistakable.

"I'll do my best," he said. "No one can't do more than that." He glanced down at Satan, who was sitting patiently by his side. "'Ow about the dog?" he demanded suspiciously. "You won't be wantin' to get rid of 'im?"

"Not likely," I said, with some feeling. "He's one of the chief attractions of the place from my point of view."

At this moment, as luck would have it, Satan rose leisurely to his feet, and, strolling across, thrust his wet muzzle into the palm of my hand. The timely demonstration evidently had a considerable effect upon Bascomb, for he looked up at me with a sudden respect that had hitherto been absent from his manner.

"'E's taken to you proper, sir," he observed; "an' wot's more, 'e's worth 'avin' as a friend, that dog is. If 'e was around, and any bloke was to try a dirty trick on you, 'e'd tear the throat out of 'im before 'e knew wot 'ad 'appened."

"I'm very pleased to hear it," I said heartily, and, having bestowed several more encouraging pats on my new and useful ally, I followed Ross into the house.

I found him in the dining-room in the act of helping himself to another whisky and soda.

"It's time we were making a start," I said, copying his example. "There are no lights on the car, and it will take us at least three hours to get back to town."

"I'm ready," he replied. "I didn't like to leave all this drink behind, though. It's putting temptation in Bascomb's way."

"You needn't have worried yourself," I explained. "There's a whole cellar full of it downstairs, and of course he's got the key."

Ross nodded his head in mock amazement. "Good Lord! And yet the silly fool hasn't even the sense to try and keep his job. I suppose you'll give him the sack now you've heard the doctor's opinion of him?"

"I daresay," I returned evasively. "I'm keeping him on for the present, though. It's no good throwing away dirty water until one's got clean."

We went down to the landing-stage and stepped into our boat, which Bascomb had busied himself in making ready for us. He and Satan remained standing on the shore as we pulled out into the estuary—two motionless black figures against the lonely background of trees and shrubs. To my imagination they seemed to me to strike a curiously grim and forbidding note, well in keeping with the reputation for unsociability that Greensea Island had evidently earned. In view of certain possible contingencies, however, this was distinctly a fault on the right side, and I looked back at them both with a certain growing sense of comfort and confidence. If my uncle's legacy was a trifle unhealthy, I was beginning to think that he had at least left me the means of dealing with it in a thoroughly practical fashion.

We had no difficulty this time in making the passage, for the tide was now at its lowest, and were able to row straight across to the jetty. We abandoned the boat to the charge of Jim, who was waiting for us, and going up to the Gunner's Arms, routed out our chauffeur from a comfortable seat in the bar parlour.

"You've got back all right then, sir," observed the landlord. "I hope you found the place come up to what you expected?"

"Quite, thank you," I said. "I think I shall be as happy and contented there as my uncle was."

He eyed me for a moment with the same air of peculiar interest, but beyond thanking me for the five shillings which I gave him he offered no further remarks.

Three minutes later we were spinning up the long incline, at the top of which we had paused in the morning to view my new property. At the very point where we had halted the road turned away to the left, winding off inland towards the railway junction at Torrington.

We were just rounding this corner when the unexpected blast of a horn caused our chauffeur to pull in hastily to the near side. As he did so a big car suddenly swept into view, coming from the opposite direction. How we avoided each other I don't know, for the fleeting glimpse which I had caught of the man alongside the driver put everything else for the moment completely out of my head.

Ross sprang up in his seat, and stared back in amazement over the top of the tonneau.

"Well I'm damned!" he exclaimed, turning to me. "If that wasn't our friend de Roda it must have been his twin brother!"

CHAPTER SIX

I helped myself to a glass of port, and, sitting back in my big armchair, looked contentedly round the dining-room. It was the third evening I had spent in my new quarters, and the refreshing air of novelty had not yet quite worn off.

So far things had been moving with admirable smoothness. I had come down on the Thursday following my first visit, and I had been happily surprised at the improvements which Bascomb had effected in the interval. He must have worked hard, for the house was as neat and clean as anyone could reasonably wish, and in addition to that he had cut the grass and tidied up the garden, both in the back and the front.

In his own queer way, too, he had seemed quite pleased at my arrival, a welcome seconded by Satan, who had evidently adopted me as a new and desirable feature of the establishment. I had put In a couple of pleasantly lazy days, rambling about the place, exploring it from top to bottom, and now on this Sunday evening I found myself sitting over the remains of supper with something of the same "monarch-of-all-I-survey" feeling which helped to brighten the solitude of Robinson Crusoe.

Like that undefeated castaway, however, I had other and more pressing considerations to occupy my immediate thoughts. Whatever way I might look at it, the fact remained that I had undoubtedly burned my boats. Here I was, stuck down alone on Greensea Island, in precisely the friendless and solitary position which Christine had counselled me to avoid. Against her advice I had thrust my head deliberately into the lion's mouth, and for any painful consequences that might follow I should have only myself to thank.

If any further proof were needed as to the soundness of her warning I had it supplied to me in a sufficiently dramatic shape by that momentary encounter with de Roda at the top of Pen Mill Hill. That it was de Roda we had so nearly run into I was in no manner of doubt. However much I might have mistrusted my own eyes, Ross's immediate recognition of him had settled the matter beyond question. I could see him now as he had whirled past us in a cloud of dust—a huddled mass of coat collar, with a sallow face and sombre eyes staring out fixedly into space. It was my impression that he had not even glanced at either of us, but the whole thing had happened so abruptly that on this point at least I might very easily have been mistaken.

Anyhow, it didn't seem to make a vast deal of difference. By no conceivable stretch of imagination could I account for his presence in this out-of-the-way part of the world, unless it had something to do with my own humble affairs. Those grim words out of the Bible, "Where the carcase is, there will the eagles be gathered together," seemed to hit off the situation with unfortunate accuracy. There was a strong suggestion of a sick bird of prey in de Roda's yellow face, and, though I had no intention of becoming a carcase if I could possibly avoid it, the parallel was too close to be anything but distinctly unpleasant.

The one point in my favour was the fact that, if trouble were coming, I was at least fully prepared for it. After the way they had bungled things in the docks my enemies would no doubt have the sense to guess that I must be on my guard, but of the extra and private warning that I had received from Christine they were, I felt sure, happily in ignorance. If only I had had the least inkling of what it was all about I don't think I should have worried in the slightest. It was this fighting in the dark that was so upsetting—this horrible ignorance as to where the next blow might come from, and why the devil de Roda himself or anyone else should be so anxious to accelerate my funeral.

For the hundredth time I turned over in my mind the few actual facts of which I was really certain, only to pull up baffled before the same blank wall of profitless conjecture. All the guessing in the world was no use until I had something more to go on, and the sooner I acquired that "something" the rosier would be my prospects of remaining on this planet.

I was just pouring myself out a second glass of port when an idea occurred to me. Why not summon Bascomb and have things out with him straight away? Up to now I had made no attempt to question him. We were bound to come to an understanding sooner or later, and from every point of view the present seemed to be as good a time as any other.

Acting promptly on my impulse, I walked across to the fireplace and rang the bell. A few moments elapsed; then the door opened and the taciturn face of my retainer appeared on the threshold.

"Are you busy, Bascomb?" I asked.

He shook his head.

"Well, come in then," I said. "There are one or two things I want to talk to you about."

Still keeping silent, he closed the door behind him and advanced to the centre of the room.

"Sit down and have a glass of port," I added. "I don't know where my uncle got it from, but it's a first-class wine."

He hesitated for a second; then in a slightly awkward fashion he took the chair opposite mine, and accepted the decanter which I pushed across.

"Thank you, sir," he said gruffly. "I reckon it ought to be all right—same as everything else in the cellar. Mr. Jannaway was very particular about 'is liquor."

"He seems to have been a good judge of most things," I said, holding my glass up to the light. "I never met him myself, as you probably know. He went abroad to America when I was quite young, and except for Mr. Drayton you're the only person who can tell me anything about him."

For a moment Bascomb stared at the table without speaking.

"I dunno wot Mr. Drayton may 'ave said," he began in a half-defiant voice, "but if anyone wants to run down the guv'nor, they won't do it while I'm around. I don't say 'e was a bloomin' saint; 'e weren't made that way, no more'n I am. All the same, 'e treated me proper, 'e did, and I ain't goin' back on 'im now 'e's dead and gorn."

There was a rough eloquence about the man's outburst which I felt would have convinced even Ross of his good faith.

"I'm glad to hear you speak like that," I said heartily. "I believe in sticking up through thick and thin for anybody who has been kind to me, especially when they can't defend themselves."

The gleam of passion died out of Bascomb's face almost as suddenly as it had appeared.

"I didn't mean nothin' against you, sir," he began with a kind of clumsy apology in his voice. "I reckon you'd deal fair with anyone till you 'ad reasons for the contrary. All I feels is that mebbe you've 'eard things about the guv'nor which makes yer think a sight worse of 'im than there's any call for."

"It isn't so much what I've heard," I said, looking him straight in the face. "It's the queer way my uncle behaved that seems to me to want some sort of explanation. Why did he suddenly shut himself up on this island and treat the place as if it were a kind of fortress? At least, that's the only description that fits in with what Dr. Manning and even you yourself have told me."

Bascomb met my glance without wavering.

"As far as that goes, sir," he said stolidly, "I dunno much more about it than wot you do. Wotever the guv'nor did 'e 'ad good reasons for, but 'e weren't the sort to talk about 'is own affairs, not even to me."

"Do you think he was afraid of somebody?" I asked. "That's what Mr. Drayton believes."

Bascomb hesitated for a moment. "Yes, sir," he said slowly, "I reckon that's about the size of it. 'E'd got it into 'is 'ead that there was some party after 'im, an' 'e bought this 'ere island so as 'e'd be out of their way."

"When did it start?" I demanded. "When did you first notice anything wrong?"

"Well, sir, it's my belief that 'e always 'ad some notion of that sort at the back of 'is mind. When I come to 'im in London, almost the first thing 'e says to me was that no strangers was to be allowed into the flat, not under no circumstances wotever. Still, 'e didn't seem to worry 'isself not to anything like the same extent. 'E used to go to the races an' the music 'alls, an' as often as not 'e'd stop out till two or three in the morning."

"But something must have happened," I persisted. "Can't you remember when he began to change?"

Bascomb nodded. "It was one mornin'," he said slowly, "gettin' on towards the end of October. I 'eard 'is bell ring after breakfast, and when I goes in, there 'e was sittin' at the table, lookin' as if 'e'd bin took ill. 'E'd bin reading the paper, I could see that, an' I remember thinkin' as mebbe 'e'd found something in it as 'ad upset 'im. 'Bascomb,' 'e says to me, 'd'you know any place where you can get me a dawg?' 'Wot sort of a dawg, sir?' I asks, an' 'e laughs in that queer way 'e 'ad which was enough to give a bloke the creeps. 'A savage dawg, Bascomb,' 'e says, 'a big savage dawg as'll look after you an' me, an' tear the guts outer any silly devil who tries to shove 'isself in where 'e ain't wanted.' 'E always spoke as if 'e was 'alf jokin', the guv'nor did, but this time I could see as 'e meant business. So I tells 'im I knows a cove in Whitechapel who could probably let 'im 'ave wot 'e wanted, an' that very afternoon I goes down there and gets 'old of Satan." He paused and glanced at me with a sudden trace of apprehension. "Not as there's anything wrong with Satan, sir," he hastened to add. "'E's as gentle as a lamb with people 'e knows, but, as the bloke who sold 'im to me says, 'e ain't got no fancy for strangers, an' you see, sir, that's just the sorter dawg Mr. Jannaway was askin' for."

"And it's just the sort of dog I'm very glad he found," I remarked thankfully.

Bascomb paused to finish his port and then carefully wiped his mouth with the back of his hand.

"After that," he continued, "the guv'nor was wot you might call a different man. 'E didn't go out no more, 'cept in the middle of the day, and although 'e says nothin' to me, I could see as 'e was busy fixin' up some plan of 'is own. It didn't take long before it come out neither. 'Bascomb,' 'e says to me one mornin', 'I think we've 'ad enough o' London. It ain't good for the 'ealth livin' too much in a town, so I've took a nice little island where we can be quiet and comfortable—just the three of us. We shan't want no furniture,' 'e says, 'but pack up everything else in the flat, and we'll go down there to-morrow.'"

"Rather a short notice, wasn't it?" I suggested gravely.

"It didn't make no difference to me," returned Bascomb. "Where the guv'nor went I went, and as it so 'appens I've always 'ad a fancy for the country, ever since me first visit to 'Ampstead 'Eath."

"And you took over this place just as it stands?" I said.

"More or less, sir. The furniture was 'ere right enough, but there was one or two things the guv'nor wanted to 'ave done, such as puttin' on extra bolts and locks, an' shovin' in that there fireplace in the 'all."

"You had the workmen staying in the house, didn't you?" I asked.

"Yes, sir. A queer lot they was too. Dutchmen, every mother's son of 'em. Couldn't speak a word o' English, or any other Christian language."

I stared at him in frank astonishment. "Dutchmen!" I repeated. "What on earth made him engage Dutchmen?"

"Gawd knows," observed Bascomb indifferently, "but Dutch blokes they was, and that's a fact. Come over from Rotterdam, and brought all their clobber with them."

"How long did they stay?" I asked curiously.

Bascomb scratched his head. "Mebbe a matter o' four or five days. I didn't take no particular notice of 'em myself, 'avin' plenty to do gettin' things straight in the kitchen. The guv'nor kep' an eye on 'em, though, and I reckon 'e seed they done their job proper."

"They must have got through a good bit if they were here for five days," I said.

"I dunno about that," returned my companion rather contemptuously. "Them furrin' blokes ain't much use at work, even when there's someone lookin' after them. They was messin' about with the fireplace pretty nigh all the time."

"Why did he want a new grate?" I enquired. "Was there anything the matter with the old one?"

"It weren't big enough," explained Bascomb. "You see, sir, 'avin' spent most of 'is time in 'ot places, the guv'nor felt the cold somethin' crool. Always blindin' at the weather, 'e was. I've 'eard 'im say it was made up outer the scraps and leavin's wot other countries 'adn't got no use for."

"Then I suppose he lived chiefly in the hall?" I remarked.

"That's right, sir. 'E never went outside the 'ouse, not after it was dark. I used to make 'im up a big fire, an' there 'e'd sit all the evenin', with Satan lyin' on the floor alongside of 'im."

"It sounds a cheerful sort of existence," I said. "How did he amuse himself? Had he got any books or papers?"

"I don't think 'e laid much store by readin'," replied Bascomb. "We 'ad the *Daily Mail* come over every mornin', but as often as not 'e wouldn't trouble 'isself to open it." He hesitated for a moment, and then seemed to decide to take me into his confidence. "You see, sir, the guv'nor 'e began shift in' a good deal o' liquor after we come down 'ere. 'E was never drunk, not wot you might call proper drunk, but most evenin's 'e'd be a bit muzzy like, an' 'e'd just sit there mutterin' to 'isself or talkin' to Satan. I reckon 'e'd fixed it up in 'is mind that someone was tryin' to do 'im in, an' when a party gets 'old of a notion like that, drink's about the only thing as'll cheer 'em up."

"And what happened?" I asked. "Did anyone put a bullet through the window or anything exciting of that sort?"

Once more Bascomb shook his head. "They didn't 'ave the chance," he observed grimly. "Before I goes to bed I always use ter slip Satan out through the back door, and I'd like to see the bloke as'd set foot on the island with 'im prowlin' around in the dark."

There was a short pause.

"Tell me about my uncle's illness," I said. "How was it he went off so quickly?"

"It was through gettin' wet, sir. 'E was out with 'is gun one mornin', an' it come on to rain sudden. Before 'e could get back to the 'ouse 'e was fair soaked to the skin. 'This cursed place 'as done for me at last, Bascomb,' 'e says. 'I shouldn't wonder if I was a corpse inside of a week.' With that, sir, 'e goes straight off to 'is bed, and when it come to five o'clock 'e was tremblin' all over an' beginning to talk wild. I reckoned 'e was pretty bad, an' 'avin' 'eard as this cove Manning was a doctor, I rows across to the barge and asks 'im to come over. I didn't like 'im, not from the moment I put me eyes on 'im, but, seein' there weren't no one else 'andy, I 'ad to make the best of it. By the time we gets back the guv'nor was worse. 'E 'adn't no notion who I was, an' 'e was throwin' 'isself about an' talkin' all sorts of foolishness. 'You'd better find me somethin' to sleep on,' says the doctor. 'If I don't stay and look after 'im 'e'll peg out in the night as likely as not.' Well, I makes 'im up a bed in the guv'nor's room, an' nex' mornin' I goes over to Pen Mill an' telegraphs to Mr. Drayton. After that the 'ole thing was out of my 'ands, so to speak. I done everything they tells me, but as you knows, sir, the guv'nor never got no better, an' two days later 'e goes off sudden early in the mornin'." He paused. "I wish 'e'd come to again, if it 'ad only been for a minute," he added huskily. "'E'd been good to me, the guv'nor 'ad, and I'd like to 'ave said good-bye to 'im."

I could not help feeling that it was probably a better epitaph than my uncle really deserved, but, all the same, there was something curiously affecting in the rough fellow's evident distress.

"What was the matter with the doctor?" I asked, after a moment's pause. "How was it you couldn't get on with him?"

Bascomb's face hardened again immediately. "I don't trust 'im, sir. It's my belief 'e's a wrong 'un."

Allowing for a slight difference in expression, they were the very identical sentiments that Manning had confided to me about the speaker, and it was all I could do to stop myself from smiling.

"Why do you think that?" I persisted.

"Well, if 'e was straight an' above-board wot made 'im carry on like 'e did? Always askin' questions and shovin' 'is nose into everything, same as if it was 'is own 'ouse." He stopped to take a long, indignant breath. "Some game of 'is own on, that's wot 'e 'ad, or else 'e wouldn't 'ave bin so blarsted curious."

"What sort of questions did he ask?" I enquired.

"Hall sorts," replied Bascomb resentfully. "Tryin' to jump me about the guv'nor mornin', noon, and night, an' as for the way 'e used to mess about, it was fair sickening. Why, after the funeral, blessed if 'e didn't come back 'ere twice an' want to look over the 'ouse again."

"Did you let him?" I asked.

"Not me! I says to 'im I'd strict orders from Mr. Drayton that no one was to come inside the place. 'E offered me a couple o' quid the second time, but I told 'im wot 'e could do with it, and after that I reckon we understood each other. Any'ow, 'e didn't show up no more, not till 'e seed you an' the other gen'leman."

"There's a fairly simple explanation of all this," I said. "He wants to get hold of the island and turn it into a yachting club. He had made an offer to Mr. Drayton before I arrived."

Bascomb looked a little sceptical. "I ain't 'eard nothin' about that," he observed. "Anyway, 'e's a wrong 'un, sir; you can take my word for it."

"I daresay you're right," I said, lighting myself a cigar. "It doesn't make much difference, because I haven't the faintest intention of letting the place and I've told him so straight out. If that's all he's after we shan't be troubled with much more of his company." I got up from the table. "I think I'll have a stroll round before I turn in," I added. "You needn't bother about the front door; I'll lock that myself when I come back."

I walked through into the hall, where I found Satan stretched out luxuriously on the mat in front of the fireplace. He cocked an eye at me as I passed, and, seeing me pick up my cap from the table, rose slowly to his feet.

"Come along then," I said. "We'll take the air together if you feel that way."

The suggestion evidently appealed to him, for he followed me out through the porch, and side by side we sauntered down the gravel path which led to the landing-stage.

It was a beautiful night, with a half moon low down in the sky, and one or two large stars shining away in isolated splendour. As I came out from the shadow of the trees the loveliness of my surroundings filled me with a kind of enchantment, and, drawing in a deep breath, I stood for a moment in absolute stillness. Everything was silent, except for the faint whisper of the reeds. A dancing pathway of silver stretched away up the centre of the estuary, and beyond it, on either side, lay the black, irregular outline of the shore.

Crossing the open with Satan at my heels, I slowly made my way down to the edge of the water. My mind was full of my conversation with Bascomb, and, coming to a halt in the warm darkness, I stood there puffing meditatively at my cigar.

Everything I had just heard had merely gone to confirm my previous ideas. There could be no doubt that, whether he had been right or wrong, my uncle had been firmly convinced that his life was in imminent danger, and in this opinion Bascomb himself seemed strongly inclined to share. I attached considerable importance to the latter point, because so far my worthy retainer had not given me the impression of being gifted with any particular powers of imagination. The only matter on which he appeared to have a slight obsession was with reference to Dr. Manning.

His mistrust for that gentleman was indeed so pronounced that I could not help wondering whether, after all, it might not be based upon a sound instinct. Unless he had exaggerated, the doctor's curiosity did appear to have been a trifle excessive, even allowing for his anxiety to get a lease of the island. I had only seen the man once, but there was something about him that I had not altogether cottoned to myself, in spite of his attractive manner and his undeniable kindness in looking after my uncle. I think it was a certain hardness in those china blue eyes of his, or perhaps it was the apparently deliberate fashion in which he had tried to set me against Bascomb. Of course it was wildly improbable that he could have anything to do with de Roda, but, all the same, I began to feel that it would be just as well to keep him on the list of suspected persons. I was in one of those regrettable situations where one cannot afford to give full play to the naturally generous impulses of one's nature!

My thoughts went back to the strange figure of my uncle as I saw him in the light of Bascomb's new disclosures. Viewed from that friendly angle, he seemed a more human sort of character than I had previously imagined; indeed, whatever he had done or been, there was something about those last days of his that stirred a belated sympathy for him in my heart. I pictured him sitting through the long winter evenings in that lonely room, with the half-empty whisky bottle beside him, and who knows what grim memories gnawing at his conscience. I could almost see him turning uneasily in his chair as the rain and wind swept up the estuary, beating on the French windows and whispering of the implacable vengeance that was lurking somewhere in the darkness outside.

It is possible that my compassion for him may have been stimulated by the fact that I seemed to be in a more or less similar predicament myself. My prospects of a long and peaceful life appeared to be quite as hazy as his own, while I laboured under the additional handicap of being entirely ignorant as to the reason for my unpopularity. I only knew that the same danger which had haunted him was now closing in on me, and that at any moment it might make itself manifest in a peculiarly abrupt and unpleasant form.

With a feeling of irritation at my own helplessness I stood staring out over the moonlit water. Except for a solitary lamp on the jetty opposite, all the long stretch of coastline on either side was wrapped in complete darkness. It looked a very suitable background for anyone with homicidal tendencies, and I was just wondering which point of the compass seemed the most promising when something attracted my attention.

Away to the left, in the direction of Barham Lock, a tiny point of light had broken out into the night. I gazed at it curiously, wondering what it could be. There was no house or cottage on that part of the coast, and in view of the shallowness of the water it was a very unlikely spot at which any vessel would have come to anchor.

For several moments I puzzled vainly over the problem; and then quite suddenly the explanation came to me.

It was the riding lamp from Dr. Manning's barge, which was moored up there in the blackness under the shadow of the trees.

CHAPTER SEVEN

"I think I shall go over to Pen Mill this morning," I said.

Bascomb, who was clearing away the breakfast things, paused in the middle of his operations.

"Will you be back to lunch, sir?" he enquired. "I got a nice duck I was thinkin' o' cookin'."

"In that case," I said, "I shall certainly be back. Better make it one-thirty though, and then we shan't run the risk of spoiling it."

"Very good, sir," he replied, picking up the tray. "I'll 'ave it ready for yer, and I reckon you'll find it'll be all right. I cooked many a one for Mr. Jannaway when 'e was alive. Very partial to roast duck the guv'nor was."

"It runs in the family evidently," I observed.

Bascomb retired with his burden, and, throwing aside the *Daily Mail*, which was exceedingly dull, I got up and looked out of the window. Two days had drifted by since our conversation in the dining-room, and so far nothing had occurred to mar the picture of rustic felicity which Ross had sketched out as my probable future. Being still fresh to my surroundings, I had found the time pass away pleasantly enough. I had gone through my uncle's papers, put in some honest work in the garden, and had a very jolly cruise or two up and down the estuary in the small sailing dinghy which I had discovered stowed away in the boathouse.

This morning, however, for some reason or other, I had woken up in a more adventurous mood. This tranquil existence was all very well in its way, but there are some luxuries for which one can pay too dearly. I am a firm believer in the doctrine that heaven helps those who help themselves, and I had no intention of sitting down and doing nothing, while my enemies quietly completed their plans for a second and more successful attempt at blotting me out.

Thinking things over while I was dressing, I had decided that something in the nature of a scouting expedition to the mainland was distinctly advisable. It would have to be done tactfully, of course, for, if my theories were right, any movement of mine was probably being watched with the closest attention. Still, that only made the idea more attractive, and I felt a cheerful little tingle of excitement in my heart as I stared out of the window and pondered over my undertaking.

The first thing to do was obviously to try and find out whether de Roda was anywhere in the neighbourhood. This ought not to be a very difficult matter, for the presence of a stranger in such a sparsely inhabited place as Pen Mill would be sure to have aroused a considerable amount of curiosity. It would be discussed and canvassed with the utmost relish, especially in the bar parlour of the Gunner's Arms, which I knew from old experience to be the rallying-point for all the busybodies in the district. One had only to drop in there for a drink, and any local gossip that was floating around was almost certain to be brought before one's notice.

After that—well, my future proceedings would necessarily depend upon how much or how little I had managed to pick up. If I found out that de Roda was really on the spot I was determined to follow the trail as promptly and thoroughly as possible. It might be a dangerous amusement, but that was an objection which would apply equally to any course I chose to adopt, and, after all, it is better to run risks when there is a decent chance of getting something for one's pains.

Besides, at the back of everything else there lurked another and much more compelling motive. Should de Roda be anywhere around, it was quite on the cards that Christine would be with him. The mere thought of this pleasing possibility was amply sufficient to outweigh all other considerations, and it was in a very contented mood that I turned away from the window and went upstairs to get ready for my trip.

A quarter of an hour later I was sitting in the dinghy, sculling across in a leisurely fashion towards the opposite shore. Except for a couple of brown-sailed barges, which were stealing out from Pen Mill to take advantage of the rising tide, I appeared to have the whole estuary to myself. I dodged in between the pair of them, and came up alongside the jetty, where two or three tousled-headed urchins were waiting my arrival.

Amongst the latter I recognised the somewhat soiled features of my friend Jimmy.

"Here you are, James," I said, tossing him the painter. "I'll be back about one o'clock. Don't let anyone sneak the sculls."

"I'll watch it, sir," he replied, with shrill confidence, and, elbowing the others officially aside, he proceeded to tow the boat along the wall and make her fast to a convenient post.

I stopped for a moment at the end of the causeway, and, under cover of filling my pipe, took a careful survey of the village green. It looked very peaceful and innocent, its only inhabitants being a small child and an ancient donkey, neither of whom seemed to threaten any immediate danger. Having struck a match and lighted my tobacco, I sauntered off across the grass, and a minute later I was mounting the steps that led up to the inn.

When I entered the bar parlour I found two other customers already in possession. One was a short, ferrety-faced man, dressed in black, with a straggling red moustache and a bowler hat on the back of his head. The second was a grizzled and elderly boatman, who was puffing away contentedly at a much used cutty. Both were seated in chairs in front of the bar, and had evidently been carrying on a conversation with the landlord, who was leaning over the counter polishing a tankard.

"Good morning," I said, with a general nod which included everybody.

I was subjected to a quick inspection, but all three of them returned my greeting civilly enough.

"I think I'll have a bottle of Bass," I said, addressing myself to the landlord. "That's the best drink for this time of day."

The little man in black blew his nose, making a surprising amount of noise over the operation.

"I envy you, sir," he remarked. "There's nothing I like better than a glass of beer meself, but it goes straight to my liver. Perhaps you aren't troubled in that way."

"I don't know where it goes to," I said, "but the result seems to be quite satisfactory."

The landlord unscrewed a bottle and carefully tilted its contents into a tumbler.

"You don't take enough exercise, Mr. Watson," he remarked. "No one can drink beer, not if they sit in an office all day. You want to be out in the open air, like George here."

The old boatman nodded affirmatively. "Beer never 'urt me," he observed with a chuckle. "I reckon I drunk enough of it in my time to float a Thames barge."

With a regretful shake of his head the little man applied himself to his whisky. "You couldn't do it, not if you were in the house agent line," he remarked. "It would have to be spirits or nothing then, the same as it is with me."

I paid for my drink, and, strolling across the room, sat down at an empty table in one of the bay-windows. There was a paper lying in front of me—a weekly rag called the *Shalston Gazette*—which seemed to consist principally of advertisements. I picked it up, however, and, opening it at the centre page, made a deliberate pretence of glancing through the local news.

For a moment or two the conversation at the other end of the bar languished; then, as if renewing a former discussion, the landlord suddenly addressed himself to Mr. Watson.

"What I don't understand," he said, "is how they come to pitch on 'The Laurels.' It ain't the kind of place you'd think a gentleman would take a fancy to."

"It suited this party right enough," returned the little man with a chuckle. "All he wanted was a house facing the water. He didn't seem particular about anything else, provided he could get that."

I felt my heart begin to beat a shade quicker, for a sudden conviction that they were speaking about de Roda had flashed instantly across my mind. The landlord's next remark put the matter almost beyond question.

"Well, I suppose, being a foreigner, he ain't used to comfort. He'll find it precious damp though, if we happen to have another summer like the last."

"That's his look-out," returned the other. "He saw the place before he took it, so I don't see that he'll have any call to grumble. Anyhow, he's paid us six months' rent in advance."

"What part o' the world d'you reckon he comes from, Mr. Watson?" enquired the boatman. "Some says he's a Frenchy, but it seems to me he's a bit too yaller in the face for that. More like some kind of a Eytalian to my way o' thinkin'."

"He's neither," said Mr. Watson decisively. "He's a Spaniard—the same as those fellers who bring round the onions."

"A Spaniard, is he?" ejaculated the landlord. "Fancy that now! Could you make out what he said?"

Mr. Watson sucked in his lip. "After a fashion," he replied. "It wasn't too easy his first visit, but the second time he come along he brought his niece with him, and it was she that did most of the talking. I didn't have any trouble with her—none at all. Speaks English as well as you or me."

"That's a fact," put in the boatman, nodding his head. "She was down to my place the day before yesterday looking after something to go on the water in. A fine young lady she is too, and a rare 'and at sailing a boat."

"I don't hold with women sailing," remarked Mr. Watson disapprovingly. "She'll be drowning herself one of these days, you mark my words."

"Not likely," retorted the other. "She can swim like a duck, that young lady can. She bathes off of the bank there before breakfast, and dang me if I didn't see 'er right out in the channel when I come round the point early this morning."

I sat back in my chair, holding the paper in front of me and making a desperate effort to appear quite unconcerned. For a moment I could hardly believe my own good luck. Without asking a single question I had stumbled bang across the very information I was in search of, and it was just about all I could manage to keep my feelings under proper control.

What excited me more than anything else was the news about Christine. The knowledge that she was close at hand—perhaps within a few hundred yards of where I was sitting—filled me with an indescribable sense of elation. I felt like jumping up from my seat, brandishing the *Shalston Gazette* round my head, and inviting all three of my garrulous acquaintances to a general orgy of free drinks.

"I ain't curious," announced the landlord, after a short pause, "but I'd give something to know what's brought 'em down into these here parts."

"I can tell you that," replied Mr. Watson, with some importance. "It's his doctor's orders. He's been ill—very ill, so his niece says—and he's been advised to take a house in a bracing climate."

"Ah! 'E's done right in coming here then," observed the boatman patriotically. "They do say Pen Mill's the most bracing spot in England."

I was just thinking how thoroughly I agreed with this statement when the outer door swung open and two fresh customers entered the bar. One was a big, red-faced man in gaiters, who came in talking at the top of his voice and slapping his leg with a riding-whip. I could have murdered him with the utmost cheerfulness, for I felt at once that my prospects of acquiring any further information were remote in the extreme. He was one of those breezy, would-be humorous gentlemen, who revel in the sound of their own voices, and, true to his type, he at once established himself with his back to the counter, and proceeded to narrate some long and pointless story.

Still holding the paper in front of me, I stuck patiently to my seat, on the off-chance that the conversation would drift back into its former channel. It was a vain hope, and, however, after waiting for several minutes, I came to the conclusion that I might as well take my departure. After all, I had found out a good bit, and if I wanted to put my knowledge to any practical use, the sooner I set to work the better.

In as casual a fashion as possible I got up from my chair and sauntered across the room. The others were all busy listening to the newcomer, and, without attracting any particular attention, I passed out through the door and made my way down the steps.

At the bottom I paused for a moment to consider my plan of campaign. I remembered something about the neighbourhood, but I had no recollection of a house called "The Laurels" or of any place that answered to Mr. Watson's description of it. I should have to make enquiries on this point, and at the same time I should have to do it in such a fashion as to avoid arousing any unnecessary gossip.

Glancing round the green, my eyes fell on the small village shop opposite, where in bygone days Bobby and I had been accustomed to purchase our tobacco. If Mrs. Summers, the old lady who used to run it, were still alive, she would probably remember me, and in that case it ought to be the very place for my purpose. Anyhow, I determined to chance it, so, knocking out my pipe, I vaulted the wooden railings and set out over the grass.

The first person I saw when I stepped in through the low doorway was Mrs. Summers herself. She was sitting hunched up in a chair behind the counter, knitting away industriously at a sock, and looking precisely as unchanged as the rest of Pen Mill. She stared at me for a moment in a half-puzzled, half-doubtful sort of fashion; then suddenly her round red face expanded into a broad smile of recognition.

"Well I never!" she exclaimed. "If it isn't Mr. Dryden!"

"That's right," I said, coming up to the counter. "And how are you, Mrs. Summers?"

We shook hands warmly, while she beamed at me through her gold-rimmed spectacles in a fashion that cheered my heart.

"Well, well, well!" she repeated. "Just to think of that now. Why, I couldn't believe my eyes when I saw you walking in through the door."

"I was wondering if you would know me after all this time," I said.

"You needn't have worried about that," she replied. "You haven't altered—not the least little bit in the world."

"Neither have you," I returned gallantly. "People who lead sober and respectable lives always keep their good looks."

"Ah!" she observed. "I might have known you'd say something like that. You were always the one for having your little joke." She continued to beam at me with the same indulgent smile. "You've come along to stay with Commander Dean, I suppose?" she added.

I stared at her in the blankest amazement.

"Why, didn't you know he was here?" she asked, in a surprised voice.

"Bobby Dean in Pen Mill!" I managed to jerk out.

"Well, not exactly in Pen Mill, though he do come around pretty often. Martlesea's his headquarters—at least, that's where he lives when he isn't in his boat."

"D'you mean to tell me he's got a job here?" I almost shouted.

She nodded her head. "He's in the Coast Patrol—the same as he was when the war was on. Fancy your not knowing that now! Why, I made certain you'd come down to pay him a visit, seeing as how you were such friends."

"I haven't had a letter from him for ages," I explained. "The last time he wrote he was up at some God-forsaken place in the North of Scotland." I paused, while the full realisation of all that Bobby's presence would mean filtered joyfully through my heart. "By Jove, that's gorgeous news, Mrs. Summers!" I added. "You couldn't have told me anything in the world which would have pleased me more."

"But if you haven't come to see him," she demanded curiously, "whatever's brought you back into these parts?"

Her question reminded me suddenly of the real purpose of my visit.

"It's my turn to give you a little surprise," I said, and then, facing towards the door, I pointed out in the direction of Greensea. "Do you know who lives there?" I asked.

"Mr. Jannaway did," she said, "but he's been dead and gone a matter of two months. There's no one on the island now, except the caretaker, Mr. Bascomb."

"Oh, yes, there is," I retorted. "There's a distinguished gentleman called Mr. John Dryden."

She shook her head at me reprovingly. "Full of your little jokes," she repeated. "Just the same as you always was."

"It's no joke, Mrs. Summers," I persisted. "Mr. Jannaway was my uncle, and he had the good sense to die without making a will. The result is that I scoop the lot—his money and Greensea Island and everything else."

Something in my manner must have convinced her that I was speaking the truth, for she threw up her hands in a gesture of profound astonishment.

"Well I never!" she exclaimed. "Why, I did hear some talk that the place was to go to Mr. Jannaway's nephew, but just to think that of all people in the world it should happen to be you!"

"It's a bit of a knock-out, isn't it?" I said sympathetically. "I haven't quite got over it myself yet."

She sat down again in her chair.

"It properly took my breath away for the minute," she declared. "Not but what I'm gladder than I can say, Mr. Dryden, and I'm sure there's no gentleman in the world who deserves a bit of good luck more than what you do."

"Thank you very much," I returned, with my best bow.

"D'you mean to live on the island?" she asked.

"I hope to," I said truthfully; and then, thinking that this was a favourable chance for making my enquiry, I added: "I suppose there have been all sorts of changes since I was here—lots of fresh people in the neighbourhood?"

She paused, as if to consider the problem. "Not so very many, sir," she said. "There isn't much to bring folks here except in the summer time. Mrs. Green at the Gunner's Arms is dead, as I suppose you've heard."

"Yes," I said. "I have just come from there."

"And Colonel Paton of Brooklands—he's gone too. The Bowden-Smiths have got his house now, and I have heard that there's a new party taken 'The Laurels'—a foreign gentleman, according to what they tell me."

"'The Laurels'?" I repeated thoughtfully. "I seem to know the name, but I'm hanged if I can remember where it is."

"Why, surely you can't have forgotten 'The Laurels,'" she persisted. "That little white house facing the estuary, away round the point." She pointed out across the green, to where the ground rose steeply behind the Gunner's Arms. "You can't see it from here," she added, "but it's almost opposite you when you're on the island."

I could have leaned over the counter and hugged her, but with another masterly effort I managed to preserve my composure.

"Of course," I said. "How stupid of me! The fact is I have been away so long that I've got a bit mixed up in my bearings." I stopped to stroke a large black cat which had jumped up on to the chair alongside of me. "So it's been let to a foreigner, has it?" I continued. "Not a German, I hope?"

Mrs. Summers positively bristled at my suggestion. "I should think not indeed. I should like to see the Hun as'd dare to show his wicked face in Pen Mill. It's a French gentleman, sir—a Mr. de Roda and his niece; very good people, too, from all accounts."

"I'm glad of that," I said gravely. "It's a great relief to know that one's got respectable neighbours." I held out my hand. "I must be off now, Mrs. Summers," I added. "There are one or two little things I have to attend to before I go back to lunch.

"You'll be in again before long, I suppose, sir? she hazarded.

"Rather," I said, "and the next time I come I hope I shall bring Commander Dean with me. It will be like old days—all three of us together again."

I gave her a parting squeeze, and, resisting the temptation to break into a step dance, I turned round and made my way to the door.

I certainly had good reasons for feeling a trifle exhilarated Not only had I picked up the information I wanted with reference to "The Laurels," but I had also made the welcome and unexpected discovery that I was no longer without a pal. If there was one man I would have chosen out of all others to take the place of Ross it was my old skipper, Bobby Dean. For the last two years of the war he and I had been cooped up together in a motor launch, pleasantly engaged in strafing Fritz, and I don't think there are many occupations in the world which give one a better chance of finding out the character of one's companions. I knew Bobby inside out, from his rough, weather-beaten exterior to the depths of his honest soul. He was one of that cheery gang of east coast yachtsmen who had flocked into the R.N.V.R. at the outbreak of hostilities, and had done so much to mess up the All Highest's brilliant idea of starving out the British Empire. So useful, indeed, had been his record that when peace came he had managed to snaffle a regular commission in the reorganised Coast Defence Force. Not being so lucky or deserving myself, I had, like most of the others, drifted away into the ranks of the Merchant Service, but ever since then we had exchanged occasional yarns, which had kept us more or less in touch with each other's doings.

His last letter had been dated from the Shetlands, where he had been chasing around in an antiquated gun-boat, and feeling extremely fed up with the universe in general. He had given me no hint then that there was any likelihood of his being transferred to a more Christian station. So the news of his presence at Martlesea had come to me as a complete and joyful surprise. A friend like Bobby was the one thing I had wanted, and as I walked across the green I devoutly thanked the gods for the kindly interest they seemed to be taking in my affairs.

It was not until I had reached the inn that my mind switched back to the immediate and pressing business in front of me. This was my first effort in the Sherlock Holmes line, and I realised that if I were going to do justice to it I should need all the concentration of which I was capable. I had no plan except for the fixed determination that I would at least have a look at the outside of "The Laurels." Beyond that point everything was deliriously vague. I could only trust to luck, and register an inward vow that if providence did throw any chance in my way, I would snap it up as promptly and efficiently as possible.

The first thing to settle was how to get to the house. There were two methods open to me—one by tramping along the foreshore, and the other by taking the narrow lane which turned away to the left about a hundred yards above the inn. I pitched on the latter as being the less conspicuous of the two, and, trying hard to look as if I had come out for a morning constitutional, I started off in a leisurely fashion up the hill.

I still had a sort of uneasy sensation that somebody was spying on me, but a glance back over my shoulder when I reached the corner gave no grounds for this ungenerous suspicion. For all the interest that Pen Mill appeared to be taking in my movements, I might have been off the earth. The white road stretched out behind me, sunlit and deserted, and, feeling that nothing was to be gained by staring at an empty landscape, I branched off without further hesitation into the side turning.

For a little distance the lane ran straight ahead of me; then it curved off suddenly to the left in the direction of the sea. I made my way cautiously round this bend, and found myself outside a high wooden paling, evidently the boundary of some private residence. About twenty yards farther on I could see a swing gate which apparently led into the drive.

Keeping well under the fence, and feeling unpleasantly like a burglar, I crept forward until I had reached the desired point. Any doubts I might have had as to the identity of the place were at once put to rest, for on the top bar, in faded and weather-beaten letters, was painted the following inscription:

"THE LAURELS."

CHAPTER EIGHT

It was in circumstances such as these that the late Mr. Sherlock Holmes always aroused my keenest admiration. No matter how puzzling the situation might be, he invariably knew what was the right line to take and exactly how to set about it. I suppose he must have been blessed with some inner sense which is denied to lesser mortals, for I know that in my own case no sudden inspiration came to help me. I just stood there gazing at the inscription with a kind of vague satisfaction, and wondering what the devil I ought to do next.

All my instincts prompted me to action, but the question was, What sort of action was the most advisable? I could not very well march up to the front door and hand in my card, much as I should have enjoyed making the experiment. There was Christine to be considered as well as myself; indeed, the feeling that whatever I did I must bring no suspicion upon her was the one predominant thought at the back of my mind.

From where I was standing I could see nothing of the house. The drive curved away sharply round a huge dump of laurels, and the whole place looked even more untidy and overgrown than my own property. If I chose I had only to push open the gate and walk in, and yet, with my hand actually on the latch, I still hesitated. Somehow or other it seemed altogether too easy. The vision of a mouse strolling unconcernedly into an open trap rose up before me with unpleasant distinctness, and, abandoning the idea, I stepped back again on to the grass.

It struck me that another and less public mode of entrance would be more in keeping with my part. The paling was only about five feet high, and offered little or no obstacle to anyone as active as myself. I could slip over quietly, just where the trees were thickest, and, unless the whole thing collapsed beneath me, the odds were that my ungentlemanly intrusion would probably pass unnoticed.

I was in the very act of turning away to put this notion into practice when a sudden sound from inside brought me up as stiff as a ramrod. It was the unmistakable noise of an opening door, followed almost immediately by the voice of a man speaking and the crunch of footsteps coming down the drive.

Thanks chiefly to my sea training, I managed to keep my head. One glance round showed me that the only available hiding-place was the thick hedge on the opposite side of the road. I made for it like a rabbit, and the next moment I had forced my way through, and was crouching down, scratched and panting, behind a welcome barrier of blackberry bushes.

As luck would have it, I could not have pitched upon a better spot. I was quite invisible myself, and through a small gap in the hedge it was just possible to command a glimpse of the gate. I found that by pushing aside some leaves I was able to enlarge the view still further, and with my eyes glued to this peep-hole I waited breathlessly for the next development.

It was not long in coming. A couple of seconds could hardly have passed when the gate swung open and two figures stepped out into the roadway. For a moment I stared at them both, hardly able to believe my eyes. One was Christine, and the other—of all people in the world—was Dr. Manning.

To say that I was knocked all of a heap would be as near as I can get to describing my sensations. I had thought of a good many things, but the possibility of Christine and the doctor being acquainted had never so much as crossed my mind. I could only gaze at them in a sort of incredulous amazement, while all the theories that I had previously built up seemed to be tumbling about like a pack of cards.

It was Manning's voice which collected my scattered wits for me.

"I will come round to-morrow about half-past ten," he said "You needn't be the least worried though. Everything's going as well as it possibly can."

Christine held out her hand. "I am not anxious now," she said simply. "Good-bye, and thank you very much."

He looked down at her in a way that filled me with a sudden and peculiar resentment.

"Don't go in for a minute," he said. "Come as far as the end of the road with me. I want to show you how to get to the barge in case you ever honour me with a visit."

I saw Christine hesitate; then, as if anxious not to appear unfriendly, she made a little gesture of assent.

"Oh, very well," she said, smiling. "But I mustn't be long. My uncle will be wondering what has become of me."

Manning glanced at her again with an expression that made me long to kick him, and, moving away from where I could see them, they strolled off together up the road.

For a moment or two I remained quite still. Then with extreme care I got up from my crouching position, and peered over the top of the hedge in the direction which they had taken. There was not much danger of their spotting me, and even if there had been I don't suppose I could have resisted the temptation.

I watched them until they reached the corner, where I saw Christine come to a standstill, as though she had suddenly decided not to go any farther. From his gestures Manning appeared to be making some sort of remonstrance, but if this were the case his arguments evidently had no effect. At all events, he seemed finally to abandon his attempts at persuading her, and they crossed the road together towards a spot just beyond the palings, which overlooked the water.

They stood there for several minutes, Manning pointing away up the estuary and apparently showing her the best method of reaching the barge. It must have been a complicated route, judging from the time he took about it, and the longer I waited the more impatient and resentful I felt.

At last Christine herself seemed to have had enough of the subject, for, stepping back from the bank, she once more offered him her hand. He took it in his, and then, in spite of a quite obvious attempt on her part to prevent him, I saw him bend down and press it to his lips.

My longing to kick him suddenly became so acute that in another second I should have jumped down into the roadway. Luckily, however, providence just saved me from this idiocy. Pulling away her hand, Christine turned round abruptly in the direction of the house, and, obeying a sort of automatic impulse, I bobbed down again behind the hedge.

There I stopped, listening intently. For a few moments nothing happened; then I heard the quick tread of footsteps in the roadway, and in the same stealthy fashion as before, I lifted my head until I could see over the top of the bushes.

There was no one in sight except Christine. She was walking rapidly back towards the gate, and was already quite close to where I was hiding. Manning had disappeared completely, and any lingering tendency to caution I still had vanished into thin air.

I leaned forward as far as I could.

"Christine!" I said softly. "Christine!"

She stopped dead. Every trace of colour had vanished from her face, and for an instant I thought that she was going to faint.

"Don't be frightened," I added quickly. "It's perfectly safe."

She stood there, staring up at me with wick-open, startled eyes.

"Oh, you're hurt," she gasped. "Your face is all bleeding."

I put my hand up to my cheek, and it came away stained with red.

"It's nothing," I said. "I scratched myself a bit getting through the hedge."

"But why are you here?" she whispered. "What made you come? It's madness—absolute madness."

"I wanted to see you," I said simply.

She gave a terrified glance round in the direction of the house.

"I can't talk to you here. Don't you see how impossible it is? You must go away at once."

I shook my head. "Not till we've fixed up something," I said. "Tell me where I can meet you, and I'll clear out immediately."

She answered me with a look of distress that made me feel an absolute brute.

"Christine dear," I whispered passionately, "I must see you and talk to you. It's the only thing in the world that matters the least to me."

For a moment there was no reply. She seemed to be making a desperate attempt to come to some decision.

"I shall be in Shalston to-morrow," she said at last, in the same hurried whisper. "There is a shop next to the station—a confectioner's shop with a small room upstairs. If you will be there at half-past three I will try and meet you."

I was about to say something, but with an almost piteous movement of her hands she interrupted me.

"No, no," she said. "Don't stop here. Go at once—please—for my sake."

There may be stout-hearted people in the world who could resist an appeal like this, but I am certainly not one of them. I let my eyes dwell in a long, refreshing look on her dear up-turned face (it was a look which had to last me for over twenty-four hours), and then, without another word, I slipped back noiselessly out of sight.

As a Yankee mate I once knew used to say, it could "snow pink" for all I cared. When you love somebody as I love Christine, the thought of meeting them becomes so absorbing that it is precious difficult to take anything else seriously. In the light of what had just happened I felt that all my previous ideas required an immediate and thorough spring cleaning, but for the time being such a mental effort was hopelessly beyond me. My brain seemed to be wholly occupied in repeating those two magic phrases, "Half-past three" and "The shop next the station," which kept chasing each other through my head like some beautiful refrain.

The only practical point which I did manage to grasp was the important fact that I must get away without being seen. As far as anyone in the house was concerned this feat appeared to be simplicity itself; the danger was that I might run into Manning. I was still very much in the dark about his relations with Christine, but, whatever they were, it would be fatal to let him suppose that I had been hanging about in the neighbourhood of "The Laurels." Besides, if I met him now I should probably be unable to resist the desire to kick him, which would certainly complicate matters to a most unfortunate extent.

Under the circumstances, it seemed to me that my best plan was to work my way round the hedge, and get out into the main road at the top of the hill. This would allow Manning a comfortable start, and it would also give me the additional advantage of being able to see whether the coast was dear.

Bending well forward, and making as little noise as possible, I set out on my journey. At the first corner I came across one of those small ponds which are a usual feature in most Essex fields. I pulled up for a moment, and, stooping down over the edge, had a good look at myself in the water. It was no wonder Christine had been startled when she saw my face. The whole of my right cheek was covered with blood, and, though the cause was nothing worse than a superficial scratch, I must have been a pretty ghastly object to bob up suddenly from behind a hedge.

Fortunately my collar was still undamaged, and with the aid of a wet handkerchief I soon managed to remove most of the gore. Even then I looked rather as if I had been fighting with a cat, but, after all, I intended to go straight back to the island, and there would only be Bascomb to criticise my appearance.

Keeping the handkerchief pressed to my cheek, I continued my journey up the hill. I had had quite enough of scrambling through blackberry bushes, and it was therefore with some satisfaction that, as I drew near the top, I noticed a gate leading out of the fields. I approached it with some care, and, after making certain that there was no one in sight, I climbed over and dropped down into the main road.

I recognised the place instantly. I was within a few yards of the very identical spot where Ross and I had so nearly run into de Roda, and I could not help regarding the fact as a favorable omen. Anyhow, it gave me a sort of renewed faith in my good luck, and, pushing forward as far as the end of the road, I peered cautiously round the corner.

It was all I could do to stop shouting out "Tally Ho!" A couple of hundred yards below me a solitary figure was crossing the village green, and even at that distance I could see plainly enough that it was Manning. He was walking rapidly in the opposite direction, evidently making for the Shalston road, which turned out of the village just above Mrs. Summers' shop.

I could feel my heart beginning to beat a shade quicker as I stared down at him. There was already an account between us which I had every intention of settling up in full, but it was not entirely the prospect of punching his head that was responsible for my sensations. I had a steadily growing conviction that for some sinister reason of his own Dr. Manning was playing a very active part in the mystery that surrounded me. Everything I knew about the man filled me with suspicion. Why had he been so anxious to get hold of the island, why had he tried to put a doubt in my mind with regard to Bascomb's honesty, and how in the name of goodness did he come to be on intimate terms with the de Rodas? In spite of his apparent friendliness I had mistrusted him from the first, and now, as I stood there gazing after his retreating figure, I felt more certain than ever that my original instinct had been absolutely sound.

I watched him until he reached the opposite side of the green, where he crossed over and disappeared down the Shalston turning. I waited for a moment, so as to make quite sure that he had really gone; and then, with a rather bleak feeling of reaction, I stepped forward from my hiding-place. It seemed to me that my adventures for the day were over. There was a painfully unenterprising air about Pen Mill, as it lay stretched out below me in the warm spring sunshine. Down in the estuary a small motor-boat was making its way rapidly towards the jetty, but otherwise the whole place was lapped in the same atmosphere of restful tranquillity as when I had landed earlier in the morning.

It was at this opportune moment that I suddenly remembered the roast duck. All my interest in life came back with a rush, and, pulling out my watch, I discovered that it was nearly a quarter to one. A brief calculation showed me that by the time I had got out my dinghy and rowed over to the island, Bascomb's masterpiece ought to be just about ready. To keep it waiting would be a very ungracious return for the trouble that he had taken, and, stimulated by this thought, I started off briskly down the hill.

As I reached the bottom I saw the motor-boat which I had previously noticed run in alongside the jetty. A short, sturdy figure in naval uniform rose up in the bows, and, tossing the painter to Jimmy and two of his companions who were waiting to receive it, stepped out on to the causeway. One glimpse of those broad shoulders was all that I needed. I had crouched down behind them too often in a smother of North Sea spray to be in any doubt about whom they belonged to. In a flash the roast duck and Manning and everything else went clean out of my head, and with a half suppressed whoop of joy I hastened forward along the roadway.

Jimmy was the only member of the group who noticed my approach. He looked round just as I set foot on the jetty, but before he could give the alarm I had marched straight up to Bobby and banged him heartily on the back.

"Hullo, Robert!" I said. "Fancy meeting you!"

It takes a good deal to surprise Bobby, but for once in a way I certainly caught him bending. He spun round as if he had been struck by lightning, and the expression on his face was about the funniest thing I have ever seen in my life.

"Dryden!" he gasped. "Jack Dryden!"

"That's right," I said. "What a memory you've got for faces."

He seized my hand and crushed it with a vigour that nearly broke my fingers.

"Good Lord!" he cried. "Where on earth did you spring from? I thought you were chasing about the Atlantic in a million-ton liner."

"You are quite out of date, Bobby," I said. "I am not a common sailor any longer. I have given up the sea and become a gentleman."

Grinning all over his face, he took a fresh look, and surveyed me affectionately from head to foot.

"I don't see any difference," he announced. "You look just as big and disreputable as ever." Then with a happy chuckle he stepped forward again and gripped me by the arm. "Did you know I was here?" he demanded. "I've never written to tell you; I've been so devilish busy."

"It wasn't altogether a surprise," I admitted. "I've been having a talk with Mrs. Summers, and she gave me all the latest society gossip."

"Ah!" he said, nodding his head; "that accounts for it. I thought you weren't half as pleased and excited as you ought to have been."

"Pleased!" I echoed. "Why, I'm so pleased to see you, Bobby, that I simply daren't give way to my feelings. I should burst into tears if I did."

"Well, don't do it here," he retorted. "Come along up to the pub and we'll sob comfortably on each other's necks."

"I can't sob comfortably in a pub," I said. "I am going to take you back to Greensea, and fill you up on roast duck."

"What do you mean?" he asked, letting go my arm.

"That's right, Capting," put in Jimmy, who had been listening to our conversation with the utmost interest. "The gen'leman lives on Greensea Island, don't, 'e, boys?"

There was a shrill chorus of assent from the two others.

"You live on Greensea Island?" repeated Bobby, staring at me. Then as a sort of after-thought he added blankly: "Well I'm damned!"

"Never mind," I said. "You'll have lots of nice people to keep you company."

He took the painter from Jimmy, and jerked his head in the direction of the boat.

"Jump in," he commanded sternly. "I've got an appointment with a fellow ashore, but he'll jolly well have to wait. I'm going to get to the bottom of this, if it costs me my commission."

There was a masterly ring in his voice which woke up all my latent sense of discipline. I drew myself up in a mock salute, and stepped down obediently into the stern sheets.

"Look after the dinghy for me, Jimmy," I called out. "I'll come back for it this afternoon."

Tossing the painter ahead of him, Bobby followed me on board. He started the engine with a quick jerk of the handle, and then, coming aft, took possession of the wheel. The next moment we were backing slowly out from the jetty, and heading round towards the mouth of the creek.

"Now, my son," he remarked, "this is your picnic. You give the orders, and I'll carry 'em out."

"Take her straight across to the island," I said. "You'll find my private landing-stage exactly opposite."

He paused for a moment with his hand on the throttle. "You haven't gone mad by any chance, I suppose, Jack?" he enquired casually.

I shook my head. "It's quite all right," I said. "I'll explain everything when we've had some lunch."

With a turn of his hand Bobby set us going, and, gliding rapidly down the creek, he ran out into the estuary. He made no further remark until we were three-quarters of the way over, when he glanced sideways at me from under his cap.

"What have you done to your face?" he asked. "You look as if you'd been trying to kiss somebody and it hadn't quite come off."

I patted my cheek tenderly to see if it were still bleeding.

"It was nothing as exciting as that," I said. "Only a slight affair with a blackberry bush."

He grunted disbelievingly, and, altering our course a shade more down-stream, swung the head of the boat round so that we came up nearly alongside the landing-stage. I leaned forward and caught hold of the chain.

"We get out here," I said. "This is where I live."

He switched off the engine, and with the painter in his hand stepped up on the planking. I followed, and held the boat steady while he made her fast to one of the posts.

"We seem to be doing very well so far," he observed cheerfully. "What happens next?"

"We go up to the house and have some lunch," I replied. "Then you shall hear the true and remarkable story of how Mr. John Dryden came into his inheritance."

He thrust his arm through mine. "Come along," he said with a laugh. "That'll suit me all right. I feel hungry enough to swallow anything to-day."

We set off up the path, and, rounding the corner, passed through the iron gate which led into the garden. I was waiting eagerly to see what effect the first sight of my residence would have upon Bobby, and it must be admitted that he rose to the occasion. He pulled up, just as Ross had done, and stood for a moment in silent admiration.

"By Gad! what a clipping place!" he exclaimed at last. "Is this really yours, Jack?"

"Every stick and stone of it," I said with some pride.

As I spoke there was a sudden scuffle in the doorway, and the huge figure of Satan bounded out on to the gravel. He had evidently recognised my voice, for with a joyful boom of welcome he came cantering across the lawn to meet us.

Bobby received the apparition with commendable coolness.

"You must introduce me to Fido," he said. "I'm very found of pet dogs."

I performed the ceremony with due state, and in a friendly group we all three advanced towards the house. As we approached the doorway Bascomb appeared on the threshold.

"I've brought a friend of mine, Commander Dean, back to lunch with me," I said. "I suppose there'll be enough duck for two?"

He ran his eye over Bobby, as if speculating on the latter's appetite.

"It ain't a very big 'un," he remarked doubtfully. "If 'e's 'ungry you'd better 'ave the cold beef as well."

"Bring up everything you've got," I said. "We'll be down as soon as it's ready."

I piloted Bobby through the hall, and upstairs to my bedroom, where, with a contented sigh, he tossed his cap on the chest of drawers.

"This is great," he announced. "Who's the sunny-looking sportsman who let us in?"

"That's my butler," I explained, pouring out some water. "You mustn't mind his manners. He's a retired prize-fighter and I took him on with the rest of the fixings."

Bobby broke into a sudden guffaw of laughter that could have been heard at Pen Mill.

"Well," he observed, "of all the giddy mystery stunts I've ever butted into this about takes the biscuit."

I nodded sympathetically. "Yes," I said, "I felt like that at first myself. It's surprising how soon one gets used to it, though."

We washed our hands and proceeded downstairs to the dining-room, where Bascomb was just bringing in lunch. It was three years since we had had our last meal together—a riotous dinner in a Harwich hotel on the night that peace was declared. I was dying to know what had happened to all the good fellows who had shared that unforgettable banquet, and while we attacked the duck I kept asking innumerable questions that Bobby answered to the best of his ability. In return I told him of one or two little adventures which had helped to brighten my own monotonous life, but it was not until we had finished our coffee and lighted up our cigars that we really approached the true business of the day.

"Make yourself quite comfortable," I said, pushing him across the port. "You have got to listen to a long yarn, and I don't want any interruptions while I'm telling it."

He filled his glass, and, getting up from his seat, settled himself in a restful attitude on the sofa.

"I'm in no hurry," he observed contentedly. "I could stop here for a month if it wasn't for that blessed appointment."

Had it been possible, nothing would have pleased me more than to let him hear the whole story, for I knew well that when it came to a tight corner no one could have a more loyal and trustworthy friend. For the present, however, until things began to shape themselves a little more clearly, I was still determined that anything which concerned Christine and her uncle should remain my own secret. By letting out the truth, even to Bobby, I might be running her into all sorts of danger, and no thought of my own safety would have induced me to take the risk.

Under the circumstances, the best plan seemed to be to repeat the same version of my adventures that I had given to Ross. So, starting with the arrival of Mr. Drayton's cable at Leixoes, I plunged straight into the story of my interview in Bedford Row, and of my eventful journey back to the docks. I went on to explain how Ross and I had come down to the island, and made the acquaintance of Bascomb and Dr. Manning. I described my first impressions of both, and finished up by giving him a full report of my conversation with the former and the various details which I had been able to gather with regard to my late uncle's peculiar habits.

Lying back, with his eyes fixed on the ceiling, he listened to me in absolute silence. Even when I had finished he remained for a moment in the same attitude, then, swinging himself up into a sitting position, he reached out for his glass and drained off the contents.

"I congratulate you, Jack," he said. "It's a damned good yarn, and you told it very nicely."

"Well, what do you make of it?" I enquired. "That's the important point."

He puffed thoughtfully at his cigar.

"I don't want to say anything rude about your relations," he observed, "but you certainly seem to have struck a peach in the way of uncles."

"It looks as if somebody had disliked him," I agreed. "All the same, I don't see why they should work off their spite on me."

Bobby brooded over the problem with a meditative frown.

"I don't imagine it's spite," he began. "People generally have a pretty good reason when they start committing murder. It's much more likely that your uncle was in with some swindling crowd who managed to bring off a big coup. He probably did the rest out of their share of the boodle, and now he's dead they're trying to collect it."

"They won't get anything by slaughtering me," I objected.

"How do you know?" he demanded. "From what this lawyer Johnny told you there's a whole heap of stuff still unaccounted for. It must be somewhere. Why shouldn't it be here?"

"Here!" I echoed.

"Yes, here on the island, stowed away—buried. A man doesn't go and invest a lot of stolen money—not unless he's a damned fool."

I drew in a long breath. "By Jove, that's a notion!" I said. "It never occurred to me."

"No, it wouldn't," he returned kindly. "You were always a bit slow in the up-take. It's just as well you've got an intelligent friend to look after you."

There was a short pause while I did some rapid thinking.

"Bobby," I said, "do you know anything about this fellow Manning?"

He tossed away the stump of his cigar and helped himself to another.

"I thought that was coming," he said drily. "Yes, I know several things about him, and one is that according to your own account he's mighty anxious to get hold of Greensea Island."

"I told you his yarn," I interrupted. "He says he wants to start a yachting club."

"Funny he hasn't mentioned it to anyone down here. I suppose he was afraid somebody would pinch the idea."

"Who is he?" I asked. "Where does he come from?"

Bobby struck a match, and with some care lighted his cigar.

"He is one of those mysterious gents that nobody seems to know anything about. According to what I've heard, he rolled up here last summer and bought *The Penguin*, an old barge that used to belong to a fellow called Collinson. He gave out that he wanted to go in for wild fowling, and, to do the blighter justice, he certainly is a first-class hand with a gun."

"It sounds to me as if you didn't like him," I said.

"I can't stick him at any price. All the same, he's very well in with the people down here. Quite a leading light among the sporting crowd. He belongs to the club at Shalston, and he's always ready to take a hand in anything that's going on."

"What's your objection to him?" I asked.

"Nothing much. I just think he's a wrong 'un."

"But why?" I persisted. "You must have some reason."

Bobby shook his head. "Not the least necessary. I can tell a scoundrel directly I see him."

"Well, I've got the same sort of feeling about him," I admitted. "Still, that's hardly a proof that he had anything to do with shoving me into the dock."

"You must try to look at it in a broad light," said Bobby encouragingly. "If he isn't up to some dirty business why did he make you that offer for the island? You can take it from me that his yarn about starting a yachting club is all bunkum. We've got two here already. Then there's another thing I don't like, and that's his suggestion that you should get rid of Bascomb. It's quite likely he's got some blackguard up his sleeve that he hopes to land you with." He reached out for the decanter and filled up his empty glass. "Besides," he added, "there don't seem to be any other competitors. Who the devil else has taken the faintest interest in your affairs?"

Not being able to answer this question, I rose from my chair and took a pace or two up and down the room. I found a curious comfort in the fact that Bobby shared my views about Manning. In dealing with de Roda I felt like a man who has one hand tied behind his back, but when it came to tackling the doctor there were no such unfortunate restrictions. The more suspicious his conduct appeared, the better pleased I should be. A way had to be found by which I could get to the bottom of the mystery without injuring Christine, and, so far, this was the only opening which suggested the least prospect of success.

"I believe you've hit it," I said, coming back to my seat. "I must take steps to improve my acquaintance with Dr. Manning. He seems to be worth cultivating."

"Well, go easy," returned Bobby. "If we're really on the right lay he's not the sort of chap to play the fool with."

"All the more reason for making the first move," I said. "'When in doubt, lead trumps.' That was Nelson's motto, and it's good enough for me."

"It's a sound plan," admitted Bobby. "The only thing is whether you're fit to be trusted by yourself. I think you had better lie low until I can come around and lend you a hand."

"I don't want to drag you in, Robert," I said. "You did your bit in the Great War."

"It doesn't matter a damn what you want," was the crushing reply. "You don't suppose I'm going to let you be wiped out while you've got a cellar full of port like this?" He paused. "The worst of it is," he added. "I am due at Harwich to-morrow, and they will probably keep me there for at least a week."

"I expect to struggle through a week," I said hopefully. "After all, there's Bascomb and the dog."

He eyed me with some mistrust. "If you take my advice," he said slowly, "you'll be precious careful what you do. Things look devilish ugly, and I know what you're like when there's any chance of a scrap about. I should hate to come back and find you with your throat cut."

"It would be still more annoying for me," I pointed out. "You needn't think I'm going to hunt for trouble. If I see the chance of having a nice little chat with our friend Manning I shall take it, but I shall try to remember that mine's a valuable life, if only for the sake of my friends."

He nodded approvingly, and, glancing at his watch, hoisted himself up from the sofa.

"Time I was off," he announced. "That chap who's waiting for me will be tearing his back hair if I don't come along soon."

We got our caps from the bedroom, and, leaving the house, made our way down to the landing-stage. Satan stalked after us with great dignity, and, following his usual custom, remained standing grimly at attention while we cast off our painter and pushed out from the bank.

"I like that dog," said Bobby. "He looks thoroughly efficient. I put more faith in him than in you or the butler."

"So do I," I said candidly. "And I shouldn't be a bit surprised if Dr. Manning felt the same."

We ran rapidly across to the jetty at Pen Mill, bringing up alongside a timber barge which had just come in on the flood tide. Bobby's appointment was at Beddingfield, a small village half a mile inland, and, having nothing particular to do, I said I would walk with him as far as the top of the hill.

"Go slow," was his parting advice, "and don't forget to send me a wire if you find yourself in a tight corner."

"Where shall I send it to?" I asked.

"The Naval Office, Harwich, will always find me. I shall be pretty busy, but you can count on my showing up within three hours of getting a message."

"That's comforting," I said, shaking his hand. "Whatever happens you ought to be in time for the inquest."

I must admit, however, that, in spite of this flippancy, there was a very real feeling of relief inside me as I strolled back down the slope. I had been quite ready, if necessary, to play this game out by myself, but the knowledge that I had a friend like Bobby just round the corner would certainly be a huge addition to my peace of mind. In a case of emergency he was not the sort to stick at trifles, and, from all I could see of the matter, that was exactly the kind of pal that I was most likely to require.

The suggestion that my uncle might have buried the rest of his money on the island was one that appealed to me immensely. There is always something stimulating in the idea of a hidden treasure, and, apart from that, it fitted in beautifully with the various other features of the situation. It explained away that regrettable absence of capital to which Mr. Drayton had called my attention, and it also went far to account for the presence of de Roda and for the embarrassment which Christine had shown in trying to warn me of my danger.

As to where Manning came in, I was still puzzled. That he had some connection with the de Rodas was obvious, but from what I had seen of him, I was strongly inclined to believe that he was playing a private and separate game of his own, in which Christine and her uncle were only partly concerned. Anyhow, I was now convinced that the most promising place in which to hunt for the key of the mystery was on board *The Penguin*, and that the quicker I got on to the job the more likely I was to find it.

With this idea in my mind I returned to the jetty, where the faithful Jimmy was patiently awaiting my arrival. The fact that I was a friend of Bobby's had evidently sent me up several pegs in his estimation, for he greeted me with a respectful salute which I was careful to acknowledge.

"I am much obliged to you, James," I said, presenting him with a shilling. "It's a great thing to have somebody that one can really depend on."

He looked up at me gravely.

"You can trust me, guv'nor," he observed. "I ain't the sort to let yer down—not if there's anything yer wants done."

"I am sure of that," I said. "And what's more, I shan't forget it."

Settling myself in my seat, I sculled off at a leisurely pace down the creek. My thoughts were still busy with the owner of *The Penguin*, and as I came out into the open I cast an instinctive glance up the estuary in the direction of the barge. What I saw pulled me up short in the middle of my stroke. A hundred yards away, and moving rapidly towards me, was a small motor-boat containing a single occupant. I recognised the latter instantly. It was Manning himself, and with a queer feeling of suspicion at this remarkably opportune appearance of his I swung the dinghy round and waited his approach.

He came up alongside, and, cutting off his engine, waved me a friendly greeting.

"I was right after all then," he said. "I thought I saw you going ashore about twenty minutes ago."

"I was just seeing back a pal of mine who's been lunching with me," I said. "Dean, of the Coast Patrol. I think you have met him, haven't you?"

He nodded easily. "Oh, yes—several times. An uncommonly good fellow from all accounts. I should like to know him better."

I thought of Bobby's remarks on the same subject, and it was as much as I could manage to keep a straight face.

"He was my skipper during the war," I explained. "I had no idea he was down in these parts. We ran across each other accidentally on the jetty this morning."

I was watching him closely while I spoke, but if my news was in any way unwelcome he certainly managed to conceal the fact.

"Just what you wanted," he said, steadying the dinghy with his hand. "It must be precious lonely for you, tucked away on that island all by yourself. I have been meaning to run across again and look you up, only I thought I had better give you time to settle in first."

I took the opening without hesitation.

"How about to-morrow night?" I said. "If you're not doing anything else, come along and dine."

For a moment he appeared doubtful. "I should like to very much indeed. The only trouble is that I shan't have my boat. There's been something wrong with the engine lately, and I'm taking her round to Bridwell now to get it seen to." He paused. "Still, that doesn't really matter," he continued. "I can easily walk along to the inn, and row across from there."

A bold improvement on my first idea suddenly came into my head. After all, if I hoped to be successful, it was no good playing the game in a half-hearted sort of fashion.

"Why not bring a bag and stay the night?" I suggested. "It will save you a tramp in the dark, and, as far as I'm concerned, you will be doing a charitable act."

Perhaps it was only my imagination, but it seemed to me that a faint gleam of satisfaction flickered across his face.

"You're very kind," he said, in that smooth voice of his. "There's n othing I should enjoy more if I shan't be putting you out."

"Just the contrary," I returned. "I don't know what sort of a meal you'll get, but I'll try and prod up Bascomb into doing his best." I pushed my sculls forward into position. "Dinner at half-past seven," I added, "unless any other time would suit you better."

"That will do me fine," he replied, switching on his engine. "I shall look forward to it immensely."

"So shall I," I said, and, with a firm conviction that for once at least we were both speaking the entire truth, I allowed the current to carry us slowly apart.

CHAPTER NINE

It cannot be said that Bascomb received the news of my expected guest with anything resembling enthusiasm. I broached the subject while he was clearing away the dinner things, and for a moment he stood at the table without replying—a study in sullen disapproval.

"Well, you knows your own business best, sir," he observed at last. "If you wants to 'ave 'im 'ere you must 'ave 'im 'ere, an' that's all there is to it."

"I am not asking him for the charm of his society, Bascomb," I said. "The fact is, I have been thinking over what you told me the other night, and I have come to the conclusion that Dr. Manning wants watching."

"You're right there, sir," was the grim answer. "'Im an' that beauty Craill, too. You couldn't find a better pair, not if you was to scratch 'ell with a pocket-comb."

"Who's Craill?" I demanded.

"Craill's the bloke wot lives with 'im, an' looks after the barge. 'E come along 'ere one day when the guv'nor was ill, and it was as much as I could do to stop Satan from tearin' 'im in 'alf."

"What was the trouble?" I asked. "Didn't he like his looks?"

Bascomb shook his head. "Seemingly not. An' wot's more, I reckon 'e felt much the same way about the doctor."

"I'm with him there, anyhow," I said. "There's some dirty, underhand work going on in connection with Greensea Island, and as far as I can see Dr. Manning is at the bottom of it." I paused deliberately. "I mean to get to the bottom of it too, Bascomb," I added. "That's the reason I've fixed up this visit."

There was a brief silence.

"Well, I don't go so far as to say you're wrong," replied my retainer grudgingly. "All the same, I wouldn't rest too easy, not with 'im sleepin' in the 'ouse. If you take my advice, sir, you'll lock 'im in 'is room, an' leave Satan loose outside the door."

"I don't want to make him suspicious," I objected. "We shan't get anything out of him by frightening him. Our only chance is to let him feel perfectly at home, and then it's just possible he'll give himself away."

"Mebbe that's so," admitted Bascomb, after a moment's reflection. "There's many a bloke trips 'isself up through bein' a bit too clever." He turned to the table again and resumed his task of clearing away the things. "I'll do wot I can anyway, sir," he added. "It shan't be my fault, not if 'e thinks 'e ain't welcome."

I was much relieved at getting this promise, for without Bascomb's co-operation the scheme would have been hopeless. It was absolutely essential to my plan that Manning should have no idea he was being watched or suspected. The first sign of anything of that sort would shut him up like a clasp-knife; whereas, if we treated him in an apparently open and friendly fashion, he might be led into taking a false step out of sheer over-confidence. I felt it would be rather a strain having to be civil to him for a whole evening, but, after all, the object in view was well worth a little discomfort, and I am always ready to suffer in a good cause.

Having regard to the important day's work ahead of me I decided that it would be a wise precaution to turn in early. A generous allowance of sleep is necessary to my constitution if I wish to be at my best and brightest, a fact which the various skippers I have served under have persistently failed to notice. Being now my own master, however, there seemed to be no point in running any unnecessary risks, so at ten o'clock precisely I let Satan out for his nightly sentry-go, and, having locked up the house, returned peacefully to bed.

As a reward for this act of virtue I woke up feeling remarkably fit and cheerful. It was another beautiful day, and as I dressed leisurely at the open window in a blaze of sunshine I kept a watchful gaze on the estuary in the hope that I might discover Christine's head bobbing about somewhere in the distance. Though vaguely disappointed by my lack of success, I managed to complete my toilet in fairly good spirits. I should be seeing her again, anyhow, in a very little while, and it does not do to be too greedy in one's demands upon providence.

A conscientious spell with the lawn-mower enabled me to get through what would otherwise have been a rather tiresome morning. Even so, I was not sorry when half-past two arrived, and I found myself once more entering the muddy creek which runs up to the Pen Mill landing-stage. As usual, Jimmy had noticed my approach, and was standing on the jetty ready to receive me. I handed my boat over into his charge, and, telling him I should probably be back about five o'clock, I strode off across the green in the direction of the Shalston road.

The distance I had to walk was about two miles and a half. I had just left myself time to do it comfortably, and to get to our meeting-place a few minutes before Christine was due. This seemed to me the most sensible arrangement, for I did not want to be seen hanging about the town, and there was no object in spending a lengthy vigil in the pastrycook's shop.

About a quarter of a mile beyond the village I passed the head of a narrow lane leading towards the water. I could not stop to investigate, but I felt pretty certain that this must be the road by which Manning was accustomed to reach his barge. I only hoped that he was safe on board, for, much as I was looking forward to seeing him in the evening, I should have found him horribly in the way if he had happened to turn up at that particular moment.

Fortunately no such contretemps occurred. I tramped on, keeping a sharp look-out ahead of me, and at twenty past three by the church clock I entered the straggling outskirts of Shalston. A few minutes' walk along the main street brought me to my destination—a quaint little old-fashioned shop, with a large supply of buns, tarts, and other delicacies piled up in the bow-window.

As I pushed open the door, a bell above my head jangled fiercely. In answer to its summons a pleasant-faced middle-aged woman glided out from behind a rampart of freshly baked loaves, and gazed at me benignly across the counter.

"Good afternoon," I said. "I believe you have a room upstairs where you serve tea?"

"That's right, sir," she replied encouragingly. "There's a nice room on the first floor. Will you step this way, sir?"

She conducted me through a door at the back into a linoleum-lined passage, whence a flight of stairs led up to the landing above.

"I am expecting a friend to tea with me—a lady," I added. "When she arrives, would you be kind enough to tell her I'm here?"

"To be sure I will, sir," was the affable answer. "And mebbe you'd rather wait till she comes before you give your order?"

"Perhaps it would be safest," I admitted. "She might have a weakness for some particular kind of jam tart."

Proceeding upstairs, I entered the room facing me, where a table in the centre was already set out for tea. It was a fair-sized apartment, furnished in that engaging style which is generally associated with the name of the late Queen Victoria. There was a piano, a large horse-hair sofa with an antimacassar over its back, and two chairs of the same material, stiffly arranged on each side of the fireplace. The grate was filled with coloured paper, and from the mantelpiece above a stuffed canary in a glass case looked coldly across at Mr. Frith's attractive reproduction of a busy morning at Paddington Station. Two or three texts, a framed certificate from "The Ancient Order of Buffaloes," and several photographs of popular watering-places mounted on red plush, lent a finishing touch to the general harmony.

Laying my hat down on the sofa, I took up a defensive position in front of the hearth. I had not very long to wait, for five minutes could hardly have elapsed when I heard the passage door open, and a sound of voices became audible in the hall below. In spite of the fact that it ought to have benefited by previous experience, I could feel my heart beginning to beat in the most curious and uncontrollable fashion. Then, beautiful as ever, Christine appeared suddenly in the open doorway, and the next moment I was holding her hands in mine.

"I can't tell you how badly I've wanted you," I said. "It seems a hundred years since yesterday."

She looked up at me in a kind of half-humorous, half-protesting fashion.

"Mr. Dryden—please!" she murmured. "They can hear everything you're saying downstairs."

I let go her hands, and took an obedient step backwards.

"I suppose they can," I said. "I quite forgot that there was anyone else in the world."

She came forward into the room.

"Besides," she added with a smile, "tea will be up in one moment. They told me that you were waiting till I arrived, so I ordered it while I was in the shop."

"You're not going to run away again at once, are you?" I demanded anxiously. "There are a whole heap of things I want to talk to you about."

The troubled expression that I had seen before came back suddenly into her face.

"I mustn't stay very long—not more than half an hour at the most."

"Half an hour!" I repeated in dismay. "You can't possibly have tea in half an hour! Why, it's frightfully dangerous to try and drink hot things in a hurry."

Before I could make any further protests I was interrupted by the creak of footsteps laboriously ascending the stairs. There was a chink and rattle of cups and then, panting slightly from her exertions, the lady of the shop emerged into view, heavily burdened with an immense tray.

She set this down on the table, and surveyed us with a motherly smile.

"If there's anything else you fancy, p'raps you'll give me a call over the banisters," she said. "My sister's gone to a funeral to-day, and I'm all alone in the shop."

I gazed at the staggering collection of pastries which we were apparently expected to consume, and hazarded an opinion that they would probably see us through.

"Well, don't be frightened of 'em, my dear," she said, addressing Christine. "They're all home made. You can eat as many as you like without takin' no harm."

She left the room again, closing the door behind her, and, having inspected the various chairs at our disposal, I brought forward the one which looked the least uncomfortable.

"You pour out tea," I said, placing it in position. "I'm so tired of doing it for myself."

Without saying anything, Christine seated herself in front of the tray. She paused for a moment to take off her gloves, while I dragged up a second chair, and, sitting down alongside, contemplated her with unspeakable contentment.

"I hope you're not very angry with me about yesterday," I said. "Spying behind hedges isn't really a habit of mine; in fact it's the first time I have ever tried anything of the sort."

She finished pouring out the tea and handed me across my cup.

"No," she answered, "I am not angry with you; why should I be? You have every reason for feeling suspicious about us, and every right to do exactly what you think best."

She spoke almost wearily, and there was a touch of bitterness in her voice that gave me an uncomfortable sense of guilt.

"Christine," I said, "I want to settle this business once and for all. As far as you and I are concerned, there must be no chance of a misunderstanding." I paused. "I don't know in the least what the trouble is in connection with Greensea Island, or what your uncle has got to do with it. It's quite clear that there's some infernal mystery, however, and, judging by what happened in the docks, I seem to be playing rather an important part in it."

Her brown eyes, full of distress, were looking straight back into mine.

"Yes," she said in a low voice. "You are in great danger. I told you so the other day."

"I know you did," I replied cheerfully, "and you can be quite sure I haven't forgotten your warning. I like this planet, and I mean to stop on it as long as I can, but there's just one thing I want you to realise. I would allow myself to be murdered twenty times over rather than do anything in the world which was the least likely to injure you."

The distress in her face became deeper than ever.

"No, no," she said wretchedly. "You mustn't speak like that. If anything happened to you I should feel that—" Her hand gripped the arm of the chair until the skin stood out white over her knuckles. "Oh," she ended, almost with a sob, "I don't know what to do. It's all so hopelessly complicated and difficult."

I fought down a sudden fierce longing to take her in my arms.

"Don't look so unhappy, Christine," I said. "I can stand a good deal, but that finishes me completely."

With a gallant if rather wistful attempt to smile she sat back in her chair.

"There's only one thing I want to know," I went on, following up my advantage, "and you needn't tell me that if you would rather not."

She made a slight movement of her head, as if wishing me to continue.

"How long have you been friends with Dr. Manning?"

I put the question quite bluntly, and I saw the faintest possible flush come into her face.

"I am not a friend of Dr. Manning's," she answered. "I dislike him intensely. If the choice rested with me, I should never see him again."

"We appear to have one taste in common at all events," I remarked with approval.

"What do you know about him?"

She brought out the words almost reluctantly, as though half afraid of making some unwelcome discovery.

"I know very little at present," I admitted, "but I hope that by to-morrow we shall be much better acquainted. I have asked him to dinner with me this evening, and he will probably spend the night on the island."

If anything, my answer seemed to increase her misgivings.

"He is staying with you? He is going to sleep in the house?"

"Why, yes," I said. "There's nowhere else he can sleep, unless I put him in the kennel. That would certainly be the best place, but, unfortunately, my dog has taken rather a dislike to him."

In spite of her apparent anxiety the corners of her lips quivered into a smile.

"If you mistrust him so much, what made you invite him to the island?"

"I thought it would be a kind action," I explained. "I suppose you know that he has a special reason for being interested in my affairs?"

She looked at me curiously.

"What do you mean? What reason?"

"Well, to be quite exact, there are two of them," I said. "In the first place, he's the family physician. He came over and stayed in the house when my uncle was taken ill, and looked after him until he died."

"But you never told me that."

Christine was leaning forward again, with a queer excitement that she made no attempt to conceal.

"We've had so little time for exchanging confidences," I objected. "Anyhow, he did come, and, what's more, he seems to have fallen in love with the place. At least, ever since then he has been making me the most sporting and generous offers, which Mr. Drayton says I'm a fool not to accept."

"He is trying to buy the island?"

"That's the notion," I said, nodding. "According to his own account, he wants to start a new yachting club." I paused. "Of course, it may be so," I added, "but do you know, Christine, at the back of my mind I've a nasty, uncharitable feeling that he isn't telling me the truth."

For a moment we sat silent. There was a strange expression upon Christine's face, as though she were beginning to understand something which up till then had baffled and perplexed her.

"Mr. Dryden," she said slowly, "for your own sake I am going to be quite honest with you. Until we came down here I had no idea that such a person as Dr. Manning existed."

I was not altogether surprised at her confession, but in spite of that it gave me a very pleasant feeling of relief.

"Perhaps he is an old friend of your uncle's?" I suggested.

She shook her head. "He was an utter stranger to both of us. My uncle was taken ill with one of his heart attacks the day after we arrived, and somebody from the hotel suggested my sending for Dr. Manning. I am quite certain that they had never met before in their lives."

"If that's the case," I observed, "he needs kicking even more than I imagined."

Once again a faint shade of colour crept into her face, and then died away again almost at once.

"Listen, Mr. Dryden," she continued, "what I want to say to you has nothing to do with anything that you may have seen yesterday. That doesn't matter in the least. You have got to think entirely of your own safety. I believe that by asking Dr. Manning to the island you are putting yourself in the greatest possible danger."

"It seems to be the general opinion," I admitted. "At least, both Bascomb and Bobby Dean—" I paused. "By the way, I haven't told you about Bobby Dean yet, have I?"

She shook her head.

"I have been carrying out your instructions," I explained. "You ordered me to dig up a friend, and I have found the one man in the world who exactly fits the part."

"Who is he?" she demanded eagerly.

"Well, to give him his full title," I said, "he's Commander Robert Dean, V.C., of His Majesty's Navy. To save time I generally call him Bobby. We were serving together during the war, and, as luck would have it, he has just been shifted back here in charge of the Coast Patrol at Harwich."

"Oh, but that's splendid," she exclaimed thankfully. "Is he going to live with you on the island??

"I should like him to," I said, "but I am afraid the Admiralty might object. They are a conservative lot, and they always expect their employees to sleep over the shop. I shall be seeing a good deal of him though," I added, quickly, as a sudden shadow of disappointment again clouded her eyes. "He is constantly round here in his boat, and if I want him in a hurry any time I have only got to send him a wire."

There was a pause.

"Does he—does he know that—" She stopped, as if not quite certain how to finish the question.

"I didn't think it necessary to tell him everything," I said. "He knows about my being chucked into the dock, and he knows what I think of Dr. Manning. As I look at it, the rest of the story only concerns ourselves."

I saw that she was on the point of interrupting me, so I went straight on, without giving her the chance of speaking.

"Anyhow, I am not going to talk about myself all the time. There are several much more important things I want to discuss, and one's the fact that you appear to be risking your life every morning before breakfast in a way that I strongly disapprove of."

She looked at me for a moment in evident bewilderment.

"Do you mean my swimming?"

I nodded. "It would be most inconsiderate of you to get drowned," I said, "just when you've become absolutely necessary to me."

I saw the corners of her mouth begin to quiver into a smile.

"I am afraid I hadn't thought about it from that point of view," she replied. "In any case, you can make your mind quite easy, Mr. Dryden. I have swum over twenty miles in the sea before now, so I don't suppose I am likely to get into trouble bathing off a beach." She glanced at the slim gold watch which she was wearing on her wrist. "Why, it's past four o'clock," she exclaimed, with sudden consternation. "I had no idea it was as late as that."

She rose quickly to her feet, and I at once followed her example.

"Christine," I said, "you're not going like this? Last time you rushed away before we could make any arrangements, and I can't leave things in the same impossible state again."

She stood hesitating, the very picture of troubled indecision.

"I don't know what to say," she answered. "I have done wrong in seeing you to-day. I only came because—well, because you didn't give me much choice in the matter, did you?"

Once more I took her two hands in mine.

"I hadn't any choice myself," I said. "It's all very well for me to make promises, but how can you expect me to keep them? I love you so much that——"

"Oh, don't, don't," she broke in pitifully. "You mustn't say that sort of thing. I am trying to help you; I want to be your friend if I can; but——"

"Forgive me, Christine," I pleaded. "It just slipped out before I could stop it." I paused for a moment to gaze hungrily into her wide-open, tear-stained eyes. "Only for God's sake let me see you again before long. I don't know what I shall do unless I can look forward to that."

"Very well," she said, almost inaudibly. "If it's possible I will write to you or send you a message."

"Do you know a boy called Jimmy who is always hanging round the quay?" I asked her. "A little curly-haired kid of about eleven, with blue eyes and a dirty face?"

She nodded.

"Well, he's by way of being rather a particular friend of mine. If you just scribble a line and give it to him, he'll bring it over to the island immediately."

She nodded again, and made a movement as if to release her hands.

"You must say good-bye—please, Mr. Dryden. I oughtn't to have stayed as long as this."

I had intended to play the game to the end, but there are times when all the good resolutions in the world are perfectly useless. A sudden feeling that I was about to lose her swept over me with overwhelming force, and then, almost before I knew what was happening, I had drawn her close into my arms, and was pressing a passionate kiss upon her soft and slightly parted lips.

"Christine, Christine," I whispered hoarsely. "I've loved you from the first moment that you came on board the *Neptune*."

I felt her body tremble all over as I kissed her again, fiercely and recklessly. Then with a choking sob she pushed me away from her, and, freeing herself from my arms, turned blindly towards the door.

I remained motionless where I was, a mingled sensation of remorse and triumph rioting wildly through my heart. I was sorry and ashamed for what I had done, but even my self-reproaches could not alter the glowing conviction of Christine's love which had come to me as our lips met. It was a revelation so intoxicating that for several seconds I stood there like a man in a trance, the faint fragrance of her hair still lingering deliciously in my memory.

At last, with a big effort, I managed to shake off the spell, and, walking back to the mantelpiece, lighted myself a cigarette. The question uppermost in my mind was what I should do next. From every point of view it seemed advisable to allow a few minutes to elapse before attempting to leave the shop. It was quite on the cards that someone who knew Christine might have seen her come out, and to emerge myself a moment later would be simply to invite trouble. Besides, there was the old lady downstairs to be considered. She was probably under the impression that we had had a quarrel, in which case she would doubtless relate the circumstances to any of her friends and neighbours who happened to drop in for an afternoon gossip. I had to find some way of lulling her suspicions, and I felt that I could hardly begin better than by making my own exit in as leisurely and cheerful a fashion as possible.

So I finished my cigarette without any attempt at hurrying, and then, leaving the canary to brood over his ghastly splendour, I descended the staircase and pushed open the side door which led into the shop. The proprietress was engaged in serving out some sweets to a youthful customer, but by the time I had passed through into the outer department this piece of business was successfully transacted.

"I should like to square up accounts," I said; and, taking out two half-crowns, I laid them down on the counter.

The good woman pushed one of them back towards me.

"It won't be as much as that, sir," she replied. "One shilling's our charge, unless the party has eggs."

"And very cheap too," I said, pocketing the rejected coin. "I am only sorry my friend had to run away so soon, but unfortunately she had an appointment at four o'clock."

I was rewarded by a glance of sympathy. "Dear me, that was a pity, sir. I hope you both enjoyed your tea?"

"I did for one," I said truthfully. "In fact, it was quite the best shilling's worth I have ever had in my life."

With a gratified smile she handed me my sixpence change, and, feeling that I had left exactly the impression I desired, I walked to the door, and stepped out into the street.

I was in no immediate hurry to get home, and, apart from that, there was the chance that if I started at once I might overtake Christine on her way back to Pen Mill. Attractive as this prospect was, I had a regrettable conviction that it would be altogether against her wishes, so, strolling across the road, I entered the open door of the White Hart Hotel, where in bygone days Bobby and I had been accustomed to refresh our war-worn energies with occasional bouts of snooker.

I found a marker in attendance, a little rabbity-faced man with an unpleasant habit of potting the black from every conceivable angle. He beat me handsomely in both the games we played, and, having paid tribute to his skill in the shape of a large tankard of beer, I set out in a chastened mood on my return journey.

It must have been close on six o'clock by the time I reached the harbour. For once in a way there was no sign of Jimmy, so, going up to where my boat was moored, I began to unfasten the painter. I was engaged on this task when he suddenly appeared from the back door of the inn, and came hurrying up the jetty wiping his mouth on his sleeve.

"Sorry I weren't 'ere, guv'nor," he began. "I'd just gorn inside to 'ave me tea."

As though in proof of this assertion, he gulped down what seemed to be a large portion of the interrupted banquet.

"Quite right," I said. "One can't do really good work without plenty of nourishment." I handed him his usual retaining fee, and stepped down into the boat. "I have got a little job for you, Jimmy," I added. "I suppose you're the sort of boy who can keep his mouth shut?"

A reassuring nod was the prompt answer.

"Do you know Miss de Roda by sight?" I asked him. "The young lady who has come to live at 'The Laurels'?"

There was a brief pause.

"Wot, 'er with the pretty faice?" he enquired.

"That's the one," I said. "Well, some day she may give you a note for me. If she does, will you bring it over to the island at once?"

He nodded again. "You'll get it all right, guv'nor; you can trust me for that."

"And don't talk about it to anybody, will you, Jimmy?" I added. "Not even to your own pals?"

"Not me," he said stoutly. "There ain't no one who can keep a secret better'n wot I can."

There was a ring of pride in his voice which inspired confidence, and, under the comforting impression that I had established a reliable line of communication, I pulled off down the creek.

When I got back to the house I found a letter for me lying on the hall table. As I picked it up the green baize door which led down to the pantry opened quietly, and Bascomb came in with a plate basket on his arm.

"The postman brought that letter this afternoon, sir. 'E 'ad to call about some registration papers 'e wanted filled in."

I turned the envelope over, and saw the name of Wilmot and Drayton stamped on the flap.

"How about this evening?" I asked him. "Have you managed to get us a decent meal?"

He nodded ungraciously. "I reckon it's good enough—considerin' the party wot's expected. I'm just settin' about laying the table now."

"Well, let me know when the doctor arrives," I said. "I am going upstairs to change, and I don't want him wandering round the house by himself."

"I'll see to that, sir," was Bascomb's grim answer, and without another word he resumed his interrupted progress towards the dining-room.

On reaching my own apartment, I sat down on the bed and opened Mr. Drayton's letter. It was not typed, but written in his own handwriting, and bore the previous day's date.

"MY DEAR DRYDEN,—If you can tear yourself away from the numerous attractions of Greensea Island, I should be glad to see your cheery countenance in town one day this week. There are several fresh papers I want you to sign, and one or two details in connection with the estate which it would be more convenient to talk over than to write about.

"I hope that you have found things fairly comfortable, and that Bascomb and the dog have proved themselves to be entertaining companions.

"I saw our mutual friend, Inspector Campbell, yesterday. He enquired affectionately after you, and was particularly anxious to know how you were getting on. I fancy he is still a little piqued—professionally—over his failure to discover anything with reference to your late uncle. At all events he seems to be under the impression that there is something remarkably mysterious with regard to the whole affair, and that sooner or later fresh developments are bound to crop up. Let us hope that they will take the pleasant shape of a bundle of missing securities.

"Ring me up as soon as you get to town, and we will fix something in the way of lunch or dinner.

"Yours sincerely,

"GEORGE DRAYTON."

Laying this genial missive down on the dressing-table, I began slowly to change my clothes.

I had no objection to a run up to town the next day; indeed, on the whole, the prospect distinctly appealed to me. I should be glad to see Mr. Drayton again and find out how my affairs were progressing, while, after a week on the island, I was quite ready for a little mild dissipation in the shape of a good dinner or a theatre.

I promised myself, too, that I would take the opportunity of looking up Inspector Campbell, who had given me his address the day we lunched at the Holborn. From the moment of my first introduction to him I had felt a curious confidence in this big, shrewd, slow-speaking Scotsman, and I derived no little comfort from the knowledge that he was still taking a friendly interest in my welfare.

There was one special matter in which his help might prove to be invaluable. He was just the sort of man who would probably be able to unearth a lot of interesting facts with regard to the past career of Dr.

Manning, and if I could only persuade him to undertake the job without any inconvenient questions, my journey to town would certainly not be wasted.

Meditating in this fashion, I proceeded to array myself in a loose-fitting suit of tweeds, which was the style of evening dress I usually patronised on the island.

I was on the point of completing my toilet when the front door bell rang loudly, and, after a short interval, I heard Bascomb ascending the stairs.

As he advanced along the passage I opened my door.

"'E's come," observed my retainer, jerking his thumb towards the banisters.

"And what have you done with him?" I enquired.

"Left 'im in the 'all," was the answer. "'E's sittin' there nice and comf'table—long o' Satan."

CHAPTER TEN

I have an idea that Bascomb's reply was intended to be ironical, but it certainly summed up the tableau that met my eyes as I came down the staircase.

Lolling back in an easy chair, with his legs crossed and looking supremely at home, was the neatly dressed figure of Dr. Manning. Satan was standing on the hearthrug a few feet away. Every muscle in his great body was tense and rigid, and his whole soul seemed to be concentrated in the stare of watchful suspicion with which he was surveying the intruder.

At the sound of my footsteps both of them looked up.

"Sorry I wasn't here to welcome you," I said, coming forward across the hall. "I hope Satan has been doing the honours for me."

Manning rose lightly to his feet, and took the hand which I somewhat reluctantly offered him.

"I expect I'm a bit early," he answered, in that pleasant, imperturbable voice of his. "The fact is, I wasn't quite sure what time you said you had dinner."

"Well, it's a movable feast," I returned, "but seven-thirty is the usual hour." I took hold of his bag, which was lying on the floor beside him. "Come along up and see your quarters," I added. "Then we shall just have time for a cigarette and a cocktail. I hate rushing at food without any preparation."

"It's an uncivilised practice," he admitted, "though I'm afraid I'm often guilty of it myself. One gets into bad habits living on a barge."

I was quite prepared to believe his last statement, but thinking it wiser to keep my opinion to myself. I led the way upstairs to his bedroom, which was two doors down the passage from mine.

Having seen that he was provided with hot water and soap, I left him to his ablutions, telling him to rejoin me in the hall as soon as he was ready.

He sauntered down again about ten minutes later, by which time I had concocted a couple of alluring stimulants that even a Buenos Aires bar-tender would have been proud to father.

"By Jove, it's a treat to taste a real drink again!" he said, smacking his lips over my effort. "The English are a fine people, but they don't know much about mixing liquors."

He put down his glass, and, lighting a couple of cigarettes, we strolled towards one of the French widows, which was partly open.

"Still, there are compensations," I said, looking out into the garden. "An evening like this makes up for a lot of indifferent cocktails."

He leaned back against the lintel and gazed deliberately round the sky—a roof of cloudless blue, tinged towards the west with the saffron after-glow of a perfect sunset.

"Yes," he admitted, "it has been wonderful weather the last few days, but you can take my word we shall have to pay for it. Unless the wind gets up we shall have a sea fog that will probably hang around for a week. It's always the way here, when you get this sort of thing in April."

I was about to make some reply when an unexpected voice behind suddenly broke into our conversation.

"Dinner's ready," it announced.

We both turned round abruptly, to find the sombre figure of Bascomb silhouetted in the doorway.

"Come on in," I said, addressing myself to Manning. "However black the future is, we can at least eat and drink."

I conducted him across the hall to the dining-room, which looked very snug and comfortable in the pleasant light of two or three softly shaded candles.

We took our places at the table, and, having served us with soup, Bascomb noiselessly withdrew, closing the door behind him.

"How are you getting on with that fellow of yours?" enquired Manning, after a moment's silence.

"Oh, well enough," I said, pushing him across the sherry. "He's a queer, surly sort of beggar, but he looks after me all right, and so far I haven't caught him pawning any of the family silver."

My companion laughed easily and helped himself to the wine.

"I daresay I'm prejudiced against him," he observed. "The fact is, he didn't exactly go out of his way to make himself civil when I was here looking after your uncle. I expect it's my profession that's responsible. Like most ignorant people, he is probably convinced that all doctors are secret poisoners."

"I think he objects to strangers on principle," I replied. "My uncle evidently suffered from the same disease, and as likely as not they infected each other."

"Agoraphobia," said Manning, smiling. "Well, I shouldn't wonder if you're right. It's a fairly common complaint, and Mr. Jannaway certainly seems to have been a typical case." He paused. "By the way," he added carelessly, "have you managed to find out anything more about him?"

I shook my head. "Not a thing," I said, "except the fact that he had a very sound taste in drink."

It may have been my imagination, but I thought I could detect the faintest possible expression of relief flicker across my companion's face.

"Greensea Island's a curious place for a man of his age to come and settle down in," he continued. "I have often wondered what brought him to this part of the world."

"So have I," I replied truthfully. "In fact, the more I think it over, the more it puzzles me. I can only imagine he must have been inspired by some happy instinct that it would suit the tastes of his successor."

At this point there was a pause in our mutual confidences, owing to the re-entrance of Bascomb with the next course. He took several minutes clearing away and providing us with fresh plates, and by the time we were again alone the conversation had wandered off into a different channel.

Whatever one's personal feelings towards Manning might be, there was no getting over the fact that he was an excellent talker. He chatted away easily and pleasantly on a variety of topics, and if he had any other purpose in view beyond that of being entertaining, he certainly managed to conceal it with remarkable success. In spite of my prejudice against him, I could fully believe what Bobby had told me about his popularity in the neighbourhood. He seemed to possess an almost hypnotic power of making himself agreeable, though in my own case his choicest efforts were so much waste of labour. I had only to remind myself of a certain incident outside "The Laurels" to feel all my old inclination to punch his head welling up with renewed vigour.

When the time for coffee arrived I made a suggestion that we should move into the hall. Manning had declined a cigar, saying that he preferred to stick to his Egyptian cigarettes, so, taking the whisky and liqueurs with us, we established ourselves in a couple of easy chairs in front of the big open hearth. I put a match to the fire—more for the sake of hearing it crackle than for anything else—and with every outward appearance of complete harmony we settled down to spend the evening.

"You've got an ideal place in its way," said my guest, looking round with a sort of lazy approval. "The old chap must have spent a lot of money in fixing it up as comfortably as this."

"I don't think he did very much," I replied. "He had some workmen here, and tidied things up generally, but I fancy the house was in pretty good condition before he took it over. This fireplace was about the only new thing he put in."

Manning's gaze wandered critically over the improvement in question.

"Those are Dutch tiles, aren't they?" he said, bending forward to make a closer inspection.

"It's quite likely," I returned. "Bascomb tells me the work was done by a Dutch firm."

I brought this out purposely in the hope of encouraging further questions, but my companion's interest in the matter did not seem to be very acute. He remained silent for several moments, staring in front of him with a curiously absent expression, as though his thoughts had suddenly taken an entirely different direction.

At last, with something that was very like a start, he seemed to come back to his surroundings.

"It's a nice piece of work," he said, "and just the thing you want here in winter. I like the old barge well enough, but there are some advantages in living on dry land after all."

I poured him out a glass of my uncle's brandy which I knew from experience to be of a remarkably mellowing nature.

"I should think a barge was great fun," I said, "What put the idea into your head?"

He took an appreciative sip at the brandy, and lit another of his eternal cigarettes.

"It was more chance than anything else," he replied. "I heard she was up for sale, and I wanted some sort of a headquarters down here, so I just stepped in and bought her straight away. The chap she belonged to was only asking four hundred, and she was dirt cheap at the price."

"I wonder what our friend Drayton's opinion would be on that point," I said. "He nearly had a fit when I told him I was coming to live on Greensea."

Manning laughed. "Oh, he thinks I'm as mad as a hatter. He can't understand anyone being able to exist unless they're within a taxi-drive of Bedford Row," He paused. "All the same, I believe it's people like ourselves who really get the best out of life. I would give the whole of what London and New York have to offer for one good evening after duck, or a stiff beat to windward round the Bridwell buoy."

The ring of genuine enthusiasm in his voice was quite unmistakable, and I looked across at him with a sudden curiosity that I did my best to hide. I have run up against a fairly representative crowd of blackguards in my life, but there was something about Manning that certainly placed him in a reserved compartment. Leaving aside his charm of manner, it seemed almost incredible that a man whose tastes lay along such simple, healthy lines as duck-shooting and yacht-racing could really be the complete scoundrel that my imagination had gradually constructed. Still, facts were facts, and this very incongruity only helped to make the situation still more stimulating.

"You must get a boat and take up racing," he continued, finishing off his liqueur. "There's no sport in the world to touch it, and the little six metre class we go in for here aren't very expensive."

He launched out into an interesting description of the craft in question, bringing in several stories about local regattas, all of which he related with point and humour. As far as I was concerned he could hardly have pitched upon a more congenial topic. Although I have never been able to indulge in it to any great extent, small boat sailing has always been a particular hobby of mine, and a very few minutes were enough to convince me that I was listening to a man who was an expert at the game. Lying back lazily in his chair, and smoking cigarette after cigarette, he continued to hold forth in such an entertaining fashion that I paid little or no attention to the time. Indeed, it was quite a surprise to me when I suddenly heard Bascomb shutting and bolting the back door, and, glancing at my watch, found that it was nearly half-past ten.

Manning, who had copied my action, sat up and stretched his arms.

"If it's all the same to you, Dryden," he said, "I think I'll turn in. The fact is I've had rather a strenuous day. I have been painting and overhauling gear ever since six o'clock this morning."

"Well, you deserve a good night's rest," I said, getting up from my chair. "Stop in bed as long as you feel like it; we have breakfast here any time it's convenient."

"You won't be too early for me," he returned. "I was never much of a hand at sleeping, and as a rule the more tired I am the sooner I wake up."

I poured out a generous tot of whisky, into which I splashed about the same amount of soda.

"That's my prescription," I said "Take it to your room and drink it off as soon as you get into bed. If you don't sleep then there must be something seriously wrong with you."

He accepted the tumbler with a laugh, and, having lit two candles, which Bascomb had placed upon a side table, I accompanied him up the staircase.

"What happens to our friend Satan?" he asked, as we paused for a moment at his door. "Do you still turn him out in that hard-hearted way your uncle used to?"

"Just the same," I answered. "He has got so accustomed to prowling about at night, I don't suppose he would be happy in the house. Besides," I added, "he's a useful guard against poachers and chicken thieves."

Manning put down his candle on the corner of the chest of drawers. "Yes," he remarked drily, "I shouldn't think that strolling round the island in the dark was a very healthy form of amusement. At least I should be precious sorry to try anything of the sort myself." He held out his hand, which I again accepted with the same inward reluctance.

"Good night," I said. "Don't forget to take my prescription. I will give you a look up in the morning and see how it's worked."

I retraced my steps to the hall, where I latched the windows and fastened the front door. I was just taking a final look round when Bascomb came in from the back regions.

"What have you done with Satan?" I asked him.

"Let 'im out," was the answer, "same as ye told me to. I can fetch 'im in again easy enough if you'd rather 'ave 'im in the 'ouse."

I shook my head. "No," I said, "I think we'll stick to the usual arrangement." Then, pointing to the table, I continued: "You can clear away those drinks and lock up the dining-room. Doctor Manning has gone to bed, and I'm turning in myself too. I will let you know in the morning what time we want breakfast."

With a significant glance in the direction of the staircase he came close up to where I was standing.

"I dunno if I ever mentioned it before, guv'nor, but that there bell alongside your bed rings in my room. Mr. Jannaway 'ad it put up special. If you should 'appen to want me any time, all you got to do is just to give it a pull."

"Right you are, Bascomb," I said, and, feeling rather surprised and more than a trifle grateful at his evident concern for my safety, I once more made my way up to my own quarters.

Reviewing the events of the evening while I undressed, I could not find much cause for self-congratulation. As far as I could tell I had managed to avoid giving Manning any hint of my true feelings towards him, but with this exception the honours appeared to be all on the other side. He had acted the part of the friendly neighbour in such an easy and natural fashion that it was precious difficult to pick any holes in his performance. His enquiry as to whether I had found out anything more about my uncle, and the two questions he had asked with reference to Bascomb and Satan, were the only incidents I could recall which appeared to be in the least suggestive. Even these were quite in keeping with the character he had assumed, and neither of them threw a very penetrating light on what was really passing at the back of his mind.

That he was meditating some mischief, however, seemed to me highly probable. Not that I had much belief in the tragic forebodings of Christine and Bascomb, for I rated our friend's intelligence too highly to imagine him to be capable of any such blunder as that of trying to cut my throat while he was a guest under my roof. I was inclined to think that it was a thirst for information rather than a thirst for blood which had prompted his suggestion of an early retirement. My opinion was chiefly based upon what Bascomb had told me about his two previous attempts to get back into the house after my uncle's death. This persistence could only be explained by the theory that he wanted to make some further investigations, and now that he was actually on the spot he was not likely to neglect such a favourable opportunity.

Anyhow, whichever view of the situation was correct, I was faced with the cheerful prospect of spending a sleepless night. It was very annoying, especially as I had to go to town the next day; but my painful experiences at sea have given me a certain amount of philosophy in these matters, and I settled down grimly to make the best of it.

Anyone who has enjoyed a similar ordeal knows with what wearisome slowness the hours can occasionally pass. In my case, I had not even the consolation of a book, for I was afraid of treating myself to a candle in case the light should be visible under the door. I just tumbled into bed and lay there in complete darkness, keeping my eyes wide open and listening intently for the slightest noise.

Through the open window, at amazingly long intervals, I could hear the church clock at Pen Mill chiming out the quarters. Nothing else broke the silence except an occasional rustle in the shrubbery, which told me that Satan was patrolling the garden with his usual trustworthy thoroughness.

Midnight struck, and after a respectable foretaste of eternity between each, one, two, and three eventually followed suit. Very gradually the blackness of night began to slip into the gray twilight of early dawn, and bit by bit the various pieces of furniture in my room emerged into shape out of the surrounding gloom.

Outside, a bird started twittering in the creeper, but everything in the house still remained as quiet as the grave. Try as I would, I found it harder and harder to fight off the drowsiness that was constantly stealing over me, and more than once I only just roused myself in time as I was on the very point of falling asleep.

Whether I eventually dropped off into a doze I can't say. If I did, some important part of me must have remained awake, for I suddenly found myself sitting up in bed, perfectly cool and collected, but with every nerve in my body strained to the utmost attention.

For a moment nothing happened. Then, once again, came the sound that I was waiting for—the faint creak of a board in the passage outside my door.

Turning back the clothes, I slipped noiselessly out of bed. A glance at my watch on the table beside me showed me that it was close on half-past four—a time at which no respectable passage board has any right to indulge in such antics. My long vigil had not been useless, and, standing there in bare feet and pyjamas, I felt that pleasant glow of rewarded virtue which comes occasionally to the least deserving of us.

I made no attempt to rush things, however. Looking round the room, my eyes fell on the poker, which was leaning up invitingly alongside the fireplace. It struck me as being a nice, companionable sort of object, and, having tiptoed across the room and taken possession of it, I returned in the same stealthy fashion to the door.

With my hand on the knob I again paused to listen. My ears are pretty sharp, and, although extreme care was evidently being taken over the performance, I felt absolutely certain that somebody was descending the staircase.

Very gently I turned back the handle. It yielded to my pressure without making the slightest noise; and then, opening the door inch by inch until the gap was just wide enough, I stepped out warily into the passage.

A quick glance up and down showed me nothing more exciting than Manning's boots. They were standing neatly on the mat outside his room, where he had evidently deposited them before getting into bed. Somehow or other this tidiness of his filled me with an increased respect for him, and, taking a still firmer grip on the poker, I set off noiselessly for the head of the stairs.

As I crept along I debated with myself what was the best thing to do. Should I try and get down without being seen, or should I make a reckless charge and leave the rest to providence? The latter course was much more to my taste, but there are times in life when personal pleasure has to take a back seat, and I reluctantly decided that I must play the game. This was the one chance I was likely to get, and it would be madness not to take the fullest advantage of it.

Still exercising the utmost care, I stole across the landing and peered over the banisters. From where I stood only the further side of the hall was visible. Everything looked exactly as I had left it the night before, and, except for the steady ticking of the grandfather clock, the whole place was wrapped in profound silence.

Unless Manning had gone through into the back part of the house it stood to reason that he must be down below more or less under my feet. The sooner I found out what he was playing at the better, so, edging my way to the head of the stairs, I very cautiously began the descent.

I knew that from the next small landing half-way down one could overlook the entire hall. There were only about a dozen steps to negotiate, and for six of them I got along very nicely indeed. The seventh, however, proved to be my undoing. As I put my weight on it the damned thing let off a terrific creak, and almost simultaneously I heard a quick movement below. It did not take me long to realise that any more efforts in the Sherlock Holmes line would be singularly futile. With one jump I cleared the intervening stairs, and the next moment I was leaning over the banisters looking straight down into Manning's face.

He was standing on the hearthrug in front of the fireplace. Except for a pair of bedroom slippers he was dressed in the same scanty costume as myself, the only other difference being the poker which I still clutched affectionately in my right hand. He had evidently turned round directly he heard the noise, and, although taken by surprise, he looked perfectly cool and self-possessed.

"Hullo, Manning!" I said cheerfully. "What the devil are you doing here?"

For just an instant he remained motionless; then with a sudden laugh he seated himself deliberately on the rail of the fireguard.

"Caught in the act," he observed. "And I took such a lot of trouble not to wake you up."

"That's all right," I said. "I have been awake for the last half-hour." I came down the remaining steps as I spoke, and walked across the carpet towards him. "What's the matter?" I enquired.

He extended his hand, and I noticed for the first time that he was holding his cigarette case.

"This is the real culprit," he answered. "I put the blessed thing on the mantelpiece last night and forgot all about it. Of course at three o'clock this morning I felt I wanted a smoke more than anything on earth. I hung on as long as I could because I was afraid of waking you up, but at last it got to a point when I simply couldn't stick it. I crawled down like a mouse, and I was just thinking I had done the trick all right when you suddenly popped up over the banisters and gave me the start of my life." He paused, and, helping himself to a cigarette, held out the case. "I am frightfully sorry," he added. "It's a rotten trick to drag one's host out of bed merely because one happens to be the slave of a bad habit."

He made his explanation with such delightful ease that if I had not known he was lying it would certainly have convinced me.

"There is no need to apologise," I said. "You gave me a really enjoyable five minutes. I had quite decided you were a burglar, and I was looking forward to breaking your head."

He eyed me and the poker with a kind of cool appreciation.

"I am glad you found out your mistake in time," he said. "There's something unpleasantly primitive about you, Dryden, especially when you're in pyjamas."

All the while he was speaking I had been taking careful stock of our immediate surroundings. As far as I could see nothing had been disturbed—indeed, I had come down so quickly on his heels that he had had practically no chance of getting up to mischief. I realised now that what I ought to have done was to have given him a few minutes' grace, and a mortifying suspicion that I had made a hash of the whole affair began to rankle in my mind.

For a moment I was badly tempted to take him by the neck and see if I could shake the truth out off him then and there. The feeling that I might be running Christine into danger still kept me in check, however, and with a masterly effort I managed to preserve my politeness.

"We had better have a drink and go back to bed," I observed, "unless you'd like to stroll round the island and admire the beauty of the dawn."

As I spoke I moved towards the French window, and at the same moment a huge black shape loomed up on to the verandah outside.

"Hullo!" I added. "Here's somebody else come to see what the matter is. Quite a family party, isn't it?"

I unbolted and opened the window, and, waving his tail in a kind of dignified acknowledgment, Satan strolled slowly into the room. He pulled up short on seeing Manning; then, apparently satisfied that as long as I was present things must be more or less in order, he proceeded to seat himself very deliberately right in the middle of the hearthrug.

I refastened the bolt and turned back to my guest.

"He always sits there," I said. "I suppose my uncle taught him to originally, and now he thinks it belongs to him. We shall find him in exactly the same place when we come down to breakfast."

Manning, who had been watching the dog's proceedings with a curious intentness, rose slowly to his feet.

"I don't think I'll have a drink," he remarked. "It's a little early and I haven't got your cast-iron constitution. Bed seems to me the best notion. I've a sort of feeling that after I've finished this cigarette I shall be able to put in a couple of hours' sleep."

"Well, as I told you before, take it easy," I replied. "The eggs and bacon will keep till we're ready for them."

We set off up the staircase, and, pausing for a moment in the passage, Manning once more expressed his apologies.

"You're a real sportsman, Dryden," he said. "I should have been horribly peevish myself if anyone had dragged me out of bed at this unholy hour."

"I generally wake up in an amiable mood," I replied. "It's only a matter of good health and having the right kind of whisky."

I watched him go into his room and close the door, and then, feeling uncommonly thankful that I had not got to be civil to him any longer, I proceeded to follow his example.

I had bungled the business beyond any manner of doubt, and I was so angry with my own stupidity that I very nearly hurled the poker into the grate. It was maddening to think that if I had only displayed an ounce of gumption I might by now have got to the bottom of the whole infernal mystery. Instead of doing this, I had allowed Manning to walk clean out of the trap, and no doubt, in the security of his own room, he was laughing to himself over the easy way in which he had outwitted me.

The only consolation that remained was the fact that there was no further reason for keeping awake. I could at least turn into bed and get a few hours' sleep, with the comforting assurance that I was not neglecting my job. Whatever else Manning might have left in the hall, he would certainly manage to do without it as long as Satan was sitting on the mat.

CHAPTER ELEVEN

"Just gorn 'aff-past eight, sir."

I opened my eyes with some resentment, and found Bascomb standing beside me, a cup of tea in his hand. I blinked at him for a moment and then sat up in bed.

"Might it be you as got up in the night and let Satan in?" he enquired surlily.

For a second I hesitated, wondering how much he knew.

"Were you awake?" I asked.

He shook his head. "No, I didn't 'ear nothin', but when I come through this mornin', danged if 'e wasn't sitting there on the mat."

He placed the cup on a small table beside me, and, crossing the room, drew up the blind.

"I changed my mind after I had gone to bed," I explained. "I felt I should sleep better if I knew that Satan was downstairs." I took a sip of the tea, and reaching out for my case, helped myself to a cigarette. "You can call the doctor in about ten minutes," I added. "I'll have my bath first and get out of his way."

Bascomb nodded and left the room without any further remark, though from the expression on his face I think he had a dim suspicion that I was keeping something back. Perhaps I should have been wiser to take him completely into my confidence, but to tell the truth I was half ashamed to confess the bungling way in which I had handled the business. Besides, faithful as I believed him to be, there was such a queer, sullen twist in his temper that I never felt quite certain how far it would be safe to trust him.

Washing and shaving are occupations which lend themselves to reflection, and I certainly found plenty to think about during the quarter of an hour that I spent in the bathroom. On the whole, as a result of my musings, I was inclined to take a slightly less pessimistic view of the situation. Although I had not exactly covered myself with glory as a private detective, I had at least established the truth of my theory that Manning possessed some strong and urgent reason for wishing to explore the house. Indeed, judging by the risks he had run, it looked as if the success of his schemes depended largely upon this particular point, and if that were the case I had apparently shoved a pretty effective spoke in his wheel.

All the same, I didn't quite like the way in which he had accepted his defeat. Even allowing for his cleverness and self-control, it was difficult to imagine that anyone who had been balked at the last moment in some vital enterprise could have betrayed so little sign of feeling. Disappointed he had certainly appeared, but it had been the disappointment of a man who has merely lost a trick which he hoped to gain, and who still cherishes a fond belief that he is going to win the rubber.

I wondered very much what he thought about my part in the performance. There had been, to put it mildly, a timeliness about my appearance on the scene which could hardly have failed to awake his suspicions. These were not likely to have been lessened by the deliberate way in which I had let Satan into the house, though in either case my action might very well have borne the innocent interpretation that I had attempted to give it. He was probably in a state of considerable uncertainty on the subject, and it was pleasant to feel that I was paying him back a small instalment of all the worry he had caused me.

What I would have given anything for was a good long chat with Bobby. I am all right in a straight-forward scrap, but I knew that at this sort of business his head was worth a dozen of mine, and that he would most likely pounce upon some important point which I had completely overlooked. Indeed, if it had not been for my appointment with Mr. Drayton I should have run up to Harwich to see him; as it was, I should have to put off our talk until my return from London.

On my way back to my room I tapped at Manning's door and informed him that the bath was ready.

He called out: "Come in," and, accepting his invitation, I discovered him in the act of sharpening his razor, which he had apparently just finished using. He greeted me with a friendly wave of the strop.

"How goes it?" he enquired cheerily. "I hope you managed to get off to sleep. I put in a couple of hours, and I feel as fit as a fiddle this morning."

"That's good," I replied. "You'll be able to do justice to Bascomb's bacon. It's one of the few things he's really sensitive about."

He smiled, and crossing to the washstand began to collect his sponge and towels.

"Did you tell him about our adventures?" he asked. "He must have guessed that somebody got up in the night when he found Satan in the hall this morning."

"I explained that I let him in," I answered. "I was too sleepy to go into details." I paused. "Besides, the whole thing sounds rather ridiculous by daylight, doesn't it?"

"Well, I suppose it might strike anyone else as being a bit comic," he admitted. "Better say nothing about it perhaps; we should be frightfully chipped at the club if the story got round."

His tone was light, almost careless, but it seemed to me that my answer had afforded him considerable relief. I made a mental note of the fact with a view to passing it on to Bobby.

"If I'm not in the dining-room when you come down," I said, "you'll find me just outside the front door. Satan and I generally take a little air before breakfast."

I left him on his way to the bath, and, re-entering my own room, proceeded to dress myself in a new suit of blue serge, which I had bought during my previous visit to London. Thus arrayed, and feeling unusually respectable, I descended into the hall, where, as I expected, I discovered Satan still occupying the same position on the hearthrug.

He got up as I appeared, and, after stretching himself elaborately, followed me to the French window, which was standing partly open. Here, contrary to his custom, he halted, looking round rather doubtfully, as though not quite certain whether it was safe to leave the place unguarded.

"Perhaps you're right, my son," I said. "We can't be too careful. You sit here and let me know when he comes down."

I patted his head and stepped out on to the lawn, where a couple of fat thrushes were hopping lazily about in the sunshine. It was another beautiful morning, hot and still as August, with an almost unnaturally blue sky, unchequered by the smallest cloud. I walked across to the border opposite, and with some care selected myself a small buttonhole. If I was going to play the part of country gentleman visiting his solicitor I might as well do the thing thoroughly.

At the very moment when I had succeeded in fixing it in my coat there came a warning growl from Satan. Strolling back to the window, I found Manning in the act of descending the staircase. He looked very cool and debonair in his grey flannels, and, in spite of Satan's inhospitable greeting, he seemed as usual entirely at his ease.

"You're a good host yourself, Dryden," he remarked, "but I'm hanged if I can say the same for your retainers. That dog resents my being here quite as much as Bascomb does."

"He is just as bad with everyone," I returned. "Uncle Richard evidently infected the entire staff."

I had hardly finished speaking when the dining-room door opened, and Bascomb himself appeared on the threshold. I don't know if he had overheard our remarks, for his face was as impassive as ever.

"Breakfast's ready," he announced curtly.

We took our places at the table, where a dish of eggs and bacon, a fresh tongue, and various other attractive items awaited our arrival. I poured Manning out a cup of coffee and told him to help himself to what he fancied.

"You look devilish smart to-day, Dryden," he remarked smilingly. "I believe I have a sort of reputation here for being the local dandy, but now you've come I'm afraid I shall have to take a back seat."

"I have to go up to town to see Drayton," I explained. "I always put on my best clothes when I visit a lawyer."

I thought it would be the safest plan to tell him the truth, for it was more than possible he might find it out for himself.

"That's rather a pity," he observed. "I was going to suggest that you should come over and have a look at the barge." He paused. "How long are you likely to be away?"

I shrugged my shoulders. "Goodness knows," I said carelessly. "I daresay I shall be back to-morrow. I believe he only wants me to sign a few papers."

There was a brief pause while Manning sipped his coffee.

"Well, as the Arabs say, 'To-morrow is also a day,'" he returned, putting down his cup. "Just get in your boat and come across any afternoon you feel like it. I'll show you the barge, and then we might go along and dine at the club afterwards."

I thanked him with every appearance of sincerity, though the sinister humour of the whole situation nearly made me laugh out loud. I felt sure, too, that under that imperturbable mask of his Manning must be appreciating it quite as much as I did.

If such were the case, however, he kept his feelings well under control, and we finished our meal without the least suggestion on either side of anything but the most perfect friendliness. After a cigar in the garden my companion went upstairs to pack his bag, and then, followed by Satan, we sauntered down to the landing-stage, where he proceeded to get out his boat.

"Thanks for a charming evening," he said, shaking my hand. "Remember me to Drayton, and mind you come and look me up as soon as you get back."

I made some suitable answer, and, settling down in his seat, he pulled off with the smooth, easy stroke of a practised oarsman. I stood and watched him till he reached the mouth of the creek, where he waved his hand to me before disappearing round the bend. Then I walked across to Satan, who was sitting by himself on the edge of the jetty staring resentfully after the vanished boat.

"It's no good looking like that," I said. "If you had been a little more civil you would probably have been included in the invitation."

I think he understood what I meant, for, rising to his feet with a disdainful expression, he strolled off ahead of me in the direction of the house. There were evidently some subjects on which he regarded humour as being completely out of place.

When I arrived back I found Bascomb clearing away the breakfast things.

"I am going up to town by the twelve-forty," I said. "I suppose I can get a trap at the inn to take me to Torrington?"

He nodded his head.

"They'll run you over right enough," he replied. "Mebbe I'd better slip across an' tell 'em though; they might be fixin' up with another party otherwise." He paused. "Are you comin' back to-night?" he enquired.

"No," I said, "I have got some business with Mr. Drayton. I shall probably be down to-morrow, but if not I'll let you know."

He finished clearing up and collected the debris on to a tray.

"'Ow about visitors?" he enquired. "I s'pose you don't want no one on the island, not while you're away?"

"There's one person I don't want," I said, "and that's Dr. Manning." I stopped, and then, feeling that I must at least make some appearance of taking him into my confidence, I added: "You were perfectly right about him, Bascomb. He's a rascal, only he's a damned clever one. I couldn't get anything out of him last night, try as I would. All the same, I'm more certain than ever that he's up to some dirty business."

A gleam of approval flickered across my companion's face.

"You can trust me safe enough, guv'nor," he returned. "'E won't set foot again in this 'ouse while I'm 'ere—not 'im nor that broken-nosed blighter Craill neither."

He brought out the epithet so unexpectedly that it was all I could do to keep back a sudden exclamation.

"Craill!" I repeated. "Isn't that the fellow who looks after his barge?"

Once again Bascomb nodded sourly. "That's 'im—an' you can take it from me that 'e's the right bloke for the job."

A vision of that furtive, sinister figure hanging about outside Mr. Drayton's office rose vividly in my mind.

"Yes," I said, with intentional carelessness, "I should think they were a very nicely matched pair. How did Craill manage to break his nose?"

"Someone done it for 'im, I reckon. Pity they didn't break his neck too while they was about it."

Lifting the tray, Bascomb marched off through the side door, and after a moment's hesitation Satan got up and followed him.

I crossed the room to the window and sat down on the sill. I felt like a man who by pure accident has suddenly picked up the very piece of a jig-saw puzzle for which he has long been vainly hunting. Ever since my first meeting with Manning I had had a suspicion that in some way or other he was chiefly responsible for that impromptu swimming exhibition of mine in the East India Dock. Bascomb's description of Craill placed the matter beyond doubt. Unless there was an epidemic of broken noses, the latter was certainly the man I had seen loafing about Bedford Row, and the odds were a hundred to one that it was his hand which had so nearly put an end to my troubles.

As to what possible motive or motives could have possessed this precious pair, I was as much in the dark as ever. They could not have been acting on behalf of de Roda, for I had Christine's assurance that until she and her uncle had arrived in England neither of them had had the least notion that such a person as Dr. Manning existed. My attempted murder must, therefore, have been a strictly private enterprise, and the only reason I could see for it was the fact that I had refused to sell the island.

Now, annoying as it is to be thwarted in a scheme of land purchase, people generally stop short of assassination as a method of expressing their disappointment. There must have been some very powerful inducement to lead Manning to such a desperate step, for, utterly unscrupulous as I believed him to be, he was too intelligent to run his neck into danger unless the stake at issue was well worth the risk.

Could it be possible that while he was on the island he had stumbled independently upon my uncle's secret? It was a new idea, but the more I thought it over the more feasible it seemed. It at least gave some explanation for his extraordinary anxiety to get hold of Greensea, and it might account for the curious dread with which Christine seemed to regard him.

If this were really the truth, the whole question of his relations with the de Rodas became one of the utmost importance. Did he know the reason which had brought them all the way from South America, and, if so, had he purposely made friends with them in order to achieve his own ends? From what I had seen of the two men I could well imagine that de Roda, broken in health and in the grip of some half-insane purpose, might clutch eagerly at the unexpected assistance that was suddenly offered him. That Manning's motives for entering into any such partnership must have been purely selfish I had no manner of doubt. Possibly he was in ignorance about some essential point on which de Roda was the only person able to enlighten him, or perhaps—and at the mere notion I felt the blood surge hotly through my heart—it was Christine's beauty which had been the lure that had attracted him. Once more the recollection of that scene outside "The Laurels" came back to me with extraordinary clearness. I could see the expression on Manning's face as distinctly as if I were still crouching behind the hedge, and with a half-suppressed oath I flung open the lattice window and got up from the sill. It was certainly fortunate for one or other of us that he was no longer on the island.

Looking back indeed, I have often wondered since how I managed to get through that morning without doing something idiotic. The temptation to jump into my boat, row over to the barge, and settle up matters with Manning once and for all, was at times so strong that it became almost irresistible. By packing my bag and otherwise occupying myself, however, I succeeded in holding out until Bascomb returned from the inn, bringing the news that a trap was in readiness to take me to the station.

"You'd better let me run yer across," he added. "Then the boat'll be 'ere in case I wants it."

"I can easily send it back by Jimmy," I objected. "Isn't it a bit risky for both of us to be away at the same time?"

"I reckon there won't be no risk," he replied grimly. "If anyone comes messin' about 'ere the next 'alf hour it's a —— certainty wot'll 'appen to them."

A glance at Satan's expression convinced me that there was some truth in what he said, so without making any further difficulties I consented to his proposal.

He carried my bag down to the landing-stage and rowed me across to the jetty opposite, where I stepped out discreetly, so as to avoid soiling my new suit.

"Good-bye, Bascomb," I said. "I shall tell Mr. Drayton how well you've looked after me."

For a moment he seemed almost embarrassed. "That's all right, guv'nor," he returned gruffly. "I ain't the bloke to go back on anyone wot's treated me fair."

He settled down again to his oars, and, picking up my bag, I started off in the direction of the shore. Outside the inn a smart-looking horse and trap were waiting my arrival. The driver, a shock-headed youth who might have been an elder brother of Jimmy, touched his cap to me as I clambered in, and the next minute we were bowling off up the hill on our way to Torrington.

During the journey to town I divided my time between pondering fitfully over my own affairs and listening to the improving conversation of my fellow travellers—a Baptist minister and his wife, who were going up to London to attend their aunt's funeral. They were a very staid and respectable couple, and, sitting back in my corner, I could not help wondering what they would say if I were suddenly to put my difficulties before them and ask them for their advice.

Such an interesting experiment being unfortunately out of the question, we reached Liverpool Street with the problem still unsolved. A porter from the Great Eastern Hotel came forward as I stepped out of the carriage, and, since I had made no arrangements to stay anywhere else, I allowed him to take possession of my bag. He conducted me up some stairs to the office, where, after a brief parley with the reception clerk, I was duly accepted as a desirable guest.

My first step, after going to my room and having a wash, was to telephone to Mr. Drayton. I was informed that he was still out at lunch, but had left a message, in case I rang up, that he would be able to see me any time between three and four. It was then getting on for half-past two, so, having treated myself to a glass of sherry and a sandwich, I started off straight away for Bedford Row.

I kept a pretty sharp look-out as I turned the corner into that respectable thoroughfare, but this time no one seemed to be taking the least interest in my movements. The street indeed was practically deserted, and it was almost with a feeling of neglect that I pushed open the front door and sought out my aged friend in his little rabbit hutch on the right. He informed me that the head of the firm had just returned, and conducted me upstairs with impressive formality. In his eyes I had evidently attained the rank of a distinguished and valuable client.

There was nothing of this about the bearing of Mr. Drayton, however, who greeted me with a cheerful lack of ceremony that was much more to my taste. As before, he insisted on my accepting one of his excellent cigars, and then, having asked me several questions as to how I was getting on, he proceeded to explain his reasons for bringing me up to town.

"I've something to tell you, Dryden," he said, "that I think you'll probably approve of. The fact is, we have been getting on with your affairs a good deal faster than I expected. For once in a way I have actually persuaded the British law to hustle itself, and, to cut a long story short, you can dip your fingers into Uncle Richard's money-box just as soon as ever you like." He leaned back in his chair and regarded me with a friendly twinkle. "I know you're tired of travelling, but I thought that this particular bit of news was worth a journey to town."

"I should rather think it was," I replied, with considerable enthusiasm. Then, jumping from my seat, I gripped his hand heartily in mine. "I'm blessed if I know how to thank you," I added. "I am no good at making pretty speeches, so you must take the will for the deed."

Mr. Drayton extricated his fingers, and examined them with a rather rueful smile.

"There's no need to apologise," he said. "Your gratitude's quite pressing enough for me." He rose to his feet and, turning towards the table, pulled forward a bundle of papers. "There are one or two things here that want signing, and then I think I had better take you round to the bank, before they shut, and introduce you to the manager. It's only just across the road in Holborn."

I sat down at the table, and scribbled my name in the spaces he pointed out. I suppose I ought really to have read the documents through, but so complete was my confidence in his good faith that I made no attempt at this elementary precaution.

"You have got a delightfully trustful nature, Dryden," he said with a sigh. "I wish I inspired the same sort of feeling in all my clients."

He rang the bell for his clerk, and, having informed the latter that he would be out for the next quarter of an hour, he picked up his hat and led the way downstairs.

"Are you staying in town to-night?" he enquired as we emerged into Bedford Row. "If so, and you have nothing better to do, come and dine with me at my club. It's very dull, but you're not likely to notice that after a fortnight at Greensea Island."

Had I chosen I think I might have been able to disillusion him on the subject of Greensea's dullness, but for the present at all events I still thought it wiser to keep my own counsel. So with a perfectly truthful remark that I was never bored in good company, I laughingly accepted his invitation, and without further discussion we turned down a narrow passage into the roar and bustle of Holborn.

Our interview with the bank was not a very formidable affair. We were shown into a private room, where a brisk, bald-headed little man with gold-rimmed eye-glasses was seated at a table several sizes too large for him.

Mr. Drayton introduced me as the heir to the Jannaway fortunes, and the manager—for such the bald-headed gentleman proved to be—congratulated me cordially on what he termed my "romantic inheritance." He announced that a sum of eleven thousand and forty-five pounds seven shillings and sixpence was lying in the office awaiting my attention—a statement which I tried to receive with becoming nonchalance. At his request I wrote out a specimen of my signature, receiving in return a useful-looking cheque-book. He then informed me that if at any time I needed expert financial advice he would be delighted to place himself at my disposal; after which he again shook hands with us both, and escorted us in state to the door of the bank.

"I like being a capitalist," I observed, as we stood for a moment on the step. "It's a much more restful life than the sea, and everybody one meets is so extraordinarily obliging."

Mr. Drayton chuckled appreciatively. "Wait till I've sent you in my bill," he retorted. "You'll have some excuse for feeling cynical then." He dived into his pocket and produced a card-case. "Here's the address of my club," he added, "in case you forget it. I must be off now, but I'll expect you at seven-thirty. Don't dress up and make yourself beautiful—come along just as you are."

With a friendly wave he disappeared amongst the traffic, while almost at the same moment a prowling taxi pulled up in the gutter. I moved forward and accosted the driver.

"Have you ever heard of a place called Angel Court, somewhere off Fleet Street?" I asked him.

He eyed me critically.

"Are you wantin' Inspector Campbell's office?" he enquired.

"Yes," I said. "Do you know him?"

He leaned across and opened the door. "Know 'im," he repeated rather scornfully. "Why, 'e pinched a bloke outer this very cab last March twelve-months. There ain't a taxi driver in London as don't know 'Foxy' Campbell."

Considerably impressed with this unexpected tribute to the Inspector's reputation, I climbed inside the vehicle. We sped away rapidly through a number of side turnings, coming out at last within a few yards of the bottom of Fleet Street. A moment later the taxi pulled up, and as I stepped out the driver jerked his thumb in the direction of a narrow archway.

"That's Hangel Court," he said. "You'll find the party you're looking for the second door on the right."

I thanked him, and, passing through the opening, entered a kind of paved yard, on three sides of which were quaint narrow little houses with old-fashioned window-panes. The second doorway bore a carefully polished brass plate, with the inscription "James Campbell. Private Enquiry Agent."

I was just hunting around for a bell when suddenly the door swung back, and, looking up, I found myself face to face with the Inspector himself. He was evidently on the point of going out, for he was wearing a bowler hat and carrying a walking-stick.

Directly he saw me his big square-jawed face lit up in a smile of welcome.

"Why, it's Mr. Dryden," he exclaimed, holding out his hand. "Well, this is a bit of luck. If you had been a moment later you'd just have missed me."

"It's my lucky day," I said "But, all the same, I mustn't keep you if you've got an appointment."

"It's nothing very important," he replied. "Come along inside. I can spare a minute or two anyhow."

He led the way into a comfortably furnished office on the right, and, pulling forward a chair, seated himself exactly opposite me. His large and very wide-awake blue eyes scanned me with friendly interest.

"I'd better start by apologising," he began. "You mustn't think I've forgotten your invitation to come down and have a bit of shooting, but the fact is I've been so busy I've had no time to write. People have been misbehaving themselves the last three weeks in a way you wouldn't believe; I suppose it's the hot weather."

"I shouldn't wonder," I said. "I've felt a little vicious myself once or twice." I tossed away the stump of the cigar I was holding and helped myself to another from the case which he offered me. "As far as the invitation goes," I added, "it's open permanently. I am not the sort of a person who wants a lot of notice. Just send along a wire as soon as the crime wave subsides."

"The very minute," he said with a twinkle. Then, putting his thumbs in his waistcoat, he leaned back comfortably in his chair. "And how are you getting on down there?" he asked. "You know, I take a special interest in your affairs, Mr. Dryden. There's something about Greensea Island that I didn't quite get to the bottom of, and no one likes to be hit in his professional pride."

He spoke in such a frank and good-humoured fashion that once again I was sorely tempted to make a clean breast of my difficulties. I stuck to my resolve, however, for the thought of Christine as the central figure in some public scandal was too utterly repugnant to be considered. At the same time I felt that in the case of Inspector Campbell a certain measure of honesty would undoubtedly be the best policy.

"As a matter of fact," I said, looking him straight in the face, "I've come here to ask you for your help."

He nodded his head.

"I thought you might," he said. "That was one reason why I gave you my address."

"The trouble is this," I went on bluntly. "I want you to do something for me, but for certain reasons which I can't explain it's quite impossible for me to answer any questions. I know it sounds pretty rotten, so I shan't be the least surprised or offended if you tell me to go to the devil."

He smiled genially. "That's the last thing I should do, Mr. Dryden. There's no sense in encouraging a rival firm." He paused. "You know your own business best, of course, but if there's any particular way in which I can be of assistance you can count on me from this minute."

"Well, there is," I confessed. "You remember a chap called Dr. Manning—the fellow who looked after my uncle when he was dying?"

Once again the Inspector nodded. "Yes," he answered. "I remember him very distinctly. He lived on a barge about three hundred yards above the island."

"That's the gentleman," I said. "He's living there still; in fact, to all intents and purposes he's my next-door neighbour. What I want you to do, if you can possibly spare the time, is to get me a little accurate information about his past life."

If my companion felt any surprise or curiosity he certainly didn't show it.

"That oughtn't to be very difficult," was his reply. "Doctors are fairly easy to trace as a rule." He reached across to the table and picked up a half sheet of notepaper. "Has he ever mentioned a particular town, or given you any idea of what hospital he was at?"

"He once told me he had been a ship's surgeon," I said. "It was probably a lie, so I shouldn't attach much importance to it."

The Inspector made a brief note. "One never knows," he observed hopefully. "People sometimes tell the truth by accident. They generally regret it afterwards."

A telephone bell tinkled sharply in the corner of the room, and with a word of excuse he rose from his seat and walked across to the instrument.

"Yes," he said. "I'm Campbell—speaking." There was a pause. "What's that?" Another and longer pause followed. "Oh, very well. Don't let him go. I'll be round almost immediately."

He hung up the receiver and turned back to me.

"I'm sorry," he said, "but I'm afraid I shall have to run away after all. I have got to meet a man who wants to leave for Scotland this afternoon." He folded up the paper he was holding, and put it away carefully in his pocket "I'll get on to this little job at once. You shall hear from me directly there's any news."

"Thanks," I said gratefully; "and, meanwhile, if the wicked should happen to cease from troubling——"

"You'll not only hear from me, but see me."

He gave me a friendly grip, and, collecting his hat and stick, led the way out into the yard. We walked together under the archway and emerged on to the crowded pavement of Fleet Street.

"There's one thing I should like to add, Mr. Dryden," he said, just before we parted. "If you ever find yourself in real difficulty or actual danger, don't hesitate to let me know. Whatever I'm doing I shan't be too busy to lend you a hand."

I tried to thank him, but, without waiting to listen, he stepped off into the roadway, and a moment later he was swallowed up amongst the traffic.

Brief as our interview had been, however, it had left me in a very satisfied frame of mind. From what I had seen of the Inspector I felt pretty sure that if there was anything worth knowing about Manning's past career he would soon succeed in ferreting it out. Apart from that, the knowledge that in a tight corner I should have him as well as Bobby at my back was the kind of encouraging thought that would have put heart into a rabbit.

My good spirits were in no way damped by one or two drops of rain, which at that moment, much to my surprise, began to dot the pavement. Looking up, I noticed for the first time that a change was taking place in the weather. A great bank of cloud was creeping slowly up from the east, and spreading in a black, threatening line all across the sky.

Manning's prophecy at once came into my mind, but, not being particularly anxious for a ducking, I wasted no time in further reflections. Hailing a passing taxi, I instructed the man to take me back to the Great Eastern Hotel, which I reached in comfort and dryness just as the rain began to descend in a steady drizzle.

There was nothing to do under the circumstances but to make the best of things indoors. I am never at a loss how to amuse myself if I can get a game of billiards, and I soon discovered that the hotel possessed a couple of excellent tables, presided over by a red-headed marker, who spoke Scotch and looked as if he drank it.

We played several hundred up with varying success; and at six-thirty, feeling quite ready to face a good dinner, I set out for Mr. Drayton's club. As an additional encouragement to my appetite I walked the whole way to St. James's Street, for by this time, although the pavements were still wet, the rain itself had practically ceased falling.

The club proved to be a big, sombre establishment, inhabited chiefly by middle-aged gentlemen of a distinctly morose aspect. What they had to be morose about I can't imagine, for a better meal than the one put before us I never wish to eat. Mr. Drayton, who was waiting for me in the hall and conducted me straight into the dining-room, confessed frankly that he had joined the place purely for the sake of its excellent cooking, and the respect which I already had for his judgment rose steadily with each succeeding course.

After dinner we made our way to the smoking-room upstairs, where, with the assistance of a couple of leather arm-chairs and a plentiful supply of whisky and soda, the time passed away so pleasantly that it was close on midnight before I got back to my own bed at the hotel.

The whisky must have been of the same high quality as the rest of the food, for in spite of the amount that I had put away, I woke up next morning feeling remarkably fit and cheerful. One of the first things I did was to pull aside the blind and have a look at the weather. The result was not encouraging, for my window faced on to a blank wall of dirty white brick, and in the intervening space a thin grey drizzle was coming down with monotonous persistence.

Once more Manning's predictions about a sudden change in the weather came back to my memory. If it were like this in London, the odds were that Greensea Island would be wrapped in a regular sea fog, which I knew from experience might last for several days. However, I consoled myself with the comforting reflection that it would save me a deal of hard work with the watering can, and that, after all, I was no longer compelled to tramp up and down a dripping bridge with a miniature trout stream trickling down the back of my neck.

I had made up my mind to go back by the mid-day train, which gets into Torrington somewhere about two o'clock. There were several things I still wanted to buy, and, now that I was actually in town, it seemed a pity to waste such a favourable opportunity. I had no wish to get soaked through, however, so on my way down to the dining-room I gave the hall porter a sovereign and told him to go out and buy me an umbrella. He returned with a sporting-looking affair, the handle of which terminated in a bull-dog's head. Though a trifle spectacular, it was a sound article for the money, and, armed with this and my cheque book, I set off after breakfast, pleasantly determined to make a good opening in Uncle Richard's life savings.

As intentions go, it must be admitted that I was fairly successful. In addition to half a dozen things I bought for myself, I discovered in a Bond Street jeweller's a perfectly charming little emerald pendant, which struck me at once as having been obviously designed for Christine. Under the circumstances twenty-five pounds seemed to be a ridiculously cheap price, but I felt that it was unnecessary to point this out to the shopman, who appeared quite satisfied with the transaction.

Returning to the hotel with my purchases, I made an early but excellent lunch off cold duck and salad, and at a quarter to one I was steaming out through the damp squalor of East London, comfortably established in the corner seat of a first-class smoker.

It was a cheerless journey, for all the way down a driving rain beat incessantly upon the windows, and most of the landscape was blotted out by drifting clouds of mist.

At Torrington things were not much better. It was not actually raining, but the little cobble-paved market-place reeked with wet, and a depressing air of forlorn moisture brooded over the entire place.

Packing myself and my belongings into a solitary growler which was standing in the gutter, I instructed the man to take me as far as the Gunner's Arms. We plodded off, and, after half an hour's drive between dripping hedgerows, came out at last over the brow of the long slope that overlooks the estuary. I lowered the sash, and, putting my head out of the window, inspected the prospect. Down below, the roof of the inn was just visible, but the harbour itself and everything beyond was hidden under a pall of fog, which stretched like a grey shroud over the whole length of the estuary. There was something singularly sinister and desolate about the whole scene, and for a moment I felt a pang of regret for the comfortable billiard-room which I had so recently quitted.

We came to a halt on the quay in front of the inn, deserted for once by its usual sprinkling of boatmen and barge hands. Our arrival had been observed, however, for scarcely had we pulled up when I saw the small figure of Jimmy emerge from the stable door and come hurrying down the yard towards us. He touched his damp curls with a cheerful grin of welcome.

"I reckoned it was you, guv'nor," he remarked "You ain't bin away long, an' that's a fact."

"Quite long enough, Jimmy," I returned. "At all events, you've had time to mess up the weather."

He took the bag which I handed out, and at the same time cast a rather disgusted glance into the surrounding gloom.

"It's a treat, ain't it!" he observed. "Come on like this yes'day afternoon." Then, drawing a little nearer, he added in a lowered voice: "There's a letter for you at the 'ouse, guv'nor. The young laidy give it me laite las' night, an' I took it across at once—saime as you told me."

I tried to cover my unseemly elation by lighting a cigarette. "Where did you meet her?" I enquired.

"She come down to the quay. I see 'er standin' there in the dark, an' I says to me self, As like as not she's wantin' me. So I just slips over alongside of 'er, an' without sayin' nothin' she shoves the letter in my 'and and orf she goes."

I looked at him gratefully. "You're a stout fellow, James," I said "I knew I could depend on you directly I saw you."

He waited until I had paid the cabman, and then, shouldering my bag, accompanied me to the boat.

"I seen 'er again since then," he continued confidentially. "I was comin' along Duke's Laine about 'alf an hour ago, an' she was waitin' to go aboard the doctor's barge."

I stopped short with a very distinct shock.

"Are you sure about that?" I demanded

He nodded a little scornfully. "Dead certain, guv'nor. There ain't no one else you'd mistake for 'er—not round these parts."

"But how do you know she was waiting to go on the barge?" I persisted.

"Why, I 'eard 'er call out, and I seed the doctor comin' orf to fetch 'er. I reckon she's there now—that's to say, if 'e ain't put 'er ashore again."

I said nothing further, but walked on to the boat in anything but a happy state of mind. The thought of Christine boxed up alone in the fog with those two scoundrels filled me with a horrible sense of uneasiness. Knowing her mistrust for Manning, and having seen something of the relations between them, I felt that only the strongest reasons would have induced her to take such a step.

It was possible, of course, that she had explained her action in the letter which she had given to Jimmy. If that were the case, the quicker I got back to the house the sooner my anxiety would be relieved, so without wasting any time I unshipped the oars and started off on my journey down the creek.

The tide was slack when we reached the mouth; and trusting to luck, for one could see only a few feet ahead, I cut straight across the estuary, and came out triumphantly almost exactly alongside the landing-stage.

Before stepping ashore I handed Jimmy a well-earned ten bob in return for his services. Then, with my bag in my hand, I strode forward through the mist and entered the narrow path which ran up through the shrubbery to the garden.

As I crossed the lawn and approached the house I noticed with some surprise that the front door was standing open. I was just thinking that it was rather unlike Bascomb to be so casual when I suddenly heard the sound of footsteps coming round the corner of the drive. I pulled up where I was, and the next moment the square, burly figure of my retainer loomed into view.

I was about to make some remark, but, whatever it was, the words remained unspoken. One glance at Bascomb's face was quite sufficient to drive everything else clean out of my head.

"Good God!" I exclaimed. "What's the matter?"

He stood there, glaring at me with sullen, blood-shot eyes—a silent and menacing figure in the mist. Then, taking a step forward, he laid his hand on my arm.

"You come along o' me," he said hoarsely. "I got something to show you."

Turning on his heel, he led the way round the corner of the house. Without saying anything further I followed him along the path until we reached the back garden, where with equal abruptness he came to a sudden standstill. Then, raising his hand, he pointed towards a dim, motionless heap, which was just visible in the centre of the lawn.

"There you are," he muttered. "You go an' look at that."

Two strides brought me to the spot, and a wicked oath broke from my lips as I stared down at the sight in front of me. It was the huge body of Satan, stretched out stiff and dead on the wet grass.

CHAPTER TWELVE

For several seconds I remained still, without speaking. The wave of grief and anger that swept through me left me sick and shaken; I could only stand there with clenched hands waiting until I could control my voice.

"Who did it, Bascomb?" I said at last.

He came up to me, and, bad as I felt myself, I was almost shocked by the sight of his face. It was like a horrible grey mask, twisted and distorted with passion.

"Who d'yer think?" he demanded hoarsely. "There's only one devil in the world who'd go fur to do a thing like that." He sank down on his knees beside the body, and, sliding his hand under the big head, lifted it tenderly from the grass.

"You mean Manning?" The words came out mechanically. I knew the answer before I uttered them.

"Aye!" he muttered savagely; "that's who I mean. It was Mannin' right enough—the blarsted, poisonin' 'ound." Very slowly he laid down his burden and got up again on to his feet. "I'll be even with 'im for this," he added in a choking voice. "You mark my words. I'll be even with 'im for this or my name ain't John Bascomb."

"When did it happen?" I asked.

He stared at me, as if only half understanding the question.

"When did it 'appen?" he repeated. "Why, las' night 'about eleven o'clock. 'E were alive an' well at the 'alf hour—that I can swear to. I was in the kitchen, an' I seen 'im pass the window—seen 'im with me own eyes. I can't say exac'ly 'ow long arter it was when I went to the back door; mebbe a matter o' five an' twenty minutes. Any'ow, there 'e was, stretched out on the path, too bad even to make a sound. Crawled back 'ome to die, 'e 'ad, pore beggar, an' me inside not knowin' nothin' about it."

His voice trembled, and, raising the back of his hand, he brushed it roughly across his eyes.

I wetted my lips, which were dry as leather.

"If Manning did this—" I began.

Bascomb turned on me with glowing eyes.

"You'll leave 'im to me," he said. "This is my job, this is; an' no one ain't comin' in between us—not till I've finished with 'im."

I saw that the man was half off his head with rage, and I felt that for the present the best thing was to leave him to himself. In the mood we were both in any further discussion would probably only end in an explosion.

"We must bury the body at all events," I said shortly. "If you want any help in digging the grave you will find me in the house."

I walked towards the back door, my mind still in a turmoil of emotion, and, crossing the kitchen, made my way through into the hall. The place was dark and cheerless, and in a mechanical fashion I struck a match and set a light to the fire. Then, pulling up an easy chair, I flung myself down, and stared at the crackling sticks.

I suppose it ought to have been obvious from the first that an attempt might be made to poison Satan, but somehow or other the possibility had never entered my mind. The dastardly act had come on me as a complete surprise, and in the first rush of anger and indignation I found it difficult to collect my thoughts. That Bascomb was right in his suspicions, however, I felt convinced, though I had no more evidence than he had in support of my belief. There was a cold-blooded ruthlessness about the whole thing which pointed clearly to Manning, and such a passion of hatred for him swept through me that for a moment I felt almost stifled.

What new threat, I asked myself, lurked behind this apparently wanton piece of spite? It was utterly unlike Manning to show his hand so clearly, unless driven to it by the most urgent reasons. He must have realised that, however easily deceived I might be, Bascomb would at once pitch on him as the author of the crime, I might or might not accept the latter's opinion, but it was at least probable that my suspicions would be aroused and that I should take prompt steps to try and find out the truth.

That he would run such a risk through sheer malice was a thing that I declined to believe. It was much more likely that he was fixing up some new and devilish plan, in which the removal of Satan was the first and perhaps the most essential step. Now that this was accomplished he was not likely to waste time, for every hour that he delayed would only add to the danger of discovery. I felt that I must act, and act quickly, but what the deuce I ought to do was another and more baffling question.

In my perplexity I suddenly remembered Bobby. A letter to Harwich would reach him first post in the morning, and unless he was up to his neck in work he would probably be with me by mid-day. I didn't want to bother him unnecessarily, but things seemed to be approaching a crisis, and if that were the case his advice and help would b& simply invaluable.

I jumped up from my chair with the intention of writing him a note at once. As I turned towards the desk, my eyes fell upon a letter which was lying on the further side of the centre table. Even at that distance I recognised Christine's hand, and at the same instant the recollection of my talk with Jimmy rushed back into my mind.

In a second I had crossed the room and picked up the envelope. Carrying it to the window, I tore open the flap, and with feverish haste pulled out its contents. There was a single sheet of notepaper, closely covered on both sides with small but very legible writing.

> "I know that you have gone to London, but I am not sure how long you intend to stay, or when you will get this letter. Anyhow, it will be waiting for you as soon as you reach the house.
>
> "I had to write to you or see you. I feel certain that something has happened—something that fills me with terrible fear for your safety. If I knew what it was I would tell you; I believe it must be connected with Dr. Manning's visit to the island, but that is only what I think, and I may be wrong.
>
> "I am *absolutely sure*, however, that at any moment you may be in the greatest possible danger. Please don't think that I am silly or fanciful in writing to you like this. You must know by now the kind of people you have to deal with, and surely you will understand that I shouldn't have sent you this second warning without some very real and serious reason for it.
>
> "Whatever happens, don't under any circumstances allow yourself to be alone on the island. I believe that your man Bascomb is honest, but it would be better if you were to have your naval friend with you as well. *Above all, be careful of Dr. Manning*. Pay no attention to any suggestion he makes, and mistrust everything he says or does.
>
> "If there is any further way in which I can help you I will do so. Should you want to send me a message, give it to the boy at the inn. My uncle has gone away for two days, so I shall have no difficulty in getting down to the quay in the evening.

"You are not to worry about me. I am in no danger myself, and I implore you to think only of your own safety.

"CHRISTINE DE RODA."

I read it hurriedly to the end, and then with a strange pleasure I turned back and went through it a second time. It was just such a letter as I should have expected her to write. Mysterious and reticent as it was, there shone through every line an honesty and personal courage which confirmed all I had felt about her ever since our adventure at Leixoes.

Of one thing there could be no doubt. Whatever had prompted her to send me this note, she had evidently been ignorant of the brutal plan to poison Satan. Had she known she would certainly have given me some warning, even if de Roda himself had been a party to the scheme.

On that point, however, I had already and perhaps quite unreasonably made up my mind. Nothing but the clearest evidence would shake my belief that it was Manning's work, and that in all probability he had arranged and carried out the whole thing for some purpose of his own. More than ever I felt convinced that he was playing a double part; that de Roda, though no doubt originally the moving spirit, was now merely a tool in the hands of a much cleverer man than himself.

Once more I glanced at Christine's letter. Her urgent pleading that I would take the matter seriously was not really needed; I should have done that even if the dead body of Satan had not been lying on the grass outside. I knew well that it was no vague or imaginary peril which had led a girl of her sense to send me this additional warning—a step, which, for anything she might say to the contrary, must have been fraught with considerable personal danger.

The last consideration, indeed, was much the most disturbing factor as far as I was concerned. I was in no mood to worry about my own safety when it was more than possible that, owing to her efforts to help me, Christine might be exposing herself to all sorts of horrible risks. People who don't hesitate to attempt murder are apt to take a particularly unpleasant view of anything which they regard as treachery. Of course de Roda was her uncle, but he looked the kind of fanatic who would attach precious little importance to family affection if it began to interfere with the success of his schemes. Besides, according to the letter, de Roda was away. In his absence Manning was presumably in charge of operations, and the mere thought of Christine finding herself in the power of that gentleman was sufficient to send a chill down the small of my back.

Suppose he had discovered that she was in communication with me! It was unlikely, but unlikely things do happen in this world, and, in spite of all our precautions, the secret might have leaked out. In view of what I had seen outside "The Laurels" my feelings can be easily understood, for he was just the sort of devil to make use of a chance like this without compunction and without mercy.

I crumpled the letter in my hand, and thrust it into my pocket. Whatever had induced Christine to visit the barge, the idea of her shut up in that lonely cabin with no one else but Manning on board was utterly unbearable. A frantic longing to do something rose up inside me, and, walking to the window, I stared out into the drifting mist.

I had stood there for perhaps thirty seconds when a really inspired notion suddenly dawned on me. In a fog like this nothing would be visible on the water more than a few yards away. If I were careful about it there was no earthly reason why I should not get into my boat and row up as far as the barge in perfect security. No matter how sharp a look-out was kept, I should be practically alongside before anyone could give the alarm.

Almost as soon as the idea came into my head I had made up my mind. So strongly, indeed, did it attract me that I did not even stop to consider what I should do when I reached my destination. I could think about that while I was in the boat. The main thing was to get started without wasting any more valuable time.

In spite of my eagerness to be off, I first of all sat down at my desk and scribbled a note to Bobby. It had to be posted at Pen Mill before six o'clock or else it would not be delivered in Harwich until mid-day, and in that case he would very probably be out of the office. I made no attempt to explain things, however; I merely told him that I was in need of his help, and that if he could manage to get down to Greensea the next day I should be uncommonly glad to see him.

I was just fastening up the envelope when I saw Bascomb go past the window. I called out to him from where I was sitting, and he stepped in through the open doorway. He was carrying a heavy garden spade.

"Where are you going to dig the grave?" I asked him.

He jerked his head toward the back of the house. "'Longside o' the shed," he answered. "I can see it there from the kitchen window."

He spoke as though the prospect of being continually reminded of the crime afforded him a kind of sullen satisfaction.

"I am going ashore to post a letter," I said. "I mean to get to the bottom of this infernal business, and I've asked Commander Dean to come here to-morrow. I think he may be able to help us."

Bascomb looked at me more strangely than ever.

"It's likely enough," he remarked. "That's to say, if there's any 'elp wanted."

He shouldered the spade as he spoke, and, stepping out on to the path, walked off silently round the corner of the house. His manner was so peculiar that for a moment I felt an uncomfortable doubt as to whether he were in his right senses. I was too anxious about Christine to worry over anything else, however, and, following him to the door, I hastily secured the bolts and made sure that the windows were properly fastened. Then, snatching up a cap from my travelling bag, I left the house by the back door.

The mist seemed thicker than ever when I came out into the garden. I climbed the wet rail which led into the shrubbery, and, having groped my way through the bushes, I struck off down the path in the direction of the water.

A few minutes' walk brought me to the boathouse, where, by gently coaxing the rusty lock, I managed to open the door without making any unnecessary noise.

The next job was to find something with which to muffle the oars. A glance round showed me exactly what I needed—a large piece of cotton waste that was hanging from a nail just inside the threshold. I tore this in two, and with the aid of some string soon accomplished my purpose. Then, pushing off quietly, I drifted out into the mist.

It was just low water, and the young tide was already running up the estuary. I knew its strength from bitter experience, so, keeping the nose of my boat well into the current, I set off hopefully on what I imagined to be the right course.

I was not far out in my reckoning, for, after about ten minutes' steady rowing, I found myself approaching a mud flat, which I recognised at once as being slightly to the east of the creek. I allowed the current to carry me down as far as the entrance, and a few moments later the rough wall of the jetty loomed into view on my left-hand side.

There was no sign of anyone about, a circumstance that was hardly surprising in view of the close proximity of the Gunner's Arms. I ferried along till I reached the nearest post, where I shipped my oars and made the boat fast. Then, climbing ashore, I started off carefully down the slippery causeway.

I got to the pillar-box, which was just alongside the inn, without meeting a soul. The knowledge that my letter was safely posted gave me a distinct feeling of relief, and, retracing my steps as quickly as possible, I was soon back in the dinghy and pulling off again down the creek.

So far all was well, but as I drifted round the point into the open water, I began to realize what a difficult job I had in front of me. In the first place, it was quite conceivable that I was on a fool's errand. Notwithstanding my fears, Christine might be in no need of my assistance, and if that were the case my sudden appearance on the scene would be about the most embarrassing ordeal I could possible inflict on her. This was an unfortunate fact that had to be faced, however; the only question was how to make certain that she was safe without giving away the whole affair.

My strongest card was the one which had been thoughtfully provided by Manning himself. His last words had been a pressing invitation that I would come and see him on the barge as soon as I got back from London, and he could hardly blame me if I happened to select a particularly awkward moment for calling. Much as he might object to my visit, he would find it uncommonly difficult to invent any reasonable excuse for not asking me on board.

What I chiefly dreaded was the possibility that Christine might betray herself before she could recover from her surprise. In that event any further pretence on my part would be useless; Manning would at once guess the truth, or something very near it, and what the consequences might be God alone knew. Was I asking too much in making such a demand upon a girl's courage and coolness? It was a trial from which very few people would emerge successfully, but then I had had ample proof in Leixoes harbour that Christine's nerve was of no ordinary quality. Her self-possession on that occasion had been truly delightful, and though she would now be up against a much more severe test I had a kind of inward conviction that I could still depend upon her. Anyhow, there was no way of avoiding the risk unless I abandoned my purpose, an alternative on which I declined to waste even a moment's consideration.

All this time the tide was carrying me steadily up the estuary, my own efforts being confined to keeping the boat as near the shore as possible without losing the drift of the current. I made no attempt at rowing, for, anxious as I was to reach the barge, I was afraid that if Craill happened to be on deck the muffled creak of my rowlocks would probably attract his attention. I wanted my arrival to be absolutely unexpected, so that I could seize the chance of getting on board before anyone was prepared to dispute my purpose.

Now that the critical moment was approaching I felt as cool as a cucumber. Nothing steadies me like the prospect of immediate action, and, although my hatred of Manning was as bitter as ever, it no longer clouded or distorted my mind. It had, indeed, precisely the opposite effect, bracing all my faculties to their clearest and sharpest pitch.

I drifted along, listening intently, and keeping a constant look-out over my shoulder. I knew by the curve of the shore that I must be getting pretty near my goal, for just below where the barge lay the estuary made a slight turn to the north.

Suddenly, a few feet ahead of me, I caught sight of a shadowy anchor chain, rising from the water and stretching away into the gloom. I was so close that in another second I should have been on top of it, but a timely dig with my left-hand scull just saved me from this calamity. Almost simultaneously the black outline of the barge towered up above my head, and, gliding round the big blunt bow, I came quietly alongside an empty dinghy which was bobbing about on its painter at the foot of the accommodation ladder.

For a couple of seconds I remained perfectly still, gripping tight hold of the dinghy's gunwale, and staring up at the railing above me. I half expected to see Craill's ugly face come peering over the top, for if he were on deck he must have heard the splash which I had made in trying to avoid the chain. No such apparition materialised, however, and with a slight pull at the painter I drew into the side and rapidly hitched up my boat. The next moment I had mounted the ladder and was safely on board.

As far as I could see, I appeared to have the whole place to myself. It was very unlike an ordinary barge, for both fore and aft a high "coach-house" roof had been built up above the deck, so as to provide the cabins below with further light and head room. Between the two, and right in front of where I was standing, a broad companion-way led down to the interior.

I advanced on tiptoe, keeping a watchful eye on the fo'c'sle, from which quarter I still feared that at any moment Craill might make an inconvenient appearance. I had taken about three steps when a sudden and unexpected noise brought me to a dead stop. It was a queer sound, as though a small but heavily laden table had been violently overturned. I stood quite still, listening intently; then, faint but clear enough to send the blood racing through my heart, came the half-stifled cry of a woman's voice.

One stride forward brought me to the edge of the companion-way, and, clearing the short flight of steps with a single leap, I found myself facing a closed door which apparently led through into the cabins. It swung open as I turned the handle, revealing a narrow passage, with another door at the end. On the farther side of this a scuffle of some sort seemed to be taking place, and a voice which I recognised as Manning's rose plainly above the confused jumble of sounds.

If there were a championship for sprinting up corridors, I think I should have some claim to be the holder. Anyhow, I covered the distance in considerably less time than it takes to write the words, and, wrenching round the brass knob with a savage jerk, applied the full force of my shoulder to the panel. Instead of being locked, as I expected, the door flew back suddenly on its hinges. How I saved myself from falling I don't know; I can only imagine that the sight which met my eyes momentarily stiffened every muscle and sinew in my body.

Amid a debris of broken cups and plates Christine and Manning were struggling together in the centre of the cabin. He had gripped her in his arms, and, in spite of the efforts she was making to free herself, he was pressing fierce kisses upon her face and neck. Beside them on the carpet sprawled an overturned tea-table, with one leg sticking up grotesquely in the air.

I had only the briefest glimpse of what was happening, for at the noise of my entrance the tableau broke up abruptly. Manning raised his head with a swift, astonished glance; and then, releasing his hold, took a step backwards. Freed in this unexpected fashion, Christine for an instant seemed to be on the point of collapsing. By a great effort of will she was just able to reach the arm of the sofa, where she stood panting and exhausted, her eyes fixed on me in a kind of half-incredulous fear.

"You must forgive me if I am intruding, Manning," I said. "You asked me to look you up, and I have taken you at your word."

Even at that moment the man's extraordinary coolness never deserted him. Whatever thoughts and emotions were passing through his mind, he seemed, after that first glance of surprise, to accept the situation with perfect composure.

"I am afraid you have chosen rather an unfortunate time," he replied. "If you would care to come back in half an hour I should be charmed. At present I have another visitor."

"So I see," was my answer. "And, if you want to know, that is precisely the reason why I intend to stop."

Manning's curious blue eyes narrowed dangerously.

"I don't quite understand," he observed in his silkiest voice.

"It's very simple," I assured him. "This lady, whoever she is, seems to have mistaken you for a gentleman." I turned to Christine. "I hope I am not being officious," I added, "but if there is any way in which I can be of use, please consider me entirely at your service."

She rose to the occasion with all the quickness and courage that I had expected.

"If it's not troubling you too much," she said quietly, "I should certainly be obliged if you would row me to the shore."

Manning stepped forward, addressing himself directly to her. His manner was politeness itself, but there was no misunderstanding the veiled threat behind his words.

"For various reasons," he said, "I think you had better allow *me* that privilege."

I saw that Christine was hesitating, so I gave her no chance to reply.

"I expect you know your way up on to the deck," I remarked. "If you will excuse me I will be with you almost immediately."

For a second she still wavered. Then with the slightest possible bow she crossed the cabin, and passed out silently into the passage. I closed the door behind her.

Only once before in my life, when Bobby and I sighted our first German submarine, have I felt the same peculiar sensation with which I turned round and faced Manning. He stood where he was, an amused and half-mocking smile playing round the corners of his mouth.

"You mustn't let me detain you, Mr. Dryden," he said. "I am sure you are full of the noblest sentiments, but it would be a pity to keep the lady waiting."

If his intention was to make me lose my temper it went woefully astray.

"I shan't be long," I replied. "I am only going to give you a damned good hiding."

I was looking straight at him as I spoke, and I saw the lightning glance with which he measured his distance from a small oak sideboard that was clamped against the wall.

"That's the worst of you primitive people," he drawled slowly, "you always—" Then suddenly his eyes travelled past me to the door, and a harsh, exulting cry broke from his lips.

"Go on, Craill," he shouted; "let him have it."

With most men the trick would probably have succeeded, but I was too old a hand to be caught in that time-honoured fashion. As he sprang for the sideboard I hurled myself after him, and at the very second that he wrenched open the drawer my fist crashed home full in his face. He lurched wildly backwards, and, stumbling over the corner of the mat, fetched up against the wall with a thud that shook the cabin.

Of the next two minutes I have a glorious but slightly confused recollection. All the rage which I had been bottling up inside me seemed to break loose at that first blow, and with a red mist in front of my eyes I leaped in to finish the business.

Whatever else Manning might be, he was game to the last inch. Hopelessly cornered, with blood streaming down his face, he yet fought back at me like a trapped and maddened wolf. He fought, too, with all the skill of a trained boxer, but science and courage were little use against the mad fury which had suddenly taken possession of me.

Keeping him pinned against the wall, I smashed home punch after punch without even troubling to guard myself. No one could stand up long under such a hail of punishment, and although he managed to land one or two blows there was not sufficient force in them to have any effect on me. At last, with a terrific right-hand jolt just below the heart, I sent him staggering sideways. He made a desperate attempt to recover, but, seizing the chance, I let him have my left bang on the point of the jaw, and down he went on to the carpet—a sprawling bundle of arms and legs.

For a moment I stood there breathing heavily, my whole being aflame with savage satisfaction. Stretched out motionless on his back, Manning presented a pretty ghastly spectacle, but there was not a spark of pity for him in my heart as I stared down into his battered and bleeding face. Christine's cry for help, and the thought of poor Satan creeping back alone to die in the darkness, were still vividly in my mind, and, turning away, I strode across towards the open drawer in the oak sideboard.

As I expected, the first thing I saw on looking inside was a revolver. It was a Smith and Wesson of the heaviest service pattern, and on taking it out I found that every chamber was loaded. I wondered grimly what my fate would have been if Manning had succeeded in reaching the drawer a second earlier. Possibly he had only meant to protect himself, but in any case the weapon would certainly be safer in my possession than in his, so, slipping it into my pocket, I strolled back to where I had left him.

Just as I came up he gave a deep groan and opened his eyes.

"Oh," I said, "you're recovering, are you?"

He gazed at me vaguely, as if only half understanding my words; then in a sudden rush the full memory of what had happened seemed to return to him, and with a painful effort he raised himself up on one elbow.

"Next time you want to insult a girl," I suggested, "you had better see that the cabin door is properly locked."

Lifting his sleeve, he tried to wipe away some of the blood which was trickling down his face.

"I always thought you were a fool, Dryden," he said in a faint voice. "Now I am sure of it." With great difficulty he struggled up a little farther, and sank back against the wall.

"I know a damned cad when I see one, anyhow," I replied. "Not that it needed much intelligence in the present case." I walked to the door, and, pausing on the threshold, took out the revolver. "You will forgive my borrowing this," I added. "I don't want to be shot in the back as I leave the barge."

His blue eyes fixed themselves on mine with a cat-like malevolence.

"You might have a worse ending," he said softly. "I am not a very safe person to quarrel with."

There was a venom in his tone which spoke volumes as to his sincerity, but unless it was intended to frighten me the warning was a little superfluous.

"I shan't grumble at the bill," I replied. "I am always ready to pay well, especially when I have really enjoyed myself."

Then, turning the handle, I stepped out into the passage, and closed the door behind me.

CHAPTER THIRTEEN

I found Christine standing on the deck at the head of the companion-way.

She looked terribly pale, and as I approached she started towards me with a little sob of relief.

"Oh, thank God!" she whispered. "Thank God you're safe!"

She took my hands, and a low cry escaped her at the sight of their scarred and bleeding knuckles.

"It's nothing, darling," I said reassuringly. "That's only a little blood from Manning's nose. He's got plenty left to go on with."

With something between a laugh and another sob she let her head sink forward against my shoulder. "Don't think me a coward. I—I'm not one really. It was just having to wait here and——"

"A coward!" I interrupted. "Why, I think you're the bravest girl that ever stepped this earth."

I put my arms round her, and for one dear moment she lay there passive and still, like a tired, contented child.

Then, suddenly releasing herself, she gazed round in a kind of startled panic.

"But we mustn't stay here," she exclaimed hurriedly. "We must go at once."

"I suppose you're right," I admitted with some reluctance. "What's happened to that ruffian Craill?"

"He went off in the other boat just after I arrived. He might come back at any moment."

"Well, I want to see him," I said; "but I don't think I'll wait now. It's a pity to cram all one's pleasures into one afternoon."

She laid her hands pleadingly on my sleeve. "Do what I ask," she begged. "Promise me you will go straight back to the island as soon as you have taken me ashore?"

"I am not going to take you ashore," I said. "You are coming home with me."

She made a quick gesture of protest, but I went on without giving her time to answer.

"There's no other way out of it," I said, speaking with the utmost seriousness. "After what's happened this afternoon you have simply got to tell me the truth. Don't you see, dear, you and I are in this together, and unless I know— —"

"Yes, yes," she interrupted breathlessly, "I must tell you; I had already made up my mind to do it." She paused in piteous hesitation. "I daren't come to the island, though," she added; "if anyone saw us— —"

"No one can possibly see us," I objected. "It's a hundred times safer than any other place. We can talk comfortably there, and I can row you ashore afterwards and land you wherever you like. This fog's not going to lift for another twenty-four hours."

I don't think I really convinced her; she seemed to give in to my will through utter weariness.

"Perhaps you're right," she faltered. "I can't argue with you anyhow. I—I'm too tired."

With a sudden remorse for my lack of consideration, I helped her tenderly down the ladder. Everything in the dinghy was soaking, and, in spite of her remonstrances, I insisted on removing my coat and spreading it on the wet seat.

"I won't try and talk to you while I'm rowing," I said. "There's a pretty stiff stream running, and I shall want all my energy to get back to the island. Besides, the quieter we keep the better."

She nodded her head to show that she understood, and, having cast off the painter, I took my place at the oars.

The first few strokes were a bit painful on account of my damaged knuckles, which started bleeding afresh the moment I closed my hands. They soon ceased to smart, however; and, keeping the same course as before, I plugged steadily along, until the mouth of the creek opened up dimly on my left-hand side. A short but strenuous battle with the current brought me safely across to the landing-stage, where I grabbed hold of the chain and waved a triumphant greeting to Christine.

"Welcome!" I said "Welcome to Greensea Island!"

She smiled back at me, such a wan, pathetic little smile that I impulsively leaned over and pressed her hand.

"My own dear," I whispered, "you have just got to be happy. Remember, you are coming home for the first time."

I felt her fingers squeeze mine gently in return; then with a sudden trace of shyness she pushed them away and got up quickly from her seat.

"You must be wet through," she said, "and as for your poor coat—" She held it up with an expression of penitent dismay. "You will have to go and change everything directly we get to the house."

"Oh, it won't hurt me," I protested. "I've been drenched so often that I can't catch a cold even if I try."

I steadied the boat while she stepped out, and then, jumping ashore myself, led the way forward in the direction of the shrubbery.

As we entered the path, and the gloom of the trees closed in about us, she slipped her arm through mine.

"It's not a very cheerful place, is it?" she said with a slight shiver.

"Don't judge us too quickly," I returned. "Wait till we reach the house. Things will seem quite different as soon as you've had a cup of tea."

She smiled again, this time a little more happily, and without any further attempt at talking I piloted her through the rest of the shrubbery and opened the iron gate which led on to the lawn. The vague outline of the roof and chimneys were just visible opposite.

"That's my ancestral home," I said. "Unfortunately it's not looking its best to-day."

Christine made no reply; she had let go my arm and stood quite still beside me, gazing ahead into the mist with a strange and eager interest.

"One mustn't grumble though," I added philosophically. "After all, if it wasn't for the fog you wouldn't be here."

We set out across the grass, and, just as we were approaching the verandah, I suddenly remembered that I had bolted the front door on the inside. I did not want to take Christine to the back entrance, for fear that she might catch sight of Bascomb digging the grave. It would be a gruesome discovery to run up against unexpectedly, especially for anyone whose nerves were already strained almost beyond the point of endurance.

"If you don't mind waiting here a couple of seconds," I said, "I'll slip round and let you in. The place is locked up, and my man will probably be out in the garden."

"I shall be all right," she said. "It was only the trees that made me fed a little creepy."

Leaving her where she was, I hurried along the verandah, and turned off down the side walk which led past the kitchen window. Directly I got round the corner I heard the sound of Bascomb's spade, but it was not until I was within a few feet of him that his figure suddenly emerged from the mist. He was standing beside a large hole, peering forward in the direction of the path.

"How are you getting on?" I asked, pulling up short.

"It's pretty nigh finished," he answered slowly. "I've put 'im down deep, so as 'e can lie quiet without bein' shifted."

I looked over into the grave, which was already partly filled in.

"Well, there's no need to hurry," I said. "I've brought someone back with me, but we shan't want anything except a cup of tea, and I can get that myself."

If he felt any curiosity about my guest he certainly did not show it.

"Aye," he remarked indifferently. "You won't 'ave no trouble about that. The kettle's on the fire, an' there's a jug o' milk in the larder."

He turned to his work again, and, resuming my way to the back of the house, I passed in through the kitchen.

I took a strange delight in opening the front door and seeing Christine step in over the threshold. At that moment everything about her seemed to become real to me in a way that it had never been before. I had a sort of feeling that we had suddenly escaped from some fantastic melodrama, and were alone together in the actual world for the first time.

She looked round, an almost childish pleasure in her brown eyes.

"It's charming," she exclaimed. "It's the kind of room one would never want to go out of."

"That's how it strikes me just at present," I said. "Come and sit down in front of the fire. You'll have time to get nice and dry while I make the tea."

She crossed the room, and, sinking down with a little sigh of contentment in one of the easy chairs, stretched out her hands towards the hearth.

For a second or two I stood watching her, too happy to move; then, wrenching my mind back to practical affairs, I started off unwillingly towards the kitchen.

It did not take me long to collect what I wanted. The kettle was already full of hot water, as Bascomb had told me, and while it was boiling I wandered into the larder, and ran to earth an appetising looking cake and a new tin of dessert biscuits. Returning with my spoils, I filled up the teapot, and then, having set everything out on a tray, I carried it carefully into the hall.

Christine examined the result of my labours with evident approval.

"I'm so glad you've got a good tea," she said. "I've had nothing to eat since breakfast."

"In that case," I answered, "we'll feed first and talk afterwards. One can't be empty and eloquent at the same time."

I sat down beside her and took control of the proceedings, sternly insisting upon her carrying out my orders. It was not until she had finished her third cup and successfully demolished two large slices of cake that I would listen to the faintest protest, by which time the colour had come back into her cheeks, and she was looking an altogether different being.

"That's splendid," I remarked approvingly. "Now you shall have a cigarette, and I'll tell you how it was that I happened to come butting in just at the right moment. You had better let me explain first; then we shall know exactly where we are."

She nodded her agreement, and, accepting a cigarette from the case which I offered her, sank back again in the chair with her head against the cushions.

I was much too impatient for her side of the story to waste any unnecessary words over my own. At the same time I felt it was vital to omit nothing which might be of real importance, so I began with a rapid description of Manning's visit to the island.

I told her all about our midnight adventures in the hall, and of how he had made a special point of my coming to see him on the barge; then, after explaining the reason for my sudden trip to London, I gave her a short but faithful account of everything that had happened since.

It was easy to see from the look of indignant horror in her eyes that she had known nothing about the death of Satan. She listened to me, however, in absolute silence, her face alone betraying the intense interest with which she was following every syllable. Even when I had finished she still sat there for a moment without speaking, as though trying to puzzle out the full significance of all she had just heard. At last she straightened herself in the chair, and threw away the half-smoked cigarette which she had been holding between her fingers.

"I have treated you very unfairly," she said in a low voice. "I ought to have told you the truth that day at Shalston. If anything had happened to you it would have been entirely my fault."

"Oh, that's nonsense," I declared. "You're not responsible for your relations any more than I am. Providence just dumped them on us, and we've got to make the best of it."

There was a moment's pause.

"I wonder how much you have guessed," she said. "I wonder if you have any idea of my uncle's real reasons for coming to England."

"I've got some notions on the subject," I admitted. "They're a little muddled, because I can't quite fit in our friend Dr. Manning. For a comparative stranger he appears to have rather an important part in the show."

With the shadow of a smile on her lips she leaned forward.

"If you tell me what you know," she said, "the rest will be easier for me to explain."

"Well, from what I've gathered one way and another," I began, "I should say that it was the late lamented Mr. Richard Jannaway who was responsible for the whole trouble. He was always a bad hat; in fact, the only decent thing he ever did in his life was to die without making a will. I know he was in South America for years, and it looks to me as if he'd managed to run up pretty badly against your uncle. He probably played the old boy some dog's trick, and Señor de Roda, being a gentleman of spirit, naturally determined to get level with him. Unless I'm much mistaken, that's how it is that you come to be sitting here at the present moment."

She nodded encouragingly.

"Now I begin to lose my bearings," I confessed. "How Manning shoved himself in is a point that's been worrying me ever since I saw you together outside 'The Laurels.' I made certain at first that he must be working for your uncle, but when you told me that neither of you had met him until you arrived in England I didn't know what on earth to think. I've turned it over pretty thoroughly since then, and I've come to the conclusion that there must be some secret about Greensea which is distinctly worth knowing. It's my belief that Manning got on to the track of it while he was staying on the island. He probably discovered that you were mixed up with it too, and for reasons of his own he decided to join forces. I've no doubt that he's playing a double game, and I shouldn't wonder if you both shared my opinion. It was probably a case of your having no choice in the matter. When you found out how much he knew you had to take him into partnership, whether you liked it or not."

Christine pushed the hair off her forehead, and looked at me with a curious expression.

"It's really rather extraordinary," she said slowly. "If you were a wizard or a fortune teller or something of that sort, you could hardly have got nearer the truth."

I acknowledged her compliment with a slight bow.

"Thank you," I said; "you've restored my self-respect. Dr. Manning told me I was a fool, and I should have been horribly depressed if I thought you shared his opinion."

"Dr. Manning thinks everyone is a fool except himself," she answered. "It's the only mistake I have ever known him to make."

"Most clever scoundrels have the same delusion," I assured her. "That's what keeps half the criminal barristers in practice."

Christine lit another cigarette, and sat for a moment staring into the fire, as if trying to arrange her thoughts. At last she turned towards me.

"Do you know that your uncle once went under the name of Stephen Gardiner?" she asked.

"No," I said, "I didn't know, but I can quite believe it. I should think he was the sort of gentleman who had probably had half a dozen names." I paused. "Where did you come across him first?" I asked.

"At Rio, two years before the war," she answered.

"What, Rio in Brazil?" I asked

She nodded. "We were living there then. My uncle had a big ranch about twenty miles outside the town, and of course he knew nearly everybody. At that time the whole of Brazil was in a frightful state of dissatisfaction. There was a great deal of feeling against the President, Gomez, who had been in for years and years, and Uncle Philip was one of the leading people who were trying to turn him out. It was through this that he and your uncle became friends."

"But what on earth had my uncle got to do with it?" I demanded. "He was an Englishman and a stranger, and I should think he must have had a pretty rotten reputation even then."

"I can't tell you that," she said. "I was only sixteen, and naturally they didn't talk about things in front of me. I suppose that somehow or other he had managed to make himself useful to them; anyhow, I know they all trusted him absolutely."

"They seem to have been a nice confiding lot," I observed. "I wouldn't mind betting they paid for it too."

She smiled mirthlessly. "Yes," she said, "they paid for it. I daresay you remember what happened; there must have been some account in the English papers."

I shook my head. "I wasn't reading the papers just then," I explained. "I was chasing about the Pacific learning to be a sailor."

"Everything that we had planned was betrayed to the Government," she said fiercely. "There was to be a general rising in Rio early one morning while the soldiers were asleep in their barracks. It was almost certain that if our people could seize the public buildings and capture the President the whole thing would be practically over. A great many of the troops were friendly, and the rest would have been quiet enough as soon as they heard that Gomez was a prisoner. That was only part of the plot, however. About a hundred miles up the Amazon there's a place called Cinatti. It's close to two or three big diamond mines which belong to the Government, and all the stones are collected and sorted there before they come down to Rio. Our people had found out through one of the sorters that a specially valuable lot would be sent off on the very morning that was fixed for the revolution. We wanted money badly, and Uncle Philip and several of the others decided that the best plan was to attack the train before it reached the capital. They knew that it would mean some terrible fighting, because the stones are always sent down under a strong military guard, but there was no difficulty in finding dozens of men who were quite ready to risk their lives. One of the first people chosen was Stephen Gardiner. He was appointed second in command, so that if anything happened to Uncle Philip he would be in charge of the party."

She paused, and drew in a deep breath.

"There were twenty-five of them altogether," she went on quietly. "They met just before midnight at the place which had been agreed upon. It was where the train had to cross a bridge over a deep gully. They blew away part of the bridge with dynamite, and hid themselves as well as they could on both sides of the line. When the train came along of course the driver saw what had happened. He pulled up, and directly the engine stopped Uncle Philip gave the signal. He was badly wounded himself almost as soon as he jumped out of the bushes, but about twenty of the others managed to reach the cars. There was a dreadful fight for a minute or two; then the officer in command of the guard was killed by a bullet, and after that the soldiers must have lost their heads. Anyhow, half of them threw down their guns, and the rest gave in to save their own lives."

"They would," I said; "it's a habit with all South-American regulars." I pushed away the tray, and leaned forward with my arms on the table. "What about the diamonds?" I asked.

"Oh, the diamonds were there," she answered, in the same curiously level voice. "They were packed in two sealed boxes, and they were a magnificent lot of stones. One of the men who knew something about jewels put their value at a hundred thousand pounds. As a matter of fact, he was altogether wrong. They were worth double that amount."

I whistled gently. "And de Roda being knocked out," I said, "Mr. Stephen Gardiner was in charge of the proceedings?"

She made a gesture of assent.

"Go on," I added grimly. "Tell me what happened."

"By the time the soldiers had surrendered," she said, "Uncle Philip had lost consciousness. Three of the others were dead and six or seven badly wounded. This man, Gardiner, divided the party into two. He left ten of them behind to look after their friends, and rode off towards Rio with the other five, taking the diamonds with him. No one dreamed that there was anything wrong. Gardiner had fought as bravely as anybody, and they all imagined that when they got to Rio they would find our people in control of the town."

Her voice shook, and for just an instant she seemed to be on the point of breaking down.

"As a matter of fact," she continued, with a kind of desperate calmness, "they were riding straight to their death. At the last moment everything we had planned had been betrayed to Gomez. He had brought troops secretly into all the public buildings, and when our people came out into the streets they were shot down like dogs before they could move a step. Six hundred of them were killed in less than ten minutes. Gomez had given orders that there should be no prisoners, and the soldiers went on firing at the wounded until there wasn't a soul left alive."

"And I suppose my infernal uncle was at the bottom of the whole business?" I broke in.

"You can judge for yourself," she answered. "When he and the other five reached the town they found troops everywhere. In the very first street they came to they were held up by a patrol. Before anyone quite realised what was happening Gardiner rode forward and said something to the officer in command. They let him through at once, and he galloped away up the street, leaving the rest behind him. Some of our men tried to shoot him, but they were too late. Directly he was past the soldiers opened fire and—" She broke off with a little mute gesture that needed no further words.

"My God! What a swine!" I exclaimed. "Do you mean to say he led all his friends to their death, and then handed the stones over to Gomez?"

She laughed again in the same mirthless fashion as before. "You are doing him an injustice," she said. "Anybody can be a traitor to his friends; it takes a genius to betray the other side as well." She paused a moment, her curious dark eyes fixed steadily on mine. "Gomez knew nothing about the attack on the train," she went on. "For once in his life he had met a man who was even more cunning and wicked than himself. Your uncle had sold him all the rest of our plans, but had kept that part an absolute secret. When the patrol let him pass they thought that he was going straight to the President. He had promised Gomez to bring in news of what was happening outside the town, but instead of doing that he galloped his horse down to the harbour, where he had a motor-boat waiting for him. Before they discovered the truth he was six miles out to sea, with the diamonds on board. That was the last that anyone in Brazil ever saw of Mr. Stephen Gardiner."

"Well I'm damned!" I remarked without thinking. Then, feeling that an apology would be rather futile, I leaned across and took her hand, which was resting on the corner of the chair. "And de Roda and the others, Christine," I said. "What happened to them?"

"Three of them were shot the next day," she answered. "They were the lucky ones. Uncle Philip and the rest were flung into prison at Rio. You can probably guess how they were treated. When Gomez died six years later Uncle Philip was the only one left alive. Almost the first thing the new President did was to release him, but it was too late to be of much service. He came out so terribly changed that none of his friends recognised him. He had been starved and tortured until his brain and body had almost given way. He had one idea only—one idea that had been burning into his mind night and day for all those six dreadful years—revenge on the man who had betrayed him."

"I can imagine his feelings," I said with considerable sympathy. "But how the dickens did he find out where my uncle had hidden himself?"

"It wasn't easy," she admitted. "Gomez had offered an enormous reward to anyone who could arrest him and get back the stones, but although the police in Europe had been on the look-out, they had never been able to discover the slightest trace of him. In the end it was just pure chance. A few of our friends had escaped after the revolution, and amongst them was a man called da Silva. He had settled down in London, and one day, when he was out walking, he saw your uncle on the other side of the street. Although it was nearly seven years since they had met he recognised him at once.

"Some people, I suppose, would have given him up to the police, in the hope of getting part of the reward which was still on offer. Da Silva was not that sort of man. He followed your uncle back to where he was living, and then very secretly and carefully he set about making enquiries. When he had found out everything he wanted, he wrote and told Uncle Philip."

"I wonder if the old ruffian guessed that he'd been spotted," I said. "If he did, that would explain why he shut himself up here."

She shook her head. "He was already trying to buy the island. I think he must have seen in the paper that Uncle Philip had been let out of prison."

I suddenly remembered what Bascomb had told me the night we talked together in the hall.

"You're right, Christine," I said. "That's what happened beyond a doubt, and I don't wonder he got the wind up. It must have been rather like reading one's own death-warrant."

"I hope it was," she said mercilessly. "I should like to be sure that he suffered before he died. When I think of the way he escaped us I sometimes feel that there's no justice in the world."

"But surely you knew he was dead before you started from Brazil?" I interrupted. "Your friend da Silva had plenty of time to write to you."

"We never heard from da Silva again," she said. "Three weeks after he sent his first letter he was killed in that big railway accident at Croydon. Until you spoke to me on the boat we both believed that Gardiner was alive."

"Good Lord!" I exclaimed. "No wonder you were a bit flabbergasted."

"It was the thought of Uncle Philip that upset me most. You see, it was impossible for me to tell him then, and I felt certain that he would never get over the shock and disappointment when he found out for himself."

"But how about you?" I asked curiously. "Wasn't it rather a relief to know that you were too late? You can't take the law into your own hands in this country without paying for it pretty heavily."

"Do you suppose that mattered?" she demanded. "Do you think I cared what happened to me as long as Gardiner was punished? Why, rather than see him escape I would have killed him myself!"

"I believe you would," I said, with genuine admiration. Then, lighting another cigarette, I added: "How long was it before de Roda discovered the truth?"

"It was two days after we landed. Directly we came ashore he left me at an hotel and went straight to da Silva's address. He had been very puzzled at not hearing again and getting no answer to his letters, but of course when he found out what had happened it explained everything. Da Silva had told us about Greensea Island in his first letter, however, so the next morning Uncle Phillip motored down here to make enquiries. The first thing he learned was that Gardiner was dead."

"How did he take it?" I enquired

"He seemed almost stunned when he came back. He sat all the evening without saying a word, and, although I did my best to comfort him, I don't think he even heard what I said. It was not until the next morning that he told me he had taken a lease of 'The Laurels.' I didn't bother him with any questions, but from the way he spoke I felt sure he believed that the diamonds, or what was left of them, were still hidden on the island. By this time he had got a kind of half-insane conviction that they were his own property."

"I am inclined to agree with him," I said. "Anyhow, I'd a jolly sight rather he had them than the Brazilian Government." I paused. "Had he tumbled across the fact of my existence?" I asked.

"Not then," she replied. "Nobody down here had any idea of what would happen to the property. I was the only one who knew, and that was why I asked you to meet me that day in Bond Street. I was afraid that directly Uncle Philip learned the truth he would suspect you of having the stones. You were Gardiner's nephew too, and in the queer state he was in that alone was quite enough to put your life in danger."

"You've acted like a brick all through, Christine," I said gratefully.

"I only did what anyone else would have done," she went on hurriedly. "I felt you ought to be warned, but at the time I little guessed the real state of affairs." She stopped, with a queer expression in her brown eyes. "You see, it was not until two days later that I first met Dr. Manning."

"Ah!" I said softly. "Now we're getting to the part in which I take a rather particular interest."

"I heard about him from the people at the inn," she continued. "I wanted to find out the address of some medical man in case Uncle Philip was ill, so I called in at the Gunner's Arms the morning after we arrived and asked the landlord's advice. He told me that there was no practising doctor nearer than Torrington, but that if I wanted anyone in a hurry he had no doubt that Dr. Manning would come at once. That very night my uncle had one of his worst heart attacks. The only other person in the house was an old Frenchwoman we had brought with us from London. I sent her to the barge with a note, and Dr. Manning got up, dressed, and came along immediately." She laughed again, even more bitterly than before. "I remember thinking at the time how extraordinarily kind it was of him."

"Yes," I said. "He's very obliging in cases of that sort."

"When I look back now," she went on, "it seems a sort of crowning irony that I should have asked him to the house myself. Not that it really made the least difference."

"He knew, of course?" I interrupted. "I suppose he had found out while he was on the island?"

She nodded. "Your uncle had been delirious for two days, and he had evidently betrayed himself a dozen times over. I think what he said must have been all very broken and confused, but it had been enough for Dr. Manning. He had guessed that the stones were hidden there, and he had made up his mind to get hold of them."

"Had he any idea that Señor de Roda was in the same line of business?" I asked.

"He suspected it certainly," she replied. "Your uncle must have mentioned the name, and no doubt he had put two and two together. He was only waiting his time. If I hadn't sent for him that night he would probably have come to see us next day."

"But what was his object?" I demanded. "From what I've seen of him I should have thought his one idea would have been to get in first and cut you out."

"So it was," she said. "Thanks chiefly to you, however, he was up against a blank wall. He had had no chance of searching the place properly while he was there, because Bascomb was always watching him, and when you refused to sell the island that finished everything."

"It certainly came very near to finishing me," I observed grimly. "I suppose there's no doubt that it was either he or Craill who shoved me into the dock."

"It was Craill," she observed. "He is only half-witted, but he's horribly cunning and dangerous, and absolutely under Manning's influence."

"A jolly sort of pair to have as next-door neighbours," I remarked. "And what was the doctor's actual proposition? He must have been counting on some pretty effectual help from you if he was ready to go shares."

"I think he had an idea that we knew where the stones were," she replied. "When he discovered he was wrong it was too late for him to draw back. Besides, he had no wish to then. He saw that he could do just as he pleased with Uncle Philip, and—and—" She hesitated as if half unwilling to go on.

"You needn't explain, Christine," I said. "I've seen something of what you've had to put up with."

"Oh, it was horrible," she whispered, "but what could I do? My uncle seemed to have no will of his own left. He believed everything that Manning told him, and in a few days he hated you quite as bitterly as he had ever hated Gardiner. I felt sure they intended to kill you, and the only way in which I could be of any help was by trying to keep on friendly terms with both of them. Even as it was, Manning never trusted me altogether."

"What are their present plans, as far as you know?" I asked.

"Unless I am wrong," she said slowly, "they mean to attack the house at once, while you and Bascomb are alone here. I believe that on the night Manning stayed with you he found out, or thinks he found out, exactly where the diamonds are hidden. He came to see us the next day, and I could tell from his manner that he was extraordinarily pleased and excited about something. After a long talk Uncle Philip went away to Harwich the same evening. He told me he would probably send me a wire, and that if he did I was to take it over to Dr. Manning at once. It arrived about twelve o'clock this morning."

"What on earth took your uncle to Harwich?" I enquired curiously.

"I don't know for certain. I think, from one or two things I overheard, that he wanted to buy a boat. The telegram was probably to say that he had got it."

"That looks like business, anyhow," I remarked. "I suppose that if they find the stones they mean to make a straight line for the Continent." I paused. "When do you think I can expect the honour of a visit?" I asked. "To-night?"

"It will be very soon, anyhow," she answered. "I believe they are only waiting until my uncle comes back. Unless everything had been arranged, Manning would never have behaved as he did this afternoon.

"He wouldn't have poisoned Satan either," I added. "It would have been a mad thing to do if he wasn't prepared to follow it up at once." I rose from my chair and took two or three paces up and down the room. Then I halted just in front of her. "Christine," I said desperately, "there's only one way out of this infernal mess. Stay with me, and let them do just what they like. I am expecting Bobby Dean here to-morrow, and he and Bascomb can take charge of the place while we go up to London and get married. After that I don't care a damn what happens. De Roda can have all the diamonds in the world as far as I'm concerned."

Her lips moved, but before she could speak I went down on my knees and put my arms round her.

"I love you, darling," I whispered. "I have loved you with all my heart and soul ever since you came on board the *Neptune*. There isn't——"

"Ah, no, no," she interrupted. "Don't—please! You make it so much harder." Then with a little heart-broken sob she suddenly pressed her face against mine, and I felt both our cheeks wet with her tears.

"Why not, Christine?" I pleaded. "You have done everything you can."

"It's my uncle," she said pitifully. "He has no one in the world except me."

"But you can't go back after what has happened to-day?" I exclaimed. "Even if Manning believes that my coming to the barge was pure chance, he knows that I took you away in my boat, and he's simply bound to suspect you. He is sure to tell your uncle, and with a madman like de Roda——"

"I am not afraid," she broke in. "However mad Uncle Philip is, he would never hurt me. Oh, my dear, I would stay if I could, I would stay with you so gladly, but when I think of all he has suffered, how can I leave him now just when he needs me most?"

"You think of everyone except yourself," I cried hotly. "I wish to God I'd killed Manning on the barge. To feel that you may be alone in the house with that devil——"

She placed her hand softly on my shoulder. "I shall be quite safe," she said. "Most likely Uncle Philip will come back this evening, and in any case there is always Marie. She is kind to me in her way. If I couldn't leave the house I am sure she would take a note for me to Jimmy, so you see there's really no need for you to be anxious or worried on my account. It's you who are in such dreadful danger."

"What, with Bascomb here and Bobby Dean turning up in the morning?" I exclaimed. "Why, if I can't take care of my own skin with the help of a prize-fighter and a V.C.—" I stopped short, as a sudden difficulty occurred to me. "How about Bobby?" I added. "So far I haven't even mentioned your name to him. He is under the impression that the whole affair is a little private speculation of Dr. Manning's."

"You will have to tell him the truth," she said "It's too late to keep anything back." She glanced up at the clock above the fireplace; then, bending forward, she took my face between her hands, and looked long and tenderly into my eyes. "I must go, dear," she whispered; "you must take me back to Pen Mill and put me ashore. I daren't stay any longer, in case my uncle comes back unexpectedly."

Every instinct I possessed rose up in revolt, but, all the same, I saw that any further protest would be useless. For a moment I knelt there, holding her in my arms, and studying every curve of her beautiful face. Then, hungry with love, I crushed her still closer to my heart, and once again our lips met in a long, passionate kiss.

CHAPTER FOURTEEN

It was in a far from enviable state of mind that I pulled back alone across the estuary after parting with Christine at Pen Mill.

By her own wish I had landed her at the extreme point of the jetty, where, with a whispered farewell, she had climbed ashore and disappeared silently into the mist, leaving me the prey of all sorts of conflicting emotions.

My chief feeling was one of anger with myself for not having prevented her from carrying out her reckless determination. How I could have done so it was difficult to see, but if there was any comfort to be drawn from that fact I certainly failed to discover it. Once more she was beyond the reach of my help, and, in spite of all her efforts to make light of the danger, I knew that the horrible misgivings which assailed my heart were only too well grounded.

Locking up the dinghy in its shed, I made my way back through the shrubbery and let myself into the house. A good fire was still burning away brightly on the hearth, and our teacups and plates were scattered about the table just as we had left them. I thought of ringing for Bascomb and telling him to clear away, but a sudden disinclination to see anyone checked my purpose. I walked across to the fireplace, and, thrusting an empty pipe between my teeth, dropped down again into my customary chair.

There I sat, thinking over Christine's story. She had told it so simply and naturally that even at the time I had felt a curious absence of surprise. Strange as the truth was, it had, too, only confirmed my own belief that somewhere far back in Mr. Richard Jannaway's chequered past lay the real source of all my present troubles. And yet, judged by any conceivable standard of the quiet English countryside about us, what an amazing tale it was! That bloody massacre in the sunlit streets of Rio, the long untiring search for vengeance, the death of my uncle at the very moment when an implacable fate was closing in about him—it all seemed more like the plot of some fantastic drama than a real sequence of actual events in which I was intimately and urgently concerned.

For de Roda himself I felt nothing but the most profound pity. I knew something of South American prisons, and I could well imagine the horrors of that six years' purgatory. To have come through it alive, and then at the last hour to have been cheated out of his revenge, was, in my eyes at least, quite sufficient to excuse the slight trace of homicidal mania with which he appeared to be afflicted.

It was no doubt chiefly due to the diabolical prompting of Manning that he had begun to confuse me with the original object of his hatred. The more I learned about things the more I became convinced that under the easy manner and smiling face of my next-door neighbour there lurked one of the cleverest and most ruthless criminal brains that was ever destined for a medical museum. His popularity in the district, and the entire absence of suspicion with which everyone seemed to regard him, only served to strengthen my belief. I wondered much what his past history had really been, and whether Inspector Campbell's researches would have any practical result. There had been an air of quiet assurance about that stolid Scotsman which had inspired me with considerable hope, and as the memory of his determined chin and his shrewd grey eyes rose up in my mind, I suddenly realised that the time had come when I should be well advised to take him fully into my confidence. After all, de Roda had committed no crime against the laws of England. If we could get him out of Manning's clutches he might yet be made to realise that instead of seeking to rob him I was only too anxious to lend him a helping hand. Of course he could not be allowed to walk off with the diamonds, much as I sympathised with his view on the subject. Still, if what Christine had told me were correct, the present Brazilian Government would doubtless be prepared to fork out a handsome reward for their recovery, and that would at least provide some compensation for all the shabby tricks that fate had played him.

For my part, I wanted nothing in the world except Christine. Some men are so constituted that they are able to fall in love half a dozen times, while with others every emotional capacity seems to store itself up for one supreme experience. It had been so in my own case. Until then the remarkable state of ecstasy, in which at various times I had seen several of my friends engulfed, had always struck me as being a little difficult to account for. I was no longer troubled by this apparent problem. My heart thrilled with a strange, inexpressible happiness, which not even my anxiety for Christine's safety was able to destroy. Everything which had been missing in life seemed suddenly to have come to me, and, almost forgetting the danger in which we still stood, I allowed my fancies to drift out into that golden future where lovers have wandered from the very dawn of time.

How long I lay there day-dreaming I really cannot say. I know that I was brought back to earth by the fall of a burned-out log, and, looking up at the clock, I saw to my surprise that the time was close on a quarter to seven. It struck me as curious that Bascomb had not yet been in to clear away the tea things, for such an oversight was altogether contrary to his usual methodical habits. Wondering what he was doing, I roused myself out of my chair and crossed the hall to the baize door. I called his name twice, and then, as he failed to answer, I walked along the passage as far as the kitchen. There was no sign of him there, nor did my investigations in the scullery and pantry produce any better result.

With a vague feeling of uneasiness I made my way to the back entrance, which I found unlocked, and stepped out into the garden.

"Bascomb!" I shouted. "Bascomb!"

Once more a complete silence was my only reply.

Puzzled, and not a little upset, I stood peering out into the fog, which still shrouded everything in impenetrable gloom. Unless he had gone down to the boathouse I could not imagine where on earth he had got to, for if he were anywhere close at hand he must certainly have heard me calling. It was so unlike him, however, to disappear in this fashion, just when he ought to have been preparing dinner, that all my former doubts as to whether he was quite in his right senses came back to me with renewed vigour.

Having pondered over the situation for a few moments, I decided that the best thing to do was to go out at once and have a look for him. It was not a particularly inviting prospect, but, on the other hand, the evening was closing in rapidly, and it would soon be too dark to see one's way about. So, stepping back into the house, I picked up a cap from the hall table, and then, after carefully closing and locking the back door, I once more climbed over the railings, and started off to grope my way along the shrubbery path.

By the time I reached the small iron gate which lead out on to the foreshore I was beginning to feel uncommonly anxious. I passed through this, letting it clang noisily behind me, and before I had taken another half dozen paces the low roof of the boathouse suddenly loomed into view.

The first thing that caught my attention was the door. Instead of being shut, as I had left it, it was now wide open, and, naturally concluding that Bascomb must be inside, I walked towards it with a considerable feeling of relief.

A moment later I was standing on the threshold staring blankly in front of me. The place was as empty as a barn. Not only was there no trace of Bascomb, but in addition to that the dinghy itself was also missing.

I don't know why it had not occurred to me till then that he might have gone ashore, but somehow or other the discovery took me utterly by surprise. During the whole time that I had been on the island he had never yet left me alone without first coming to ask my permission, and I suppose I had begun to regard this as a kind of inevitable rite. At least I can think of no other way to account for the sensation of aggrieved astonishment with which I remained there gazing round the deserted shed.

Being eventually struck by the futility of my proceedings, I came out on to the landing-stage, and stepped forward to the very edge of the water. In all directions a solid blanket of grey mist stretched before my eyes, while, except for the sound of my own footsteps, everything was as silent as the grave.

That Bascomb should have deserted me in this extraordinary fashion was a thing which even now I found it hard to believe. There was only one conclusion to be drawn from the evidence, however, and that was that as soon as he had heard me return he had slipped away quietly with the extra key of the boathouse and had gone off alone in the dinghy. Why he should have chosen my dinner-time for his excursion was a mystery, but, queer as he might be, I felt convinced that he must have had some very definite purpose at the back of his mind.

I tried to put myself in his place, and all of a sudden a startling but far from impossible idea suggested itself. Supposing he had gone to the barge! Supposing that, in his mad fury at the death of Satan, he had set off single-handed to try to wreak his vengeance upon Manning and Craill!

Straining my eyes, I stared vainly through the mist in the direction he would have taken. If I were right there was no saying what cheerful work might even now be in full swing, for I knew enough of all the three principal actors to be quite certain that none of them would stick at trifles, and yet, without a boat, I was powerless to interfere. Until Bascomb returned or somebody else came over from Pen Mill I was as much a prisoner as Napoleon on St. Helena.

At the very moment when this unpleasant truth was forcing itself into my mind the almost uncanny stillness was broken by a low whistle. I turned round sharply, and then six times in quick succession the same sound repeated itself from somewhere close about me. It was the call of a whimbrel—that queer, mournful note which, according to every fisherman along the east coast, is the sure herald of death or disaster.

For a sailor I don't think I am particularly superstitious. All the same, there was something so weird and ominous in that unexpected cry that just for an instant I felt as if a cold hand had suddenly been placed against my heart. Then, by a big effort, I managed to pull myself together. With a kind of impatient anger at my own idiocy I stepped down off the landing-stage, and, walking back to the boathouse, had another look at the interior.

There was nothing further to be learned there. Bascomb and the dinghy had both vanished beyond a doubt, and the only thing I could do was to await their return with such philosophy as I had at my command. After all, it was just possible that he had crossed over to Pen Mill. In view of his somewhat distracting day, he might have overlooked the fact that we were short of food, and have hurried off to remedy the deficiency at the last possible moment. I can't say I had very much faith in this conjecture, but it did at least provide me with a gleam of hope. Anyhow, having once more closed the door, I abandoned the shed to its own desolation, and set off in a shade better spirits on my return journey to the house.

The first thing I did on getting back into the hall was to go to the sideboard and mix myself a drink. I have always found that I can bear suspense better with the aid of a good stiff whisky and soda—a peculiarity which I share with Bobby Dean and most of my naval acquaintances. Carrying the tumbler to the hearth, I placed it within convenient reach upon a neighbouring table, and then, having thrown another log upon the fire, I sat down deliberately to wait upon events.

For the best part of an hour I maintained my solitary vigil, the only interruption being the chiming of the clock, which hammered out every quarter with what sounded to me like a kind of malicious amusement. I bore it doggedly until close on half-past eight, by which time I had begun to feel so devilish empty that my stock of patience was rapidly exhausting itself. It was long past my usual dinner hour, and the experiences I had been through that afternoon were scarcely the sort to blunt the edge of a naturally healthy appetite.

A tour of inspection to the larder resulted in the discovery of half a cold chicken which had apparently been left over from my last meal. In addition to this I also succeeded in routing out a stale loaf and a promising-looking Cheddar cheese. Though not quite up to my usual standard, it was a good enough banquet for a really hungry man, so without bothering about a table-cloth or any other superfluous details, I carried the whole lot back to the hall, and settled down to repair my wasted energies.

By the time I had finished nine o'clock had already struck. Except for the flickering gleam of the fire I should long ago have been in complete darkness, and, feeling that a little extra illumination would not be amiss, I got up to light the lamp. Before doing so, however, I took the precaution of closing the shutters. In the absence of Satan anyone could steal up to the verandah without being detected, and it would be a sideways sort of ending to be shot through the window just when my affairs seemed to be approaching a really interesting climax.

Having guarded against the possibility of this disaster, I proceeded to make myself comfortable for the evening. Tired as I was, I had no intention of going to bed as long as there was any reasonable chance of Bascomb's return. Even if I did so, I should certainly be unable to sleep, and I should probably have the additional joy of being hauled out in the middle of the night in order to unbolt the door and let him into the house.

So, providing myself with one of Uncle Richard's biggest cigars, I refilled my glass again, and wheeled the sofa round in front of the fire. Then, taking Manning's revolver out of my pocket, I laid it carefully on the table beside my tumbler. Although its original owner might still be too indisposed to threaten any immediate danger, there were always Craill and de Roda to be considered. Either of them might take it into his head to pay me a surprise call, and, mentally afflicted as I believed them both to be, they were the sort of visitors for whom it was just as well to be fully prepared.

The warmth and stillness of the room soon began to affect me with such a pleasant sense of drowsiness that I found some difficulty in keeping myself awake. In order to assist in the process, I started going over again in my own mind the whole tangled skein of events which had led up to the present crisis. It was an interesting exercise, and, apart from that, it served a double purpose. I was determined to make a clean breast of everything to Bobby the next morning, and, if his advice was to be of any value, it was highly essential that the version I gave him should be an absolutely correct and unprejudiced one.

Ten, eleven, and twelve all struck in turn, but outside the house the silence of the night remained unbroken by the faintest sound or movement. Towards one o'clock my desire for sleep became positively overwhelming. By this time any hope I had ever had of Bascomb's putting in an appearance had practically ceased to exist, and it seemed worse than useless to tire myself out to no purpose just when I might need every ounce of energy and intelligence that I could possibly rake together.

I debated for a moment as to whether I should go upstairs and get into bed. The prospect had its attractions, but, on the other hand, I felt extremely comfortable where I was, and from a strategic point of view the position could hardly be improved upon. As long as I remained in the hall no one could break into the house without waking me. If I were fast asleep upstairs in my bedroom the odds would be altogether in favour of the visitor, and since the safety of my throat appeared to be the stake at issue, this consideration was quite enough to turn the scale.

By an heroic effort I roused myself sufficiently to make a final inspection of the back premises, in order to be quite certain that all the window fastenings were properly hasped. Satisfied on this point I returned to my couch, and, taking off my collar and tie (the only form of undressing that I attempted), I dropped back on to the cushions with a little grunt of contentment. I just remember seeing the gleam of the lamp reflected on Manning's revolver, and then, as far as I was concerned, that weapon and all the remaining troubles of life were suddenly and completely blotted out of existence.

When I woke up again it was to find myself in semi-darkness. The lamp had gone out, and the only light there was filtered in dimly through the cracks in the shutters. Everything looked very cold and depressing and for a minute or two I lay there staring vaguely round the room, and wondering how long I had been asleep.

At last, with considerable reluctance, I sat up and pulled out my watch.

I expected the time to be between six and seven, but to my utter amazement the hands, which were just visible pointed distinctly to a quarter past ten. I thought at first that the damned thing must have stopped, but on putting it to my ear I found that it was ticking away merrily.

Thoroughly roused now, I scrambled to my feet, and, crossing to the window, unbolted one of the shutters. As I threw it back a flood of daylight poured into the room, and an instinctive glance up at the clock merely helped to confirm the previous verdict.

Under the circumstances the fact that I had managed to oversleep myself was not without its comic side. It was the sort of thing that would tickle Bobby immensely, but, as far as I was concerned, there were too many other pressing considerations to give my own sense of humour a sporting chance.

Opening the window, I stepped out on to the verandah. Though still leaving a good deal to be desired, the weather had actually improved during the night. In place of the fog there was now only a thin drifting mist, which barely obscured the opposite trees. One or two birds were chirping away in the shrubbery, while overhead a lemon-coloured, watery-looking sun was striving bravely to make its belated appearance.

Slightly cheered by these discoveries, I walked back into the hall. Unless things were very much worse out at sea there was nothing to prevent Bobby from running down the coast in his motor-launch. It would be necessary for him to go a bit carefully, of course. Even under such conditions, however, the passage was a comparatively short one, and, provided he had been able to get away in good time, any moment might bring him to the island.

Knowing Robert, it seemed to me that the sooner I fixed up something in the way of breakfast the better. He would probably have contented himself with a cup of coffee before starting, and I could hardly expect him to listen intelligently to a long story until he had backed it up with a little solid nourishment.

As a first step towards this desired end I set about lighting the fire. It proved an evasive job, but, having at last persuaded it to burn, I opened the remainder of the shutters and carted away the debris of my previous night's feast. Leaving this on the kitchen table, I prowled off once more to the larder, where I had noticed a basin of eggs during my former investigations.

Heaven knew how long they had been there, but it was no time for indulging in any false delicacy. I brought them into the hall, together with a pot of marmalade and what was left of the bread and butter, and then, after laying the table and putting on a kettle to boil, I began to think with some favour of a well-earned wash and shave.

I had actually reached the foot of the staircase when a sound from outside pulled me up short. It was the unmistakable clang of the garden gate, and, hurrying towards the verandah, I saw to my delight a sturdy figure in naval uniform advancing across the grass.

With a joyous shout I flung back the window and stepped forward to meet him.

"This is splendid, Bobby," I said. "You're just in time for breakfast."

He came up to me, grinning cheerfully, and wrung my hand in a double-fisted grip.

"I'm glad to hear it, my lad," he said, "and I'm still more glad to see you looking so devilish well. After your alarming note I expected to find nothing but a nasty mess on the carpet."

"You were always an optimist," I remarked. "Come along inside and make yourself useful. You can attend to the tea while I run upstairs and have a wash and shave."

He followed me over the threshold, and, tossing his cap on to the sofa, established himself in a comfortable position in front of the fire.

"Where's that sunny-faced butler of yours?" he enquired. "Doesn't he like early rising?"

"For the time being," I replied, "Bascomb is off the map. You shall hear everything if you'll wait a minute, but it's a long yarn, and I don't want to start telling you in bits and pieces."

"Right you are," he drawled. "You bung along off and wash your face. I'll look after the kettle and answer the front door."

Leaving him in the act of lighting a cigarette, I retired upstairs to the bathroom, where with the aid of a cold swill and a hasty shave I managed to make myself a little more presentable.

I got back to the hall just in time to catch Bobby emerging through the baize door with a saucepan in his hand.

"You must excuse the liberty," he remarked, "but I couldn't find anything to boil the eggs in."

"I am afraid we are a trifle disorganized," I confessed. "The fact is we have had a lot of trouble in the family in the last twenty-four hours." I paused. "By the way," I added, "what have you done with your crew? I suppose you didn't come down here single handed?"

"I brought one chap with me," was the reply. "I left him on board down at the landing-stage. He's all right. He'll sit there on his little behind until further orders."

I took the saucepan away from him and motioned him towards a chair.

"That's your programme also, old dear," I said. "I'll finish getting the breakfast ready, and I'll talk to you at the same time. You freeze yourself into that pew and listen to me as you never listened to anyone in your life."

There must have been something in my manner which showed that I was in dead earnest, for without another word Bobby seated himself at the table.

I put the saucepan on the fire and stood up facing him.

"It pains me to confess it, Robert," I said, "but the last time you were here I'm afraid I wasn't quite straight with you."

"I had an idea you were keeping something up your sleeve," he replied. "It takes a lot of practice to make a really convincing liar."

I nodded a little sadly. "Yes," I said, "honesty was always a handicap of mine—especially in the Service."

A sudden hiss from the kettle attracted my attention, and, stepping forward, I picked up the teapot.

"You're going to hear the real truth now, Bobby," I added, "and don't you dare to open your mouth again until I've got it off my chest."

Long and complicated as my story was, the whole thing had burned itself into my mind so vividly that I was in no danger of forgetting the smallest detail. I enjoyed, too, the additional advantage of having rehearsed it the previous night, and when once I started I found myself going ahead with amazing fluency. Without attempting to skip anything, I told him exactly what had occurred from the fateful moment when Christine and her uncle had arrived on board the *Neptune* in Manaos Harbour. He already knew, of course, about my interview with Mr. Drayton and my adventure in the dock, but all the rest of it was, so to speak, fresh ground, and I did not think there was much chance of his finding my narrative either tedious or redundant.

To say that this confidence was justified would be putting it at its mildest. Munching his food and sipping his tea, he followed every word with an expression of absorbed interest that never varied from start to finish. Once or twice he interrupted me to ask a question, but otherwise he sat there in profound silence, his blue eyes fixed steadily on mine.

Bit by bit I proceeded to unravel the whole tangled skein of my adventures, until I at last reached the point when the clang of the garden gate had announced his own arrival upon the scene.

"I don't want to appear emotional," I concluded, "but I must admit the sight of your ugly mug filled me with the most inexpressible joy." I paused to moisten my lips, which were as dry as parchment. "That's as far as we've got up to the present, Robert," I added, "and now for heaven's sake let's have a drink."

"Well, the first thing's easy," remarked Bobby, as he accepted the tumbler which I offered him. "Here's to Christine, and if she's half as nice as she sounds you're the luckiest beggar that ever trod this planet."

We drained the toast in silence, and then, putting down his glass, he hoisted himself out of his chair and walked across to the window.

"That's that," he observed grimly, "and——"

I saw him pull up with curious abruptness, and stand there perfectly still staring out into the garden.

"What's the matter?" I demanded.

He looked back over his shoulder with a queer smile on his lips.

"I don't know if you're expecting any visitors," he began.

Before he could conclude his sentence I was standing alongside of him.

Crossing the lawn and coming directly towards the house were two figures. One was an enormously stout, broad-shouldered man, whom I recognised immediately as the landlord of the Gunner's Arms; the other was a police sergeant in uniform.

Bobby was the first to break the silence. "We seem to have finished the story just in time," he said drily.

Without making any reply, I unlatched the window and threw it open.

The two men came up to the verandah side by side and halted exactly in front of us.

For a moment nobody spoke; then the landlord, who was breathing heavily, stepped forward and touched his cap.

"Beg pardon, Mr. Dryden," he said huskily, "but this is Sergeant 'Umphries of Torrington. He wants to have a word with you."

"Why, certainly," I replied. "Come inside, both of you."

I moved back, and, mounting the verandah, they tramped in heavily over the threshold.

"I expect you know Commander Dean," I added, "at all events by sight."

There was an exchange of salutes, followed once more by an embarrassing silence.

"Well," I said encouragingly, "what is it? Anything I can do for you?"

Sergeant Humphries cleared his throat

"I'm afraid I come on rather an unpleasant business, Mr. Dryden," he began. "I believe you have a man in your employment name of John Bascombe?"

A sudden feeling of impending tragedy tightened round my heart.

"That's right," I said. "He has been with me ever since I came here."

"Do you happen to know where he is now?"

I shook my head. "He went ashore last night without my permission, and so far he hasn't returned."

There was another pause.

"He won't return," said the Sergeant, "and if you want to know the reason why I can tell you, Mr. Dryden. At the present moment he's lying dead in the stable at the Gunner's Arms."

CHAPTER FIFTEEN

Although I was half prepared for what he said, the announcement left me momentarily dumb.

"Dead!" I repeated at last. "Bascomb dead! How in God's name was he killed?"

The Sergeant looked at me with a certain sympathy in his stolid features.

"We reckon he must have run into the jetty in the fog last night, and upset his boat. As like as not he stunned himself at the same time; anyhow, he was found lying on the mud this morning with a gash in his head that you could shove a couple of fingers into."

"We got the dinghy all right," put in the landlord. "It was floatin' about the estuary bottom upwards."

I caught Bobby's eyes fixed upon my face, and I knew that the same thought was in both our minds.

"This is pretty bad news, Sergeant," I said. "What do you think I ought to do?"

The man rubbed his chin thoughtfully. "Well, sir, I take it the first thing's for you to come ashore with us and identify the body. There'll have to be an inquest, of course, but seein' as the Coroner's away at Ipswich I don't suppose it will be until the day after to-morrow." He paused. "Per'aps you know where the poor fellow belonged, mister? If so we shall have to write and tell his relatives."

I shook my head. "I haven't the slightest notion," I said. "He had been with my uncle for some time, and I re-engaged him on the lawyer's recommendation. He wasn't the sort of man to talk about his own affairs."

"That's a fact," added the landlord emphatically. "If ever there was a bloke who kept his mouth shut——"

"It ain't of no real consequence," interrupted the Sergeant with some dignity. "The police can always find out what they want sooner or later." He turned to me. "If it's convenient to you, mister, I reckon we'd better get across at once. The doctor's examinin' the corpse, and mebbe 'e'd like to have a talk with you."

"The doctor?" I repeated. "What doctor?"

"Doctor 'Ayward of Torrington," was the answer. "He came over in the car with me as soon as we got the message."

I remained silent for a moment, thinking rapidly.

"Very well, Sergeant," I said. "I will be ready almost at once. I must have a word with Commander Dean first; we are just settling up some rather important business." I crossed to the sideboard and fetched a couple of glasses. "Help yourselves to a whisky," I added. "I shan't keep you more than two or three minutes."

They both murmured their thanks, and, motioning Bobby to follow me, I walked into the dining-room and closed the door behind me.

I couldn't have controlled myself much longer.

"The devils!" I said hoarsely. "The infernal devils! They've murdered him, just as they murdered Satan."

Bobby laid his hand on my shoulder. "It's a rotten business, but we mustn't lose our heads, Jack. We've got to decide what we're going to do."

"I feel as if it were all my fault," I muttered. "I ought to have killed Manning yesterday when I had the chance."

"What the hell would have been the good of that?" demanded Bobby impatiently. He thrust his hands into his pockets and took a couple of rapid turns up and down the room. "Look here, old son," he went on quietly. "We haven't any time to spare, so the sooner we fix things up the better. In the first place, what are you going to tell the police?"

"Nothing," I said curtly. "There's only one other person in this beside ourselves, and that's Inspector Campbell. I shall go up to London as soon as I can and put the whole thing in front of him."

He nodded his approval. "Just what I was about to propose. There'll be the very devil to pay if these local people get hold of the faintest idea of the truth." He paused. "You must lie to them for all you're worth," he added. "You must make them believe that no suspicion of foul play has ever entered your head. I'll stop here and look after the place until you get back."

"You're sure you can manage it?" I asked.

"Easily," was the comforting rejoinder. "There's next to nothing doing in our line at present. I must run over to Martlesea some time to-morrow; otherwise I'm at your disposal for the next three days."

Considerably cheered by this assurance, I led the way back into the hall where I found our two visitors in the act of wiping their moustaches.

"Very good whisky that, sir," observed the landlord approvingly. "'Tain't often you get a taste of the pre-war stuff nowadays."

"Well, I'm ready if you are, gentlemen," I said.

With a regretful glance at the decanter the Sergeant picked up his helmet, and, leaving Bobby standing in the window, we all three set out across the lawn.

We found the motor-launch lying about twenty yards out in the estuary, and a dilapidated dinghy tied up alongside the landing-stage.

"I had to bring one of me own boats," explained the landlord as he unfastened the painter. "We got yours all right, sir, same as I told you; but the rudder's broke and two of her planks stove in."

"She must have been smashed up pretty badly," I remarked. "It seems to me as if she'd been run down."

"I should have said the same," put in the Sergeant, "but accordin' to what they told me at Pen Mill there wasn't a craft afloat yesterday. That's so, ain't it, Mr. Robinson?"

The landlord nodded. "None of our folks was out, at all events," he observed. "Might 'a' bin a stranger goin' up to the lock, but it don't seem likely—not in a fog like that."

"Well, we can find out, I suppose," I said, taking my place in the boat. "The point is sure to be raised at the inquest, anyhow."

We sculled rapidly across to the opposite shore, and disembarked on the jetty, close in front of the inn. It was easy to see that something unusual had happened, for the whole population of the village had apparently collected on the hard, and were hanging about in small groups eagerly watching our arrival.

Through a fire of curious glances we marched up to the stable, outside which a solemn-looking constable was standing on guard.

Lifting the latch, the Sergeant opened the door just wide enough for us to enter; and then, following on our heels, closed it carefully behind him.

We found ourselves in a large, dimly lit coach-house, which had evidently been emptied for its present tragic purpose.

Stretched out on a bundle of straw was the dead body of Bascomb, and stooping over it a tall, grey-haired man who bore the unmistakable stamp of a country doctor.

In a businesslike fashion the Sergeant stepped forward.

"Well, here we are, doctor," he said. "This is the gentleman I was speaking about. Mr. Dryden—Dr. 'Ayward."

The doctor straightened himself, and, having surveyed me for a moment through a pair of gold-rimmed spectacles, came up to where I was standing.

"I am pleased to meet you, sir," he said. "I only wish it was under less distressing circumstances."

We shook hands.

"It's a very sudden and shocking business," I said. "Bascomb was the sort of man who ought to have lived to be a hundred." I paused. "Have you any idea how it happened?" I asked.

Dr. Hayward pursed up his lips and looked at me a little queerly.

"I am quite certain of one thing at least," he answered, "and that is that the poor fellow didn't meet his death by drowning. He was dead before he ever reached the water."

There was a brief silence.

"Then the idea about his having run into the jetty—" I began.

The doctor shook his head. "He was killed by a violent blow on the back of the skull. If you think you can stand a rather unpleasant sight, I'll show you the actual injury."

I contented myself with a nod, and, moving forward, followed him across the stone floor.

Bascomb's body was lying on the straw, face downwards. It had been stripped to the waist, and in the grey light which filtered in through the glass roof the enormous muscular development of his back and shoulders was plainly visible.

My companion took out an electric torch from his pocket, and, bending down, switched on the current.

"See that?" he enquired briefly.

Hardened as I was by my experiences in the war, I was unable to repress a shudder of horror. Right in the middle of the close-cropped hair the bone had been smashed in like the top of an eggshell.

"Not much doubt about the cause of death—eh?" The doctor switched off his torch, and stood up facing me. "One doesn't do that sort of thing without a little assistance," he added grimly. "He may have been struck by the prow of a boat or the screw of a steamer; the only other explanation I can offer is that he was deliberately murdered."

"Murdered!" The Sergeant strode forward, and then, suddenly pulling up, stared incredulously from one to the other of us.

"We must at least consider the possibility," I remarked.

The Sergeant rubbed his chin in the same thoughtful fashion as before.

"It's a startlin' notion," he observed at last. "There's never been a murder in Pen Mill yet—at least not in my time."

"I don't say there has now," interrupted the doctor, with a slight touch of impatience. "It all depends upon whether any vessel went up the estuary last night in the fog."

"We can find that out easy enough," chimed in the landlord. "Only a matter of enquiries at the lock. She couldn't 'ave got no farther—not till this mornin'."

The Sergeant looked at him with a certain severity. "I know my business, thank ye, Mr. Robinson. When I want any help I'll ask you for it." He turned to me. "What's your opinion, sir? Any party in your knowledge as had a grudge against the deceased?"

I shook my head. "I am absolutely ignorant about his private affairs," I answered. "As I told you before, he was one of the most reserved men who ever lived. For all I know he might have been at daggers drawn with the entire neighbourhood."

"Was he violent tempered or quarrelsome?" asked the doctor.

"I never saw any sign of it," I replied. "We were alone together for a month, and I couldn't have wished for a better servant."

"I reckon our first idea was the right one," announced the Sergeant. "It must have been some craft coming up in the fog that did it. The odds are they thought it was an empty boat they had run down, and, seeing as they'd be liable for damages, they made up their minds to say nothing about it." He took out his note-book and sucked the stump of a pencil. "What time was it when the deceased left the island?" he enquired.

"I couldn't say exactly," I replied. "It was probably between five and six."

"Just about high tide," he observed, in a satisfied voice. "That more or less settles it to my way of thinking."

He asked me one or two other questions, to all of which he noted down the answers; then, with the air of a man who has efficiently discharged a difficult duty, he snapped together his book and replaced it in his pocket.

"I don't think we need detain you any longer, Mr. Dryden. If the Head Constable comes over he'll probably wish to speak to you, but as like as not he'll leave the case to me. I'm going along to the lock straight away now, and it's my belief that before to-night we'll have our hands on the party that's wanted."

"I shouldn't be surprised, Sergeant," I said untruthfully. "All the same, it will be a smart bit of work if you do."

The doctor, who appeared to have lost interest in our conversation, picked up a piece of sacking and spread it across Bascomb's body. I had an idea that he was very far from satisfied, and the moment we left the coach-house my suspicions were confirmed.

Drawing me slightly to one side, he glanced impatiently at the Sergeant, who was engaged in giving some instructions to his subordinate.

"The man's a fool," he said in a low voice, "but there's nothing more to be done at present. We must wait until the Head Constable comes over."

Before I could make any reply we were joined by Mr. Robinson, the landlord.

"Excuse me, sir," he began apologetically, "but if you 'appen to be wantin' a boat while that dinghy o' yours is under repair, you're welcome to the use o' the one we came across in."

"That's uncommonly good of you," I said, "and, what's more, I should like to thank you for all you've done this morning. I am very sorry you should have been put to so much trouble and inconvenience."

"There ain't nothing that calls for mention," he objected. "You and me are neighbours in a manner o' speakin', and quite apart from that, sir, I'm always ready to do me duty by a corpse."

I was still searching for a suitable rejoinder to this sentiment when I was released from my embarrassment by the Sergeant.

"I'll wish you good morning, Mr. Dryden," he remarked, coming across to where we were collected. "Don't you get upsetting yourself over this business; you leave it to me, and I'll see that it's brought home to the right quarter."

I shook hands all round, and, followed by the fascinated glances of the public, made my way down to the jetty, where I proceeded to re-embark. On the whole, in spite of Dr. Hayward's suspicions, the affair had gone off as well as I could possibly have hoped, and it was with feelings of considerable relief that I ran in alongside the landing-stage and stepped out once more on to my own territory.

I found Bobby lying in a deck chair on the verandah awaiting my return. He jumped up as I appeared and came forward across the lawn to meet me.

"Welcome home, my lad," he observed. "I was just beginning to be afraid they'd clapped you into the local dungeon."

"Anything fresh happened while I've been away?" I asked.

He shook his head. "It's been positively dull. I've spent the time sitting in the sunshine, brooding over your family affairs."

He led the way back to the verandah, and, taking the chair alongside of him, I plunged straight away into an account of my experiences at Pen Mill.

"I hope I handled the thing right, Bobby," I concluded. "The doctor was evidently inclined to think it might be a case of murder, and to have set myself up against him would have been simply asking for trouble. If he felt the least suspicious about me, he'd probably have wired bang off to the Head Constable. As it is, thanks to that fool of a Sergeant, we ought to have at least twenty-four hours' breathing space."

Bobby patted me approvingly on the back. "You displayed a surprising amount of tact," he remarked. "It looks to me as if falling in love had considerably sharpened your wits."

"I think it was falling into the dock," I retorted. "Anyhow, the question is, What are we going to do now? According to the Sergeant the inquest will probably be on Friday morning, and unless we make pretty good use of our time— —"

"We shall," interrupted Bobby. "I've been chewing the whole thing over while you were ashore, and I've come to one or two highly intelligent conclusions." He leaned across the arm of his chair, and knocked out his pipe against the side railing. "In the first place," he continued, in a rather more serious tone, "we've got to face the fact that Bascomb's death puts us into a devilish awkward position. I'm not very strong on law, but there's such a thing as being an accessory to murder. If we suspect Manning and de Roda we've no right to keep the fact from the police merely because we don't want to get your girl into trouble."

"But it was your advice," I protested. "Besides, I don't believe that de Roda had anything to do with it. I'm almost certain that Bascomb went over to the barge with some mad idea of revenging himself upon Manning. He probably found Craill there as well, and between the pair of them— —"

"Exactly my idea," broke in Bobby. "All the same, we've got to be precious careful what we do or the police will end by nabbing the whole damned lot of us."

"Well, what do you suggest?" I asked.

"I think your notion's the right one. You must cruise up to town first thing to-morrow morning and get hold of this detective Johnnie. Tell him everything, just as you have told it to me. He is evidently a long-headed sort of bird, and he'll probably see some way out of the difficulty. Even if he can't we shall have put ourselves on the right side of the fence."

"Hadn't I better go at once?" I proposed.

Bobby glanced at his watch. "You may as well wait till the morning. He would most likely have left his office by the time you got there, and it's quite on the cards you might be missing all sorts of fun down here."

"Not much chance of that," I said regretfully. "They'll give us a fairly wide berth as long as your motor-boat's lying off the jetty."

"One never can tell," observed Bobby philosophically. "If Manning has found out all he wants to, and if he and Craill really did Bascomb in, you can bet your boots they won't hang about any longer than they can possibly help."

"I wish I could guess where the diamonds are hidden," I remarked.

Bobby looked at me with that queer provoking grin of his.

"Well?" I demanded.

"You're not very good at riddles, are you, Jack?" he said slowly. "I suppose it's never occurred to you that your uncle must have had some damned good reason for putting in a new fireplace?"

"By God!" I cried, jumping up from my chair; "I believe you've hit it." I paused for a moment, as a whole stream of significant memories rushed back into my mind. "It explains everything," I almost shouted. "Bascomb told me he had workmen over from Holland to put it in, and——"

"Why the devil didn't you say so before?" interrupted Bobby. "Of course, if that's the case, it absolutely settles the matter. I was merely going on the fact that directly Manning thought you were asleep he made a bee-line for the hall."

"I'm an ass, Robert," I admitted humbly. "Manning told me so yesterday, and I'm hanged if for once in his life he wasn't speaking the truth." I glanced in through the open window in the direction of the hearth. "Have you got as far as making a search?" I asked.

He nodded. "I went over every inch of it while you were away. It's my belief they're bricked up behind one of the tiles. You don't want much space to hide a packet of diamonds in."

"Well, come along then," I exclaimed. "There's a good hefty chisel in the kitchen, and if we can't——"

"Don't be in such a hurry," drawled Bobby. "We've an uncommonly tricky course to navigate, and we can't afford to run aground."

"But where's the harm?" I objected. "It's my property. I've every right to hack it about if I want to."

"I'm not questioning your title deeds," returned Bobby languidly. "What we've got to consider is how it will look in a Court of Law. If there's any trouble we shall be more or less dependent on this detective merchant of yours to get us out of it, and that being so, I don't propose to do any treasure-hunting until he's actually on the spot."

"I suppose you're right," I said after a short pause. "I only hope Campbell will be able to come."

"Hoping's no good; unless you find him and bring him back with you to-morrow night we shall have to tell the Head Constable the whole truth. If the Coroner knows his job something's sure to come out at the inquest, and you don't want to see your girl stuck up in the dock alongside Manning and Craill."

"It's the one idea that's been haunting me all through this ghastly business," I exclaimed. "I'm not talking rot, Bobby, but I'd hand in my ticket without a kick as long as I could keep Christine out of it."

"Of course you would," he replied. "Otherwise I shouldn't be wasting my time trying to help you." He hoisted himself out of his chair and put his hand on my shoulder. "You have my blessing for what it's worth, Jack," he added. "I don't know much about girls—not what you call nice girls; all the same, I'm absolutely certain that you've struck a regular prize-packet."

Compliments were so rare in Robert's vocabulary that I appreciated his effort at its proper value. We shook hands solemnly, and then, with a little grunt of satisfaction, he reseated himself on the arm of his chair.

"Well, that's that," he observed; "all we've got to do now is to carry on till to-morrow morning. You'll trot up to town by the first train, and I'll stop here and look after the treasure."

"I don't quite know how we shall manage about the housekeeping," I said. "There's tons of liquor, but the grub's running devilish short."

"It doesn't really matter," replied Bobby cheerfully. "Drink's very sustaining, provided one has enough of it."

As things turned out, I think we should have contrived to get through the rest of the day successfully, even without the help of Uncle Richard's well-stocked cellar. Although Bobby had heard my story from start to finish, there were still so many points on which he was anxious for further enlightenment that it took me all my time to answer his innumerable questions. He cross-examined me with a dogged persistence that would have done credit to a prosecuting counsel, and in more than one instance I was extraordinarily impressed by the shrewdness and insight of his comments.

At seven o'clock we adjourned the discussion in favour of a scratch meal, which consisted chiefly of champagne and biscuits. The former being Pol Roget of a particularly good vintage, we were able to give

Bobby's nutriment theory a really convincing test. It worked out most successfully, for resuming our conversation over a couple of cigars, we talked on for the next two hours without the faintest feeling of exhaustion.

About ten Bobby glanced at his watch. "You'd better turn in now," he remarked firmly. "You've got a long day ahead of you, and the more sleep you have the better."

"Hang it all!" I protested. "I'm not going to dodge my share of the work. Somebody's got to keep awake."

"That will be all right," he interrupted. "I shall have nothing to do to-morrow after you're gone. If I want to I can sleep the whole blessed morning."

"But how about to-night?" I persisted. "Suppose Manning and Craill pay us a visit?"

Bobby smiled grimly, and, putting his hand in his hip pocket, pulled out a vicious-looking Mauser pistol.

"You'll probably hear the shooting," he replied. "You can come down in your pyjamas and help me throw out the bodies."

I saw that it would be a waste of time to argue any further, so, having made sure that he was provided with plenty of smokes and drinks, I assisted him to close the shutters and lock up the house. This done, I wished him a pleasant vigil, and, retiring upstairs to my own room, I was soon safely between the sheets, with Manning's Smith and Wesson tucked away under the pillow beneath my head.

I must have dropped off on the spot, for the next thing I remember is suddenly sitting up in bed and finding Bobby standing beside me with a cup of tea in his hand. He had drawn back the curtain, and the grey light of early day was coming in through the open window.

"Here you are, my son," he remarked cheerfully. "You shove this down your neck and tumble out at once. It's getting on for six o'clock."

"Anything happened?" I enquired. "I've been sleeping like a log."

"The champagne's finished," he announced with a grin. "There's no other news that I can think of at the moment."

I gulped down the tea, and, scrambling out of bed, proceeded to commence a hasty toilet, while Bobby, who looked very unshaven and disreputable, seated himself on the window sill and puffed contentedly at a cigarette.

"I've never spent a more peaceful night in my life," he continued. "If we can't find the diamonds you might do worse than turn the place into a rest cure. I believe you'd make a pot of money."

"It's not a bad notion," I admitted. "We could have Manning as a resident physician."

I ducked my head into a basin of water, and emerged from the process feeling considerably refreshed.

"How's the weather?" I enquired, seeing that he was looking out of the window.

"Better than it was. There's still a lot of mist hanging about the estuary, but the wind's south-east, and it will probably get up later in the day." He turned back into the room. "What time are you due in town?" he demanded.

"Just after nine," I said. "I ought to be in Fleet Street by half past."

He sat there swinging his foot and meditating while I rapidly pulled on my trousers and laced up my boots.

"It all depends whether the sleuth-hound's in his kennel," he observed. "If he is you'll be through by about ten-thirty. Send me a wire directly you've fixed up your arrangements. I want to let them know when to expect me at Martlesea."

"You couldn't put off the trip till to-morrow?" I suggested.

He shook his head. "I must look in for an hour. It doesn't matter what time though; there's always someone there till eight o'clock."

"I shall try and bring Campbell back with me by the mid-day train," I said. "Then we can have a hunt for the diamonds before you start."

"That's the idea," he replied approvingly. "With any luck it ought to be a very interesting and profitable afternoon."

He hoisted himself off the sill, and, coming up to where I was standing, helped me on with my coat.

"I'll row you ashore now," he added, "and if you'll let me know when to expect you I'll be waiting for you at Pen Mill."

"But how about the house?" I objected. "We oughtn't to leave it empty."

"I've only got to tip the word to my man Jenkins," he replied. "He'll take damned good care that nobody lands on the island."

We made our way downstairs, and, shutting the front door behind us, we set off at a brisk pace for the landing-stage.

The motor-boat, which had slewed round with the tide, was now lying with her nose towards the island, and Jenkins himself—a stalwart figure in white slops—was leaning pensively over the iron railing. As soon as he saw us he drew himself up and saluted.

We paddled alongside, where Bobby gave his instructions; and then, pulling straight across the estuary, ran in under the end of the jetty.

Except for an aged fisherman mending his nets the place was entirely deserted.

With an encouraging "Good luck" from my companion I jumped ashore. I expected any moment that the landlord would appear at his door and waylay me before I could pass the inn, but by the mercy of providence his attention must have been otherwise occupied. Anyway I reached the village green unchallenged, and a few minutes later I was half way up the hill and safely beyond the reach of any such unfortunate encounter.

It was a full hour's tramp to Torrington, even for a quick walker like myself. Bobby had timed things perfectly, however, and just as I arrived at my destination the train came steaming in alongside the platform.

I made a rapid inspection of my fellow-passengers, and, having discovered that to the best of my knowledge they were all complete strangers, I took my seat in the corner of an empty smoker. The doors banged, the guard waved his flag, and with a triumphant whistle we slid slowly forward on our fifty mile journey to London.

I don't know whether the Great Eastern is generally punctual, but on this occasion its performance was beyond criticism. The hands of the big timepiece at Liverpool Street were pointing to exactly nine o'clock as I stepped out of the carriage and, hailing a taxi, instructed the man to drive me to Angel Court. He put me down outside the entrance, and with a queer feeling of excitement at my heart I walked up the narrow passage and pressed the bell of the Inspector's office.

My ring was answered by an alert-looking youth in his shirt-sleeves.

"Mr. Campbell hasn't come yet, sir," he said, in answer to my enquiry. "I'm not expecting him till half past ten this morning."

I suppose he saw my disappointment, for he added civilly: "Was it something important you wished to see him about, sir?"

"It was important enough to get me out of bed at six o'clock this morning," I explained.

"Well, perhaps you could look in again, sir," he suggested "If you like to leave your name I'll give it to him directly he arrives. He'll be here for certain by ten-thirty."

"I'll come back in an hour then," I replied. "If he turns up before tell him that Mr. John Dryden wants to see him."

I had met with the first hitch in my programme, but as I walked back into Fleet Street I consoled myself by reflecting that things might very easily have been much worse. Even if we missed the earlier train there was another, an equally good one, at two-fifteen. This would get us to Pen Mill shortly after four, which would still give Bobby plenty of time for his trip to Martlesea.

It occurred to me that the best thing I could do while I was waiting was to lay in a stock of fresh provisions. I could hardly expect Campbell to subsist entirely upon a diet of dry biscuits and champagne, so summoning another taxi, I told the driver to take me to Fortnum and Mason's. Here I purchased a number of delicacies, including a couple of cold chickens and a fresh tongue. I gave instructions that they should be packed in a hamper and sent off to the cloak-room at Liverpool Street to await my arrival, and then, still having half an hour to spare, I strolled across to the Piccadilly Hotel and treated myself to a glass of sherry and two or three caviare sandwiches.

At ten-thirty exactly I was back once more in Angel Court with my finger on the Inspector's bell. It had scarcely rung before the door was pulled open and the burly figure of Campbell himself appeared in the passage.

"Glad to see you, Mr. Dryden," he exclaimed, giving me a hearty grip. "My clerk told me you'd be along in a minute. I'm sorry I wasn't in when you called before."

"It was my fault," I said, following him into the office. "If people will come at such unholy hours they can hardly expect to find you at home."

"We're used to early visitors in this line of business," he replied with a laugh. "Besides, you couldn't have come at a more convenient time anyhow. As a matter of fact I was just going to write to you."

He pulled forward a tattered arm-chair, and, relieving me of my coat and hat, laid them on the sofa.

"Are you busy this morning?" I asked. "Can you fix things so that we shan't be interrupted for at least a couple of hours?"

He glanced at me sharply from under his bushy eyebrows.

"I daresay I can if it's really essential. Do you mind waiting a minute while I speak to my clerk?"

He stepped out into the passage and entered the opposite room. A minute later he returned, and, having shut the door behind him, took the chair opposite mine.

"Now," he enquired genially, "what's the trouble?"

I suppose that the task of listening to the most incredible stories is just part and parcel of a detective's business. Few men had probably had more experience in this line than Campbell himself, but as I began to speak I wondered in my own mind if he had ever encountered such a strange yarn as the one which I was about to unfold.

Following the same course that I had adopted with Bobby, I once more described my first meeting with Christine and her uncle that sunny afternoon in Manaos Harbour. Then, step by step, and taking infinite pains to omit nothing which might be of the least significance, I laid bare the whole amazing train of incidents which had led up to my present visit.

As a feat of uninterrupted talking (for, unlike Bobby, Campbell made no attempt even to ask a question) it was the nearest approach to a record that I am ever likely to achieve. Long before I had finished my voice was as hoarse as a crow's, and even now I can remember the feeling of relief with which I lay back in my chair when it was all over, and gazed expectantly into the shrewd, wide-awake eyes of my apparently unwearied companion.

It was he who was the first to break the silence.

"I congratulate you on a really remarkable performance, Mr. Dryden," he observed. "I have never met anyone who would make a better witness."

"Well, if that's the case," I replied, "I hope to God my abilities will be wasted."

Campbell looked at me for a moment with a queer, half-quizzical smile; then very suddenly his expression changed to one of the utmost gravity.

"Aye," he said in his harsh North country accent, "it's a serious enough matter in all conscience. The pity is that you couldn't come to me before. It might have saved one poor fellow's life anyway."

"You believe that Bascomb was murdered then?" I answered slowly.

"I'm sure of it," was the grim reply, "and, what's more, I'm practically certain that every word which that young lady told you is the Gospel truth." He sucked in his upper lip, and sat there for a moment gnawing the end of his short stubbly moustache.

"It's curious what a fool one can be at times," he continued. "I've been looking out for those stones ever since the Brazilian Government sent round their first notice. Twenty per cent was the offer they made, and on their own original estimate that would have worked out at something like forty thousand pounds. There isn't a police officer or detective in Europe who hasn't tried his hand on the job—and to think that for the last three months I've been walking around with the blessed things right under my very nose!"

"Oh, hang the diamonds!" I exclaimed. "We've got something more important to think about than them."

"Quite so," assented Campbell drily. "All the same, you may find the subject of some interest—after we've settled with Dr. Manning."

"Have you any doubt in your own mind as to whether he killed Bascomb?" I asked.

"I should think it's more likely to have been Craill," was the answer. "There was a touch of crudeness about the affair which doesn't quite fit in with our friend's record."

I leaned forward eagerly. "You've traced him?" I exclaimed. "You've found out who he is?"

Campbell pulled open a drawer in the table beside him and took out a piece of paper.

"I've managed to dig up one or two interesting little details. I was going to send them along to you this morning if you hadn't saved me the trouble." He glanced at his memoranda. "The gentleman's right name," he continued, "is not Manning at all. It's Francis Maitland Winter. He is thirty-six years old, a graduate of Harvard University, and I should say one of the most complete scoundrels that ever infested this earth."

I looked at my companion with open admiration. "How on earth did you discover all that?" I demanded.

"It wasn't difficult. The cleverest criminal makes a slip at times, and when our friend let out to you that he had once been a ship's surgeon he was actually speaking the truth. It was an unpardonable piece of carelessness, and he has probably regretted it bitterly ever since. Of all people in the world a ship's surgeon is one of the easiest to trace. A few enquiries in the right quarter convinced me that Dr. Manning was the same person who, under the name of Francis Winter, was tried for murder some years ago in New York and triumphantly acquitted by a well-meaning but remarkably thick-headed jury."

"Whom did he murder?" I asked.

"Well, he was charged with having poisoned one of his own patients—an old gentleman who had been ill-advised enough to make a will in his favour. He seems to have carried the whole thing through with extraordinary cleverness. Anyhow, he was not only acquitted, but he actually got away from America with the money. I believed it amounted to about a hundred thousand dollars."

"He must be a greedy devil," I observed. "If I'd made a coup like that, I'm hanged if I'd risk my neck a second time."

Campbell shrugged his shoulders. "I don't suppose he's well off. According to the evidence that came out at the trial, the man's a born gambler. He's probably lost the whole of it by now."

"But what are we to do?" I exclaimed, getting up from my chair. "I'm tied hand and foot for fear of dragging in Christine and her uncle. Unless you can help us— —"

"I'll help you, Mr. Dryden, that's what I'm here for." The Inspector had risen to his feet also, and somehow or other the sight of his burly figure and the fighting gleam in his hard grey eyes sent a fresh wave of hope and confidence through my heart. "Our first job," he continued, "is to get Mr. de Roda and the young lady out of the hands of these ruffians. We must do that immediately. As soon as we've made quite certain that de Roda had nothing to do with the murder of Bascomb we can put the Yard on to Manning straight away. That will keep them busy while we're looking for the diamonds."

"I'd better go out and wire to Bobby that I'm bringing you back with me," I said. "I promised to let him know as soon as I could."

Campbell glanced at the watch which he was wearing on his wrist.

"The only trouble is that I can't leave here until after five. I've asked a man to come and see me this afternoon, and there's no possible way in which I can put him off."

I did a moment's rapid thinking. "Have you got such a thing as a time-table?" I enquired.

He handed me an A.B.C. off the mantelpiece, and, hunting up the right page, I soon found what I wanted.

"The best plan for you," I said, "will be to come straight through to Martlesea. There's a six o'clock train from Liverpool Street which gets in at seven-fifteen. I'll go back this afternoon and arrange with Bobby to pick you up at the station. Then he can bring you over to Greensea in his motor-boat."

Campbell nodded. "That will do me all right. What time shall we get in?"

"Oh, somewhere about eight-thirty," I replied "It's not more than a dozen miles, and you won't hang about on the way—not if Bobby's driving her." I picked up my hat and coat. "I'd better be clearing off now," I added. "That will give you a chance to settle up your affairs and make your will."

With a twinkle in his eyes Campbell held out his hand.

"Well, good-bye for the present," he remarked. "Don't do anything rash while your friend's away, Mr. Dryden. If you take my advice you'll just lock yourself in the house and wait there till we arrive."

He walked with me to the front door, and, leaving him standing on the steps, I made my way back down the alley into the roar and bustle of Fleet Street.

In answer to my enquiry a friendly policeman directed me to the nearest post office, where, after a brief deliberation, I sent off the following wire to Bobby:

> "Business satisfactorily arranged. Meet me Pen Mill four o'clock."

By the time I had handed this in it was already a few minutes past one, and, feeling that whatever else I had accomplished I had certainly earned a good lunch, I turned into the Cock Tavern, which was only half a dozen yards away.

Here I feasted sumptuously on roast saddle of mutton and a bottle of Burgundy—an excellent wine for anyone who is suffering from the after-effects of two hours' continuous oratory. There being no occasion for hurry, I dawdled away another pleasant half hour over a cigar, and then at a leisurely pace I walked back through the City to Liverpool Street. At five and twenty to three I was watching the panorama of East London slip by the carriage window, with Fortnum and Mason's hamper reposing safely in the opposite rack.

On reaching Torrington station I was fortunate enough to secure the same ramshackle cab which had carried me to Pen Mill two days before. Packing myself and the hamper inside, I requested the driver to repeat the performance, and at a stumbling trot we once more jogged off through the wet and narrow lanes.

Bobby had evidently received my wire, for as we descended the hill I caught sight of him strolling in solitary state up and down the hard. He came forward to meet me, and opened the door of the cab when we drew up.

"Hullo!" he exclaimed. "Where's the sleuth-hound?"

I stepped out, clasping the hamper in my arms.

"Don't worry," I said, "I've got him all right."

Bobby looked round blankly. "Well, where is he?" he demanded. "In the basket?"

"No," I explained. "That's a little addition to the larder. Campbell couldn't get away till the six o'clock train. He's coming straight through to Martlesea, and I've arranged for you to pick him up at the station."

With a satisfied nod Robert relieved me of my burden, and having paid the cabman, we started off together up the jetty.

"There's no reason why you shouldn't shove off at once," I added, "not if you're in a hurry. We can't do anything here till Campbell arrives."

"I suppose I ought to," said Bobby rather doubtfully. "All the same, I'm not over keen on leaving you alone."

He stepped down with the hamper into the dinghy, and I took my place at the tiller.

"I shan't get into any mischief," I assured him. "I shall take Campbell's tip and lock myself up in the house with a loaded revolver. He's heard the whole yarn and he quite approves of our present arrangements."

As briefly as possible I went on to describe my interview in Angel Court and the dramatic news which the Inspector had given me with regard to Manning's real identity.

"I always knew he was a bad egg," grunted Bobby, tugging away grimly at his oars. "It's uncommon lucky for you that you happened to make a hit with that girl of yours. If it hadn't been for her— —"

He left the sentence unfinished, and with a few vicious strokes ran up alongside the motor-boat, where Jenkins was awaiting our arrival.

"Well, you pop off," I said, preparing to take his seat. "I've told Campbell to look out for you on the platform, so you can't very well miss each other. I'll expect you back here about eight-thirty."

Bobby clambered on board, and, waving him farewell, I rowed on to the landing-stage, where I proceeded to disembark. I stood there until they had cast off their moorings and were heading out into the estuary; then with the hamper on my shoulder I trudged off towards the house.

The first thing I did on getting inside was to lock the front door and close up all the shutters. It was rather an undignified business—barricading oneself in one's own house in broad daylight—but, as somebody says in the Bible, "there's a time for everything," and it seemed to me that this was the right occasion for a little judicious cowardice.

Having secured my defences, my next step was to unpack the hamper. I arranged its contents in a tempting array on the empty shelves of the larder, and then, after boiling a kettle and making myself a cup of tea, I settled down on the hall sofa with a bundle of papers which I had brought down from town.

For any use they were to me, however, I might as well have left them behind. Try as I would, I was quite unable to fix my attention on what I was reading, and in a very little while I gave up the attempt in despair, and finally abandoned myself to my own thoughts.

Now that I had done everything I could I was once more beginning to feel intensely worried about Christine. Not a word or message had come from her since she had disappeared into the fog at Pen Mill, and knowing, as she must have done, the state of anxiety I should be in, this complete silence was all the more ominous and suggestive.

The murder of Bascomb and the facts which Campbell had discovered with reference to Manning's past history added to my misgivings. Except for the poor protection afforded by her uncle and the old French servant, she was at the mercy of one of the most cunning and pitiless scoundrels who had ever escaped the gallows. Every evil impulse in his nature must have been roused to life by the events of the previous afternoon, and still more bitterly than before I cursed my own folly and weakness in ever having permitted her to leave the island.

I was sitting there gnawing my lip and staring at the empty grate when a sudden sound in the verandah outside attracted my attention. Faint as it was, every muscle in my body stiffened instinctively. In one rapid movement I whipped out Manning's revolver, and the next moment I was crouching forward, my eyes fixed on the shutters.

For perhaps a couple of seconds the silence remained unbroken. Then, clear and unmistakable, came a low whistle, followed almost immediately by two sharp taps upon the pane.

CHAPTER SIXTEEN

By a great effort of will I remained exactly as I was. I had to decide what to do, and I had to decide in a hurry, but it was obviously one of those situations in which one could not afford to make the least mistake. If I called out, the answer, for all I knew, might take the shape of a Mills bomb. On the other hand, if I kept silent, how could I discover the identity of my visitor?

Tap, tap, tap.

Once again came the mysterious summons—this time more imperative than before.

As the last knock died away, an idea flashed into my mind. Rising to my feet, I moved stealthily across the hall, and, creeping up the staircase like a cat, I turned into my own bedroom, which looked out on the front of the house. The window was still open, and, advancing towards it with infinite care, I was just preparing to make a cautious reconnaissance when I suddenly heard a shuffling movement down below. I paused, and, almost at the same second the loud jangling peal of the front door bell echoed up from the kitchen.

Somehow or other, the sound acted on me like a tonic. Without hesitating any longer, I thrust my head out over the sill, and there, right underneath me, I saw the ragged, curly-haired figure of my little friend, Jimmy.

"Hullo, James," I called out, "what are you doing here?"

He took a step back, and looked up.

"I gotter letter for you guv'nor—a letter from the young laidy."

"The devil you have!" I exclaimed eagerly. "You hang on there, my son. I'll be with you in half a tick."

Thrusting the revolver into my pocket, I hurried downstairs again, and with feverish haste unchained and opened the front door. Jimmy wiped his boots noisily on the mat, and with a cheerful grin advanced into the hall.

"I seed the light through the shutters," he explained, "and I guessed you was inside. That's why I knocked at the winder."

"Quite right, Jimmy," I said. "Where's the note?"

He dived into his pocket, and produced a crumpled and dirty-looking envelope, which he handed to me.

"When did you get this?" I demanded, refastening the door.

"On'y just now, guv'nor. It was give me by the old Frenchwoman wot lives at 'The Laurels.'"

I crossed to the lamp, and, tearing open the flap, pulled out the enclosure. It consisted of half a sheet of notepaper closely covered in Christine's small writing.

> "DEAREST,—I am giving this note to Marie, who has promised to deliver it to Jimmy. I believe she is to be trusted, but I dare not say more for fear that it should fall into the wrong hands. At the present moment I am a prisoner in my own bedroom. I expect to be free again, with Marie's help, at half-past eight this evening. If all goes well I shall come across to the island immediately. Will you be on the landing-stage at twenty minutes to nine? Come straight down across the garden and through the iron gate, *but on no account leave the house a moment before it's necessary*. I will explain everything when I see you. With all my love,
>
> "CHRISTINE."

I read it through to the end, and then turned back to Jimmy, who was still standing where I had left him.

"Did the old woman say anything when she gave you this note?" I asked.

"On'y as I was to let 'er know whether you'd got it," was the answer. "She's going to wait for me at the corner o' Butcher's Lane."

"Well, you can tell her it will be all right," I said, thrusting the letter into my pocket. "I suppose you haven't heard whether Mr. de Roda is back at the house—the young lady's uncle, you know?"

Jimmy nodded. "'E's there all right. 'E come up in a motor-boat about mid-day. She's lying out in the tideway round the point."

"How do you know it was Mr. de Roda?" I asked.

"Why, George Ellis, the boatman, seed 'im and Craill rowin' ashore. I 'eard George tellin' my dad. She's a fine boat, too, guv'nor—the old *Seagull*, wot used to belong to Captain Stainer of 'Arwich. George reckons 'e must 'ave bought 'er while 'e was away."

"Big enough to go to sea in?" I asked.

He nodded his head. "That's a fact," he answered in the usual Essex idiom. "The Capt'n run across to France in 'er once, and George says she done the trip in a reg'lar treat."

I pulled out my pocket-book and extracted a ten shilling note.

"Here you are, Jimmy," I said, "you cut back and give the old lady my message. Just say that I've received the letter, and that I'll do exactly what Miss de Roda wishes."

I conducted him to the door, stammering his thanks, and assuring me that my errand should be faithfully discharged, and having watched him hurry across the lawn and disappear into the shrubbery, I once more turned the key and shot home the bolts.

I felt that if ever I had cast my bread successfully upon the waters, it was in picking out Jimmy as a trustworthy confederate. Except for him, Christine would have had no chance of sending her letter across to the island, while the news he had brought with regard to de Roda was perhaps of even greater significance than anything she had dared to write.

There was only one explanation which would account for this sudden purchase of a sea-going motor-boat. Manning and de Roda must have made up their minds that the time had arrived for their final effort. Believing that I should be alone in the house that night, they had evidently decided to seize the diamonds by force and to make a bolt for the continent, where their plans were no doubt already arranged. Having become suspicious of Christine, they had apparently taken the simple course of locking her in her own room, so that she should have no possible opportunity of communicating their designs to me.

The one weak point in their otherwise excellent scheme had been the old French servant. Her affection for Christine had manifestly overridden her fear of the others; and, while pretending to carry out their orders, she had secretly consented to assist her young mistress.

If only the suggested plan worked successfully, nothing would fit in better with my own arrangements. To get Christine and de Roda into our hands was, as Campbell had said, the first and most essential step in our future proceedings. By eight-thirty, or soon after, he and Bobby ought to be back from Martlesea, and matters would be enormously simplified if they were to find half of the opening task already accomplished.

I was under no delusion, however, with regard to the dangerous nature of the undertaking. Should Christine's attempt fail, she would be in greater peril than ever, while even if she succeeded it was more than probable that her escape would be immediately discovered. In that event the house might be attacked before Campbell and Bobby returned. It was impossible to foretell to an exact certainty what time they would arrive, and, with everything at stake, Manning was not the sort of gentleman to allow the grass to grow under his feet.

I took out my revolver, and, having emptied the contents, carefully tested its mechanism. There was a comforting efficiency about the ensuing click, click, click, which left nothing to be desired, and, picking up the cartridges one by one, I reloaded it in every chamber. After all, if it came to a fight, the odds would be in my favour. I am a pretty safe shot, and, unless they blew the whole place to pieces, I ought to be able to hold the house against half a dozen assailants. No one could force an entrance without exposing himself to a bullet, and I was cheerfully prepared to shoot both Craill and Manning at the very first opportunity that presented itself.

A glance at the clock showed me that it was close on half-past six. There were still two hours to spin out before the appointed time—a prospect which certainly demanded all the patience that I possessed. I took the precaution of going upstairs again and fastening my bedroom window, and then, having filled a fresh pipe, I settled down grimly to my long vigil.

With exasperating slowness the minute hand crept up to seven, and began to drag round again on its interminable circle. By the time it had reached eight the strain of sitting there and doing nothing had become unbearable—so much so, indeed, that if it had not been for the very emphatic warning contained in Christine's letter I could hardly have resisted the temptation of starting out for the landing-stage. Her instructions had been too definite, however, to admit of any doubt as to their importance, and I felt that it would be madness to run the risk of endangering the whole plan for the lack of a little extra self-control.

At last the half hour struck, and with a sigh of relief I got up from my seat. Being careful to avoid any unnecessary noise, I unlocked the front door, and for a moment I stood on the step, revolver in hand, taking a rapid survey of the garden. Viewed from there in the gathering dusk, it presented a singularly peaceful and deserted appearance. A faint rustic in the tree-tops was the only sound which disturbed the silence, and, closing the door quietly behind me, I set off across the lawn in the direction of the iron gate.

On reaching that point I came to a temporary halt. The path beyond—always a sombre and depressing place even in broad daylight—was now so dark as to be hardly distinguishable from the rest of the shrubbery.

I peered ahead into the blackness, listening intently, but except for the occasional creak of a branch everything was as still as the grave. It was about as uninviting a route as one could very well imagine, but there was no other method of getting to the boathouse unless I disobeyed Christine's instructions, and I had been along it too often to be in much fear of losing my way.

Opening the gate, I passed through. For another second I again paused to listen; then with my revolver ready for immediate use I stepped boldly forward into the gloom.

As I did so my foot struck against a piece of wire, which was stretched across the path a few inches above the ground. So sudden was the shock that I had no chance of recovering my balance. The revolver escaped from my hand, and almost before I realised what had happened I had pitched forward full length on the point of my shoulder.

At the same instant there was a crash amongst the bushes and two men hurled themselves on top of me. One of them fell across my legs, clutching me by the knees; the other landed with his full weight right in the middle of my back.

Half dazed, and almost entirely winded, I still had strength to make one desperate effort. Twisting myself sideways, I jabbed back my elbow into the face of the man above me, and a smothered oath told me that the blow had gone home. Before I could repeat it, however, his fingers sank into my throat, and I felt a cold ring of steel pressed against my forehead:

"If you move again, I'll blow your brains out."

It was Manning's voice, and, low as the whisper was, there was no mistaking its savage sincerity.

I ceased struggling, for beneath that suffocating hold it was impossible to do otherwise.

"Hurry up, de Roda," came the sharp command. "Tie his arms and legs and be quick about it, we've no time to spare."

I felt my ankles being lashed together, and then a thrill of pain darted through my shoulder, as somebody jerked my arms roughly behind my back. A minute later I was as helpless as a trussed fowl.

Manning let go my throat and rose to his feet

"The first sound you make," he observed softly, "I'll shoot you like a dog."

"Better knock 'im in the 'ead," suggested a hoarse voice, "it'll save a lot of trouble."

I heard Manning laugh, as though he found the suggestion amusing.

"I have a better plan for dealing with Mr. Dryden, Craill," he remarked. "Do you think you can carry him to the house?"

The other made no answer, but, stooping down and gripping me round the waist, hoisted me over his shoulder as though I had been a sack of flour. Considering that I turn the scale at fourteen stone, the fellow's strength must have been prodigious.

Manning opened the gate for us, and we passed out on to the lawn.

Every step Craill took gave me a fresh thrill of pain, but the physical suffering I felt was nothing to the agony of rage and mortification that was tearing at my heart. The devilish ingenuity by which I had been trapped only added to my torture, for since the contents of Christine's letter were known to my captors, it was only too probable that her position was as dangerous as my own.

As we reached the verandah Manning's voice once more broke the silence.

"You had better put our friend down for a moment," he said. "We shall have to borrow his key to get into the house."

With a heave of his back Craill let me fall heavily on the stonework, and moving up to where I was lying Manning ran his hand quickly through my pockets.

"I've got it," he announced. Then, turning towards the silent figure on his right, he added almost mockingly, "Quite a dramatic moment, isn't it, de Roda?"

I heard the sharp click of the lock, and almost simultaneously a flood of light streamed out through the doorway.

With a strange gasping sob de Roda thrust his companion aside, and, trampling on my foot as he passed, stumbled blindly ahead of us into the hall.

Manning shrugged his shoulders. "You must make allowances for the old gentleman, Dryden," he said. "He has been very hardly treated, and I'm afraid it's affected his manners."

He stepped forward, laughing quietly to himself, and, without waiting for further orders, Craill dragged me roughly in after him and closed the door behind us.

"I think that end of the room will be a good place for our host," observed Manning, pointing towards the staircase. "You can tie him up comfortably there, and then he will be able to get a nice uninterrupted view of our researches."

Powerless to resist; I was hauled to my feet and lashed securely with my back to the banisters—a proceeding which gave me such pain in my injured shoulder that I had all my work cut out to remain silent.

With a cruel smile upon his lips Manning stood watching the operation. One side of his face was still bruised and swelled almost out of recognition, and even in the midst of my own suffering the sight filled me with fierce and exulting pleasure.

"You are not looking quite at your best, Manning," I remarked, "I am afraid you must have had another sleepless night."

"Shall I give 'im a wipe across the mouth?" growled Craill. "That'll stop his jaw."

Manning silenced him with a gesture.

"I don't think I shall be very much in your debt by the time I have finished with you, Dryden," he replied pleasantly.

A queer exclamation from de Roda, who was crouching in front of the fireplace, broke in suddenly upon our conversation.

"You were right," he cried hoarsely, "you were right, doctor! It is here! I see it myself."

He pointed with trembling fingers towards a small ornamental knob in the centre of the grate, which I had noticed on several occasions bore a rough resemblance to a bull-dog's head.

Manning glanced round unconcernedly, and then turned back to me.

"You must excuse me for a moment," he said. "Mr. de Roda is naturally impatient."

He walked across to the hearth, and the gaunt, huddled figure of the other moved aside to make room for him.

"Now we shall see," he remarked. "It will be very disappointing if I am wrong after all."

He caught the knob in both hands, and, bending forwards, gave it a sharp wrench. Instantly, and without the least noise, the whole front of one of the side pillars swung open like a door, exposing a high narrow cavity lined with brick.

In a second de Roda had flung himself on his knees and was groping in the aperture.

"They are here!" he screamed wildly. "My God, they are here!"

Sobbing with excitement, he began to drag out handful after handful of rough uncut stones, which rolled about the floor as he dropped them in his frantic haste.

Manning stood looking down on him as though he were regarding the antics of a child.

"Don't get too excited," he said soothingly. "You will only make yourself ill if you do." He beckoned to Craill. With staring eyes fixed upon the treasure, the latter shambled across the room. "Go into the kitchen," he added, "and see if you can find something to put them in. There's pretty sure to be a bag or basket about, and I don't suppose Mr. Dryden will object to giving us the loan of it."

Craill turned obediently towards the baize door, but he was checked by another gesture.

"I shall also want some paraffin oil," continued Manning in the same dispassionate tone. "Let me have all you can find, and if you come across any old newspapers bring them as well."

He glanced once more at de Roda, who was gloating over the diamonds and babbling to himself, then with his hands in his side pockets he strolled back to where I was pinioned.

"And now, Mr. John Dryden," he said, "I have time to attend to you."

For a moment we stood face to face, his china blue eyes fixed upon mine with a kind of pitiless satisfaction. I felt sure that I was very close to death. Even though Bobby and Campbell arrived in the course of the next few minutes, it would make no difference to my own fate. Manning would certainly kill me if it were his last act on earth, and in the absolute conviction that whatever happened I was a doomed man, a curious and almost detached calm seemed to find its way into my heart.

I looked back at him with a smile on my lips.

"For an expert, Manning," I said, "you take a long time about committing a murder."

He laughed easily. "I am sorry to keep you waiting," he replied. "It won't be very long—I can assure you of that—but there are just one or two little bits of information which I should like to give you first." He came a step closer. "I don't often take people into my confidence, but, you see, in your case I can afford to make an exception. Dead men are notoriously reticent."

I realised that every moment he indulged in the luxury of trying to torment me the more slender became his chances of escape.

"Go ahead, doctor," I said cheerfully. "Your conversation is always stimulating."

Provoking as my attitude must have been, he managed to control himself admirably.

"In the first place," he began, "it may amuse you to learn that the letter which brought you blundering out of the house in that singularly convenient fashion was written by myself."

Incredible as his statement seemed, something told me that he was speaking the truth.

"I congratulate you," I said coolly. "I knew you were a murderer and a thief, but I had no idea that you were an accomplished forger as well."

"You flatter me," he replied. "As a matter of fact it was a very hurried and rather clumsy piece of work. Any intelligent person would probably have seen through it at once." He pulled out an envelope from his pocket and held it up mockingly in front of me. "This is the touching and affectionate original," he added. "It was given to Marie by Christine, and, like a good servant, the old lady promptly handed it on to me. Very trustworthy domestics the French, Dryden."

For a moment I made no answer. The sight of Christine's letter in that brute's hands sent such a fresh wave of anger surging through me that I was afraid I should be unable to control my voice.

"I won't read it to you," he continued. "You might find it upsetting, and I should like your last moments to be really peaceful and happy." He paused. "Besides, you would probably be more interested to hear about my own future arrangements, especially as, to a rather important extent, they involve those of Miss de Roda."

He put the letter back into his pocket, and once more surveyed me with the same Satanic enjoyment.

"I have been fortunate enough to get hold of a really nice little ocean-going steam yacht, Dryden. At the present moment she is lying in the harbour at Rotterdam, and by to-morrow night we hope to be well on our way to the South Seas."

He glanced round again carelessly at de Roda, who was still scrabbling amongst the treasure, apparently blind and deaf to our presence.

"For Christine and myself," he continued softly, "the voyage will be full of romance. It will be our honeymoon, Dryden; a rather unwilling one on her part, perhaps, but none the less enjoyable for that."

I bit my lip until I could feel the blood trickling into my mouth.

"A pleasant family party at first," he went on, in a still lower voice; "but between ourselves, I don't think we shall be troubled with the old gentleman's company for very long. It would be sad, of course, if anything were to happen, but I shall do my best to console Christine. I fancy she has one of those rare natures which will respond to affectionate treatment."

God knows how much more of this I could have stood, but at that instant the baize door opened and Craill re-entered the hall. He had a bundle of newspapers under his arm, and was carrying a large tin of paraffin and a canvas bag.

Manning relieved him of the latter, and held it up to the light.

"That will do, Craill," he observed, handing it back. "You can put down the other things and help Mr. de Roda pack away the stones. We shall be leaving very shortly."

He turned towards me again, brushing off a patch of mud which he had apparently just noticed on his sleeve.

"By the way, Dryden," he added, "in the excitement of the moment I have clean forgotten to thank you for telling me where to look for the diamonds. It was the one point in which I was utterly at a loss. Your late lamented uncle was always babbling about a dog's head, but somehow or other I never connected it with the hiding-place. I always thought he was talking about that brute Satan. It was only when you confided to me that he had had the fireplace specially put in that I happened to notice that ingenious little bit of carving in the centre of the grate. Curious that I should have been so stupid, but the best of us make mistakes at times. *Non semper arcum tendit Apollo*, as our delightful friend Horace used to say."

He looked deliberately round the room, as though in search of something, and then walked across to the writing-table, where there were a couple of candle-sticks with stumps of candles in each.

He took out one of them, and, strolling back, picked up the bundle of newspapers which Craill had deposited on the floor.

"I have devoted considerable thought towards providing you with a fitting exit, Dryden," he remarked. "One or two very attractive ideas have occurred to me, but I think on the whole that the best plan will be to burn down the house. I trust that in the throes of courtship you have not overlooked the precaution of insuring against fire?"

His fiendish purpose had been obvious ever since he had sent Craill for the paraffin, and if he hoped for any sign of weakness from me he must have been singularly disappointed.

"I am afraid there will be no premium this time," I said. "You can't expect all your murders to be equally productive."

In spite of his wonderful self-control the shot went home. I saw the fingers of his left hand tighten sharply, while a sudden look of surprise flashed across his face.

"So you have been making enquiries into my past history?" he observed almost caressingly.

"Just a few," I admitted. "It was an unsavory business, but I have managed to dig up one or two quite interesting facts. At the present moment they are in the hands of the police."

He laughed gently. "I was doing Christine an injustice," he replied. "You seem to have occasional gleams of intelligence after all."

We were interrupted by Craill, who, leaving de Roda and the diamonds, lurched menacingly across the room.

"You 'eard wot 'e said, boss! Shove 'im through it, quick, and let's be off. We got to fetch the girl an'——"

"Don't upset yourself, Craill," came the imperturbable answer. "We shall have plenty of time to carry out our original programme."

He took another leisurely inspection of the room, and then, walking across to the opposite corner, dropped the newspapers in a tumbled heap alongside the grandfather clock.

"You can pull up those two tables," he added, "and empty out the log basket against the wall. I don't think we shall have much trouble in starting a really satisfactory bonfire. That's the best of these old panelled houses: they burn beautifully when they once catch alight."

With an evil grin upon his face, Craill set about the business, while de Roda, clutching the bag of diamonds in his trembling hands, stared vacantly at all three of us.

As soon as his instructions had been obeyed Manning picked up the paraffin. Taking out the cork, he poured half the contents of the can on to the wood, and splashed the remainder over the two tables and the wall. Then, bending forward, he placed the stump of candle in the middle of the pile of newspapers.

"You see the idea, Dryden?" he remarked, turning to me. "Something after the principle of a delayed fuse. Bar accidents, it will take the candle about ten minutes to burn down. That will afford you a nice comfortable opportunity to say your prayers. It will also give us plenty of time to call for Christine and be well on our way down the estuary before anyone has grasped the important fact that you are in need of assistance."

He struck a match, and, having carefully ignited the wick, stepped back to contemplate the result.

"For Gawd's sake 'urry up, boss," repeated Craill, more insistently than ever. "There ain't no sense in messin' abaht 'ere—not now we've got the stuff."

"You two can start now," replied Manning, "I shall catch you up before you reach the landing-stage."

Craill made a movement as if to take the diamonds from de Roda, but with a snarl, almost like that of a wild animal, the latter started away.

Manning laughed again. "Mr. de Roda will carry the stones, Craill," he said. "They will be quite safe in his charge."

Still hugging the bag fiercely in his arms, de Roda followed his companion to the hall door, and without any further remark from either of them the two men passed out into the darkness.

Directly they had gone Manning sauntered up to me. "I think we had better gag you, Dryden," he said thoughtfully. "I want to leave the window open so as to ensure a good draught, and it's just possible that somebody might hear you squealing."

Twisting his handkerchief into the shape of a bandage, he stepped up on to the staircase behind me, and, drawing the broad part tightly across my mouth, knotted the ends together at the back of my head. Then, coming round in front of me again, he took a last smiling survey of his handiwork.

"Good-bye, my friend," he drawled slowly. "I am afraid you are in for a rather uncomfortable time, but you must try to regard your suffering as a kind of disguised blessing. If there is any truth in what the church teaches us, you will probably find it an excellent preparation for the next world."

He made me a low mocking bow, and then with a final glance at the candle walked quickly across to the doorway and strode out into the garden after his two companions.

CHAPTER SEVENTEEN

SILENCE!

Silence so complete that I could almost hear the beating of my own heart as I stared across the room at the little cone of flame which burned away steadily amongst the tumbled pile of newspapers.

Five minutes had passed since Manning had left me—five ghastly, interminable minutes that had seared themselves for ever into the very fibre of my being. Twice I had tried to close my eyes, but on each occasion the hideous fascination of that ever-shortening stump of candle had proved far stronger than my own will. I had wrenched at the ropes which held me until my wrists were bleeding, and, now, utterly exhausted and almost sick with pain, I leaned back waiting for the end.

I had no feeling of fear for myself; all my thoughts were of the horrible fate that awaited Christine if Manning succeeded in getting her on board the yacht. I tried desperately to imagine what would happen when Bobby and Campbell reached the island. As far as I was aware they knew nothing of Manning's intentions. They would probably arrive only to find the house a mass of blazing ruins, and unless by some miracle they guessed the truth, they would be powerless to interfere until it was too late.

With straining eyes I watched the little yellow flame as it began to flicker ominously in its final stages. The end was very near now. A minute—forty-five seconds——

Clang!

Merciful God! What was that?

A stifled cry broke from my lips, and, jerking my head round, I stared through the open doorway into the darkness outside.

Someone had passed through the garden gate and was hurrying towards the house. I heard a rustle on the lawn, the swift pad of footsteps across the verandah, then, breathless and dripping wet, a slim, solitary figure stumbled into the light.

It was Christine.

Dressed only in the scantiest of swimming costumes, with the water still trickling from her bare arms and legs, she stood there, white-faced and horror-struck, gazing at the sight before her.

"The candle!" I stammered wildly. "Quick, put it out!"

With a faint splutter the wick suddenly heeled over, and a thin wisp of smoke shot up into the air.

In a flash Christine seemed to realise the peril in which we stood. Almost before the words left my lips she had darted across the room, and the next moment she was stamping out the smouldering paper with her bare feet.

I remember making a queer sound which I think was intended for a protest. For an instant she leaned against the wall, trembling and sobbing from the reaction; then with a kind of pitiful blind haste she groped her way to my side and began to unfasten the handkerchief which Manning had knotted across my mouth.

"What have they done to you?" she faltered. "Oh, what have they done to you?"

I gulped down a mouthful of sorely needed fresh air.

"Christine, my darling," I whispered, "how in heaven's name did you get here?"

"I swam over from the shore," she answered breathlessly. "I landed on the saltings just opposite the garden."

"You did *what*?" I exclaimed. I stared at her in amazement. "You swam in the dark across the estuary?"

She nodded.

"There was no other way of reaching the island. Marie had promised to send you a message by Jimmy, but instead of keeping her word she must have given it to Dr. Manning. He came to my room and told me what he was going to do. I made up my mind then that as soon as they started I would try to follow them. I got out through the window and I managed to climb down by the creeper. I thought the tide would be too strong for me, but I didn't care either way. If I wasn't in time to help you, I just wanted to be drowned."

She stopped, and her eyes fell upon an old-fashioned American bowie knife which was hanging from the wall at the head of the stairs. With a quick movement she stepped forward, and, unhooking it from the nail, began to saw away feverishly at the ropes which fastened me to the banisters.

She had just cut through the first strand when I suddenly realised that at any moment Manning might return.

"Shut the door before you do anything else," I explained. "Lock it and bolt it top and bottom. If they guess where you are——"

I had no need to finish, for Christine hurried off at once, and, forgetting my injured shoulder in the excitement of the moment, I gave an impatient tug at the nearly severed cord. I was rewarded by such a stab of pain that before I could stop it an involuntary grunt broke from my lips.

"What is it? What's the matter? You are hurt after all!"

With a face whiter than ever, and her eyes full of concern, Christine had hastened to where I was standing.

"It's nothing much," I said. "I blundered over a bit of wire they'd stretched across the path and I rather think I've cracked my collar-bone. It will be all right as soon as I've tied it up."

She knelt down beside me, and with trembling fingers set about the task of freeing my wrists. I heard her give a sudden gasp of horror as she saw the state they were in.

"Oh, the brutes!" she sobbed. "The utter brutes! How can God allow such people as Manning to exist?"

"He won't allow it much longer," I replied grimly.

The cut ends of the rope pattered down on to the floor, and, shaking myself loose, I stepped forward, a free man. Christine dropped the knife and rose unsteadily to her feet. The next moment I was crushing her soft wet body in my uninjured arm, and pressing kisses upon her bare neck and shoulders.

"My own dear love!" I whispered. "I must have been mad ever to let you go."

I strained her to me, kissing her again and again, until the little round oilskin cap that she was wearing slipped off her head, and her slender beauty was almost hidden by a rippling torrent of dark brown hair.

At last a faint recollection of our rather precarious position began to intrude itself into my mind.

"I hate to stop kissing you, Christine," I said, "but would you mind helping me load my gun? I don't believe I can manage it with one hand."

She released herself from my embrace, and stood there like some lovely sea Naiad, her breast rising and falling and her lips slightly parted.

"Where is it—where do you keep it?" she asked.

I nodded towards a leather case which was standing up on end in the opposite corner.

"That's it," I said. "Do you think you can put it together and shove in a couple of cartridges? I want to be ready for Manning in case he comes back."

She started towards it, and for the first time the gaping aperture in the fireplace suddenly attracted her attention.

"Yes," I said, "they got the diamonds all right. Your uncle went off hugging them in a bag. I should feel quite pleased about it if I only thought he would be allowed to keep them."

Christine stepped forward to the case, and, laying it on the floor, began to unfasten the straps. In spite of her agitation there was a promptness and efficiency about all her proceedings which filled me with admiration.

"Why were you alone here?" she asked, as she snapped the barrels into their place. "Has anything happened to your naval friend?"

"Something must have happened to him," I replied, "but goodness knows what. He and Campbell, the detective, ought to have been back by eight-thirty. They may turn up any moment now, and——"

Christine rose hastily, holding the loaded gun in her hand. A delightful little tinge of colour had suddenly crept into her face.

"They mustn't find me like this," she faltered. "Could you lend me a coat or something?"

She gazed desperately round the room, as though in search of some likely garment.

"My entire wardrobe is at your service," I assured her. "You shall come upstairs and take your choice." I paused. "All the same," I added regretfully, "I shall never make you look as nice as you do now."

She blushed again, and, moving impulsively towards her, I once more slipped my arm round her waist.

"My own darling," I exclaimed, "you must be simply frozen to death; and your poor little feet——"

"No, no," she protested, "I'm quite all right, really I am. It's your shoulder we've got to think about."

"Oh, bother my shoulder!" I objected. "It only wants a little support of some sort. A scarf or a handkerchief or any old thing will do. I'll come upstairs with you, and you can fix it for me while I'm routing you out some clothes."

I tried to relieve her of the gun, but with a shake of her head she insisted upon carrying it, and side by side we mounted the staircase which led to my own bedroom. There was a box of matches upon the dressing-table, and, having leaned her weapon carefully against the wall, Christine proceeded to light the candles.

"Now we'll see what we can find," I said. "I've got any amount of kit, but I'm afraid none of it will fit you very well."

"I'm going to attend to you first," she answered, pulling open the top drawer. "Why, here's the very thing I want! This will make a beautiful sling."

She took out a large silk handkerchief, and, crossing to the washstand, picked up the wet sponge. Then with an air of almost professional gravity she came back to where I was standing.

"I learned something about accidents when I was living on the ranch," she went on. "You must let me put this under your arm before I fasten you up. That will keep the collar-bone in position until we can get it properly set."

With a neatness that would have done credit to Harley Street she rapidly completed the operation, and, feeling considerably eased as far as the pain was concerned, I moved over to the wardrobe and threw back the door.

"Here you are, dear heart!" I said. "Coats, shirts, trousers, underclothes—anything necessary to a person of taste and fashion."

She laughed softly, and, taking a step forward, peeped in at the crowded shelves.

"I expect I shall find something that will do," she said. "I only want to feel a little more respectable and just a tiny bit warmer."

"Well, help yourself to whatever you like," I observed. "I shall take the gun and go and sit on the staircase until you've finished."

"But you can't use a gun now," she exclaimed, "you've only got one arm."

"That's quite enough to shoot Manning with," I returned; and, without waiting for any further remonstrances, I picked up the weapon and walked out into the passage.

A moment's consideration convinced me that the finest strategical position was the small landing half-way down. At that point I should be practically invisible from the hall below, and at the same time I should command a full view of the front door. Crippled as I was, I could certainly lay out anyone who attempted to ascend the staircase, and with this consoling thought I made my way down, and seated myself comfortably on the first step of the next flight.

In spite of everything, an inexpressible joy was rioting through my heart. What the devil did such details as a cracked shoulder and the loss of the diamonds matter when compared with the glorious fact that I had recovered Christine? From the blackest depths of despair I had been lifted suddenly to the very heights of human felicity, and the most carefully balanced human nature is apt to be a trifle upset by such an abrupt and dazzling transition.

The one disturbing factor in the situation was the thought of de Roda. His mind had evidently given away entirely, and the memory of his haggard face and those strange burning eyes of his haunted me like a reproachful ghost. Manning and Craill were not likely to burden themselves for long with such a companion. Even if they spared his life, or what was left of it, they would almost certainly abandon him at the first possible opportunity. They would go off with the treasure, leaving him robbed and helpless in some out-of-the-way-corner of the world, and I knew what suffering it would mean to Christine unless we were able to save him from such a fate.

Until Bobby and Campbell arrived, however, there was absolutely nothing to be done.

I was staring at the door, and asking myself for the tenth time what could have happened to them, when a thundering rap on the knocker nearly made me jump from my seat. With an instinctive movement I thrust the barrel of my gun through the banisters.

"Who's that?" I called out.

"Who the blazes d'you think it is?" came the cheery answer.

It was the one voice in the world that I was longing to hear, and, scrambling to my feet, I plunged recklessly down the staircase. The next moment the door was open, and two stalwart figures, clad from head to feet in glistening oilskins, stepped forward into the light.

"We're very late," began Campbell, "but——"

The sentence died on his lips, and with a sudden sniff he stood gazing first at me and then at the tumbled heap of logs and furniture on the further side of the hall.

"Good Lord!" exclaimed Bobby. "What have you been doing? Playing football?"

I looked at them both, and for the life of me I could not help laughing.

"You were quite correct about the diamonds, Bobby," I said. "Manning found them without the least difficulty."

I pointed to the fireplace, and with a queer exclamation Campbell strode across the room and peered into the recess.

"Are you serious, man?" he demanded. "D'ye mean to say he's got them?"

"Yes," I said, "he's got them all right, and it's only by the mercy of God and her own pluck that he hasn't got Christine as well."

"When did this happen?"

Campbell shot the question at me so savagely that it sounded like the bark of a dog.

"Twenty minutes ago," I said.

"And where is he now?" This latter from Bobby.

"Unless he's mad," I replied, "he's probably half a mile down the estuary on his way to Rotterdam."

There was a moment of pregnant silence.

"So it was their launch we saw," observed Bobby coolly. "I thought it must be."

Campbell closed the door in the grate with a vicious swing, and came swiftly back to where we were standing.

"Let us have the facts, Mr. Dryden, just the bare facts and nothing more." He caught hold of a chair and thrust it towards me.

"Better sit down, man," he added in a gentler voice. "You're looking as if a rest would do you good."

I took his advice, accepting at the same time the somewhat battered silver flask which Bobby lugged out hastily from an inside pocket. It was full of neat brandy, and, having gulped down a generous mouthful, I proceeded to give them a compressed but faithful description of the evening's entertainment. The whole recital only occupied a short while, for in spite of its amazing nature neither of them attempted to interrupt me.

"So you see what comes of not keeping your appointments, Robert," I finished. "The diamonds have gone; here am I with a cracked collar-bone, and——"

A sudden sound attracted our attention, and we all three turned round abruptly. Christine was standing at the head of the staircase, with her hand on the banister. Dressed in an old sailing jersey of mine, with a pair of white flannel trousers rolled up over her bare feet and ankles, she presented such a delightfully unexpected picture that for perhaps a couple of seconds none of us moved or spoke.

"Let me introduce you," I said. "Christine, this is Bobby, and this is Inspector Campbell. I have just been telling them how you saved my life."

She came down the staircase, and with a simultaneous movement both my companions started forward to meet her. Bobby, however, arrived first.

"Put it there," he exclaimed, burying her slender hand in his huge brown fist. "I told Jack he'd got a prize-packet, and, by God! it's the truth."

Campbell's greeting was a shade more formal

"You're a very gallant young lady, miss, and I'm proud and honoured to make your acquaintance."

With shining eyes Christine looked from one to the other of them.

"I knew that you wouldn't fail us," she said. Then, coming towards me, she added eagerly: "But what are we waiting for? Why don't we start at once?"

I got up from my chair.

"Christine's right," I cried. "How about your launch, Bobby? Has anything gone wrong with her?"

"Gone wrong with her!" he echoed indignantly. "Of course it hasn't."

"Then why were you late?" I demanded.

"I was kept for an hour at that cursed office. There was some Admiralty business that had to be attended to."

Christine turned to him, her face alight with excitement.

"We have still time." she said. "If we can catch them up before they get to Holland——"

She was interrupted by Campbell.

"She's talking sense, the young lady," he exclaimed. "They can't be very far ahead of us, and there's twenty thousand pounds reward if we get the stones."

"It's my uncle's life I'm thinking of," declared Christine passionately.

Campbell made an obvious effort to appear sympathetic.

"Never fear, miss," he rejoined. "We'll bring him back to you and the diamonds as well."

"I am coming too," said Christine quietly.

The Inspector stared at her in dismay.

"But, my dear young lady——" he began.

"You may as well save your breath, Campbell," I remarked. "If three hundred yards of water can't stop Miss de Roda——"

"Why the blazes shouldn't she come?" demanded Bobby indignantly. "She's got more pluck and grit than all the rest of us put together."

"Have it your own way," returned Campbell. "I'm thinking there'll be some bloody work before we get the bracelets on Dr. Manning, but if you choose to run the risk—" He broke off with a shrug of his shoulders, and Bobby stepped forward, glancing down at Christine's bare feet.

"Haven't you got any shoes?" he asked. "You can't go through the shrubbery like that."

"Yes, I can," she replied. "I've done it already."

"Well, I'm hanged if you'll do it again," he retorted. "You're all cut about and bleeding as it is. You hop up on my back like a sensible girl."

He stooped down, and, without making any fuss or protest, Christine at once accepted the proffered lift.

Campbell's grim eyes watched her appreciatively.

"You stick close to me, Commander," he said. "I'll go ahead of you with the light, and then you can see where you're putting your feet. I wouldn't have you drop that lass, not for a twenty pound note."

He produced an electric torch from his pocket, and switching on the current, led the way out into the garden. Bobby followed, with Christine on his back, and, just waiting to close the door, I hurried after them and ranged myself alongside of Campbell.

There was very little mist left, and the moon, although occasionally obscured by clouds, was now shining brightly. We passed through the iron gate and entered the shrubbery, where I showed them the broken wire which had been the cause of my downfall. Then, step by step, we moved cautiously forward along the winding path, until a glimmer of light in front of us showed that the trees were coming to an end.

As we emerged on to the saltings Christine slipped lightly to her feet.

We could see the launch lying out in the tideway, and a dark figure, silhouetted sharply against the water, standing on guard over a small dinghy.

"There's Jenkins!" said Bobby, in a relieved whisper.

At the sound of his voice the sailor wheeled round quickly; and then, seeing us advancing across the grass, drew himself up to the salute.

"Anything happened?" enquired Bobby.

"All quiet, sir," came the curt answer.

"In you get," continued Bobby, motioning us towards the dinghy.

He turned to Jenkins, who was moving away to unhitch the painter.

"We've got to catch that launch, Jenkins," he said, "the one we saw coming out from the opposite shore. She's making for Rotterdam, and no matter if we break the blasted engines we're going to overhaul her before she gets there."

"Very good, sir," returned Jenkins indifferently.

He waited until we had scrambled in, and then, unfastening the rope, took his place at the oars. Two or three strokes brought us alongside, where Bobby held the boat steady while we clambered on board over the low iron railing.

I shepherded Christine and Campbell to the cockpit, and, leaving them there, lent what assistance I could to the others in the task of getting under way.

Within five minutes of our feet touching the deck the anchor was hauled in, and we were heading out into the open estuary, with the black water rippling past our stern.

Bobby, who had taken the wheel, signalled to me to come aft.

"You'll find a pair of night glasses in the cabin," he observed. "You'd better go up into the bows and keep a look-out."

I nodded. "If you've got such a thing as a spare gun," I said, "I'll borrow that too."

"There are a couple of Webleys about somewhere," he replied. "Ask Jenkins for them and give the other one to Campbell."

I dropped down the narrow hatch, and, having discovered the glasses, made my way forward to where Jenkins was busy with the engines. He left them for a moment, to reappear with a brace of useful-looking revolvers, and thus equipped I crawled back to the cockpit.

I found Christine and the Inspector sitting side by side, apparently on the most friendly terms.

"Here you are, Campbell," I said, offering him his choice. "I promised you a bit of shooting, and the odds are that you'll get it."

With a significant gesture the detective tapped his hip.

"Not for me, thank you," he replied. "If Dr. Manning wants to argue I've got an old friend here who'll do all the talking that's necessary."

Christine stretched out her hand.

"I'll take the other one," she announced.

Campbell made an attempt to interfere, but he was too late to be effective.

"You needn't worry about me," said Christine reassuringly. "I know how to use a revolver."

"I'm not surprised to hear it, miss," was the answer. "All the same, if it comes to a shooting match, the proper place for you is in the cabin."

"He's right, Christine," I added. "For heaven's sake keep under cover when we run alongside."

She looked up at me eagerly.

"You think we shall catch them, then?"

"Of course we shall," I answered. "It's not likely that they can do more than twenty, and Bobby can knock nearly forty out of this old jigger." I squeezed her hand comfortingly in the darkness.

"I'm going up forward now to keep a look-out for them," I continued. "As soon as you hear me let off a yell you'll know that they're in sight."

With surprising tact Campbell turned away his head, and, having taken full advantage of the opportunity, I swung myself up on to the deck and started off in the direction of the bows.

We were now racing through the water at a tremendous speed, the whole frail shell quivering and rocking beneath the powerful beat of the engine. On either side a great rolling wave curved away from the ship's stern, and behind us a broad wake of white foam gleamed and tossed in the fitful light of the moon.

I crept forward to the end of the deck, and, crouching down in the angle of the railing, stared long and steadily through my glasses.

As there was no sign of our quarry it was clear that she was already round the point. Manning had doubtless seen Bobby's launch returning up the estuary and had wasted no time in getting away from "The Laurels" directly he had discovered Christine's flight. At the lowest computation he must now be at least six miles ahead of us. Provided the moonlight held, however, he would still be in sight by the time he reached the bar, and I glanced anxiously at heavy masses of cloud which were gathering ominously from the south-east.

On we went, the water becoming rougher every minute as we forced our way into the trough of the incoming tide.

Bit by bit the coast opened out on our right, until at last we were almost opposite the big clump of trees which marks the extreme end of the southern shore.

Clutching the rail to steady myself, I once more raised my glasses. Then, in a lather of spray and foam, we suddenly shot out into full view of the sea, and at the same moment a wild, involuntary shout broke from my lips.

There, not half a mile ahead of us, was the launch. She was lying broadside on under the full light of the moon, and one glance was sufficient to show me she had broken down. Even at that distance I could make out two figures working frantically at the engines and another huddled shape in the bows.

"We've got 'em!" roared Bobby, above the throb of the pistons.

He spun over the wheel, and, swinging round like a greyhound on the trail, we leaped seaward straight for our helpless prey.

I found Campbell standing beside me, a revolver gripped in his hand.

"If there's any sign of trouble," he said quietly, "shoot at once. You keep your eye on Craill and I'll look after Manning."

I had rather it had been the other way on, but there was no time for arguing.

Even as he spoke I saw Manning fling down his useless spanner, and, wiping his hands coolly with a piece of cotton waste, step up into the stern. Craill followed, his evil, scowling face in strange contrast to the smiling calm of the other.

Slackening speed at just the right moment, Bobby brought us alongside with masterly precision.

Campbell leaned forward, his eyes fixed grimly on the pair of them.

"It's no use, doctor," he said, "your luck's out this time."

With a ghastly sound, half-way between a sob and a scream, the gaunt figure of de Roda rose suddenly from the deck. A torrent of Spanish curses burst from his throat, and, dropping the bag of diamonds which he was still holding, he staggered to the side, shaking his fists at us in a frenzy of maniacal rage.

I heard a low cry of anguish beside me, and, as I half turned round, I saw Manning and Craill whip out their revolvers.

I think we must all have fired simultaneously. The only thing I actually remember is a blinding crash in my head as I pitched forward against the rails.

*

For a little while I thought that I was still dreaming. Then the low murmur of voices became so persistent that at last, with a tremendous effort, I managed to open my eyes.

"What's that?" I demanded.

There was the scrape of a chair, and the next moment Bobby and Christine were standing beside the bed.

"It's all right, old lad," said the former soothingly. "We're both here."

I looked up in bewilderment. I had a vague feeling that I was back in my cabin on the *Neptune* and that somehow or other Bobby ought to be Ross.

"Some blighter pushed me into the dock," I said irritably.

Then, with the same startling abruptness as before, a wave of memory surged through my aching brain.

"Good Lord!" I cried, starting up. "Where am I? What's happened?"

Christine sat down beside me, and very tenderly took my hand in hers.

"You are back on the island, dear, in your own room. There's nothing to be anxious about or worried over. It's all finished, and we are just here together—you and I and Bobby."

I let my head sink back on the pillows.

"I remember now," I said. "I stopped a bullet, didn't I? I've a sort of recollection of seeing a lot of stars, and after that everything's a blank."

Bobby seated himself on the other side of my couch.

"This is splendid," he remarked. "You'll be asking for a whisky and soda before we know where we are."

Christine leaned forward and rearranged the pillows.

"Tell me," she whispered, "is your head hurting you very much?"

I put my hand to my forehead and found it encircled by a wet bandage.

"It's aching a bit," I admitted. "What's the damage? Anything serious?"

"Well, it was rather a close shave," said Bobby drily. "Manning's bullet ripped along the side of your skull and knocked you out as clean as a whistle. A devilish good shot—under the circumstances."

There was a moment's pause.

"Go on, Robert," I said, "you're just getting interesting."

Christine made a faint movement of protest.

"The doctor will be here in a minute. Hadn't we better wait?"

"No, no," I protested. "I must hear what happened."

She glanced across at Bobby.

"Very well, then," she said quietly, "you tell him."

"I don't know if Manning saw you fall," continued Bobby, "but if so it was the last thing he did see on this earth. We all fired directly he raised his hand. He got three bullets, one from Christine, one from Campbell, and one from me. It will be a very interesting point as to which of us killed him."

"And Craill?" I asked.

"You laid Craill out all right. At the present moment he's in the Pen Mill Police Station nursing a sick elbow."

For an instant I hesitated. Christine must have guessed my unspoken question, for when I looked up at her her eyes were wet with tears.

"We found my uncle lying dead on the deck," she whispered. "Dr. Ross had always told me that any great shock or excitement——"

Her voice faltered, and, breaking into a pitiful little sob, she buried her face in her hands.

"My poor darling," I said hoarsely. "I'd have given anything in the world——"

With a brave effort she raised her head and brushed away the tears which were running down her cheeks.

"I know," she said, "I know how you feel. I can't help crying, it's all so sad and terrible, but even if it were possible I don't think I would wish him to be alive. It nearly broke my heart to see him as he was. Now at least he is at peace."

She turned to Bobby.

"Don't bother about me," she added. "Just tell him the rest before the doctor comes."

"There isn't much more to tell," said Bobby quietly. "We towed the launch to Pen Mill, and Campbell went ashore and rang up the police. The Head Constable came over at once and brought the doctor with him. There was the devil of a fuss, as you can imagine. Fortunately, however, the old boy knew all about Campbell, and after a lot of jaw we were allowed to bring you back here and put you to bed. It was nearly midnight by then, and we've been taking turns sitting up with you ever since."

"What's the time now?" I demanded.

Bobby glanced at his watch.

"Close on twelve."

"And where's Campbell?" I asked.

"He stopped ashore with the police. There's going to be an inquest on Manning this afternoon, and——"

He was interrupted by a loud ring at the front door bell.

Christine rose quickly.

"It's probably the doctor," she said. "He promised to come over as soon as he was free."

She motioned Bobby to remain where he was, and, crossing the room, disappeared into the passage.

"We got the diamonds all right," added Bobby cheerfully. "Campbell had a squint at them, and he says there are only about a third missing. He reckons you ought to get at least twenty thousand out of the Brazilian Government."

"I've had my share," I said. "You and he and Christine can split it up between you."

"I'll do nothing of the sort," began Bobby indignantly. "If you like to give Campbell—" He stopped short at the sound of returning footsteps, and a moment later Christine entered the room.

"A man has called with a message from Mr. Campbell," she said. "He wants you to go over to the hotel at once."

Bobby got up from the bed.

"Something to do with this infernal inquest I suppose."

He reached for his cap, which was lying on the dressing-table, and, having patted Christine paternally on the shoulder, walked to the doorway, where he turned round and surveyed us both.

"So long, my children," he observed. "Settle it for when you like, but don't forget that I'm to be best man."

*

For just a second after he had gone we both remained silent.

"I suppose we must let him have his way," I said. "We can't very well refuse after all he's done for us."

Christine stood looking down at me with a world of love and tenderness in her eyes.

"I don't know why it is," she said helplessly, "I feel as if I wanted to laugh and cry at the same time."

I stretched out my hand and drew her down on to the bed beside me.

"It's only this house, dear heart," I said gently. "As soon as it's all over we'll go away together and——"

She stopped me with a little gesture.

"But I don't want to go away," she whispered. "I think Greensea Island is the only place in the world that I was ever really happy in."

I sat up, and, putting my arms around her, pressed my lips to hers.

"Oh, but your shoulder!" she faltered. "Your poor shoulder! The doctor said——"

"Hang the doctor," I exclaimed, and with this ungrateful sentiment I kissed her again.

THE END

Printed in Great Britain
by Amazon

55937865R00138